JUDGING ATHENA

JUDGING
Athena

PERRIN LOVETT

GREEN ALTAR BOOKS
SHOTWELL PUBLISHING

Produced in the Republic of South Carolina by

GREEN ALTAR BOOKS
An imprint of Shotwell Publishing LLC
Post Office Box 2592
Columbia, South Carolina 29202
WWW.SHOTWELLPUBLISHING.COM

ISBN: 978-1-963506-39-6

FIRST EDITION

10 9 8 7 6 5 4 3 2 1

For the love of unworthy men and women, who might still be joined as one in bliss, prosperity, and salvation, and for the merciful Lord God Who made them for each other in furtherance of His Supreme will.

Contents

Grace and loss, and so she fell.
Shame, penance, and justice,
Somewhere between Heaven and Hell,
Hope and love? A love for hope?
Myriad emotions and tasks foretold,
What would it take to make complete,
A heart so warm withstands the cold.
How be she judged?

One

Made of Finest Nickel

The temperature slowly descended as the oppressive gray of twilight gave way to another early New England night. The young man sheltered beneath the lofty portico, between sturdy stone columns afore the entrance of the impressive structure. He looked some distance down the long, dark sidewalk and across the street, back towards the parking lot and his car. The distant lamp was well-placed and provided nearly ample lighting, though, of course, the time and the weather failed to fully cooperate. At just a tad after six o'clock, the afternoon, or the evening, held a darkness better suited to a damp midnight. It was, after all, if he had reasoned, the middle of November. And the chill threatened to give way to hard cold, a stern preview of the approaching Winter. Not the first snowflake had he yet glimpsed that Fall, but that afternoon, or since he'd left work some thirty or so minutes earlier, a healthy if depressing sleet had presented itself in force. Even where he stood, the rise, fall, and whip of the wind brought more tinkles of slush to his face and coat. The resulting sensation, along with a semi-long squint of a look at his older Honda Civic, brought recent words back to his mind.

'Yeah, you're gonna need it sooner or later. Maybe sooner than later,' the mechanic had told him. 'For you, I can get a new radiator in there for, lemme just say, give or take, about seven-fifty. Could do it in one day. If they got the parts, of course.'

'Seven-fifty,' he'd quoted back somewhat hazily to the kindly man.

'Give or take.'

'With the— If I needed any related tuning or if something else needed replacing, would I be safer budgeting a flat thousand?'

'You know your car, young feller,' the mechanic said. 'Heater core, worn tires, *et cetera*. Eventually, it'll be more like a couple grand. But, yeah, a thousand would make it easy for now. And just so you know, I think she's got a few more miles and maybe months left in her. I do know money is tight. Just keep an eye on the gauge and the reservoir level until you're ready. I'll be here, so lemme know.'

'Thank you very much.'

'And back to the flakes,' the mechanic said, 'nobody claims they like 'em, but in a case like this, I say just sprinkle as needed and trust the good Lord to get you through.'

They both laughed at the time. Back under the awning, the young man suddenly wondered if he had any flakes left in that little jar. He simply couldn't remember. He needed to budget— even more than he usually did—but the poor man's antifreeze fix was pretty cheap. He looked and squinted again now that the wind had died just a bit. From his vantage point, he didn't see any steam coming from under the hood. That was well. He didn't have a thousand dollars or even the suggested seven-fifty. The situation made the Lord's trust mandatory and, accordingly, something else to be grateful for. Turning to go through the large, heavy doors, he thought a little more about his finances.

Once inside both sets of doors, he stopped just inside the little entry alcove before the main landing and rotunda. After shaking slush from his hair and water-resistant medium-weight jacket, he momentarily took out his phone. In a jiffy, he'd punched up his meager checking account. Based on what he needed to set aside for rent and the basics until the next payday, he simply didn't have the money for major repairs. Not just yet. He said a quick trustful prayer about it all and then turned off his analytical mind; he had a different kind of necessity to purchase, one that wasn't about him, and, thus, to his mind, far more important. With a sigh of determination, he pocketed the phone and walked deeper into the main hall.

Fully surrounded by its environment, he was reminded how much he enjoyed the Gallery. In addition to so much visual detail and subdued excitement, it had the pleasant smell of a good museum or library, and the temperature and humidity were always perfect. But on that evening, and at that hour, he felt like he was all alone there. He saw no one else and he couldn't make out the first voice or footfall. Regardless, he walked on toward fulfilling his little mission. Just before taking his next step, he thought, perhaps prophetically, certainly fortuitously, to pop a breath mint into his mouth. A turn to his right and he saw the main reception desk. No one was there. Walking just past it and turning again to his right, he found the gift shop. Still observing no one about, he slowly walked inside.

It was as he remembered it: well-lit, modern, comfortable, and full of interesting merchandise, though he understood more than a few of the wares were a little pricey. He was just beginning to earnestly look around, wondering exactly what he wanted and how much it would set him back, when he thought he heard sweet, soft music playing. As if in a dream, he tried to listen to the melody. Suddenly, he realized the song had lyrics. Or were they plain spoken words? Something suggested they were. In fact, he almost thought some enchanting voice was speaking to him, saying, 'Just a moment, and I'll be there.'

And just like that, someone was there. He saw her coming from the corner of his eye. 'Hello,' she said, approaching him with a smile. 'My sincerest apologies if I've kept you waiting.'

He just looked in the direction of the voice and froze, staring in disbelief. The sound of her speech was enough to bend time; it was clear, concise English, but it bore the subtle hint of an accent he simply could not place. Given enough time, he might have reluctantly, unimaginatively decided it could have been a French accent. But the temporal temporarily evaded him. If her voice slowed perception, then the sight and beholding of her brought time and space to a complete standstill. Before him was, as best he could describe her, the most beautiful woman he'd ever seen. Or even dreamed of seeing. In fact, he instantly decided he was looking at the most beautiful woman in all the world, maybe of all time.

He discerned a nearly supernatural being, one of impossible, definitional, and divine beauty made or forced to be painfully visible, almost palpable, visceral. She was tall for a woman, about his height. He wasn't sure if she was wearing heels. If so, then she might have overtopped him by half an inch. Her proportions were simply perfect as displayed by way of proffer through the elegant gray dress or skirt suit she wore. She had the longest, silkiest, blackest hair imaginable. Piercing eyes shined forth from an angelic face without flaw. Her irises flickered like lightning, though he was unsure of their exact color, at one imperceptible millisecond appearing blue, then gray, then hazel, and then some alluring, undefinable combination. If she wore any makeup, it was minimalistic. Her face and body defied any sign of age; if he had to guess, if his life depended on it, he would have said she was a little older than him, perhaps in her late twenties. She was a young woman in her utter prime, the ideal specimen. And somehow he felt as much as saw a glow about her. She was smiling, friendly, honestly, and kindly with rich red lips as she slowly advanced towards him. Before her wafted a smell sweeter than any flower, a scent that, even as it demanded attention or even adoration, almost physically pushed him away like the strong breeze at the edge of a hurricane. Helpless and deprived of his clear senses, he took a step backward. He felt his pulse begin to race. The rapid beat felt so good, if the feeling did cause him additional slight confusion, possibly alarm, something between fear and glee. Yet, truth be told, it was probably much closer to pure glee.

'How may I help you, sir?' she asked.

'I, I—' he stammered even as he felt his back touch something. Quickly turning, virtually in a panic, and with no time to spare, he was just able to grab the little green porcelain vase before it fell off the short white marble stand. As he handled it, he caught a glimpse of the price tag - *$999.95*. 'Oh, wow,' he stuttered as he gingerly replaced the vessel. 'I, I, I—'

'I'm so sorry, I didn't mean to startle you,' she apologized, still through a bewitching smile that now intimated kind laughter.

'No, I'm sorry,' he said as he turned once more to face her. Maybe it was the lighting or a trick of his mind, but it appeared that she had melted into a more ordinary form of extreme beauty, still seemingly too perfect, but, at least, earthly. 'I, I—I'm just looking for a little g-g-gift.'

'I'm Athena,' she said, extending her right hand to him.

He nervously took it and then openly if thinly gasped. Upon their touching, upon the grace of a short, formal handshake the kind proper ladies receive and dispense, he was taken by a sudden calm that swept his whole body, mind, and soul. And just like that, he was back to being himself, back to being able to see, think, and speak again, and back on his minor gift quest. He was keenly aware, however, that he felt greatly gladdened, or joyous even.

'Athena,' he said with a warm smile and a subtle blush. 'Athena? Like the winged Nike Athena? Wow. I'm Josh.'

'It's very nice to meet you, Josh. And, yes. Shhhh—I've never heard anyone guess my secret identity before,' she said with an open laugh, soft, sincere, and perhaps flirty. 'Now, you're looking for a gift? You're in the right place!'

'Well, yes,' he said more affirmatively, finally feeling like he'd come back to having his feet on the ground. 'I'm looking for something small and simple for a lady friend.'

Athena strolled a few feet into the assorted shelves and stands, one finger to her lips as she thought. 'Your friend, is she a special lady? I take it she is.'

'Yes, very much so, very dear to me. My sweet Isabella,' Josh said. 'I suppose I want something she can wear, something to remind her of the exhibit and our seeing it. It's also for her birthday in a few weeks.'

'Are you coming to see it together, the Gallery, or have you recently browsed?' she asked.

'Oh, I've been here before. But this will be her first visit. We're coming tomorrow, about this time, as part of a little group. We're taking a guided tour of the Patterson prints.'

'I see,' she said with another delicious smile. 'Please give me a second while I think. With the flu season hitting early, we're a little short-staffed tonight. The shop, while I know most of what's here, isn't my usual station. Patterson— I fear we don't have anything directly related to his works, certainly nothing like apparel.' She paused as she looked around thoughtfully.

'Oh, I didn't mean to keep you from anything,' Josh said. 'Do you work at the desk, or back in the gallery?'

'Yes, the latter. I'm the curator,' she said, still looking and thinking.

'Of the whole museum? Wow, that's impressive!'

'Yes, and thank you,' she said, turning again with that smile. 'Something she can wear. But I take it not a hat or t-shirt, correct?'

'Well, no, maybe something a little more special or formal than that, more meaningful.'

'I've just the thing!' she said, snappily striding towards the back wall. 'Or, just the set of items. How about jewelry?'

Josh joined her in front of the wall and a case full of adornments and treasures. His money woes uneasily hinted at the back of his mind. 'Maybe something, uh, something affordable? Small?' He looked at her hopefully.

'Just the thing!' she almost sang. She reached down to the end of a shelf and picked up a short necklace with a small oval locket, the assembly of which appeared to be made of slender loops of some shiny if slightly tender metal. 'This is our Doris Harper limited collection. Mrs. Harper makes every piece by hand in her Maine cottage. No two pieces are ever the same—each is a unique triumph. And she only makes them of the very finest nickel. A gift to thrill Miss Isabella for a lifetime.'

Josh understood exactly zero about jewelry, or metals, for that matter. But he instantly loved what he saw and happily envisioned it hanging around someone special's neck. 'Nickel?' he asked somewhat timidly.

'Not so brash or commonplace as gold or silver. Or platinum. And there is great art in these designs. The craftsmanship, the presentation is what sets them apart. We regularly ship them coast to coast and to Europe,' she explained. 'I don't know what it is, some secret, but they're treated with a patented clear protective layer or electroplating that preserves their so-slightly muted luster and prevents any unwanted allergic activity if that would be a problem. I just happen to be wearing one of her bracelets.' She raised her other hand in demonstration. Josh looked at the bracelet, not knowing exactly what he was supposed to look for. He also took the chance to observe her left hand, seeing smooth lineless skin, polished hard nails, and, he noted with a quiet thrill, no rings. He gave a quick glance back to her neck and head. He couldn't see a necklace though he saw she wore simple earrings that complimented the bracelet, her outfit, and her flawless face.

'I do like that locket,' Josh said, his thoughts still resting on her appearance and bearing. 'Dare I ask how much it costs?'

'Far less than one would think,' she said knowingly and kindly. 'This is only one-fifty!'

Josh quickly calculated he could afford it, that it would only delay his repairs but a short month if that, and that the purchase would be well worth it. '*Isabella will love it forever,*' he happily thought to himself, her sweet, cute face temporarily replacing Athena's in his whirling mind. He smiled at the notion of presenting it to her the very next evening around the corner in the traveling exhibition room. 'I'll take it!'

As he reinserted his debit card into his wallet, he watched Athena wrap the little white box holding the locket. They were both smiling throughout the transaction. But through the whole process, Josh thought to himself: '*I wonder what Isabella would think of Athena? I wonder what I think? What do I think?! Is this love at first sight?! Oh, my Lord! What, if anything, do I say? What do I do?*' He felt his heart rate accelerate again.

Still with that smile to thaw any heart, Athena handed him the little wrapped package. 'I'm sure she'll love it. I will be in, this time tomorrow. If you get the chance, I'd like to see you again, Josh. I'd like to meet you and your special little lady!'

'*And that will be something!*' he thought. 'It's a deal,' he said. 'We'll, hopefully, see you tomorrow.' He turned to go but then paused. Turning back to her, he reached out for her hand. Shaking it lightly, again feeling that delightful calm and warmth, he said, 'Thank you so very much, Athena. Well met, and I look forward to seeing you again.'

She smiled once more, though this time the look went much deeper and higher than before, a touch of giddiness added to her existing pleasant transcendence. He left and she watched him until he exited through the main doors. As a matter of common courtesy, she immediately decided against further observing his movements outside.

'Wow,' she said openly. She then reflected on their brief meeting. He was an inch or so above average height for a man in those times. His hair was dark brown and well matched his keen sparkling eyes. She could tell that beneath his blue coat he was slim though not thin. Below his coat, she'd seen clean, neat casual slacks over well-loved walkers. He was, to her eyes, very cute, adorable even. She had, even when she first approached him, sensed he was sweet, kind, gentle, and pure. That boy. That man of what? He's probably only in his early twenties. Yet he seemed so timeless. And sincere. Wonderful. And ... she then thought very deeply: '*Could he have actually seen me? Even for a second, could he have seen me as I really am? As best his eyes might contrive? If so, he is a great rarity. Regardless, his lady friend is most fortunate. He didn't say what kind of special friend she was. He wore no ring, nor did he mention her romantically. I dared not read his thoughts, settling for a woman's guess instead. And what do I now guess? Isabella. I know not about her, but is this? For me, is this? Could this be love at first sight?!*' A feeling she had not known or even thought of in an age took her for the barest moment. She closed her eyes and breathed deeply. Then, as she gave thought to the night's closing, she decided to check the computer registry for the following evening and any scheduled guest groups.

Outside, seated in his small, older economy car, pelted by more sleet that, by the sound, hardened as the temperature continued to drop, Josh thought for a quiet moment. Then he spoke to the night, 'I know Isabella will love this gift. And our visit. All of them will.' He smiled, crossed himself, and then spoke to his Father, 'Thank you, O Lord, for this gift, for Isabella, and for my meeting Athena. I don't even know what I want to ask. Or even what to think. You know my heart and all things. Thank you, thank you, thank you! For all this and Your continuing mercy. Amen.' He smiled just before adding, 'And please, God, please keep the wagon wheels turning!' With that, he turned the key and watched with relief as all the gauges rolled into place. He backed out and drove on and all was well in the deepening night.

A few hours later, at his bedside in his little apartment, he said another prayer. It was one of thanksgiving for his life, his blessings, and for tomorrow evening. He almost sang it out, so glad was his heart.

Two

Two Women

The next evening, Friday evening, the weather was much the same as the day before. It might have been a degree or two cooler, somewhere right around the genuine freezing point. Outside, while the sleet and rain had abated, at least for the night, sloshy little mires and ridges of wet ice lurked around the puddles. Inside the Gallery, where the ambiance never changed, a few more bodies bustled about here and there. It was a moment after six when Athena looked out into the first large exhibition room.

'I knew it,' she said to herself very quietly and with a slight smirk. She'd looked and found only one group for that evening, a party of eight to ten, though with very little other identifying information. The only contact was for a Sister Maria Francisco, with or without the name Isabella. Her intuition, or something deeper, had formed an impression in her mind. Now, upon seeing them all together being led about by Margarette, she knew her guesses had been right. '*I knew it. I felt it in my heart about you and yours, young master Josh, you rascal. I could have assumed or guessed blind,*' she thought. She then smiled broadly and watched them further.

Before two of Patterson's larger, wall-length 1970s retro-agrarian lithos, the little ensemble loosely gathered as Marge discussed colors, lights, and sentiments. An elderly nun, Sister Francisco obviously, stood at the rear of the pack, nearer to the center of the room. Close by her, and turned to talk with her, was a middle-aged woman dressed for a typical fall outing. Beside the woman, looking about almost rebelliously was a young girl of maybe twelve or thirteen. She might have been going on twenty-five, or completely innocent; it was difficult to predict from the distance upon a first glance. Two little boys swayed and murmured nearby in the company of three little girls. All of the children looked like ordinary little siblings, each wearing slightly worn hand-me-down clothes. And finally, standing just to the side, and kind of in between the crowd and Marge, was Josh. Tonight, presenting exactly as Athena remembered him from the previous night, he was wearing the same blue coat, though with faded jeans and brown hiking boots.

Marge told one of her patented art jokes and the adults laughed along with one or two of the children. There was an impromptu break and then it happened. One of the small girls, a child of maybe seven, dainty under her curly brown hair, shyly, though rather expectantly, made her way over to Josh. He made some very happy exclamations and then dropped down to her level on one knee. From inside his coat, he produced a little wrapped package. They opened it together. The girl squealed with delight. Athena watched, transfixed, as Josh slowly raised and then lowered the locket over the girl's head and neck. She practically jumped into his arms with a crushing hug. He returned it while kissing her head and rubbing his face through her locks. And so Athena beheld special little Isabella.

'I knew it,' she whispered to herself as her eyes moistened.

The other children looked on, their attention spans doing the best that children can muster. Marge was smiling and holding her hands over her chest. The nun and the other woman raised high grins, spoke together, and happily pointed to the presentation. The teenage girl cracked an open-mouthed smile which seriously threatened her seemingly rebellious character. In a moment, Josh stood up and took Isabella's hand. The girl swayed and pranced while constantly touching and looking down at her new locket of finest nickel. Together they and the whole group resumed their tour. Athena, her mind racing and her heart tingling, made a decision.

As they moved towards the far end of the hall and the opening to the larger gallery beyond, she cloaked herself and followed them, intent on hearing and seeing more.

Marge now introduced the small throng to Patterson's post-farm period works, pausing to hand out a smattering of little color sample flyers on raised card stock. Josh and Isabella moved to the front of the strolling assembly with the rest of the children and the young woman in tow. The nun and the other woman brought up the rear. The nun paused and looked back to where Athena stood shadowing their passing, though she did not directly see her. Nonetheless, the older woman smiled gladly before speaking again to her companion about some pending change of procedure or logistics.

Athena edged closer to Josh and his special girl, as close as she felt comfortable.

'I love it!' Isabella half whispered, half shouted. 'You're the best big brother ever! I love it and you!'

'I love you too, babydoll,' he almost cooed while squeezing her little hand in his. 'But, shhhh, Miss Margie, here, is talking about palettes.'

The child softly laughed, gave an extra round sway, and then, latching on to Josh with both hands and arms, said, 'What about the little round box?'

'On the necklace?' Josh clarified.

'Yes.'

'That's called a locket,' he said. 'And what about it?'

'Can you put our picture in it?' she asked, not quite pleading. 'Then I can remember you wherever I go.'

'Well, I suppose we could, if we can take a picture and print it,' he said. Then, somewhat more thoughtfully, or kindly, he whispered, 'Or, if you want, you can wait and add a picture of two, well, more special people. If you know what I mean.'

'Do you mean—' she started to ask.

'I do, kinda,' he said, somewhat knowingly and hopefully.

'Have you met— Do you know something?' the child asked innocently but expectantly.

'I do not know, exactly,' Josh said. 'But I've been praying extra hard, and I have a little feeling. And I like it!' His smile simply beamed down on her.

'Oh, my goodness,' the little sweetness sighed. 'That's my dream! But, I love you so much, Joshy.' She paused for a moment, obviously thinking about some weighty matter. Then, she asked, 'If we wait for that feeling, my dream to come true, could we have all our pictures in it? That way I and they could never forget all you've done for us. You're the sweetest, Joshy.'

He actually picked her up in his arms and held her. 'Issy, I'll do whatever you want.' He kissed her head again and said, 'It's your birthday, after all.'

'And you're the bestest man in the whole world,' she said.

He set her back down and she began to hop and dance with glee. While she jumped and twisted, he took a step backward and watched her. Athena held her breath as she watched; Josh was crying. She touched her heart and then her own wet eyes. She continued to watch as Sister Francisco made her way to the pair and gave them each a hug. She paused holding Josh for an extra second. 'You are the dearest of them all, my baby,' the older woman whispered in his ear before kissing his cheek.

Josh (and Athena) recovered a bit and the show meandered along. Towards the end of the tour, during a little free time in the long hall beyond the main gallery, Josh spent a little extra time with everyone. Athena stood in the shadows and watched. He paid Margarette a few high compliments. Then he did some ridiculous but marvelous little dance with the smaller children, ending with the little boys and that swish arm move the kids love to make. He paused with the older girl, pretended to lecture her, and then, in a flash, mocked to steal her nose. She was left in stitches as he stealthily made his way to the adult women. He snuck up behind them and made them jump. Next, he took them in a hug and made some remark that caused them to cackle with laughter. Athena stood on her toes as she watched the women chase him down the hall in a little series of circles. He was finally caught, by Francisco, in a habit-ed standing tackle. The children, even the older girl, gathered in force and took him to the floor. When the pile cleared, he was left on his back laughing and sobbing almost uncontrollably. Athena felt a fire burning in her breast.

He slowly heaved himself upright, straightened his coat, and moved to join the gang at the end of the hall. Just before they all returned to the main entrance area, Athena, her heart kindled with interest and desire, flashed into place ahead of them. She dropped down on her knees in front of the little girl. 'You must be Isabella!' she exclaimed.

'You must be the lady who sold Joshy the round bo— the locket, I mean,' Isabella answered. 'I love it.'

'Hello, there,' Josh said as he approached. 'I see you two have met. I was wondering how this would go. Issy, this is Athena. Athena, Isabella.'

'You said she wears a gray dress, Joshy,' Isabella said somewhat emphatically. 'Her dress and skirt are red!'

The two adults looked at each other, smiling, before Josh interjected, 'It must have changed colors overnight. But I'd say it's maroon, not plain red.'

'Crimson, the color of hearts afire,' Athena said to Issy, though she looked up into Josh's eyes. As was becoming somewhat commonplace in this woman's presence, he blushed for an instant.

Athena was then introduced to the rest of the little crowd while they enjoyed a short reception break. By then, the children, minus the older girl, were becoming a little tired. Sister Francisco said something about the van, a movie back home, and a late evening snack, and with that, they prepared to depart. At the last moment, Josh walked over to where Athena stood alone.

'I have to see them out and into the van,' he said. 'If you'll be here for a second, and if it's not an imposition, may I come right back and talk to you for a moment?'

'Of course!' she said with her biggest smile yet. 'I'll be right here waiting … Joshy.'

He started to respond, blushed again, and then quickly eased to the doors. 'I'll be right back.'

She looked out through the large window next to the doors. Outside, a few new drops of some precipitation fell here and there. Josh helped each child climb inside and buckle up. He gave Isabella a long hug and another kiss on her head. Then he walked around to the driver's door, and hugged Sister Francisco as they had a few parting words. After that, we walked the middle-aged woman to her nearby SUV, bid her goodnight, and closed her door. He watched both vehicles drive off towards the main road and town. Finally, shaking the sleet or rain off his coat as he came, he bounded back up the stairs and re-entered the Gallery.

'You're amazing, Josh, a real gentleman and a sweetheart,' she said, reaching up to dust a few drops from his hair. He did not blush, though a boyish grin overcame his face, followed by a short, faint, choked chuckle.

Just then, Margarette passed behind them. 'All clear, A, and I'm outta here for the night,' she said. 'Sam and Milley said they'd do the finals and lock 'er down. I'll see you on Monday, Missy.' Turning to Josh, she said, 'And thank you, young man, for bringing such life into our artsy world. Please come back and bring your friends anytime.' With that, she walked away into the evening air.

'Thank you, Athena, for what you said. And for everything, tonight and yesterday,' he said.

'My pleasure.'

He hesitated for a split second before some new courage steeled his mind and voice. 'Athena,' he said, looking deep into those keen fierce eyes, the exact color of which still could not be gauged. 'I've never been very good with this kind of thing. Not really. But, I have to say this or risk bursting: you are, without equal, the most beautiful and fascinating woman I've ever met, like the real goddess Athena. And I was wondering if you had, if you have, that is— Are you seeing anyone, or—'

'No,' she quickly replied, staring back into the gentle eyes of an overgrown teddy bear. 'Not at all. I am completely unspoken for and unattached.'

'Well, then,' he almost stammered, his new courage still powering through. 'Would you like to go out to dinner with me, to go on a date with me, sometime soon?'

'I'd love to, Josh!' she said without a second thought. 'How about tomorrow night?'

'Really? Tomorrow? Tomorrow will be great!'

'It's settled then,' she said, her warmth truly beginning to melt his being. 'Give me your number, and I'll text you my address. You can pick me up tomorrow at seven. I can see you're very good at surprises, so line up something special for our date. Deal?'

'That's perfect! And thank you. Thanks again for everything.'

'My pleasure. I've been looking for an opportunity to get out, and I couldn't have found a better reason or person. Now, if you'll tell me your number, I'll text you. Then, would you be available to help me close out here and walk me to my car?'

'Absolutely,' he said, his head slowly beginning to spin.

They exchanged information and then he walked with her the extremely short distance to her office which was on the other side of the doors opposite the gift shop. 'Josh Williams, it is wonderful to meet you. I'll give the guard gate your full name for tomorrow,' she said as they walked.

'Athena Naonikis—that's a name—the pleasure is all mine,' he replied. '*Did she say guard gate?*' he quickly thought.

As she fetched her slim, neat purse from behind her desk, she asked, 'Your group, those dear children were from an orphanage, weren't they?'

'Yes, they were. Are. It's the Catholic home over in Pottsville.'

'What, if I may ask, is your connection with them?' she asked of sincere interest.

'I'm a volunteer, a big brother. We were supposed to have a few more chaperones with us tonight, but things have been a little crazy lately. There's some change brewing I don't really understand. I had a boy, a little brother, but he got lucky and was adopted by a couple from Tewksbury. Wonderful young couple, already with another little boy of their own. Issy, Isabella came back recently from a foster situation and she didn't have a sister. So ... she got me as a brother.' As he spoke, his expressions ranged from perplexed, to concerned, to exuberant. She saw them and found him all the more fascinating.

'How did you find the home?' she asked. 'From your church? Catholic? I don't mean to pry.'

'No, it's fine. Pry away,' he said, leaning against her office door. 'I grew up kind of Catholic, but in college, thanks to the Orthodox Christian Fellowship connected with a nearby parish, I joined the Orthodox Church, the OCA. But I know the home very well because it was my home for most of my life. I'm an orphan too. I know what they're going through and I love them all very much.'

She could tell he was becoming slightly emotional and moved close to him, looking him in the eyes. She placed her hands on his shoulders and, immediately, that inexplicable calm fell over his mind and body. 'Prying and giving,' she said kindly. 'I know the OCA; I'm a member of the Greek parish just down the road. Don't ask me how, exactly,' she said, 'but I almost sensed that this was the case. I think it was reconfirmed in my mind when I saw the nun hug you and call you her baby.'

'You heard that?' he asked.

'Yes. Er, sound carries in these halls. I wasn't eavesdropping.'

'Well, it's okay even if you were,' he rejoined with a kind look. He dared to place his hands atop hers for a moment. 'You're very perceptive, Athena.'

'You're not alone, and we have so much to discuss tomorrow and, perhaps, beyond. I'm an orphan of sorts too.'

Almost at the same time, they broke their mutual embrace and separated a step or so. Josh almost whispered to her, the calm and warm feeling still flowing through him, 'I really want to get to know you better. You're so different. I can't quite explain it, but I feel, well, drawn to you. If that makes sense.'

Both of their breaths became eerily audible at that moment. 'I feel it too, Josh,' she said, her musical accent shattering the silence like a warm wave rolling over a beach. At the same time, and with the same intensity, effort, and focus, they smiled at each other. And they laughed.

After a quick intercom word with Milley, and after she locked the front doors, he walked her around the corner to the employee parking lot. He couldn't help but notice that she approached and opened the door of a new Mercedes GLS, a Maybach edition no less. For a fast second, he reflected that she was a station or five above him, maybe above anyone he knew; but she held herself out with no hint of pretense. Whereas part of his mind might have been tempted to yield to trepidation, he instead found the whole affair mildly encouraging, intoxicating, even.

Standing with the door open and the engine heating up, she reached out to him. He was surprised (and overjoyed) when she simply wrapped her arms around him and held him for a good minute. 'Josh, thank you for everything this week,' she told him. 'I'm genuinely looking forward to tomorrow evening.'

'Thank you, Athena. I'm really loo—' His words were cut short when she leaned in and planted a small sweet kiss on his lips.

That done, she simply said, 'Goodnight, Josh,' and entered her SUV. Another moment, a wrinkling-nosed smile, and she drove off.

Josh could only get a weak, 'G-g-g—,' out as he stared off into space. He didn't even notice her leave as he stood there trying to process the intense smell, taste, and overwhelming sensation he'd just experienced. In fact, he stood frozen for a few minutes before he was able to shake himself back into reality. Heedless of the night, the cold, and the world, he zombie-walked back to his little Civic. The caress of her lips still bit into his and reverberated throughout his whole head and into his very soul. He came fully to somewhere on the road, surprised to find himself at the wheel.

He also noticed the radio on and the station was playing Real Life's "Send Me An Angel." He didn't really know the song, though he sang along, semi-mesmerized by the lyrics. At a red light, he suddenly let fly a thundering, 'WOO!!!' Then, as was his habit, he began to pray. But this time, he prayed openly and rather loudly, the kind of excited speech any lovestruck teenage boy might give to a good, listening father.

And the prayer, while it changed several times in pitch and scope, rambled on until he was back in his apartment and even when he tucked himself into bed. A few tears of triumphant joy fell on his pillow as he drifted into the deepest sleep he could ever recall. If he dreamed, if he could imagine remembering it, then he dreamed of a most happy day to come.

Athena did dream. And in her sleep, as was often the case, she said a long prayer of her own, though this one was substantially different from the ordinary. While it, as usual, centered on praise and forgiveness, she thankfully entertained her nascent ideas about Josh. Thanks were mostly all she could express at this early point; owing to her uncertainties about him and any potential possibilities, she reserved any requests for the future, notions she hoped would not be too long delayed. Alternated with her nightly appeals and innovations, she lucidly conducted a review of the past two evenings and a cursory exploration of her feelings. She was tempted to delve deeper into who Josh was and what he felt, but she deemed the notion inappropriate. After contemplating every word they had spoken, together to each other, or apart about each other, and upon rereading both their expressed emotions, she settled into a quiet slumber. The smile remained on her silent lips until dawn.

Three

First Date

Josh watched the sunlight build and intrude through his bedroom window. He'd found himself stark awake long before the dawn or even before the first blared notes from his alarm clock. But he had forced himself to lie there waiting on the light. Her face, her scent, her touch, and that one amazing kiss encroached on his thoughts constantly. But even as he relished the memory from last night, he tried to focus on planning for this evening. He had an idea, not the most imaginative, but one that might hopefully lead to something of a novelty in dating. And he reasoned with himself that he needed a little rest as he wanted to be fully alert and energized around seven. In truth, with the light now falling around him, he was overflowing with energy. So he hopped out of bed and bounded into the new day.

A pot of coffee brewed while he preplanned the morning. He also had the presence of mind to double check his phone. Sometime during his drive or in his prayers, he'd managed to leave her a short text: 'Thank you, Athena. Can't wait for tomorrow. Joshy' She had replied just a little later with a kissing heart emoji. That did something for him, though it again set those effervescent memories swirling madly around his head. Listening to the coffee drip, he temporarily tried to tune those out—a process he never fully accomplished. Still, with a fresh cup and an English muffin, he settled at his computer.

His first order of business was to look up her address, check it on his phone maps, and then memorize the route by going over it nine or ten times. That part was easy as he knew the general area pretty well. He then thought about the logistics of getting there and back. The Civic was holding up pretty well; he still couldn't afford to have it properly repaired, not that there was enough time that day, but it should, he optimistically reassured himself, work well enough. He thought to top off the tank and properly clean it, and he aimed to make that his next priority—after he made dinner reservations.

He first thought about dining at Sanders, his informal go-to steakhouse. It was a nice enough place and, while not a regular, he'd been there enough times to appreciate the atmosphere and menu. Then he had a slightly better idea, to try a place he'd always looked at but had never ventured into: Meadowbanks Food & Tavern downtown. As he dialed their number, praying someone would be available that early, he pondered if it was good enough for Athena. She was, he adjudged, the classiest person he'd ever met. He was hoping this was the right call when someone did answer. And they happened to have a nice nook table overlooking the river that night at seven-thirty!

He then departed to work on his car. Driving up to the car wash, he caught himself drumming on the steering wheel and singing along with Journey and "Ask the Lonely." 'Not my song, today!' he laughed out loud as he counted quarters for the vacuum cleaner. While he was out, he stopped in and got a refresher haircut. He was almost home when something else important occurred to him. Forty-five minutes later, he walked back in his door with the roses he'd just purchased. It was still early afternoon when he returned home. Next, he looked at his wardrobe. It was far from perfect, but with a load of laundry running, he knew he could make it work. At some point he did have wits enough to eat a light snack for energy. After that, still waiting on the laundry, he showered and shaved. He brushed his teeth, brushed them again, rinsed with mouthwash, and then brushed a third time. A little after six, he stood in front of his mirror admiring his handiwork. He wore a blue blazer over a white shirt (sans a tie), his best gray slacks, and his newly polished dress shoes. He figured if the weather kept up, then his blue rain jacket would make a decent enough overcoat. After a quick prayer over the matter, mints in his pocket, he grabbed the roses and headed out for his date. *'My date with Athena!'* his mind sang.

In fact, his mind kept happily singing the whole way as he drove to her neighborhood. It was one town over, a short hop, and it was one of the tonier neighborhoods in the area. That detail was cemented when he pulled up to the guard house beside the large sliding iron gates.

'Good evening, sir,' a uniformed guard said. 'Are you expected?'

'Yes, sir,' Josh said politely. 'I'm here to visit Miss Athena Naonikis.'

The man studied a computer screen for a second. 'Mr. Josh Williams?' he asked.

Josh placed a one day permit on his dashboard while the gate opened with a creak and clang. He didn't even have to consult his phone, instead navigating by his memory of that morning's map readings. With a few turns, he drove down several short, picturesque streets, each lined with larger, affluent-looking houses. Towards the back of the development, he found a cul-de-sac adorned with a circular row of stately detached townhomes. He eased up to Number Seven and saw her Mercedes. The townhouse had a double garage though her SUV remained parked in the short driveway. He parked beside it, got out, and glanced around in the growing darkness punctuated here and there by a number of old-fashioned street lamps. He looked at her home, a regal three story house, her Maybach, and, then, at his little Civic. A few sprinkles of sleet began to land on him and he had the feeling again that he might be punching above his weight class. Undeterred, again steeled with some previously unknown fortitude, he carefully handled the roses, and walked up the short flight of brick steps to her door. He rang the doorbell and took a half step back.

After a short moment, there was a click, the door opened, and there she stood smiling. If it was physically possible, she looked, to his wide eyes, twice as beautiful as he'd remembered her from the gift shop where she'd deprived him of his senses. She was wearing black leather boots that reached almost to her knees. Under a dark fur coat, she was wearing a sleek black dress that, like the boots, almost reached her kneecaps, which themselves were semi-obscured by dark hose. Her hair was down and flowed over her shoulders. Gold glinted here and there from a necklace, earrings, and a bracelet. A perfect angelic face grinned at him following a laser-like path of focus from her keen eyes. He stared blankly at her and perhaps uttered something like, 'Bee—'

'Hello, Josh,' she said sweetly. 'Are those for me?'

'For you?' he said stupidly before recovering a little. 'Oh, of course! Roses for my goddess Athena.' He tried to laugh at his excuse of an ice-breaker but his mouth suddenly felt dry. He held them out and she accepted them, giving him a little hug that ended by her placing one hand on his forearm. Suddenly, he recovered and found his voice. 'You look incredible! I must be the luckiest man on earth!'

She laughed it off and waved for him to follow her. 'Thank you for these. They're incredible. Come with me to the kitchen so I can snip and set them. It'll only take a second.'

He followed her towards the back of her first floor to the well-appointed kitchen. He noticed, among many other nice things, that she kept a healthy crop of very happy looking plants. He watched as she deftly snipped the stems, placed them in a crystal vase, and added a little plant food to the water in it. She briefly explained what she was doing though he found it hard to reply. Almost as soon as he'd started watching her, in awe, she was finished. 'Now they'll be beautiful for at least a week! And we can move on to dinner and our date, Josh. Ready?'

He walked her down the steps and to the passenger door of his car. There, for a microsecond he felt a little awkward. 'Pardon me, I have to run around and unlock it from my side,' he said as he moved away. 'One second.'

She waited, smiling, until he returned and helped her inside. Once he was in, he explained, 'That lock and, well, my key clicker stopped working so well. I'm sorry I don't have a nicer car, something you deserve to ride in.' He looked a little embarrassed.

'Is this your car?' she asked sweetly.

'Yes, it's all I have.'

'Then I like it!' she said. 'I like everything about you, malfunctioning clicker and all.' She wrinkled her nose at him.

'Thank you,' he said sheepishly. 'I need to get a few things fixed though.' He started backing out and explained a little more: 'The heater is, well, it's related to my radiator situation. The fan works okay, but the heat is kind of intermittent. I've gotten used to it. But I hope it's not uncomfortable. I use this thing to defrost the windshield.' He looked a little rueful as he pointed to a little heater on the dashboard next to his permit. It was connected via a cord to the car's 12 volt plug.

'Heater core?' she asked knowingly. 'Are you running flakes in the radiator?'

'Uh, yeah. That's all I can do until I can afford to get it fixed.'

'Well, if you don't mind, may I take a crack at the heater controls?' She already had her fingers circling around them.

'Sure...'

He watched as she turned the system completely off. Then she reset the fan, adjusted the flow to split between heat and defrost, and dialed the heat all the way over. She might have tapped the console one or twice for some reason. He was a little doubtful, somewhat bewildered, in fact. They drove in silence for a few moments before he noticed something. He felt heat, warmer than he'd felt since the previous winter, on his feet and his hands on the wheel. She'd somehow fixed the thing!

With a cocked eyebrow and maybe a little smirk to him, she unplugged the heater, wound the cord, and placed it behind her seat. 'You won't be needing that now. All it needed was a woman's touch!'

'Wow,' he said. 'You don't just look incredible. You are incredible. I was embarrassed to admit this, but ... I'm a little intimidated by you. I feel like a puppy dog in your presence. But everytime you shake my hand or just lightly touch me, it's like you fix everything that's wrong inside. Must be your universal manner, that.'

She turned fully and gave him the sweetest look. 'Anything I can do to help, Josh. And, you might not know it, but you, well, fix things for me just by being you. No touch required.' Then she added with a soft laugh, 'But the touches are nice too. And I love puppy dogs.'

They enjoyed almost cooing smalltalk until they arrived at Meadowbanks. 'I've never been here,' she said as he opened the car door for her. 'Have you?'

'No. I've been looking for a special occasion and this one is just perfect!'

Together, they walked inside and were soon seated at a cozy little table in a back nook. By candlelight on the table, they looked out at the small, slowly flowing river reservoir outside.

'This was a wonderful choice, Josh,' she said as she turned her attention to the menu.

'I've only heard good reviews about it,' he said, one eye on her, the other on the wine list.

'You're thinking red, aren't you?' she asked.

'Well, yes,' he said with a little contemplation. 'I'm not the best with these pairings. I'm not the biggest drinker anyway. I was thinking about a steak, maybe the fillet, so I suppose one's supposed to order red with that. I, uh, take it you're just a little more worldly than me. Any ideas?'

'As a matter of fact, yes, and a delightful idea,' she said. 'Steak is perfect, and I'm in the mood for veal. So, yes, again, we should have a red. And—this is incredible—they have the *perfect* one!'

'Really? Which one?'

'It's called *Agiorgitiko*, and it's a Greek classic from Peloponnese. Some might say it's a wee bit too fruity for red meat, but in my opinion, the subtle contrast only adds to the mutual taste experience. Whatcha think, Joshy?'

'I think you're the solemn, uh, solemn, the wine person among us.'

'The sommelier. Just trust me on this one!'

'Implicitly,' he said, setting aside his wine list. 'Are you really an expert? On wines?'

'No, but I've tried this one in Greece and I'm surprised and delighted to see it here. An extra star for Meadowbanks!'

'You've been to Greece?' he asked even as he tried to peruse the steaks.

'Oh, yes,' she said. 'Well, I'm kind of from Greece, kind of originally.'

'Oh, wow,' he said, looking intently and admiringly at her. 'That explains the accent. I would have guessed it was sort of French. Shows what little I know.'

They both snickered, then she added, 'You might know a little. Before I took my current position, I worked at the Louvre in Paris. And I have an art degree from the Sorbonne. Bits and pieces of influence, one might call it.'

Just then, a waiter appeared, and took their wine request. Just when Josh tried to think of anything to ask about her obvious travels and cosmopolitan life, the man returned with a bottle. He left two glasses, the bottle, a basket of fresh, warm bread, and departed again with their dinner orders.

'Take a sip of water and swish it around to clear the palette,' she instructed. He did as he was told. 'Now, swirl it in your glass, sniff it, and then take a sip. Hold it on your tongue and inhale through your nose. As soon as the breath is in, swallow, and then fully breath to assess the entire effect.'

They both undertook a formal taste testing at the same moment. 'That is good,' Josh said, genuinely impressed with the velvety grapes. 'I can see what you said, but I think it'll hit the spot behind a morsel of meat.'

'Told you so. And I'll say it again while we're eating.'

In preparation for their meal, Josh led her in a short Blessing. '...Christ our God, please bless this food and drink of Thy servants, for Thou art holy always, now and ever and unto ages of ages...' He made it right to *Amen*, when he added, 'And thank you, O Lord, for this fellowship, for our blessed meeting and for our time together. Please continue to bless Athena and I and the two of us together. Glory to the Father, and to the Son, and to the Holy Spirit. Amen.'

'That was lovely, Josh,' she said. 'The two of us. Together. Amen, again and again.' He looked softly at her for a moment, a look she returned to him. A look that turned into a short mutual fixation.

They stared across the table at each other for a moment. Her look was one of a master gardener inspecting a prize flower. His was more akin to a little boy seeing something exciting for the first time. His lips moved a few times though they made no sound. He blinked a few times. Finally, she broke the silence, 'I don't mean to be forward, Josh. But I've been thinking about this since I first met you. You're just so cute. Handsome, very masculine, but with the innocent charm of a lad. And from what I've gathered and seen of you, and your interactions with others, I sense the look goes through and through. I just wanted you to know that.' She reached out for his hand, tenderly taking hold of it with hers.

He passed through two shades of pink, but with her touch he again found his voice. 'Thank you,' he said quietly. 'As I said, you're an incredibly beautiful woman. Perfect, even. And I hate to admit this, but I can't help but think you're way too good for me. I'm just little me, and you're so, so sublime. I can't believe you're not married or in a relationship. You must have a thousand rich, powerful, model-looking men constantly vying for your attention. I'm not putting myself down or questioning your judgement, but, really, why me?' He looked like a puppy to her, a sweet helpless puppy. She smiled again, sighed, and answered him.

'I like you. I love the idea of you, Josh. You're one in a million, and I fear I might be falling for you. Don't let it go to your head, and I know you won't. Just know that I don't date or show this kind of affection often. In fact, I almost never, ever do so. Yes, I've had a few suitors. But none of them offered me anything meaningful, if that makes sense. Something about secular or earthly society, especially modern or postmodern society, precludes or attempts to stifle legitimate companionship between men and women. And mine has been a rather peculiar case. This may sound strange, but I frequently try to mask my appearance so as to not be that attractive to men. I love people, and I respect men, but I never really thought I'd find someone like you. Just trust me, and you owe me nothing, but I feel a connection with you. You feel right, Josh. Very rare and precious.'

'Wow,' he said, somewhat stunned.

'I know, I know,' she said. 'Tell me a little more about yourself. Part of me felt jealous at the idea of Isabella—before I met the sweet baby—and I didn't like feeling that part. But, to put it on you, how come you don't have a girlfriend? I can plainly see that beyond being a cutie you're very popular and adored.'

'That's, uh, that's easy and difficult to explain,' he said with a slight stammer. She rubbed his fingers and he continued, 'I guess I've been waiting on the right woman. Being who I was, I never had much luck with girls when I was younger. Which might have been for the best. In college, I went on a few dates. I'm a little awkward, I suppose. And I really always wanted to hold out for Mrs. Right. I don't even know much about families and relationships, but I don't like all of the, uh, what do they call it, the *hooking up* that goes on. I never had anyone to talk to about this, so I always turned my thoughts to God. I pray. A lot. I've never gotten a direct answer, but that little voice always told me to wait. For someone very special. I never thought, or dared to think, she might be as special as you.' He became very bashful and a tear might have hovered at the bottom of one of his eyes.

Suddenly, without any warning or explanation, she stood up. He tried to stand for her, but she was too quick. In an instance she was leaning down beside him, her hand on his head. 'You're so sweet, Joshy,' she said. Then she kissed his lips again, squeezed him, smiled, and returned to her seat. Once there, she simply said, 'And we'll discuss that further, maybe tonight or later. Just now, tell me more about you! You mentioned college and your time with the orphans. What kind of work do you do? Tell me everything!'

He started out of order and again told her of his own time living at the group home and his newer volunteer work. She appeared to delight in every word, especially those concerning Isabella. She sensed a sadness from his childhood, something that reminded her of her own ancient past, but which she was overjoyed to notice he had compartmentalized or adjusted to and overcome. All of his concerns centered on Isabella and the other children. In fact, he appeared far more preoccupied with others in general than with himself. Yet, she delighted in his humble telling of the National Merit scholarship that had taken him to Dartmouth for a Bachelors in English with a minor substitution in analytical research. As they ate, she probed him about his support job at Merrimack College.

'So, you're on loan sometimes? From the department?'

'Sometimes, yeah. I'm the English go-to research assistant. A glorified gofer, really. I do some grant work too. But they, yeah, loan's the word; they loan me around to the rest of Arts and Sciences as needed or as I'm available. The way I see it, at least I'm popular.'

'As I noticed! I saw that with the ladies and the kids, Joshy. Josh. And will you take them up on the graduate school offer anytime soon?'

'I'm considering it. I'd have to have another scholarship or a grant. I guess I could write my own in the latter case. Ha! But while the idea of teaching is attractive, I kind of just like working. I finally feel like I'm contributing, if that makes sense. But we keep talking about me.' He stopped, put his fork down, and looked deep into her lovely eyes. 'The curator who used to work at the Louvre. Tell me more about your background. How'd you find us all the way over here? And what, if I may ask, is your academic background? The Sorbonne?'

'How'd I get here?' she asked back with a laugh. 'Oooo, and how about dessert with this chat?!' They ordered a chocolate tart for two and she continued: 'I'd wanted to come back to North America, so when I saw the opening, I took a gamble. I hope I haven't disappointed. But as for the qualifications, I have a Doctorate in Archeology from ETH, in Zurich. And, as for arts, I had a few years as an assistant in the Louvre galleries, and my Sorbonne degree is a Masters in Art. A concentration in portraits, but for whatever reason I wrote my thesis on a particular sculpture.'

'Which one?'

'Bernini's *Apollo Chasing Daphne.*'

'Yikes. That was the ultimate case of playing hard to get!'

'That's what I always thought too! And don't you go turning into a tree on me, Josh.'

'I'm more of a shrub kind of lover...' They both chuckled at his sophomoricism. 'And you have a PhD too?' he asked. 'Wow. How many degrees do you have in total?'

'Seven, I think. At last count.' She paused to think about them, evidently deciding to dismiss the precise thought.

'Seven?! That's incredible!'

'Two Doctorates, four Masters, and two Bachelors. Well, eight, now...'

'Athena, you have me outgunned at every turn! How many languages do you speak?'

'Several. How about you?'

'English, if I'm lucky and in the mood. And I can half babble in Spanish!'

'*También hablo español, mi dulce hombre!*'

'*Buen hombre? ...Yo también hablo... Quizás... No?*' He didn't seem quite as certain as she was.

'*Puedo decirte que te amo?*' she asked with a coo, but a rather serious coo.

'Does that mean *love*?!' He was legitimately shocked, both that he thought he understood her and by what he thought he'd heard.

'Maybe,' she said with a playful little grin. 'And may I ask if you like to dance?'

'Like?' he stuttered. 'I might like to but I really don't know how.'

'Neither do I,' she said. 'But I noticed they have a little floor and a band happens to be playing. I would like to give it a shot, if you'd be so kind.'

'Thank God we're even on the dance score,' he said with a relieved laugh. 'And I'd love to dance with you!'

With that, they made their way over to the dancefloor and simply moved around in a circle while holding each other and softly whispering in each other's ear. They were one of six of seven couples slowly swaying about; and it appeared that none of the others were professionals. Twice, Josh was asked if he'd allow a man to cut in with her, yet both times she had quickly replied, 'No thank you. I'm only here for my Josh tonight.' '*Her Josh?*' he thought, amazed. More amazingly, as he saw it, at one point another woman, and not a bad looking one, asked him for a dance. Athena had smiled allowingly, though he had immediately but politely declined. Instead, they kept dancing, holding, and whispering. Josh felt his heart trying to race again. Maybe it was the constant slow movement, such a sweet athletic activity, that kept it in check. He repeatedly thought about the soft warmth of her touch and the indescribable joy he found in it. He also considered the inexplicable calming nature of her touch. Finally, after she'd told him more of her thoughts about seeing his interactions with Isabella, he murmured into her ear, 'This is so wonderful, Athena. This has to be the most fun I can remember. Ever, maybe. I'd never imagined ever being able to, well, hold onto someone like this and have this kind of quiet communication.'

As it turned out, she was thinking similar thoughts around the same time. 'I know what you mean. I could do this all night, Josh. Yes, when the bodies touch, like this, it's like our minds act as one. Who knew?' She dropped her last pretense of formality and cuddled against him. They held closer, talked a little less, and simply enjoyed the thrilling moment. They could not, of course, continue then and there for the entire evening. An hour or more passed and many songs rolled by. Finally, they decided together, more unsaid than in any overt way, that they wanted to continue their quiet talk alone.

'Time for a little fresh air?' he asked. 'If it's not too frightful out, would you like to stroll around downtown for a little bit, Athena?'

'I'd love to. And with you here, I can't imagine anything frightful enough to stop us.'

For another hour or so, they walked, hand in hand, around the scenic little town center. The night was rather cold and damp, though their feelings were anything but. For whatever reason, he kept worrying that her unprotected hands would get cold. Yet, the whole time, they remained warm and comfortable. She brushed it off and he dismissed the concern. Their talk centered on each other, faith, families, children, and childhoods. While she might have appeared somewhat reluctant to discuss her upbringing, she instead held rapt attention as he described his. After a good time walking, chatting, and looking in shop windows, they made their way back towards his car.

They were crossing Main Street, without any cares or real concentration on the world outside their own conversation and company, when he started to ask her something. 'Athena, do you think— I mean, if you're not too busy, would you like to—' He didn't finish the question or his thought at that moment. As they entered the crosswalk, he might have seen it at a distance. It should have commanded his utmost attention, though, due to his extra pleasant circumstances, he could have been forgiven for ignoring it. Now, suddenly, it was a dire emergency. The dump truck, its plow blade tucked and raised high, was right on top of them. And it was moving far too fast for any proper reaction. All he had time to do was latch onto her in as protective a fashion as was possible and utter, 'Oh, my God!'

As best he could remember it, they had suddenly spun around several times. In an instant, it was all over and they were back in roughly the same spot they'd been in when he had finally noticed the speeding menace. They had turned a little, now facing down the street, and he plainly saw the truck driving on, flying into the darkness. She had her hands on his chest as if to soothe him. He was gasping. 'Athena! Are you okay?'

'I'm fine, Josh. We're fine.'

'Oh, Lord, I thought we were dead. Are you really okay? Let me feel you. Tell me you're all-right.'

'Josh, take a breath. We're both okay. He missed us entirely. We're fine. He's fine too. Working overtime, afraid of black ice, and he didn't even notice us. We're all fine. It's over, baby.'

He found it momentarily impossible both to understand how they had escaped unscathed and how she remained so utterly unflappable. But her touch did its magic and restored a calm sense over his whole being. He recovered and they made their way back to the car. On the ride back to her house, she finally convinced him she and he were both going to live. She even got him to laugh at the little incident. And it slowly faded from his mind, in its place there remained only a warning and life lesson about paying attention to roads and one's surroundings. A child's lesson. And that's how he almost began to feel as he pulled into her driveway, again like a giddy child.

At the top of her steps, she fully turned to him and placed her arms around his shoulders. 'Thank you for everything, Josh. This was a simply marvelous evening. But ... I'm not quite ready for it to end. If you're not tired of me, may I invite you to come in? Maybe to have another drink and talk some more?'

'That's a great idea! I'd love that!'

With another soul-warming hug and a smile bright even by her high standards, she led him inside. She bid him to make himself comfortable in the well-appointed and tasteful living room. 'Another red? Or maybe a nightcap toddy?' she asked.

'A toddy might be nice,' he said, not quite sure what he was talking about. 'Lady's discretion.'

She quickly returned with a little tray. On it, Josh saw a little cake with two small forks, and two glasses of some creamy looking concoction. She explained the drink was a colder toddy, a self-designed mixture of brandy, Irish creme, and a secret ingredient. Yet upon setting the tray on her coffee table, she stood still for a second before saying, 'Stand up, if you don't mind. I'd like to get to this sooner than later.' He sheepishly stood and stepped close to her. She then seized him in an embrace beyond passionate. For a minute, an hour, or an eternity, he felt their bodies melt together. The hug would have been an experience to best anything he'd ever know, except for the kiss. This time, the lip lock lasted and lasted. It was not a lecherous kiss; rather, it was utterly deep, intimate, sensuous, and loving, a kind physical expression of pure spirituality. While it lasted, Josh couldn't think of anything or move beyond his caressing of her, his part in their mutual bliss. He felt like he was on fire, though it was the warming fire at the end of a cold, hard day, something to ease the mind, spirit, and senses. When it was finally over, he could barely move or see straight. He came to, discovering that she must have led him back down to the couch. The little cake was already gone. She was snuggled up next to him with her feet tucked beneath her legs. They talked as she ran her fingers through his hair. And they were sipping her delightful toddy creation.

Time stood still as their discussion grew quieter and deeper. He had no idea how many hours passed. He only knew that, while he felt a little sleepy, he never wanted the moment to end. As his eyes became heavy, he was aware they had just happily planned a second date, the subject of which had been on his mind and lips just before their truck encounter. There might have been a second drink, if he later remembered correctly. All he could really feel was an intense happiness the kind of which he had never known and could hardly describe with words. The next thing he really knew and understood was that he had fallen asleep and was temporarily reawakened. And he was lying down. There was a soft light in the room, a bedroom, he took it. He was in bed, his clothes still on, sans his sport coat and shoes. A comforter was being placed over his body. Then he looked into her eyes again.

'Where—' he tried to ask.

'Shhhh, baby,' she cooed. 'You fell asleep. I don't want you driving, so you're staying here with me. Platonically, of course. In a second, you might want to properly undress, but I had to tuck you in. So cute and snug.'

'How did I get in here?'

'I carried you.'

'You did? No.'

'No, you're right, silly. You, uh, sleep-walked, and I guided you. Now, let's get some real rest so we're ready for tomorrow's second big adventure.'

Feeling very relaxed, he didn't protest. In a moment, after she had gone to her room, it had taken him a few minutes to reluctantly get up and remove his pants and shirt. At the moment, all he had mustered was, 'Yes, Athena. And thank you for the most wonderful night of my life.'

She had smiled gently and said, very close to his face, 'Thank you, Josh. If you need anything in the night, just call for me and I'll be right here. Close your eyes and I promise you'll be refreshed when the sun rises for our new day. Goodnight, my sweet, kind soul.' With that, she had kissed his forehead, tucked the covers around his shoulders, and walked away, closing the door behind her.

With his clothes off, with the light off, feeling more cared for than ever before, he had just the time and wits to say a short, overly heartfelt prayer. Then he closed his eyes and walked through a small, lush garden of the most pleasant dreams.

Four

Second Date

Part of him, maybe the subconscious part, was trying very hard to wake up as the light of an early morning peeked inside the windows. But they were not his windows. And it wasn't his room. Or his bed. He couldn't think clearly, but he almost felt that he liked the bed he was in better than his own. At least his back did. He kept opening and closing his eyes, attempting to decide where he was and what he wanted to do. Something strongly suggested doing nothing; he felt more rested and more relaxed than he had in years. He felt beyond comfortable. Suddenly, he smelled something very sweet and inviting. There was a warmth flowing over him and the bed. Something soft and silky fell on his face in multiple places. It tickled a little and he couldn't help but smile. Then he opened his eyes and saw hers.

'Good morning, Josh,' she whispered just before lightly kissing his lips. 'How do you feel?'

'Athena,' he said, leaning slightly closer to her already very close face. 'I feel great! Oh, my goodness.' It all came flooding back to his brain. He sighed contentedly and lay back on the pillow.

'Are we still on for our date today, Joshy,' she asked with a happy smile.

'Absolutely! What time is it?'

'It's still quite early. Early enough. I'm going down to make our breakfast. Anything you like, dear. I have coffee and tea and anything else to suit. Take your time. I've placed a new toothbrush and a few items in the bath. Come on down when you're ready. When we're all set, I can change and be ready in a flash. Then we can pop back by your place and you can change.'

'Okay,' he said sweetly, boyishly.

'And did you decide? Mine or yours?'

'I did, now that I remember,' he said through an extra boyish grin. 'Yours! I've always liked it and a little change is good for me.'

'Very good. Coffee or tea? I can have it prepared when you come down.'

'Coffee is fine. Thank you very much.'

'Cream? Sugar?'

'No, thank you. Just black.'

'See you in a few.'

With that, and a tapping of his nose with her finger, she left. Josh got up and put his clothes on again. In the spacious bathroom, he found all she'd set out for him. He freshened up a bit and then found his way downstairs to her kitchen. The morning was still cold and gray, but a healthy and growing light intruded through numerous high, wide windows. He fondly remembered the scene from the previous night; and now, he found it even more appealing. Two steaming cups of black coffee were already waiting on the counter. Athena was nearby, looking into a bay window handsomely appointed with a few plants. The roses he'd given her were in the center of the display in their crystal vase. She was studying them rather intently.

'Hello, handsome!' she said, looking at him for a second. Her gaze returned to the roses and she ushered him to come closer. 'Grab your coffee and look at this. We have an intruder!'

Josh took a sip of his coffee—which was perfect—and looked down at the roses. She pointed to a green leaf below a flower. 'See him? I have no idea where he came from, but here's Mr. A. Fid!

I wonder if Charlotte knows he's here? I wonder if she's seen the roses yet?! And thank you, again, they're so lovely.'

'Thank you,' he said. 'Charlotte? Who is she?'

'Oh, she's one of my roommates,' she said. Then she added in a hushed voice, 'Don't tell anyone, but she might be my favorite. I call her Charlotte for reasons that will be obvious.'

'Roommates?' Josh was a little confused.

'Oh, yes. You can meet her now. She lives in that crack in the windowsill.'

They both moved over half a step and Josh watched as she tapped her painted fingernail on the sill just in front of a small crack. He was already bewildered before she made a soft humming sound, which he could have sworn was punctuated with very light, rapid clicks. He was about to say something when he almost dropped his coffee. Right in front of him, he watched as a small gray orb spider cautiously crawled out of the crack. The spider did a little dance, seemingly waving her front legs up towards Athena. She hummed and clicked something to her unusual roommate. Josh stared, his mouth open, as the little spider crawled right up onto her fingernail.

'Say good morning to Josh, Charlotte. He's special!' she said as she gingerly held her friend aloft.

Josh stared wider, his eyes threatening to pop right out of his head. The spider turned to face him and one of its little fore legs raised up as if to wave. He nodded back. The spider did another little dance and then Athena carefully held the tiny creature near to the even smaller insect. The spider appeared delighted and, hopping off of Athena and onto the leaf, did what hungry spiders do at breakfast time. They watched as she spun a little web around her meal, one she evidently intended for a later lunch or, possibly, supper. Athena again offered a ride on her finger, but they were both a little surprised when Charlotte simply jumped off the stem and rode a lone thread of silk down to the sill.

'She's independent like that,' Athena whispered to Josh. 'Getting a little older and loves to exercise her prerogatives. Good girl!'

Josh took another sip of coffee and watched Charlotte wander back to the crack. She turned, did another little dance, kind of saluted the larger couple, and re-entered her home.

All Josh could manage was a weak, 'Uh— Uh— I—'

'So, sweet darling, what would you like for breakfast? I'm afraid we're just a little short on other bugs. Some fruit and an omelet, perhaps?'

His mind utterly incapable of processing what his eyes had just seen, he decided to just roll with the idea of eating with this most astounding woman. It turned out to be an excellent decision. If he had had the wits to worry, she did not leave the doomed aphid out of her concerns, quickly adding a word for his cocooned sacrifice to the end of Josh's blessing of their breakfast. Her cooking turned out to be its own blessing—fast, professional, and extremely tasty. While they ate, they continued some of their conversations from the previous night. He helped her clean up, and then she announced she would need just a moment to change for their new date. She showed him to her library, also giving him the choice of waiting in the living room. When she disappeared upstairs, he plodded around both rooms. The library was hedged with elegant shelves, mostly full of rarer-looking texts, many in a wide variety of languages. He noticed boxes full of other books everywhere. '*She out-reads me too*,' he thought. He'd just entered the living room, sat down on the couch, and once again tried to make some sense of his meeting little Charlotte, when Athena appeared again. She hadn't jested about the "in a flash" part. And she looked amazing!

He stared at her, seeing her wearing a long dress topped with a short coat. Her hair, freshly washed and dried, was pulled back in a ponytail. In one hand, she held a small purse, in the other she held a veil. Both items matched her outfit. The whole outfit was simple and conservative, and yet it augmented her feminine charm and power. And, again, as if Josh could see her any other way, she did look amazing.

'I'm all ready, dear,' she announced.

'How did you do all that so fast?!'

'I'm not a fussy girl,' she said with a grin. 'Now, you'll have a few extra minutes for you!'

They left her house in his little Civic again. For some reason, the heater and defroster started without hesitation, which he found odd but comforting. He also silently noted that, despite two days without attention, the temperature gauge stayed right on center.

He opened his door and welcomed her to his little apartment. 'I'm not quite as fast as you, but I won't be long. I'm sorry, but I don't have a TV. It's not much, but please make yourself at home and I won't be too long.'

'Not to worry, dear,' she said as she took a seat on his couch. 'I don't have a TV either. I watched a few shows years ago just to see what all the hub-bub was about. It did nothing for me and I've never watched anything since. Nice place, by the way.'

He wasn't sure if she was being honest about his little home, though he sensed she was, but he delighted in her dislike of television. 'No TV? Glad I'm not the only one! I'll be right out.' He turned but then added, 'It's not as well stocked as your place, but you can have anything in the kitchen you like, Athena.'

'I'm fine, Joshy,' she replied. 'Oh, and, if you don't mind, don't shave this morning. I kind of like the shadow on your cute face!' He blushed for a second and then hurried off.

Not shaving saved him a few minutes. He was not nearly as fast as her, but he was a fairly low-maintenance man. Before long, he returned to the living room wearing his best blue slacks, a gray tweed sportcoat, and his new accessory of pride, a Thanksgiving tie. She liked it immediately.

'Where'd you get the tie?' she asked as she stood to greet him. 'Nice look too!'

'It was a birthday gift from a little someone! Any guesses as to who?'

'Could it be...' she said, pretending to think in exaggerated fashion, 'Isabella?'

'You got it! She's the sweetest baby girl ever. The gift was almost as exciting for her as it was for me. It's so much better that you've met her now, so that I can further share the turkey joy with you.' They both laughed at the sweet, honest sentiment.

'We've got a little extra time,' she said. 'Running early, even for Hours. Would you like to be early? Or maybe continue our chat for a minute?'

'Well,' he said, 'we can keep talking in the car. But there's one more important thing I need to do first. We can take care of it on the way. Only be a second, really.'

Without asking more, she agreed and they were off. After a few turns, Josh headed down the main highway. They talked but he seemed preoccupied with his little mystery errand. In only a minute, he pulled into a shopping center, stopping in front of his favorite Market Basket location. Athena looked puzzled, so he quickly explained. 'I need to run in for something. I'd invite you to join me, but that would ruin the surprise. I'll only be a second, so please wait here if you don't mind. And, gee, I sure hope they have some on an early Sunday morning.' She nodded acceptingly and he literally ran off to the front doors.

He was really only gone for a few minutes. She saw him coming back, though he had his left hand behind his back, evidently holding something. He was smiling the biggest, cutest puppy dog smile she could imagine. In a second, he was there and motioning for her to roll down her window. She did, her mouth open a little. He beamed and handed her another dozen red roses, still in their cellophane wrapper. 'For you, my sweet Athena. No date for my girl without flowers.'

'Oh, Josh!' She accepted them and then actually opened the door, stood up, and hugged him. The rest of the drive, she made over the flowers, thanking him profusely. In short order, she somehow managed to peel back some of the packaging and rearrange them. She certainly had a knack for enhancing beauty.

In a few more minutes, they came to a stop in the parking lot of their destination. She carefully tucked the flowers, standing them in place behind her seat. Then she put her veil on and looked at him. 'You're so beautiful,' was all he could say, his breath momentarily taken.

'Thank you. You're not so bad yourself,' she said, adding, 'And we're right on time! Ready?'

He walked around and opened her door. Then she accepted his hand and they walked towards the front doors of her home away from home, Saint Athanasius Greek Orthodox Church. More than a few families and singles were already milling about the entrance or making their way inside. More than a few gave interested looks to Athena and her dashing young companion. No one was more surprised, or gladdened than Father Andreas, who happened to be on duty by the doors that morning. He happily walked over to them with his hands outstretched.

Taking one of each of their hands in his, he said, 'Good morning, Athena! And may God bless you and—'

'This is Josh Williams, Father Andreas. He's a very special friend of mine.' She winked at Josh and smiled gleefully at the priest. 'Josh, this is Father Andreas, our stalwart emeritus priest.'

'Pleased to meet you, Father,' Josh said, shaking the older man's hand.

'And I, you, young man,' the priest said. 'And, yes, I'm the gray, old backup around here. I'll make sure Father Josias knows you're here together! And welcome!'

They arrived inside the Church a few minutes before Hours commenced, taking a place, side by side, near the rear, along the wall. A few folks stopped by briefly to whisper hello and, seemingly more importantly, to meet Josh. A large family, the Morrisons, joined them near the wall, all of them evidently well-known to Athena. Josh liked everything and immediately felt at home. While he had been to several Greek services before, a few in that very Sanctuary, in fact, he would have admitted, as to language and custom, his Greek was a little rusty. And if pressed and if the services were mixed, he might have described his linguistic skills as non-existent. Yet he found something, then and there, strange but wonderful. From the Psalms through the Liturgy, and with all the Prayers, while he did not understand each and every word not offered in English, all of it made a great sense, in his heart as much as in his mind, as if it had been all delivered in English and very clearly. He chalked it up to universality and his rather devoted participation in those companion American-English services. And he was especially moved by Athena that morning. Out of the corner of his eye, he watched as she prayed, sang, and rose and fell from their kneelings. All those around them, along with Josh himself, did the same or made the same motions. But there was just something in her performance that he couldn't resist, a vision of liturgical excellence and obedience he almost thought. He did not know, but she was essentially running the same observation of him; she was especially taken with the small kind offerings he kept making of holding her hand as they knelt together, a kind but stern mark of deferential compassion. *'The way of a man,'* she thought. *'My man.'* She had also turned her thoughts, and a small prayer, towards his embrace of the, to him, interspersed foreign language.

Father Josias, the parish's priest delivered a short homily or reflection he entitled, "Crowns of Glory." It followed the teachings of Christ, as witnessed in the Gospels, along with the works of the early Patristic Fathers, particularly Saint John Chrysostom, as they embraced the blessed union of marriage. In short order, the very kindly mannered man covered the three basic principles of the betrothed: joint release of carnal desire; the concurrent blessing of children, and; joint salvation through that unbreakable and most dear friendship between a man and wife. As the words progressed, Josh felt himself tremble slightly. Then he dared to glance sideways at Athena. He marveled that she was already looking at him. They smiled upon making eye contact and he let his hand rest lightly between her shoulders. He might have heard her sigh. No words, of course, were spoken, but during Holy Communion, they each took an added interest in the acceptance of the other. Both noticed the priest had what appeared to be an added sparkle in his eye.

When the service concluded, they made their way outside with the throng. Father Josias sought them out and greeted them. 'My, my, Miss Athena, I was told you'd brought a guest, and I could not be happier to meet, Mister—'

'Williams. Josh Williams,' Josh said. 'Just Josh.'

'Welcome, just Josh! And, I see you are a Christian man— excellent! What, may I ask, if I may, what brought you here with our favorite curator and beloved sister, Athena?'

'We discussed the visit, to my Church, the OCA, or to yours, and, well, here we are,' Josh said.

'This is a date!' Athena added. 'Our second date.'

Father looked astounded for a moment, a look that melted into utter joy. 'Wonderful!' he said rather loudly. 'That is wonderful and most blessed news! Now, I trust you'll be joining us for a little bite to eat in fellowship?'

'Absolutely,' the couple said together.

On their way to the fellowship hall, they spoke with many people, all friends of Athena's and new, instant friends of Josh's. Back inside, they were temporarily separated. Mr. Morrison and a few other men asked for Josh's input on certain matters. And Father Josias, having joined them once again, ushered Athena a short distance away for a quick chat. Once in a quiet corner, they smiled deeply at each other.

'Not that it's directly my business, dear sister,' Josias said. 'But is this?'

'I hope so,' she said with a wide smile. 'I really do. And, of course, this does directly concern you, dear brother.'

'Then I hope so too, and I hope that I can help, the Lord willing,' he said. He then looked from side to side before addressing her in a whisper, 'I step perhaps out of my reckoning, here, but, Josh, does he— Does he know yet?' His face was still kind and happy though it was now touched with seriousness and questioning.

'No. I have not found it in myself to tell him yet. But I certainly will, Father,' she said. 'He deserves to know. He has to before he can decide anything. And then—'

'And then,' he said. 'We pray and consult. And pray. Here, again, I fear I must defer to your authority in some of these matters.'

'The authority is not mine, and my own is subdued, as you know. No, all authority is His alone,' she said. 'The prayers. For and from all of us. And we, Josh and I, if this is my love of loves, and his, and I hope it is, we will need your help, you dear man.'

'I will need your prayers for my strength and guidance,' he said.

'You will have them,' she answered. 'And I will need yours. So will sweet Josh.'

'Sweet Josh,' he replied. 'Well, I like him! I see he's already passed a very high and mighty test. Crowns of Glory!'

'Crowns of Glory,' she repeated. 'My stirring hope and longing!'

'Here, several matters may be intricately bound together!' he said. With that, he hugged her, and they wound their way back to where Josh stood with the other men. They found him ankle-deep in a discussion about the Pats' chances and prospects, post-Brady. Several shoulders shrugged and several sets of eyes rolled, and the men went their respective ways.

'Important topics?' Athena asked as they made their way down the little buffet.

'It started as a hello and what do you do conversation. Then we all lightly talked about our respective jobs. Then, it got serious,' Josh said with a laugh. 'They're all really good guys. It's a very nice parish you have here.'

'All the nicer today!' she rejoined.

They sat down with the priests and their families. Josh got the impression that, while she remained somewhat of a local mystery, most of those present held Athena in very high regard. After they ate, they enjoyed coffee and a bit of talk. A little after two o'clock, they excused themselves and headed towards Josh's car.

'Thank you for another lovely date, Josh,' she said. 'Or, are we still going?'

'I'd love to keep this up!'

'Good, that's just what I had in mind, my dear. Any ideas of how to spend the rest of the day?'

They decided to spend the afternoon meandering around the same streets they'd walked the night before. The bookstore was open, and so they also spent a little time browsing. Josh was amazed that Athena seemingly knew everything about most of the books they saw and about their authors. With her input, he picked up a few children's books for Isabella's birthday. They stopped and enjoyed coffee together. Then Athena invited Josh to come back to her place for a homemade dinner.

'Are you sure I won't be keeping you from anything?' he asked as they drove.

'No, of course, not. I have a couple of things to look at for the week, but I can glance at them tonight or in the morning before I go in. I review things rather quickly when necessary. And I hope I'm not keeping you from any homework.'

'Oh, no,' he said. 'We're slowing down for the Thanksgiving break. Anything I need to do for tomorrow will be waiting at work when I get there! And I'd much rather spend more time with you.' Once inside, she asked what Josh's favorite food was. As an American boy, he didn't surprise her too much when he said, 'pizza.' So, in rather short order, she whipped up what she called a fusion pie influenced by Greek and Italian takes on a Chicago classic. He didn't quite follow all of her explanations, but he loved the food. When they finished, cleaned up, and moved to the living room to chat and sip wine, it was dark outside. Neither one of them wanted the evening to end, though they both knew it must eventually.

Josh took another sip of wine and started, 'So, Athena, last night you said something to the effect that you quote-unquote *might* be falling for me.'

'I did, and I think it's a distinct danger, Josh.'

'Well, then, we're walking into this danger together,' he said. 'Like I said in the Gallery, I've never been very good with relationships. And I almost feel overwhelmed by this one. If this is one. And to be completely honest, I love the feeling! I know we just met, and when I compare myself to you, I think I should feel like a real nobody. But, I kind of don't. Please be patient with me as I really want to get good and deep into what we have. If we have—'

'I think we do have something, Josh. What you just said; I feel the same way. And I don't know what you mean by the comparison talk. Believe it or not, but I'm in your relationship history boat! And I too love this feeling. And I don't want you to think I'm rushing, or that we're rushing into this. Into us. By the way, I hope there is an *us*.'

'Athena, the heck with it! Let's rush in, full steam ahead,' he said. They both laughed and then hugged. 'And let's keep talking. And doing things! Can we call these dates?'

'We can. Yes, yes, and yes, sweetie. We'll take it fast, if we like, though with, shall we say, all proper cautions,' she said.

'That's the thing!' he said happily. He hugged her again and she came to rest her head on his shoulder.

As they cuddled for a little while, she asked, 'Outside of work, do you have any major plans for this week?'

'Well, I need to stop by the home one of these days. One afternoon. Something is going on that might affect things, and I'd like to learn a little more. And speaking of, Isabella's birthday, proper, is this coming Saturday. I absolutely have to go to that for my little sweetheart. Love her so much.

'And, then, there's this new woman in my life. I don't want to pester her, but she's rapidly becoming very important to me. I have to find a way to keep seeing and talking with her, fast, but not too fast. I'm hoping she and I can do a few things this week. Maybe a few more dates. I think we're calling them dates now.'

'Anyone I know?' she asked. They squeezed each other tighter. 'I have some ideas to help you. I take it you know best about the kids, though I hope you'll apprise me of anything you learn. I'd also love to come to the birthday party if I'm allowed. That would make an extra sweet date. And, if there's any time on any week nights, I'm available. Most of them, really. Except for Tuesday; we have this function that evening at the Gallery. Just some thoughts.'

'Thoughts I can adopt,' he said. 'You're definitely invited on Saturday. Maybe we can catch dinner somewhere fun afterward. And as for the other evenings, let's count on making a few of them work. Work any way, with any activity.'

'How about all of them? Or at least most? Anything, even just coffee or a walk, anything would be wonderful. I really want to keep talking with you, Josh, and see where this goes. I have a great feeling I like the idea of the destination!'

'Me too! It's a deal: I will call and text incessantly and make a regular nuisance of myself.' They both laughed again, though this time they reluctantly began to part.

'You better call and text. And we'll play it by ear, day by day. How's that?'

'Perfect. But, unfortunately, I think this play, this evening, had maybe better come to an end. Work and all awaits tomorrow.' They both very reluctantly stood up together. He continued, 'And, I have to again thank you for—'

Like the others, Josh, poor Josh, simply didn't see this kiss coming. And it was a doozy, the most passionate they'd shared. When she finally released him, he stood there almost catatonic and shaking. But she patted his shoulders and somehow it felt like he was released from a spell. Then all he felt was a happy tingling all over. 'And that,' he said. 'We need to do more of that! And how on earth do you do it? It's like you completely take control of me!'

'I have my secret ways, baby. I hope it doesn't scare you.'

'Scare? I'm scared witless! And I'm loving every second of it!'

'Good. There's more where that came from. And at some point, I'll let you in on my little secrets,' she said with a wink. 'But now, my sweet Josh, you'd better go home so you'll be rested for the week.'

'I will. But if it's okay, can I think about and dream of you when we're away?'

'You'd better! That will match what I'll be doing.'

With more laughter and a few gentle touches, she walked him out. At his car door, she said, 'Thank you for everything, Josh. I can't really describe what you've come to mean to me in such a short amount of time. It's like the wait of a lifetime is over!'

'Then we're together in our inability to accurately explain this. But, dear Lord, I'm so happy about it! Thank you, Athena, and goodnight.'

With one final short electric kiss, they parted. It wasn't too long before they were each beside their respective beds. Each said a heartfelt prayer that lasted for some time. Some say that some prayers go unanswered. It may be that some do. And it may also be that some do not.

Five

Guess Who I Met

Monday came, cold but bright. The forecast called for a deepening chill, and possibly a little snow towards the end of the week. For now, a clear calm lay over the area, Merrimack College included. Yet around mid-morning, there was a stir in the English Department. 'Lisa! Have you seen Josh this morning?' Allison practically shouted when she found Lisa, Professor Lisa Dawson, in the break room.

'I might have seen him. Can't exactly recall. Why do you ask?' she asked the department secretary.

'Something's up! Something good. It's the way he's acting. The way he's walking around this morning. Heck, he's not walking, he's floating! Should we investigate?'

'Let's go find him,' Lisa said, a sudden interest tinged with womanly nosiness building inside her.

Ever in high demand, Josh wasn't always easy to physically locate. But at that hour, they found him at his desk in his little office in the basement. Allison and Lisa, now joined by Mary, an assistant professor, crowded in his doorway and looked in at him.

'Hello, everyone!' he said with a smile as soon as he saw or sensed them. He then noticed the way they were acting, as if their very thoughts projected themselves into the room.

'Whatcha smiling about, Josh?' Mary asked.

'How was your weekend, Josh?' Lisa asked at the same time.

'What's her name?' Allison asked just a second behind the others.

Josh started laughing—his happiest laugh. He was known as a lighthearted soul, which, along with his work habits and competences, made him popular in addition to valuable. He often laughed. But this was, to the women, a new note. There was a child's silliness and innocence to it. And it immediately brought them straight into the office, each taking a perch close to the near-hysterical boy wonder.

'Okay, wow, girls, lemme see,' he said, breaking his chuckles. 'I'm smiling about her. I spent the weekend on dates with her. And her name is Athena.' He went right back to laughing. His ways were contagious and they soon burst out laughing with him.

'Details!' Lisa demanded.

'How'd you meet her?' Mary asked.

'How beautiful is she?' Allison asked.

'One at a time!' he faux scoffed. 'Okay, I'll give a few details. Allison's question first.' Here, he grew very serious, continuing, 'On a scale of one to ten, she's a one hundred. She's literally the most beautiful woman I've ever seen or imagined. And it's not just her looks; everything about her is a ten-plus. Or a one hundred. Plus. She's the most interesting person I've ever met. Almost alarmingly interesting. I've been buzzing around—I suppose you've all noticed—because I still can't process everything that's happened to me in the past few days. I keep thinking it's a dream I'm about to wake up from.'

'Ohmygawd, girls! This is serious,' Allison said. 'Keep going, baby. More!'

'Really, where'd you meet?' Mary asked.

'It was last Thursday night. You remember, maybe, that I was going to the Anderson Gallery at the Academy on an advance mission to find a gift for Isabella?'

'Of course, we do, silly,' Mary said. 'We kinda take notice of all your sweet ways. Did Miss Athena take notice too?'

'Well, sort of,' he said. 'So I went to the gift shop Thursday night, and there she was. She kind of snuck up on me. And when I told her what I wanted, she helped me find it. A locket on a necklace for Isabella. But not before shocking me completely witless. I almost didn't know what to do. In fact, if she hadn't calmed me down, I probably would have fainted or something. Right then and there, I said to myself it was love at first sight. Or really wondered as much.

'Then the following night, we all went back for our tour. I gave the locket to Isabella and I suppose Athena saw us interacting. And at the end, she was waiting to meet everyone. She kept talking, very nicely, to the kids, but she always looked at me. Something came over me, and I plucked up the courage to ask her out. I almost fainted again when she said yes. She even suggested the next night, time and all. But she left the details to me.'

'Where'd you take her?' Allison asked.

'Wait a second, Josh,' Lisa said. 'Athena. The Athena at the Anderson. Right? Isn't she the new curator? The director of the Gallery?'

'Yes, she is,' Josh said. 'She told me when we—'

'Hold on, Josh,' Lisa interrupted again. 'Ladies, he's not kidding about the one hundred over ten thing. I met her at a gala last month, and she is, no holds barred, INCREDIBLY beautiful. And I mean like making supermodels look ugly beautiful. Her name is appropriate; she literally looks like an immortal goddess.'

'I know, right? Part of me keeps asking what she sees in little old me. I asked her, and she just laughed it off that I was special,' he said. 'By the way, I walked her to her car Friday night, and she gave me a kiss before she left! A burning kiss.' All three women squealed at that part.

'She's right, Joshy. You are a special man. And not at all bad looking. No wonder she kissed you!' Mary said, adding, 'HR, don't hear us now.'

'He is also right that it's not just looks,' Lisa said. 'She has a presence about her. Something beyond what we're supposed to be capable of. But, Josh, Mary's right too; you might be exactly what she needs. And wants. Maybe wants in a burning way.'

'And the date?' Mary asked.

'So, I picked her up at her place—with roses! And we went to Meadowbanks.'

'In Andover?' Mary asked. 'Nice choice!'

He continued: 'Yep, it was great. Always wanted to eat there, and I couldn't have picked a better partner. We had wine. She's a bit of a wine expert. And we ate. And talked and talked. Then we even danced. And talked more. Then we walked around town for a little while. I took her home and she invited me in. There, we had more wine and talked for a looong time. And she did give me another kiss, a kind of big one.'

'Did you spend the night?!' Mary asked.

'MARY!!' the other two said at once.

'Well, I mean...' Mary said.

Josh suddenly turned into a blushing bashful puppy. 'Yes, but! We slept in separate rooms. I, um, I don't believe in, you know. I don't think she does either. I know she doesn't.'

'We know, Josh. We know you. The perfect gentleman,' Lisa said. 'But— What happened on Sunday?'

'We had already made plans, so that morning, yesterday, we went on another date. To her Church.'

'That's our Josh!' Allison said. 'That's the most civilized, manly date I've ever heard of.'

'It was really great,' Josh said thoughtfully. 'I met some of her friends and her priest. That's kind of important, you know. Then we spent the day, lazily touring around, always with conversation. To finish it off, she made me the best pizza I've ever had. Then I floated off to dreamland and I woke up here. Answering women's questions.' They all laughed.

They kept laughing as the women dug for a few more details. They'd never seen him so happy, nor could they think of anyone they'd rather see so ecstatic. He told them whatever they wanted to know, minus a few personal feelings. And he kept to himself, of course, his occasional thoughts about little things he still couldn't explain away: things like his heater, the speeding truck, and Charlotte. Throughout the day, they kept finding him and made more small talk about his new love life. At one point, around noon, he had made them wait while he ordered something on his cellphone. At intervals, they were joined by a few more women and two younger male professors, Bert and Tom. Tom and Bert were both newly married to wonderful young women, and they each thought of Josh as a little brother. Really, the whole department thought of him as the perfect kid sibling. With one exception. And the exception spoke with him, in a slightly different manner, a little later in the afternoon.

Josh was called over to a lecture hall in one of the classroom buildings towards the end of the afternoon. When the class, English Lit. 101, was released, he approached the professor. 'Dr. Johnson, you wanted to see me?' he said.

'Yes, son, Josh, and thanks for coming in and sitting through the second half,' Johnson said. Professor Hale Johnson was the Department Head, longest tenured member of the faculty, and a slightly rotund man pushing seventy. He bore very gray hair and an almost entirely white beard. If he wore red, which he didn't usually, he would have looked like a collegiate Santa Claus. And with Josh, in lieu of an elf, he'd always thought of the young man as more of a son.

'Two things,' Johnson said. 'First, I'm going to be out Wednesday and Friday. We're just reviewing the lecture notes in advance of finals. It's not a hard week seeing as how we're all off next week. So, I was wondering— Heck, I know you're up for it. Will you please conduct the review classes for me? Be my TA for two days?'

'Absolutely, sir! I'd be honored.'

'Great. Many, maybe not most, but many of the kids already know you. Or know of you. And they all think highly. Almost as highly as I do. I know you'll handle this with aplomb. Another score for the resume, and maybe, just maybe, we can use the experience to coax you, you know, towards a secondary degree, or two, and, one day, classes of your own.'

'I know,' Josh said. 'Thanks for the vote of confidence. All of them. Was the tenure-track the second thing?'

'No. That was just a bonus. Gotta nag you about it whenever I get the chance.' Johnson laughed at his makeshift cleverness. 'No, son. The second thing is a rumor I've been hearing all day. All those nosey women, and the two do-gooder boys, haven't let up about *her* all day. I know you, and I know you're different. Different in an old-school way that we'd all benefit from if it again became the social norm. So, I'm just going to ask and let you tell me what you will. Athena, is she? The new director of the Anderson? Is she, Josh, special?'

Josh blushed despite himself. And he sat on the edge of the presentation desk where Johnson was busy packing up papers. 'Sir, do you believe in love at first sight? Real love? Not all the fake Hollywood, twenty-first-century lust nonsense?'

'Yes, I do, son. I've been lucky to have lived in it for most of the past half-century. Is that what you're feeling?'

'It is. Right from the first second I saw her. Or when I heard her voice before I saw her. She's kind of blinded me, or taken control of my autonomy, if that makes sense. I just feel like I'm already one with her. Or that I want to be. I'm not sure what I'm saying, but if there is real love out there, then I hope this is my part in it. You know, sir, my love life never really existed, and I don't have any direct examples from a family to rely on. I'm flying blind. Blinder now because of her. I'm a little scared, but I want to love her. Really love her. That's what my heart says. I keep praying about it constantly.'

'Good. Keep doing that. That is, as with most things, the best answer. Love is real, my boy. And if this is it for you, then I couldn't be happier.'

'How will I know?'

'You probably already do. Perhaps. In the end, it'll hit you in a way that's unmistakable. Again, I know you, so you only have the best and most honest intentions. I don't care how pretty, or well-bred, or lofty, or even supernatural she is: any woman, any real woman, would be out of her mind with happiness to have you. As a man and as a husband.'

'That's what I've been afraid to say to myself!' he said excitedly. 'I keep asking if I'm worthy to be a husband. Especially to her. That's a powerful role to step into if I understand anything. It's like the relationship of Jesus to His Church. Powerful. And I'm just—'

'Just way stronger than you think,' Johnson said smiling.

'Do I, do we take it fast? Or slow and careful? Or what?'

'That's the easy part, Josh. You both take it as it comes. The trick is making something of what you come by. That's the secret, and the basis for all the needed prayers. And asking old curmudgeons for advice, if you happen to know one. You help me with the classes, and I'll be available for any talks or advice you need, son. How's that?'

'That's a deal, sir!'

They started walking out. Johnson laid his hand on Josh's shoulder, and said, 'Two things, for now and later. First, always be good to her. I know that'll be the easy part for you. The second, and more weighty item, is to always consider the awesome responsibility that comes with being the man of a relationship. It is exactly as you described it, a concurrent commitment of Divine importance.'

'Heavy,' Josh said.

'But, if it is to be, worth it. Oh! And, a third thing—have fun!'

Athena hung up the video call with the board and rectors. Then she restacked her proposal papers—all of them accepted now—and prepared to place them in her file cabinet. That's when she caught sight of Marge and Milley standing just outside her door, intently looking in. Just behind them stood a sleepy-looking Sam and stuffy-nosed-looking Bridget from the gift shop.

'So, how was your weekend, A?!' Marge asked.

Athena wiggled her nose and said, 'It was great. Why do you ask?'

'Oh, no, sweetie. You don't get away with just *great*. Ever since you got in, you've been acting super serious. With you, that means you are super excited about something,' Marge said. 'Milley and I, and these two, want to know if it has something to do with that handsome young hero who was here Friday night.'

Milley giggled, Marge stared at Athena, and Athena opened up a huge, happy grin. 'It does, in fact,' she said.

'Was his name John?' Marge asked.

'Josh.'

'Josh!' Marge exclaimed. 'Josh was the sweetest, kindest, cutest man I've seen in forever. I mean cute! The way he lit up that little group and kept them moving and laughing. And the way he treated that baby girl! He made her whole year, and he stole my heart!' Athena was about to say something, but Marge added, 'You'll expect some competition from her, you know. And, yep, even Sam could have seen the way he was talking to you when I was walking out. And the way you looked and acted. Smitten!'

Athena quickly brought them up to speed on the Thursday night shop encounter and how she'd wondered about Josh's relationship with the then-mysterious little Isabella. The three women crowded close around her desk, while Sam held up the doorpost. She then told them all about the extended, weekend-long date.

'Roses twice?' Bridget sniffled.

'Yes, he's an old-fashioned romantic,' Athena explained. 'He likes to open doors, he stands when I stand, offers his hand, and so much more. He's so complimentary too, in a shy, sweet way. And best of all, we just have so much in common.' She sighed.

'And he's hot!' Marge put in.

'Sounds like me when I was young!' Sam added. The girls giggled and doted on him for a second.

'And he took you to Church?!' Milley said.

'Yes, my Church. It felt so natural and homey having him there. At the same time, I don't know … I felt complete, or more at home than I normally feel. Everyone liked him.'

'That's huge,' Marge said. 'One never hears about that kind of date. The first one was awesome-sounding enough. But only a real gentleman would suggest something overtly Christian.'

'That's him!' Athena said. 'Josh is a real Christian gentleman. One I'm so lucky to have met.'

'Well, sister, we're all so happy that you've found him,' Marge said. 'I, for one, thought it was a small shame that the prettiest, most accomplished woman on the East Coast didn't have a Mr. Right in her life. But you were waiting, weren't you? And I get the feeling that maybe the two of you were brought together for a reason. By Someone Above!'

'Thank you, yes. In a lot of ways, I suppose I have been waiting. And I pray he is a gift to me from Heaven. I'm not sure how these kinds of things work, but I really hope it does work out.'

'Trust the Lord, baby,' Milley said.

Not wanting to be overshadowed by the women, Sam spoke up again, 'Do the two of you have plans for this week?'

'We do. There's something with those sweet children on Saturday, and he's going to surprise me during the week. Everyone, please keep your fingers crossed.'

'Will do, A, will do,' Marge said. After a few more words, the gang departed and Athena was left alone, thinking about her luck, not only with Josh but also with having such delightful friends. '*If only all Mankind were given to such kindness and happy generosity,*' she mused. Later, for her lunch break, she sat in her SUV and had a phone chat with Father Josias. While the words were different, and there was a far different tone to the conversation, it ran along much the same lines as Josh's talk with Professor Johnson.

When she walked back inside, Marge was waiting for her at the main desk. 'Roses, THRICE!' she said as she pointed to the newly arrived bouquet sitting on the ledge. 'I'll guess he's a keeper, and he definitely has a thing for you, A.'

'Oh, my goodness,' Athena said as she examined the flowers. There was a note attached, and she read it as she walked the roses back to her office:

> *Dearest Athena,*
>
> *Maybe you're starting to understand a little about me. My words simply cannot capture how happy you've made me over the past four days. So - it's more roses! Their beauty reminds me of you. If I may, just for a moment, I'd like to see you again this evening after work. This all feels like a dream, so I need you to pinch me! I also hope you're having the same wonderful day that I am, the day you've made so special.*
>
> *Sincerely, and I fear I am falling too,*
>
> *Josh*

She stifled a mixture of tears and laughter for a second. Then she sat down and typed him a text message:

> *Josh, you silly boy! I love the roses, and, yes, I also risk falling — even further! I'd say you shouldn't have, but I'm so glad you sent them. I will agree to "pinch" you, but only if you help me with something. I was a little busy this weekend, and I neglected to go grocery shopping. Meet me at Butcher Lad's at*

six and help me pick up a few things. If you make good choices, in addition to the pinch, I might cook for you again.

XOXO

Athena

She then added a second text: *PS: Marge was most impressed with you! I take it that is the common reaction! SIX at BLs!*

Promptly at six, Josh pulled into the little parking lot of the area's swankiest grocery store. He saw Athena just as she drove up. They got out of their cars simultaneously, and, to him, it was like seeing her again for the first time. He stood there for a moment, temporarily dumbfounded. She cured that by marching right up, kissing his nose, and taking him in a long, amorous embrace. When she released him, and he began to smile and make cute purring noises, she reached under his coat, aiming for his upper arm, and gave him a slight pinch through the fabric of his shirt. 'There. You're not dreaming,' she said before taking his hand and making for the doors.

She walked just ahead, not quite like she owned the place, but, obviously, as a seasoned regular customer, turning this way and that and, at intervals, selecting an item or two. Josh dutifully followed pushing a little cart. 'This is the nicest little supermarket I've ever seen,' he said. 'Is this luxury? And are you a, uh, a foodie?'

'Yes,' she said, 'and maybe. It depends on what that means. I've just found that the quality here matches my tastes.' She then turned and winked at him, adding, 'And I hit the Basket sometimes too.'

In the rear of the store, where the fresh meats and foods were kept under glass cases manned by men in aprons and neat paper hats, she quickly assembled something for their meal. 'Do you like lobster rolls, Josh?'

'Oh, yes, I love seafood of any kind. I never get to eat much of it, except for the frozen stuff. Is that a real lobster?!'

'Yes, the poor thing. We will honor him as he nourishes us, you'll see. Now, come help me get a few more things. You're gonna love my rolls. Nothing frozen about them.'

Back near the checkout stand, she paused and picked up a bottle of wine. 'Perfect for lobster,' she said. 'A Chianti. I would go with a rose, but you keep covering those.' They both chuckled.

Just before he started loading the food, and their poor little claw-bound friend onto the conveyor belt, he said, 'They have roses, right here! Should I—'

'Josh, no!' she said. 'I love the ones I have, and I really love the sentiment behind them. But I can't have you spending all your money on flowers for silly me.'

'Money well spent, I'd say, silly,' he said with a smirk. 'But can I help with this?' He pointed to the groceries and started to remove his wallet.

'Again, no, Joshy. This is my treat. More than roses, money, all of it, what I want is to spend a little time with you. Let me pamper you and you make it up by being mine.' There was something in the way she said those last words that made his heart flutter. She noticed, and for that reason, or no reason, she gave him an Eskimo kiss before paying.

Shortly thereafter, in her kitchen, Josh helped her prepare the food as best he could, as that was not his strongest ability. He took great interest in how one prepared a lobster, something he'd heard of but had never seen. And it turned out that no one had ever seen Athena's method. When the time came, and the pot was boiling, she held up the lobster. She prayed over or with it, and then she made a series of squeaks that reminded Josh of spider talk. Lastly, and it stood out to Josh as another inexplicable Athenaism, she said something in a language he couldn't place. Then she tapped the crustacean on his head. At that, the little beast went limp and still. 'Now, from a better place, he won't feel a thing,' she explained before getting down to the art of cooking.

For most of the process, Josh merely stood by, doing as he was told. She moved around like a blur, and, in what seemed to him a ridiculously short time, she announced they were ready and asked him to open the wine. After his Blessing, with an added word for the departed main ingredient from her, they settled down for the best seafood dinner Josh had ever had or imagined was possible. They talked about their respective days, the various reactions to news of their dates, their hopes and aspirations, and more. The more they spoke, the deeper they were drawn each into the other. Upon eating the last bite of the last roll, and feeling his stomach tighten pleasantly, Josh asked, 'Were you ever a professional chef or something? This was amazing. Even by your standards, which I've quickly come to see are exceedingly high.'

'A lot of experience, my dear Josh,' she said. 'And I took some courses a while back in Europe. And a girl has her secrets, you know.'

A few minutes later, relaxed on the couch with their wine in reach, she fed him the last morsel of tiramisu by hand, pausing to lick her fingers, an act that seemed very normal from his semi-hazy point of view. 'Stuffed!' he said. She then took a sip of her wine and actually began rubbing his tummy.

'There, there, baby,' she cooed to him.

'Athena, why are you doing this?' he asked softly and innocently.

'For better digestion, silly.'

'No, I mean, the dinner and all tonight.' He once again started to look a bit like a puppy.

'Well,' she said, taking another sip. 'I agreed with your rose note: I just had to see you. We're having a thing tomorrow night at the Gallery, so I decided this was the right time to have you over. Wednesday through Friday, I'm hoping, trusting, we can enjoy some similar moments together.' She batted her eyes at him.

'No. I really mean ... why are you so good and kind to me?' The puppy looked utterly lost now. And utterly adorable.

'Because, Josh, you are good and kind. Like you, I find some of my words failing me. So it's up to my actions. Let me care for you, sweetheart.'

'My words do come up a little short. And I'll let you care for me if I can care for you,' he said gently.

'It's a deal! Now, enough talk. Come here to me.'

'Like a hug?'

'Shhhh— Let me hold you.'

That is exactly what she did, an experience he simply couldn't describe. Time stopped, as did his conscious thoughts. They merely held a continuous embrace. He closed his eyes—as did she—and together they felt, smelled, and listened to each other's being. If he could remember it, amidst great bliss, the last thing he could recall was falling asleep. The way a contented little puppy might. At some point, and maybe it was only a dream, though it felt more like deliberate speech, he found time for his usual evening prayers. That night, it was as if they had come to him, that they had come to listen as much as he normally came to tell, ask, and praise. A dream or not, he awoke with a smile on his face. That smile gave way to mild bewilderment when he realized he was snuggly tucked into his own bed at home. His panic subsided when he discovered the evening had not been a dream. Upon reading her text on his phone, which he found in its usual place by the clock on the bed stand, it all made sense, even as there was no explaining it rationally. She had written, only a few minutes earlier:

Dearest Josh, thank you for another wonderful evening. I hope you enjoyed the lobster, the wine, and our time. Thank you most of all for caring for me and allowing me the courtesy of returning the same to you. Falling further, harder, and happier, Athena.

He sent her a short reply, adding a heart emoji to the ending. Then the smile returned and he drifted back into the deepest, most comfortable slumber a mortal man might achieve.

Six

Thinking of You (and Roses)

W hen Tuesday morning dawned, cold and clear, and she reported to work, Athena relived the previous day's giddy talk about Josh. He, of course, was just about all she thought about, what she really concentrated on, all day; even as she recounted their short relationship and happy exploits, in the back of her mind she mentally reviewed him on a much deeper level. Around mid-morning, still locked in her private contemplations, she started reviewing and rehearsing for that evening. At lunchtime, she again sat alone in her SUV, first speaking to Father Josias and, then, praying to his Boss. The afternoon brought a series of staff and Academy-related meetings which were punctuated by more rehearsals. Around five, she bid the day staff a good afternoon and had yet another Josh talk with the girls and Sam. Upon their devising a late closing procedure, she was called away to discuss matters with the event personnel.

When she left the office, Sam listened to the silence for a moment, before addressing the ladies: 'So I was in the building, last week, with him, and I missed this Josh fella? The younger me, and almost as good-looking? Even without meeting him, I get the idea that he's really something special. Someone I'd like immensely. You gals know he'd have to be par excellence, right? He's made a supreme impression on a downright power and force to be reckoned with. I've never said it, and never heard any of you say it either, but I know deep down that all of us realize there's always been something very, very different about Miss Athena. She's, to speak plainly, just ... better. Or higher. If you know what I mean.'

The ladies did know, even if they'd never mentioned it to each other. To them, their relatively new boss, who was the best ever at what she did, wasn't just a coworker. She was something else. Not quite a friend, nor like a sister, nor a daughter. It was a relationship that defied explanation, though each of them felt richer for it. If Athena had known, and it was never something she considered, then that was essentially the way all of her acquaintances viewed her—with the exceptions of Father Josias and, now, sweet Josh. The latter remained in her inner thoughts throughout the night's main event.

Around six-thirty, the large and influential crowd began to arrive. Present were a number of artists, faculty members from the Academy and several better New England colleges, a select few members of the media, and the all-important class—the donors who kept the art rotating and the wheels turning. Here and there lurked a politician or two, though security kept an eye on them. The whole building had been repurposed both as a showcase and as a party center. Champagne and hors d'oeuvre flowed freely among a gathering clad in black ties and formal gowns. And no one had seen her change, but of all the fanciness and beauty, nothing and nobody outshone Athena, even as, in her mind, she had somewhat diminished her visual appearance.

But she was most certainly noticed. As the show progressed, she tried her best to meet and greet everyone. More than a few of the gentlemen, particularly those of higher standings, tried their hardest to speak with her. A rare bold few even attempted some form of romantic initiation. Yet each time, as she very politely but effortlessly let them down, almost as if by a form of mind control, the only face she could really see or wanted to see was Josh's. And when her time came to act as mistress of ceremonies in the large auditorium, even as she wowed the gathering with her extended plans and the coming year's exciting new schedules, all she could still genuinely contemplate was him.

At the end of it all, a massive success, there had been raucous applause and great promise of continuing patronage. Still, she thought of him. As the reserve staff later departed and the cleaning crews went to work, she kissed him in her mind. Driving home not long before midnight, he still filled her with happy thoughts. Her concentration was only broken by the neighborhood guard who had flagged her down as she auto-passed through the gate: 'Miss Athena, a moment if you please. A package came for you this afternoon, and I did not want it waiting outside on your steps.' She waited while he fetched something from the little house by the gate.

'The FTD man came around four, madam. Someone thinks well of you!' He smiled as he handed her a custom arrangement of roses, reds mixed with fall foliage-themed additions. On the top were two white roses, side by side, and touching each other as if in an embrace.

'*JOSH!*' she thought, before telling the kindly man, 'Thank you very much, Mr. Dalton. I think I know who they're from. Such a lovely ending note for an eventful day!'

Inside her home, after arranging the bouquet on the kitchen window sill (and alerting Charlotte of the arrival), she poured herself a glass of wine and started typing him a text message. Around seven words in, she stopped and simply dialed his number. She was on fire with a raging smile when he answered, 'Hello, my dearest goddess Athena!'

'Good evening, Joshy. Thank you so much for the beautiful arrangement. I just left them in Charlotte's care. And I hope it isn't too late to call,' she said.

'It's never too late for you! And I missed you so much today. You're just about all I could think about.'

'I know the feeling, Josh.'

'Well, how did the gala go?'

'Perfect! We wowed everyone, and I think it's going to be smooth sailing into next year. They all concurred with my plan to update our operations by stepping back in time a little, a retro overhaul,' she said.

'I'm impressed, and I'm not even sure what that means.'

She proceeded to tell him a little more. Then she lovingly reminded him that he didn't have to buy her roses every day. He made no promises in that regard. They then discussed the rest of the week.

'Well,' she said, 'since we're both going to be a little late tomorrow and probably have eaten, how would you like to meet for an after-dinner coffee, maybe with ice cream—as crazy as that combo sounds—at the new little place by the bookstore? Sip and chat a little?'

'I'd love that!' he said. 'I can meet you there when?'

'How about seven? I can't wait to hear how your first day of lecturing went!'

'Seven it is, and I'll be excited to tell you all about it, hopefully. Oh! And that reminds me of something for Thursday night! Are you free, again around seven?'

'I will be, yes. What will we be doing?'

'This is so cool. Can you meet me at the reception center at the college?'

'Sure.'

'Awesome! I've never been invited to anything like this before, but since I'm a guest or substitute teacher for the end of the week, they invited me to the faculty break party! And I get to bring a guest.'

'Who are you taking, Josh?'

'Gee, I hadn't thought of that...' They both laughed as was their merry habit.

'I'll be there, pleased to be on your arm, my dear,' she said. 'And that only leaves Friday night to round out. Listen, I'm taking off Friday so I can run down to Boston and do a little shopping. I want to get something for Isabella, and I want to give some nice gifts to all the children. Would you be available to go with me?'

'I'd love to, but I'll be in the lecture hall again that afternoon.'

'Oh, right! Well, trust me to pick up some wonderful things for the sweethearts. And how many kids are there?'

'Just the ones you saw at the Gallery. Two little boys, three little girls, and thirteen-year-old Michelle.'

'Got it, thanks! And when I'm done, I'll be a little tired from my adventure, so I have an idea of what you can do for us for supper.'

'I'm all ears.'

'I'll come to your place when I'm finished. Let's just say seven once again. And I want, no, I expect you to have prepared your usual dinner. For you and me. Whatever you normally have by yourself, even if it's frozen.'

'Really?'

'Yes. Friday night is Josh night. Impress me. In the most ordinary Joshy way you can. Great faith in you, kid.' They laughed yet again.

'Deal. Now, I'll need to plan my roses accordingly...'

'I would say, *no roses*, but I know what you'll make of that. So do as you like. But just know that tomorrow, in your little War of the Roses, I'm going to have to retaliate!'

'Bring it, sister!'

'Oh, yes, dear Joshy. Consider it done. And, now, do consider some sleep. I want you up and at 'em in that class tomorrow.'

'Yes, ma'am. If it's okay, I'm going to dream about you.'

'I might do something similar, my sweetie. Have a blessed evening, Josh.'

'You too, Athena. And a very good night to you.'

'Good night, Josh.'

Not long after their call ended, it so happened that, their prayers said, they did dream about each other. And both awoke the next morning ready to take on the world.

Josh had a little special project waiting on him in the morning, the kind he was now famous for handling with great expertise. Around noon, he popped down to the cafeteria for a grab-n-go lunch, planning to spend the next few hours going over his class materials. When he walked back into the department, Allison immediately flagged him down. 'Hey, you! Lemme look at your outfit. No tie, huh? It's a staff policy that all male professors wear ties to class, you know. I can't let you disappoint us by going in there so casually. Like a slob or something.'

Josh went a shade of red for a second. 'Oh, my,' he exclaimed. 'You're right, even if I didn't know. I didn't think about it. I need a tie. Where can I get one fast?!'

She started laughing. 'I made that policy up, baby. You look fine as usual. But to answer your question, you can get a tie or four of them right here!' She reached down and picked up an odd but fancy-looking parcel from the floor, then handed it to him. He looked at it. For a moment, it looked like a flower arrangement. But upon closer inspection, he saw that in place of roses or carnations, someone had carefully, artfully gathered four neckties in the central display. Two were Christmas-themed, and the others geared for Thanksgiving. 'You better wear the one with the Pilgrim man on it!' Allison said with a chuckle, adding, 'And guess who they're from!'

He already knew, but he happily read the little attached note:

My dearest, sweet Josh,

Roses are nice,

When they're from my mate,

But just as I warned,

I RETALIATE!

Take that, baby!

All tied up,

Athena

As luck would have it, Mr. Pilgrim happened to match his outfit. And it caught the eye of two girls seated in the front row of Johnson's class. One spoke up during a pause in the review presentation, 'Mr. Williams? Dr. Johnson said you were great. By that tie alone, we happen to think he's right. Where'd you find it?'

'Oh,' Josh said sheepishly. 'It came today. A gift from someone.'

'Someone special?' the other girl asked. Several of the other kids now took notice of the conversation.

'Yes, very,' he answered.

'From your girlfriend?'

'Well, yes,' he said with a grin. 'We just started dating. I keep sending her roses, so this tie and a few others were retaliation, as she puts it.'

'So sweet!' the first girl said. 'Do you have a picture of her?'

'No, I don't. I'm not much of a shutterbug. But I tell ya what, I'll try to get one and show her off on Friday. Deal?'

'Deal! And I bet she's beautiful!'

'She is so beautiful I can't even describe her.'

One girl then whispered to the other, 'And she's lucky! I want him.'

'I know, right?' the other said.

The rest of the class went perfectly with Josh blissfully unaware of his rising stock among the co-eds. Johnson was the favorite professor in the whole department, one of the most liked in the whole college. And his kind recommendation, along with meeting him, cemented Josh's worth in the students' minds. He told Athena all about it over their late evening coffee.

'We haven't mentioned titles yet, but can I call you my girlfriend?' he asked her.

'I don't see why not ... boyfriend! And all thanks to my tie bomb!'

He got a little quiet, sentimental almost. 'I've never had a girlfriend before.'

She took his hand in hers and said, 'Well, now, I've never had a boyfriend before either. I guess we're even.' She smiled so sweetly at him.

'So we are,' he said, coming back to life. 'But ... not for long are we even. Rose time!'

'What? No! No roses!'

'Okay,' he said. 'I don't have roses anyway.'

'Whew. I was just about—'

'I have one rose!' He then pulled a single flower out of the little bag she'd noticed him bring in. He stood up, walked over to her, and presented it. After she smelled it, cooed a little, and berated him for his sweetness, he loosely affixed it to her jacket lapel. Just as he was about to stand upright, she grabbed him by the collar and pulled him in for a latte-flavored kiss. 'Even, again?' she asked as she released him. He made a funny little noise and returned to his seat. They spent the rest of the evening talking softly and exchanging loving gazes. He even got a second kiss and a long, warming hug when he walked her to her car.

Thursday went by in a flurry for both of them. At seven, he met her at the doors of the reception center at the college. Part of him had expected to be almost used to her by then, but when he saw her, she once again took his breath away. She had a similar effect on the rest of the regular faculty.

'Is that her?!' Allison said to her little group.

Lisa looked and then said, 'That is Miss Athena from the Anderson! Even prettier than I remember her. Wow, and go, Josh.'

The new couple made a small splash at the gathering, and both had a dandy time. He was, of course, proud to introduce her to any and every one, and she gained a new and expanded appreciation and respect for him. The high point of the event was a bit of an oddity, an academic riddle, and it led to a resolution of sorts that defied the very concepts of high and odd. For many years, it would be a source of bafflement, later giving way, at Merrimack, and at other language and philology departments, to a legend. Before leaving for his early Thanksgiving break, Professor Johnson, the academic's academic and a known joker, had left a conundrum for the attendees to ponder and, if they dared, to try to solve. Professor Lisa Dawson read it out for the gathered intellectuals, a matter almost none of them had ever considered or even thought to consider: a hypothetical question allegedly postulated in parts by J.R.R. Tolkien, John Gardner, and Seamus Heaney about a case shift in the first known original manuscript of *Beowulf*. 'And, of course, the crazy man couldn't be here in person to see the looks on all of our faces,' she said. 'Any guesses?'

Instead of guesses, witty remarks, or any other form of verbalization, all she received in answer was a host of blank looks. There was, however, a lone exception. After what felt like a short eternity had passed, Athena whispered to Josh, 'Are you going to have a go?'

'What?' he said. 'Heavens no. No idea whatsoever.'

'Would you mind if I answered?'

'Hey, knock yourself out.'

Athena then raised her hand and stepped forward into an opening at the center of the crowd. 'May I?' she asked Lisa.

'Certainly, Miss Athena?' Lisa said.

'Thank you,' Athena said. 'I think the portion in question is towards the end of the Old English text, I'll say from lines two thousand seventy-five through twenty-one hundred and ten, two key lines and five critical words to be exact. If none of you mind, I can quickly recite them for reference.' There were no objections and so she began to quote the passage in question from memory in the original tongue.

Lisa, who was holding an original language book, whispered to Allison, 'My God, that's verbatim.'

Athena continued, and upon finishing her recital, further remarked: 'There is no evidence of a shift in those words. However, we must consider the base source of the words where the problem allegedly lies. Some, like Professor Tolkien, I think, might have said the issue came from a juxtaposition of Old Saxon, as later reckoned Germanically. The German issue, if that was it, would still persist in similar verses, in the general lexicon, even into modern times.' Here, she repeated the two key sentences in both Old English and Old Saxon. All eyes were on her, and a complete silence had fallen. 'The problem is the relative lack of declension, which I suspect Tolkien, and perhaps Heaney, and maybe even Raffel would have taken into consideration. So, of course, the real answer to this little riddle lies not in those languages, but in Old Norse.' She then quoted the offending sentences in Old Norse, followed by a comparison of the five critical words in all the mentioned languages with a modern English reference thrown in. A few heads were being scratched. 'And that's it. With or without declension, which I've always thought superfluous, it is the ancient Danes who give us the answer.'

When she finished there was a long period of quiet. Lisa, who'd been looking at the notes Johnson left behind, finally said, 'Sweet Jesus, that's exactly what Hale thought the answer was, not, as he said, he ever expected anyone to understand the question to begin with. B-but, your explanation goes so much deeper, I can't even—Bravo, Athena!' The room broke into applause while Athena merely nodded shyly while holding Josh's arm. He was completely speechless, as were several others around them. At length, a few professors came over and congratulated her, with two asking if she was an independent Geats scholar. She only replied, politely, 'Oh, no. I just have a knack and some free reading time. That's all.' Though Josh kept looking at her as if he'd just met a beautiful female Aristotle or Newton, the party resumed as it had been before

Hale's brain buster was unveiled. At some point, a photographer took a few pictures of them, together as a pair, and as part of several smaller groups. Another wonderful evening, another date ended with another kiss.

Just before they separated in the parking lot, she asked him, 'What? No roses?'

'Not tonight, sorry. And you do deserve some for your brilliance if nothing else. But, uh,' he said, 'this time, it's just ... rose petals! For the tub.' He beamed as he handed her a little jar full of dried leaves meant for enhanced bathing.

'You—' she said. 'You *clean up* well! Oh, and happy one-week anniversary!'

'The happiest week of my life!' he said. They shared a laughing hug and then headed off for more thankful prayers and additional sweet dreams.

Friday afternoon, in the lecture hall, the same girl immediately confronted Josh as the class commenced. 'Did you remember the picture?'

'Oh, no! I totally forgot!' he said ruefully. 'And we were at this thing last night and had our pictures taken. I never thought—'

He was cut off when the entire class of a hundred or so eighteen-year-olds started to laugh. 'Brah!' a fraternity brother-looking boy called out. 'You seen the *Monitor*?!'

Josh looked confusedly at the projection screen for a second. The class kept laughing. 'I haven't turned it on yet,' he started to say.

'No, Mr. Williams,' a girl said. 'The *Merrimack Monitor*. The paper?'

'Whuu—'

'Brah,' the boy said. 'They got your picture. Dude, you're on the front page. Pull up the online edition!'

Josh fumbled with the screen controls while the kids chuckled knowingly. He found the *Monitor* and pulled up their site. And the first thing he saw was a picture of Athena and him at the party the night before, both of them holding each other, leaning together, smiling, laughing at something.

The girl in the front read the image caption: '*Mr. Josh Williams, lecturer of English, with his date, Ms. Athena Naonikis, esteemed curator of the Anderson Gallery...*'

'She is beyond description!' another girl said.

'Brah, you the man! The man's man! Heck, dude, you're beyond THE MAN!'

'Congrats, brah!'

'Doc Johnson made the right call!'

'LUCKY!'

'He's not bad, himself! Lucky lady.'

Josh blushed and grinned as his new friends and admirers gushed over his love life. When they calmed down, with simmering smiles on their faces, he told them a few heartfelt words: 'She's very, very, very special to me. Thank you. Now, you guys are just a few years younger than me. I was just in classes like this not long ago. I know how life and the times can be. But things can be pretty wonderful too! Maybe you already have that special someone, or maybe he or she is coming to you soon. Pray, and God always delivers in His time. I'm so happy to know all of you now, and I want the best for each of you. I love you guys.' A few tears fell here and there. Several 'aws' echoed about.

'We love you too, brah! You're just awesome!'

'Okay, then,' he said, pulling up the day's material. 'Show me you love me by reading off these Chaucer notes in turn, round robin.' The kids exceeded his expectations, as he kind of suspected they would. The class and the rest of his day went swimmingly. Then he hurried home and put on his new cook's apron.

Right at seven, there came a rapping at his door. He opened it and looked at her. For the first time since he'd met her, she was dressed slightly casually, in a manner that matched his appearance that evening. Her hair was up in a ponytail, and she wore trendy jeans and a flowing sweater. Again enamored, he swept his new love into his arms. 'Come on in, girlfriend! I gotta show you something!' He led her inside. 'And tell me all about the shopping trip in a bit.'

'Something smells good,' she said. 'Something besides you. But what do you have to show me?'

'This,' he said, pulling up his phone. 'This is the college newspaper. We made the front page today.' She looked at it happily and quickly read all about their event.

'We're famous,' she said.

'No, we're legends,' he said. 'I had mentioned you to the kids in the class on Wednesday. And they were the ones who showed me this today. Here's a big selfie one of them took. He then showed her a photo: their picture was on the big screen in the background; Josh was front and center, surrounded by fawning kids, one of whom, the girl from the front row, had snapped the selfie. 'They're the best kids!' he said proudly.

'And you're the best boyfriend,' she rejoined. After a moment, a few more lovey-dovey words, and upon putting her purse down, she asked, 'So, what smells so good?' She didn't say, but she saw that there had been a conspicuous effort to tidy the apartment up from her last visit on Sunday. He led her to the kitchen and started explaining, picking up a box from the counter as evidence.

'First off,' he said with a little embarrassment, 'it's meat. I forgot when I was shopping, and, uh, it's not Friday-friendly. In a strict sense. But—'

'Do you observe fasting?' she asked, in a more excited voice than one might have imagined.

'I do try,' he said. 'That's one area I really need to work on improving. However, on days like this, when or if I do catch myself in a mistake, I try to fast in the daytime, at least until three. And I ask for forgiveness with the provision that I'll do better. Do you fast?'

'Yes, and I find it refreshing you do as well. Another pleasant Joshism.' she said. 'I find it a little easier than most people, in a number of ways or for a few reasons. But all of us have room for improvement, Josh. You have a dedicated heart, so don't be too hard on yourself. And, if I may, I kind of assume part of your bachelor frozen dinner way has something to do with simplicity, correct? If so, that's a decent marker of not putting oneself too high in the order of eating or drinking. And it would generally fit with all your sweet, innocent ways.'

He smiled and said, 'Thanks. Uh, as for the TV dinners, thanks, again, but that might be more pure bachelorism. But you could be kind of right, and I hadn't thought of it that way. Maybe all of this is something we could help each other with in the future?'

'Why, I think we might be able to do that!' she answered with a bright face. 'Now, for tonight? What's behind box number one?'

'Right!' he said. 'Tonight, my dear, we will enjoy the finest frozen lasagna Market Basket has to offer, a special by Mrs. Marie Callender!'

'Oooo—,' she said. 'Yummy meat and ricotta!'

'That's not all. With it, I have just sliced up a healthy fresh bell pepper. And, in this very bag—that I'm having trouble opening—is our salad. A bistro mix! How's all that?'

She wrapped her arms around his neck, leaned in, nose to nose, and said, 'That, or anything made by you, my sweet baby, is beyond perfect.' She then nibbled on his nose, an action that made him giggle like a bashful child. Then he backed up, with her stealthily following him, almost cornering him by the fridge that he hastily opened. He reached in and pulled out another box.

'Instead of our usual wine, I thought a choice sampling of beer would go well with our meal. Well, that and I don't know much about wine. But I give you the Sam's Seasonal Holiday sampler!' The box top was already opened, and after poking around for a second, he produced a dark glass beer bottle. 'Might I recommend Old Fezziwig? Or another one; there's a few to choose from.'

'Baby,' she said, 'this is all beyond perfect. Kindly pour me a Fezzi at your leisure.'

He promptly produced two new, just purchased a few nights before glasses and poured two frothy draughts of the ale. Together they watched the bubbles subside. Then, with a swirl and joint sniff, they each took a sip. 'Perfect!' she said.

'Wait til you try my patented frozen Italian!' he said with a laugh.

After she helped him with the near-impossible task of opening the salad bag, they sat down to eat. He said another Blessing and almost choked up when it came time to give thanks for her presence in his life. 'Amen,' she said with him, then adding, 'And now a toast! To Isabella, the children, and to us!'

'Hear, hear!' he said as they clinked the new glasses.

They ate slowly and talked about the day, their budding feelings for each other, and, especially, about plans for the next day. 'Come over about an hour early,' she instructed. 'I'll have the gifts wrapped by then and you can help me load them back into the Benz. I'll even let you drive since you know the way.'

'Me, drive a Mercedes! Heavy.'

'It's a machine like any other, baby.'

'Okay. And what did you get for them? I found Isabella a few more little things, like those books from the other night.'

'Mostly clothing,' she said. 'Very nice stuff, very traditional. For some reason, I was thinking extra about the older girl, Michelle.'

'Kind of you. She's, uh, maybe had it rough.'

'I got the feeling.'

'But how'd you know about sizes and so forth? Details?'

'One doesn't rush a woman about shopping details, Joshy. You'll see and learn all tomorrow.' She winked and then blew him a kiss across the table. Thereafter, they tidied up a little and then he led her to the couch.

'I'll be right back,' he said with a smile. In a moment, she heard a dinging sound from the kitchen. A minute after that, he returned with a tray. Rather, it was more of a one-by-twelve pine board with items on it, a bachelor's tray if ever she'd seen one. He presented two more beers and two little previously frozen pies. They chatted, sipped, and munched on the pies, which were surprisingly good chocolate mousse numbers.

With a bite remaining, she put down her fork. Josh was already finished with his pie, and he looked at her expectantly. 'Stuffed!' she said.

'Oh, no,' he said as he lifted the last bite on her fork and brought it to her lips.

She ate it, swallowed, and then let out a little 'oof,' with one hand on her stomach.

'Perfect,' he said, admiring her. 'Now, I get to rub your tummy! For digestion and such.' They both grinned, and he slid over next to her. As his hand gently rolled across and around the sweater, he suddenly remarked, 'Oh, wow. I've never touched a girl's stomach before. I'm sorry. Maybe—'

'It's okay, and better than okay,' she said. 'As long as it's through my sweater and no more. And it's soothing, you sweetie. I like it. So, what was it? So good and kind.' She tenderly returned the rubbing affection. That turned into a kiss, a long reclined hug, followed by cuddling. They had established a knack for holding each other, an act of communication without words as much as a show of endearment. Their eyes were closed and they both enjoyed being close and comfortable. And just when Josh was afraid he would fall asleep in her arms again, she kissed him wide awake and prepared to stand up. 'It's a big day, tomorrow, and we both need to be rested. I should head out.'

'You're right, Athena, my perfect girlfriend. Thank you for coming over, for holding me again, and for being in my life!'

'You're so welcome, baby boyfriend. And thank you for everything.' In a minute, by the door, she turned to him, and held his head in her hands, standing very close. She looked exceedingly deep into his eyes. 'I love you, Josh!' she said before she gave him a small kiss.

It was like his world had ended and instantly begun again, far better than before. No one had ever spoken those words amorously to him and he let her know that fact. Then, placing his hands on her head, with tears falling down his face, he said, very softly, 'I love you too, Athena. I love you. And I'm so hopelessly in love with you.'

They held each other, almost rocking for a little while. Finally, she said, 'I know, baby, I know. And this is just the beginning. Soon, we're going to have more wonderful words for each other. For tonight, dream about the ones we've just spoken. I know I will.'

With that, they said their gentle goodbyes and she left. He had to sit down with another beer so as to process the moment. Then, after an extra long prayer, and a little weeping for joy, he did indeed dream of the happy scene over and over until dawn. Not so far away, she had an identical experience.

Seven

Presents and Presence

Saturday morning rolled around with a damp, gray sky that threatened to unleash an early example of winter's frigidity. The temperature was then as high as it was forecast to go, and throughout the weekend and into the next week, it was supposed to become even colder and inclement. There was now a decent chance of a white Thanksgiving. Josh took note of it all as he walked to his Civic, hoping that the heater's late turnaround would hold a little longer. He had half zipped up his blue coat against the chill, and he was carrying a square paper bag containing a few more gifts for Isabella. Stopping along the way at a certain shop, he purchased another kind of gift. And he took both the bag and the new gift with him when he approached Athena's door.

'Your daily dose,' he said as he handed her a bottle from the top step. 'Biltmore Estate's Dry Rose! For a little later, of course.'

'Rose wine!' she said, looking at the bottle. 'You never give up, do you?'

'Nope!'

'Well, good, then,' she said. 'I'll set this in the kitchen for later, and then, if you'll be so kind, I have all the presents in the garage. And I need to give you something.' She soon returned with whipped cream-topped, hot, chocolatey coffee for him and her, then led him to a side door in the hall.

In the garage, Josh saw why she parked her SUV in the driveway. The floor was completely covered with large cardboard boxes. And every box appeared to contain at least a hundred books. 'Doing some reading?!' he asked.

'A little, here and there,' she said. 'The row nearest the door here is incoming. The others on the far side are outgoing. I read them when I have a chance, keep the ones I like, and donate the rest to libraries and schools. He quickly calculated there had to be at least five thousand books present, and maybe closer to ten. Taking a cautious look inside three of the closest boxes, he saw that, like the works in her office, the books came in many different languages and covered a remarkable range of subjects. He gave her another quiet dumbstruck look. 'I'm a speed reader,' she said.

She then opened the overhead door, ushering in a cold air, and walked him to the opening. There, on top of some of the incoming book boxes, sat a host of large Lord & Taylor shopping bags. Each bag was full of wrapped gift boxes of different sizes. 'It's basically one bag for each baby, one for the home and Sister Francisco, and one is for extras split between Isabella and Michelle. And this, of course, is for Isabella too!' She picked up a huge, floppy teddy bear.

'Oh, my!' Josh exclaimed. 'And I see you've added labels with all of their names! How'd you know?'

'A good memory, sweetie. I met them all the other night, remember?'

He could not remember, exactly, but they nonetheless proceeded to load the bags (and bear) in the back of her GLS, essentially using all of the available room. As he helped her into the passenger door, she handed him the key fob. Inside and behind the wheel, he looked around at the elegant but complex-looking displays and controls. 'This is quite the car,' he said.

'Take a second and look it over, get to know it,' she said, sipping her coffee. 'And the end of the driveway, it's much the same as any car. Maybe a few more horses than your Civic, but it'll handle the same. I disabled all of those annoying driver-assist gadgets. Oh! And I programmed the second seat control for you, tailored to fit you.' She leaned over him, tapped a button, and he felt the seat move back and down slightly. He might have noticed the mirrors tilt a little too.

'How'd you know how to do that?' he asked. 'Without measuring me or letting me sit here first?!'

'I have excellent spatial awareness,' she said smartly before giving him a little kiss. 'Forgot that. Happy morning, Joshy!'

After a short study of the controls, he backed out and they headed towards the children's home. 'So, what'd you buy for everyone?' he asked.

'Mostly clothing,' she said. 'I just wanted them all to have a few nicer things to wear, especially for winter. Traditional articles, like I said last night. And I got a few school items and toys too.'

'Again, how did you know what the sizes were?'

'Well, I saw them at the Gallery that night, silly,' she said, adding, 'Or, I guessed, aided by my spatial senses.'

'Those must be very good,' he said. 'My seat's perfect. Comfy too. It's heated, isn't it?'

'Yep! Cozy?'

'Can I live in here?' he asked. They laughed and chatted all the way to the orphanage, with the chat becoming a little serious and the laughter subsiding only once they neared the address. 'I'm not sure, but I think there's a big change coming,' he told her. 'And sooner than later. I'm afraid the powers that be are planning to close the place and consolidate operations elsewhere. That'll mean any remaining kids will have to move. Again. It's what we, what they do. Way too often, poor things.'

'See what you can find out,' she said. 'Do any of the children have placement prospects?'

'Not that I know of. The whole system is out of whack, even by the usual standards. Isabella and Michelle, and maybe a few of the other little kids have done the foster home musical chairs routine lately. With not-so-decent results. Issy is like my baby girl, and

I feel so bad for her. And, I don't know what, but Michelle—' He stopped his thoughts, a pained expression flashing across his face.

'We'll find out together, my dear,' she said reassuringly. 'Thank the Lord they have you and the good nun.'

'And you, too, now,' he added as they pulled into a driveway.

While taking the bags out of the back, he leaned close to her and said, 'Our words, last night at the door—the happiest I've ever heard or said.'

'I know, Josh. I love you. Today more than ever.'

'I love you too, Athena.' He kissed her cheek before picking up as many bags as he could handle. When he turned around, she draped the bear over his shoulders. And in one trip, they carried everything inside, depositing most of it with Sister Francisco.

'We bought a few things for everyone,' Athena told her. 'I'd like to wait until after the party to give a few things to the other kids. And to you.'

'Athena, you are a wonderful woman! A match for my dear little Josh. And I am so happy to see you again,' the nun said happily. In a moment, she privately added to Josh, 'Well! Is this—'

'I really hope so!' he said.

Francisco then had other news, which would have a slight impact on their auxiliary gift plans. 'We're down by three,' she said. 'Three of the little kids, the two boys, and Wendy have all been pre-placed in advance of the great potential. They've been approved—you know about that, Josh—for real homes, though those homes are outside the area. It just came together this week, and they all left yesterday. I really think, hope, and pray that it's going to work.'

While they were certainly happy for the three absent children, Josh and Athena were still a little crestfallen. 'Well,' Josh said. 'We still have the other girls. On with the party!'

Sister added, 'But I do have good addresses for all three of the adoptees. I'll make sure what you've brought gets to them. I promise.'

'Thank you, Sister. And everything will work out in the end!' Athena said.

The party did go on, and it was loads of fun. Sister aside, Josh and Athena were the only other adults present. Michelle overcame her budding teen angst and doted on and played with Isabella and the other small girl, Kara. And truth be told, Josh did a fine job standing in for another little boy, playing, acting out, and rolling around with the kids, evidently as much to his satisfaction as theirs. Pizza was on the menu as their main lunch course, and Isabella blew out all eight candles on her big creamy white birthday cake decorated with frosting puppies and kittens.

'It's so soft and warm!' she said as she modeled her new coat, one of three Athena had picked up. 'And it fits me perfectly!'

'See,' Athena whispered to Josh. 'Spatial recognition.'

Isabella also thought the coat accented her new necklace well. So, as they were together, there were phones present, and Sister Francisco had a higher quality printer in her office, she demanded, and finally received, a picture of Josh and herself. They posed for Athena, with Josh holding a giggling Issy in his arms. And as there was space for a second small photo, Josh took one of Francisco surrounded by the three girls. The pictures were scaled down, printed, cut, and installed. 'See, Joshy, now we'll be together forever, all of us!' Issy clamored as she (repeatedly) showed Josh the locket's contents.

After they ate cake, after Isabella opened the rest of her presents, and after they played a few more games, one of which threatened to turn into Pin the Tail on Joshy, Francisco asked if they'd like to present their gifts to the other girls. 'Yes, Sister, but first, this one's for you,' Athena said. Francisco looked gratefully at the shoes and other items she saw in her bag, but she was most taken with the envelope full of cash and a rather large check. 'Just for whatever,' Athena said as she hugged the woman.

Kara received a number of articles that matched and complemented Isabella's trove. They took to playing, dancing, and modeling together, lost in a little world of princess wardrobing.

Josh and Francisco followed them around, making a general fuss while also trying to pick up the assorted wrappers and gift papers. Athena took the opportunity to approach the older girl. 'Michelle, is it? We've brought you a few things too, my dear,' she said.

'Really?! I wasn't expecting anything. You didn't have to.'

'No, but I wanted to. A young woman—what an exciting time— has to look her best. Building confidence and having fun at the same time is a blessing. Would you like to see what I brought?'

'Yes, please, ma'am. And are you the woman we met at the museum tour? Are you, uh, are you and Josh, you know, an item?' Michelle was smiling innocently and happily.

'Yes, and yes!' Athena said. 'And please call me by my name, not ma'am! I'm Athena.' She extended her hand to Michelle. A slight awkwardness overcame the girl, they both smiled, and Athena simply decided to joyously take both the teen's hands in hers. Suddenly, the smiles vanished. Athena gasped and the girl turned white then red. A look of horror swept over Athena's face and Michelle looked guilty and afraid like she'd just revealed a deep and horrible secret. The girl began to shake and cry.

'No, no! It wasn't supposed to be that way! He told me if I pleased him, then he'd love me. I did something wrong. I did! It was all my fault!'

Athena quickly took her in a powerful hug, whispering in her now very red ear, 'No! Nothing was your fault! You are pure. You are innocent. You are a young woman, greatly loved, who has extreme value. Let me hold you.' They continued to embrace and both cried. Slowly Athena moved her hands, one to the girl's back, centered over her heart, and the other to her head. As she did, a sense of peace fell over Michelle, the same calm Josh had experienced from Athena's angelic touch. Her tears dried, followed by Athena's. They stood there, head to head for some time. Whether they were only standing, or whispering private words to each other, no one else knew.

At length, with Athena still holding the girl's arms, they backed up a step from each other. They were smiling again. 'Come, show me your room, Michelle. And I want you to try on a few things. We can play with a little makeup too if you like!' With that, they went away for a little while. About an hour later, when the two little girls started watching a movie, Josh informed Francisco he was going to track down the missing womanly duo.

He knew where he was probably supposed to look first because, by chance, Michelle now occupied his old lodgings, a small bedroom at the back of the house. Going down the hall, he heard their voices. Smiling, he reached the door and looked in. And he froze in place with his mouth agape. Michelle was facing away towards the window, swaying and holding up a long blue dress covered with printed flowers. A small pile of new clothes, shoes, and girly items sat on the bed before her. It would have been an ordinary happy scene except for Athena and the glow. Outside the window, Josh could plainly see the sky and air were overcast and gray. The small light in the ceiling did its job, but nothing rational could explain the other, greater light emanating from the corner. He could never be sure, but he almost imagined the light held the image of a woman, a woman looking silently toward Michelle with her arms outstretched. Michelle appeared to notice none of these circumstances, nor did she take much note of Athena.

And Athena was near the door, facing the girl who faced away from them. Josh saw his new girlfriend, the most wonderful person he'd ever met, down on one knee. Her head was bowed and she clasped her hands to her breast. And, unmistakably, she was repeating over and over, '*Sancta Maria, protege eam. Sancta Maria, protege eam...*' Josh immediately and silently knelt behind her out of unconscious reverence, though he kept his head up and his eyes open. He couldn't have watched for more than three seconds when Michelle turned towards the door and the two adults. 'I love it all!' she yelled out happily. And just like that, the light receded, Athena was standing, and Josh, still kneeling, felt the world return to normal. 'Hi, Joshy!' Michelle said. 'Why are you on your knee, silly? Did you know your sweet girlfriend was doing all of this?! I feel like a real woman for once in all my life. I so love you two!'

89

They led a beaming Michelle back to the living room. After several hugs, and after taking Athena's contact information and a promise she would always be available no matter what, the young woman joined the two smaller girls and their exciting cartoon movie. Josh and Athena sat and talked with Francisco in the kitchen for a little while.

'I'm not sure, Josh,' she said. 'It has to do with the budget, the changing times, and a lot of things. But, unfortunately, I've been told by the end of the year. These three dears will be the last to come to live with me. I'm afraid my time has come to go out to pasture. And if they're not placed before, then I think the girls will be moving on. Probably to the central house or even out of state. I've been a little depressed about it.'

'Don't be,' Josh said, holding her hand. 'You've been the best mother any child could ever want. Trust me, because you know I know. And the good Lord has a plan for everyone. I'm twenty-four, and until last week, your love and some friendships aside, I'd never even seen the hint of a real family or true belonging.' He looked at Athena as he spoke.

'You two, whatever comes, are so special,' the nun said. 'I'm so happy I've gotten to see the beginnings of what may be a great and righteous marriage. The spirit of the sacrament just oozes from the two of you! Two of the kindest people I've ever known. And I've started praying for and about youse pretty hard and heavy. I love prayers like that.'

'Thank you,' Athena said. 'What Josh said, is what I've experienced in my life, or, rather, haven't, for maybe just a little longer than him. It's such a wonderful feeling to finally find it. I just wish more people, like all these babies, could get to know it, feel it every day.'

'Well,' Francisco said, looking at the clock, 'I suspect you want or need to go talk about a few things. And I have to wrangle dinner and pry the girls away from the tube eventually. Thank you for adding so much to her special day! And when your special day comes, if you know what I mean, I expect an invitation! Her Church, yours, mine, no schisms here.'

'None whatsoever, and never!' Athena said.

'You'll be at the top of our list, if or when,' Josh said. He looked at Athena, smiled, and added, 'When.'

After a few hugs and kisses, they found themselves outside by her SUV. 'Please drive again, Josh,' she said before he opened her door.

Inside, with the motor running, he asked her, 'Are you all right? Did you find out something? Something unpleasant?'

'Yes, I'm fine, thank you, though I am frazzled. And, yes, she told me what happened to her, the poor baby. It makes my blood boil.'

'I didn't want to say anything, and I really don't know, but I heard it was bad. Like the Staties and the FBI were involved bad. A few arrests were made.'

'Not enough,' she said. 'The main demons, the cretin—pardon my language—the louse of a so-called man, and his friend and conspirator, the degenerate social worker, the one who supervised the whole ring, are still on the run.'

'Is she still in counseling?' Josh asked as he started to drive away.

'Yes, and she's starting to come around. My prayer is that she'll become stronger for all of the evil and trauma. But it will take time.'

'Did you calm her?' he asked. 'The way you calm me? I've noticed that, by the way. And a few other things.'

'Yes. Call it my woman's touch of healing. And she's protected now, by the authorities and Something Greater. I just wish someone could find those two. I hate, literally hate the evil done by the wicked against the innocent. But my judgement is clouded. I'm not thinking as I should. Or could. Fogged over by grief and RAGE!' As she said *rage*, Josh could have sworn he'd glimpsed, from the corner of his eye, a white fire springing up in hers for only a second. He sensed that just as she was brilliant, dedicated, kind, and caring, she was also fierce. But she continued, 'And I'm no warrior. No idea where they got the spear and helmet idea from! I've never been able to endure strife, pain, or suffering. I am not Michael, he who would be most needful at this time. And forgive me, I'm not thinking straight about an earthly substitute. Who, I wonder, could deliver justice tinged with a mercy aimed at reconciling and redeeming all? Who?!'

Josh honestly didn't follow all that she was saying, though he certainly sensed and endorsed her primary sentiments. He, too, was no warrior. For an instant, not knowing what else to do, he thought about changing the subject. And at that moment, he saw it ahead as they sat at a red light. 'Now, that's a weird billboard. Call him? Who on earth is he?'

Athena looked up and saw it too, an attention-getting yellow billboard with *'Call Christian.'* written in black letters. Beyond the period was a picture of a telephone. 'That's it!' she exclaimed. 'Exactly who to call. Josh, do you believe in literal signs from God?'

'I mean, I do, but I honestly don't think I've ever seen one. Well, maybe there was a light in a corner recently.'

'I think you just did see one, or another one. Now if you'll excuse me, I need to make a call.' He nodded as he started driving through the intersection and she dialed a number on her phone. After three rings, someone picked up on the other end. In turn, Athena said, *'Hei, Christian. Dette Er Athena. Min gamle venn, jeg trenger din hjelp.'* She then carried on her half of a perfectly fluent conversation in yet another language Josh didn't understand. He thought many parts of it sounded a bit like English, but despite her wonderful, musical voice, he found it virtually impossible to follow along. When he cocked an eye at her for the second time, she looked at him and said, 'Norwegian. Modern.' Then she went right back to what sounded like a very serious talk. The call lasted for maybe ten minutes. Not knowing precisely where they were headed, he looped around several streets in order to stay in the general area of her house and a few of their favorite places. As the sky grew darker, and as he noticed real snow beginning to fall, he felt slightly hungry.

Finally, he heard her say one word he certainly knew, 'Josh!' And around that time, her demeanor changed, from very serious back to extraordinarily kind, happy, and becoming. After a few more sentences in Norwegian, she suddenly shifted to English: 'I suppose he can hear this part, as it's about him. Yes. I really hope so. He's the sweetest, kindest, most knowing and accepting, and cutest man I've ever met in all these long years. Yes. He might have been the reason I waited. Yes. I am in love with him, completely. One day—oh, he's looking at me with those puppy eyes—one day, I hope we have what you and your queen enjoy.' The gushing talk, that made Josh smile and blush at the same time, continued for a moment before she wrapped up the call, 'Thank you, ten thousand times over, my friend. Please let me know what comes of it, or when it is accomplished. May God Almighty guide, protect, and bless you as always. Amen, thank you, and goodbye. *Farvel!*' She hung up with a contented sigh.

'I take it you have a few powerful friends?' Josh asked.

'While I talked, I sent him some information. And he already has a lead on an address! He can do this, whether the police can't or won't.'

'How or when did you send him anything?'

'Just now. I, uh, never mind that part.'

'And where is he? In Norway? How could he have jurisdiction in Massachusetts?'

'Let's just say he has unlimited license to handle certain matters, for his house and for all of Ours. And he has a few compatriots here in the States. Not to worry. And I feel so much better about *that* now. I know he'll do it the right way. A Christian response from Christian.'

'Okay,' Josh said, still not fully understanding anything. 'And now?'

'And now, it's Saturday, you know. How about we crash Meadowbanks again and see if we can't get in without a reservation?! My treat, sweet boyfriend. Or, is it *fiancé* yet? Sister Francisco appears to have moved us along.'

'Yeah, I noticed that,' he said with a chuckle. 'And in a direction I like.'

'Let's have a bite to eat, at the Banks, or anywhere, and then, can we go back to my place? I want to talk to you alone about something. You can't guess what it is, though I know you've caught hints of what I'll reveal to you. Ideas?'

'I'd love to dine and dance again if it's possible. We could skip the careening truck this time though.' They smiled but were quiet for the rest of the short ride. When they parked, he looked over at her, took her hand, and said, 'The hints. Would those have to do with you knowing every language there is, spider and lobsterese included, the spatial anomalies, your woman's touch, and things like that?'

'Yes, perhaps,' she said. 'Do you trust me, Josh?'

'Completely,' he said. 'It goes with the love I have for you.'

'Good. Then trust me now. Let's have a fun time and I'll fill you in at home.'

'Home,' he said. 'I was about to regrettably say I'd finally forgotten the roses, but then I remembered I took care of it and they're, or it is waiting at home! Trust with fun! Let's go, Athena.'

They walked in, hand in hand, just like the week before. And somehow, and maybe it was another hint, a reservation was waiting on them, a table for two for Mr. Josh Williams. They sat at the very same table, though the wine pairing was different that night and the food a little lighter. Later, they danced as only they could, once more wrapped up in their own little world of just them. On their way back to her house, she asked, 'Josh, what are your plans for next week? For Thanksgiving?'

'Well, I didn't really have any. I suppose I wanted to see Isabella again, on the big day or around it. And I was just going to microwave Market Basket's finest frozen turkey and loaf around. But now—'

'Yes, but now, that simply won't do. Will you please spend the week with me? I hope we can continue our journey together. And, if it all works out, I'd love to have the three girls and Sister Francisco over for dinner on Thursday. I might even buy a big screen and a recliner so you can, ahem, enjoy the Big Bird parade and some football games! Eh???'

'Minus the TV, I'm all in! The gang would love it, and I'll see if they're available. And, more than anything, I'd love to spend the whole time with you, my goddess Athena! And you really are just like her. Like a myth come true and to life. You've jumped right to the top of my list of many things to be thankful for,' he said. 'Is that what you wanted to tell me?'

'No, not exactly. Let's go home, drink some North Carolina roses, and talk.'

'We're almost there, sweet girlfriend!'

Eight

Higher Revelations

'Can you spend the night again, Josh?' she asked when they were inside and walking back towards her kitchen. 'Maybe a couple of them?' She had taken his hand and was looking at him intently as they walked.

'Sure, I'm free,' he said. He knew and fully trusted her (and himself with her), but he still didn't grasp exactly what she was leading up to or why she had just asked him. At no point, however, did he consider saying no. 'I want to spend all the time I can with you.'

'Good. That gladdens my heart, Josh. Let's get the wine and then talk in the living room.' Together, they rounded up two glasses and the bottle, without any cake that evening, and then proceeded to the couch. There, they sipped tentatively, being delighted with the flavors Josh had picked, and made a little small talk. Roundabout, she paused and lightly kissed him, an action that, as ever, sent an electric thrill down his spine and deep into his soul. She then put her glass down and held his hand. 'I love you, Josh Williams, and I am head-over-heels in love with you. I want you to know that and believe it!'

He put his drink aside and looked into her eyes. 'I love you, Athena. I know and believe what you say, and I want you to believe me. I'm completely and hopelessly in love with you too!'

'But, Josh,' she said, becoming rather serious. 'Do you love our Trinitarian God more than me?'

'Yes,' he said slowly and deliberately. 'Do you?'

'Yes,' she said emphatically. 'And that's where we begin this. Where we should and must. We need to discuss a few things tonight, and it may linger beyond the night or even tomorrow. And there is one thing in particular you must know. But first, I want to explain, as best I can, how much, or, rather, just how I love you. Is that okay?'

'Sure,' he said as he wrapped her into a reclined hug. 'Tell me anything.'

'Okay, Josh. More than once, you've mentioned or hinted that you think I'm above you, or that you're somehow unworthy. Is that right?' He nodded and she continued, 'And that is how I feel about you. You've sweetly admitted to me that you have had next to no romances, correct? At the same time, and I get it, you seem mystified that I'm not married, don't have, or haven't had until now, a boyfriend, or that I don't have a line of suitors waiting.' She paused, then continued again, 'The truth is that whatever limited love experience you have is probably an order of magnitude beyond my own. It'll make more sense, I think, in a little while. And for now, just know that I'm as awed by you, or I am even more so than you are of me. I think the reason I haven't had any romantic relations is in large part due to my waiting for you to walk into my gift shop and my life. Trust me on that, Josh.

'Moving along a bit, Sister Francisco mentioned something I think you really agree with and which lit a fire in my heart. I would love nothing more than to be your wife. Would you, Josh, like to marry me? To be my husband?'

'Yes!' he happily said, almost shouting. 'I'd love nothing more than to live my life complete with you. As one being. I don't know the first thing about proper family formation or any of it, but trusting the God I love more than anything, even you, I want this. I know we can make it work.' He was on the edge of joyful tears.

'Wait! Don't get on your knee just yet,' she said with a laugh. 'More talk is needed first. A little personal or intimate talk first, if that's okay.' He nodded along happily. She then said, 'I'm a virgin, Josh. Are you?'

'Yes,' he admitted quietly.

'Do you lust for me, Josh? Or do I tempt you?'

'No,' he said quickly, honestly, as if he'd just had a stern realization. 'I mean, with my lack of experience, I have had those kinds of sinful thoughts before, you know. The kind to confess and guard against. And with you, I admit you are beautiful and I relish any, well, touch we make. But, no, I almost can't believe it, but thinking about it, I haven't lusted for you. Not sexually. I know what's underneath your clothing, and just the notion of that knowledge fills me with a thrill I really can't explain. It's like I just accept it as what could, hopefully, be, and I hope that what happens, well, happens for the right reasons, like those Father Josias mentioned last Sunday. I don't lust for a woman's body, I long for her ultimate companionship.

'And you keep impressing me, like with this talk. Part of me is terrified by it all, but something far greater is pushing me through, turning the terror into affectionate action. I hope that makes sense. And I also appreciate your virginity. And for whatever reason, this isn't that hard to discuss, and I don't feel like I'm blushing or that my heart is running a marathon. I know the world would see your charm, accomplishment, and extreme beauty, and find it impossible to believe you've never given into anyone. But I don't care about the world, and it all makes happy sense to me. I hope my words properly convey my thoughts here.'

'They do, sweet, strong man,' she said with a tear in her eye. 'With every sweet word, you make yourself clearer as what I've waited so long for. Waited even as I never expected or understood. I reciprocate everything you've just said. You slept a door down from me last weekend, and I never once thought you'd appear at my door desiring anything premature. You didn't disappoint, my love! And I happily admit, that while I find you beautiful and desirable, I have stowed any untoward thoughts and remained faithful to myself second, and to Our Lord first.

'If we are to do this great rewarding thing, on our approach, I think we need boundaries. And, most happily, I think we've already set them as we go along. I don't expect sexual pleasure from you before we are one, and I would never impose myself on or tempt you otherwise. Our kisses, and caresses, our, uh, tummy rubs, and this very embrace, are, to my mind and heart, gentle and innocent displays. I've never dreamed of such bliss, but at the same time, I feel nothing but an honest, righteous longing in it all. A mere promise and hope of what may come. Do you feel the same way?'

'I do, my love,' he said, nuzzling against her cheek. 'With all of it. As if you can complete my thoughts and feelings. I know you're the woman I've waited for. Oh, how I love you, Athena!'

'Now,' she said, 'for stronger words. I'm not sure if we should sit or stand for this. What I'm about to tell you, I've ever only told a few mortal men and women, and never before has it been in such a romantic circumstance.'

'How about we sit up?' Josh said. They did sit up straighter and they separated a little from their hug, though they remained close together and still touched each other with their hands and arms.

Athena spoke again, slowly and almost with uncertainty, 'I have to tell you something about me. You must know and understand it before you can decide what to do or how you want to proceed with me. Maybe I should have said all of this a few days ago, but there's no time like the present. Josh, I know you've noticed certain things about me and about how, well, I affect you. And our relationship. You are very perceptive, and I think I'm partly malleable under your influence. Am I wrong?'

'No,' he said, sensing he knew what she meant. 'I don't know how I could influence you, or, maybe you really mean, do something to make you drop your guard. But I have noticed what I can only describe as, well, supernatural ways. You're so beautiful it should hurt, though it doesn't. It would appear you know everything, read everything, and you can speak any language. You have, I just know, some power in you; you can calm with a touch, for instance. Your seemingly random guesses suggest something beyond sentience, an alternative perception of reality. Twice you moved me to a bed in my sleep, once over a distance. Little, or not-so-little things like that, right? And, you saved us from that truck, didn't you?' He had moved in very close to her face, his eyes peering intently into hers.

'No,' she said, returning his gaze, 'I saved you from the truck. It couldn't have hurt me.' For an instant, she looked around, almost as if at a loss for words. But then, she looked even deeper into his eyes, into his mind, and into his soul even. 'Josh, a few times, you've referred to me as your goddess Athena. You've said I'm like her. While it sounds so sweet, I'm about to tell you why I have always taken offense at that comparison. You see, I am not like her.' She grew silent for a moment, and then said, '*I AM her.*'

Josh nodded along innocently, and it took a few seconds before it hit him. Then it hit like a sledgehammer. Beyond what she had said, there was the overwhelming way she'd said it. She had just communicated with him telepathically, and he was more certain of that alarming fact than anything else! Suddenly, his eyes went wide. His heart leaped into a race against his mortality. He began to tremble and hyperventilate. He couldn't think or speak, a real terror wrestling with the love in his heart.

'*Baby, baby, peace, be still,*' she said directly into his mind again. '*I will never harm you, kind child, gentle son of Adam, you dearest man. Breathe, and then think. Whatever you process in your brain I will hear and understand. Tell me anything. And know I won't hurt you.*' She now had her hands lovingly wrapped around his head. Her forehead rested on his, and their eyes were so close their lashes criss-crossed, meshed together.

At last, he thought, pleadingly, '*Please have mercy on me. You're a goddess?! An immortal goddess?! I didn't know, but yet I did. Please don't— Please help me understand. I'm so lost! Don't hurt me. Don't kill me, Athena. I am beneath you but I love you!*' At their ultra-close range, her eyes were a blur to his. And yet, somehow he fathomed he could in a way fully see them, and almost inside them. She, on the other hand, saw perfectly and clearly:

of him, within him, and beyond him. Feeling his utter confusion and his fright, and seeing him crying from both, she very tenderly leaned up and kissed his eyes, then his forehead, and then his lips. She was still holding his head as a mother might cradle an infant.

'No,' she said, once more in an ordinary audible manner. 'No, no, no, a thousand times, and for eternity, no, I will never harm you or cause you pain, let alone kill you. I love you more than you can guess, and I'm sorry, so sorry that I scared you. I never intended that. Please let me explain myself. There are no goddesses, my love. All the old pantheons are false rumors at best.

'And this part is painful for me ... and embarrassing. I know you and all others mean well, but I do not like being associated with pagan myth, even if I had a hand in creating it. Please don't call me a goddess again, my love, for our love and for our love of God—the notion, once deprived of any innocence, is blasphemous.' She touched her head to his again and drew him closer to her, wanting nothing more than to soothe his tremors. 'That title is a sad misnomer, born of ancient misunderstanding caused by very regrettable indiscretions on my part and the parts of my fellow beings. And something else. What I am, what you may consider me, and this is the most difficult part— Josh, I am a suspended angel. An earth-bound angel. I am one member of a small host who refused to take a side or a part in the Great War so long ago.

'Rather, we took too long to take the right side. Our lament for all times. For our recalcitrance, for our pitiful, delayed obedience, we were punished. With love, but with force. We were not cast down with lucifer and his kind. Instead, to compel us to witness what we had helped foster by standing by so reluctantly, to see the effects of our original rebellion and hate poured upon Creation, we were sent here to earth. For punishment and atonement, we have walked among Mankind, seeing, hearing of, and feeling the pain and suffering loosed on that day of our failure. Every sin, cardinal and venial, we have sadly witnessed. We live and have lived among you, as adopted facsimiles of you, and yet not so. Our chance for redemption comes through our acknowledgment of our misdeeds, our failures in what we did and did not do, through our constant pleas for mercy, and through any assistance we might give Men while they endure.'

Josh began to recover a little. And as usual, he took pity and interest in others. 'Is this your form of Purgatory? To be cleansed in our fires?' He stopped shaking and wrapped his arms around her.

'In a sense, if not in such terminology,' she said. 'I will try my hardest to explain everything to you. But first, please don't fear or hate me. I really do love you as a woman should love a man, and as we were taught to respect your kind and your souls. I am immortal. But so are you, my love. Please tell me you're not afraid. Or, if you are, what I can do to ameliorate the fear.'

It took him a minute that felt more like an hour, but he was able to slowly answer her. 'I'm not afraid. Well, I am terrified, in fact, but I think it has more to do with not knowing or understanding. I trust you, and I love you. And just as importantly, I know you love me. Please forgive me, but I've never been so close to any woman for so long, certainly one of such power. I don't fear you, per se, though I think I might fear displeasing you or, worse, offending God by intruding into matters I don't understand. But I do not hate you, and I never could. Have you ever told this to anyone else?'

'Only to a very select few in all the years Mankind has walked outside the Garden. And I've never told anyone like you, who I have such feelings for. I think those cares affected the way I just handled things, and, again, I'm sorry if I frightened you. All of my other disclosures were made under much different circumstances and with a different delivery,' she said.

'Does anyone alive right now know, other than me?'

'There are a very few who guess or otherwise treat me with an unspoken or unquestioning deference. But they do not fully or completely understand. As for the full truth, only Father Josias knows at present,' she said. 'I usually do not tell this secret to even my spiritual fathers or advisors, though with him, perhaps in anticipation of meeting you, I felt it was safe and right for him to know. And one thing you should know now is that, in my experience, it is somehow impossible for the human keeper of this knowledge to disclose it to another who does not know. You will always remember it, and be able to discuss it with me, and possibly with Father Josias, but you won't remember or think to inform anyone else. I don't understand that quirk, though I suppose it is a form of protection for you. And there is so much more I want to share with you, that you need to hear and consider. Part of it, any part you like, I can delve into here and now by speech or by thought. And I know of another simple means of conversation that will be both pleasant and very informative. But all of this is to be determined by your desires and comforts, Josh.'

They sat still and silent for a few more minutes. She kept rubbing his head, and at intervals, massaging his shoulders and back. He maintained his caress of her upper body, a grasp that alternated between affection stroking and holding on for dear life. Finally, he again lowered his face to touch hers, pausing to gently rub his nose back and forth against hers. Then, ever plain, kind, and lighthearted Josh, he thought to inject just a little humor into the most unusual night. 'So, Charlotte,' he mused, 'she's always been just a spider? You didn't turn a poor woman into a bug out of jealousy or anything, did you?' Even with their eyes so close, she observed that his mouth was curled into a little smile, timid under the circumstances, but still very sincere.

'NO, silly!' she laughed out. 'Even I can't explain that one! We made some mistakes, but it was the collective imagination of the world that ran wild with them. And, well, they were assisted by the fallen spirits, ever keen to capitalize on any misfortune.'

'I would like to hear more about how the myths started, if you know and will tell me. I'd like to know as much as possible, even if I can't understand it,' he said.

'In any order you like, Josh.'

'Tell me this, if you will,' he said, becoming rather serious again. 'Have you seen God? Not in His works, but in His original Face or Being?' It sounded like a child's question, which, of course, it was.

'Yes,' she said with an air of deep sadness. 'Time is really irrelevant, being especially so during and before Creation, so there are elements you may never understand until you are in His presence. But I was there. I know of no real way to convey the Glory and Majesty. Or my regret that I have been absent from it for so long, relatively speaking. Your best estimation is the same as my great hope—a hopeful, apophatic matter of faith and trust.' She sounded and looked truly contrite and sad. He took his turn to comfort her.

'In time and as we're able,' he said. 'I have one major question that I can think of, but thinking is rather difficult at the moment. Maybe we should work into it. Uh, tell me—'

'Would you like to know more about The Fall? Or my time wandering? Or just, for starters, how the moniker Athena and that sort of legend came to pass?'

'If it happened in our world, on earth,' he said, 'maybe that part is more relatable to me. What were the mistakes you mentioned?'

'Ah,' she said. 'Those of us in between, and more than a few of those I call the Regulars, those who obeyed honorably and timely in Heaven, at intervals made the mistake of allowing ourselves to be seen by various early peoples. The fact of the Regulars' involvement is one of the few things that ever made me feel a little, well, less fallen. But all of us should have known to be more careful. And, again, the seeing of us, partly in our natural states, led to the exploration of many vivid imaginings. Not that poor men and women could be blamed as they had no way of understanding. I could tell you a thousand stories, and in a more ready means of communication, later, I will. But one example, which you know something of as a myth, might be a helpful illustration. Do you know about Apollo or Hyperion?'

'I'm vaguely versed in some of the classical stories.'

'And, Josh, do you know anything about the various contrived hierarchies of we angelic beings?'

'Not so much,' he said. 'I know there are angels, and archangels, and powers. But I'm not really sure who is who or who does what.'

'Well, let me go with that, Josh. Those above my order, named by you, the Powers, have several primary functions. One of them is to act as technicians and keep the mechanisms of the universe humming along. And one of the Powers, a long, long time ago, was tasked, as he still is today, with operating the stars. He pays, of course, particular attention to our star, the Sun. One fine day, thousands of years ago, he came down for an inspection.

'He could have performed it from anywhere, but as the Sun is crucial for the Earth, and as all of us are and were naturally curious about what happens here, he saw no reason not to perform his checks directly from the planet's surface. He picked a mountain in Greece as his observation post. I was aware of him at once, knowing who he was. With him being a Regular, I could not initiate direct contact with him. There are a few such rules or parameters of our exile. But I watched, fascinated and gladdened. Mortal eyes saw him too, though they did not understand what they saw. And what he did was dial up the brightness of the Sun just a little, dim it, and then return it to its normal radiance. Nothing more than a simple test for him, as a man in a factory might perform with a clipboard or a tool. But to the ancient Greeks, well, he became known as the sun god.

'He became aware of his mistake, as all of us who made similar errors did in turn, but there was no way to unring that bell. Even as it caused great consternation, it was forbidden for him to undo the perceptions of man, to hold them accountable for his mistake. We are permitted to take certain actions to protect or conceal, but to cover over such blunders is impermissible. Sometimes, I have wished it was not so. Evil cannot create. Demons can only mock. As testified by the darker elements of paganism, they certainly mocked our lack of caution. Along with others, I made similar mistakes. And life—'

At that moment, he stopped her by squeezing her tight and kissing her, deeply and passionately, and for a very long time. When they breathlessly broke the smooch, he held his face against her cheek and whispered into her ear: 'If I can, like the little mouse to the lion, I'd love to help you atone for your mistakes, Athena. But I've just decided something I have to say right now. I love you! I love you more than I've ever thought one person could love another. I want to marry you. I want to be your husband and to have you as my wife. But in order to do that, I have to know, or to find out, if this is permissible. Are you and I, with our differences, allowed to so love each other?'

'Josh,' she said in a slow, deliberate answer, 'I have considered that question since I first met you. I asked Father Josias, but he did not know. I doubt any man, no matter how pious, would. I've read the Bible many times since, along with many Patristic texts and other various works. But my answer, which I will say is a yes, came from my prayers. And I have prayed and prayed like never before. Tonight, and into the morning, and in the days that follow, I will explain it further. But for now, please know a few things. Ever since I departed Paradise, I have prayed unceasingly. I know my pleas are heard, and considered with love. Just as those of any man or woman. Despite my heightened senses and abilities, I have lived essentially as a mortal woman for six thousand or so years.

'Part of my explanation is that as I have so lived and experienced, part of me thinks that the experience of love and marriage an ordinary woman—and they are all really extraordinary—might know or enjoy is not forbidden to me. And when I poured my heart out to our Father about this, just the other night, I got something back I have never received before. It was not a concrete yes or no, but it was an answer, in two ways symbolic. I asked if I might have you, Josh, to become your wife and the mother of any children we might ever be gifted. And suddenly, in answer, a calm descended upon me, a feeling I have not known since before the ejection and punishment. To me, it was a signal that my request was received and sanctified.

'And then, that feeling of bliss, which I reckon is similar to the calm I may grant you in your times of distress, was replaced by another feeling. One I have never felt before or even imagined. I have never felt physical pain or seen my own blood. And so I cannot exactly describe or understand those concepts. Or I couldn't. What happened did not really hurt, it was not painful. But it was strong, as it felt to me. It started as what I can only describe as a cramped feeling in my belly. I explored it, and later discovered I was beginning to bleed. Down there, if you know what I mean, Josh. I'm, right now, having my period.'

Josh, like any other young, inexperienced man, did not know exactly what those words meant to a woman. But he thought he generally caught what she was saying. 'I get it. As they say, and I don't mean to be crude, it's that time of the month again? Forgive me, but I would have never known. We don't, you know, uh, I'll be extra nice and respectful and—'

'No, Josh,' she said. 'In all my ages of existence, this is my first period. Ever! As with any other woman, it means my body is preparing itself for maternal possibilities. I'm being allowed to prepare to become a mother! Of your children, Josh. That is the second, and most ordinarily visible sign of a positive response to our questions. And by these two proofs, I know we are destined for each other. I also know you will need to seek your own independent verification. I hope I can help you along that path, starting now or later tonight.' She gave him a small kiss.

While she talked, when she came to the maternal aspects, his hand had unconsciously drifted to her tummy. He was slowly, tenderly rubbing it at that moment. He slowed further, only allowing his fingers to stretch and contract lightly across the fabric of her blouse, when he exclaimed, 'That's wonderful! That's a miracle, Athena!' Tears of joy filled his eyes and then hers too. 'Well, then, tonight I want to try to satisfy my mind as well. Or to start doing so. We should, of course, go to Church in the morning, and talk to Father Josias. But first, with your help, I'd like to ponder a few things. And when the time comes, maybe it would be best if I asked your Father for your hand in marriage. You know, that would kill two birds, or, rather, catch two pleas with one angel. Or something like that. What are the other means of communication you mentioned? And it is now getting a little late. You also mentioned me spending the night again in the guest room?'

'Yes, you must ask Him. And that may be the total solution all the way around. I'll help you in any way I can. And it is late, so it is all the more conducive for our alternative speaking method, which will practically explain itself when we start. Are you familiar with the practice of bundling, as practiced by the Amish and a few other sects? They say it started, Biblically, with Ruth?'

'Not really,' he said. 'Does that have anything to do with our unusual method of talking?'

'Well, let me just suggest it this way: Josh, I'd like you to sleep with me tonight. In my bed.'

He stared at her for a moment, feeling he was happy to gauge, no lust in his heart, though there was some excitement, mainly at any thought of just being near her even as he didn't understand exactly what she was asking or why. He simply said, 'Athena, I trust you. And myself. So tell me what you mean.'

'No, I'll show you. Come on!'

After putting away the bottle and glasses, and after tidying a few loose ends, she led him upstairs. They stood just inside the door of her master bedroom looking at what Josh took for a regal king-sized bed made of some rich dark wood and set with nearly lavish-looking coverings. She said, 'Fully clothed, and without any intimacy, we will lie together comfortably under the covers, side by side. We will both talk and sleep, both things deeply. Now all we have to do is perhaps shower and change into more homey attire!'

'But,' he said, 'I only have these clothes I'm wearing.'

'Not exactly,' she said. 'Come with me.' She led him down the hall to the guest room where he'd slept one week earlier. Several outfits were laid out on the bed. 'I took the liberty of gathering a few of your favorite worn comfortable night clothes,' she said. 'Thin sweatpants, a t-shirt, a long sleeve sports tee, et cetera. All right here. I even washed them with my special brand of detergent and softener. And I grabbed a few more general items for the next day or so.'

'When did—' he started to say. 'Oh. Your ways again?'

'No apologies,' she said with a wink. 'And I also bought you a few garments when I was in Boston. You might like those nice, soft pajamas there. Whatever you want to wear, my dear, so long as you're fully covered.'

He thought for a moment, and then said, 'No apologies needed. But with this display of, well, power, how does it fit into your restrictions or parameters or abilities? Or whatever you call it all?'

'Well,' she said, 'in addition to protective matters and con-cealment—which is usually geared towards protecting someone, I have, as a condition of my dual nature, the ability to make cer-tain adjustments for convenience. So long, that is, as it furthers some greater purpose. His, not mine, mind you, sweetheart. I'll explain it a little more when we're under in a bit. The ostentatious or the self-aggrandizing is forbidden; however, the expediting of common recourse is not. It will, I hope, make sense when I fully explain it. And who knows? If our union is blessed and assured, then maybe you can teach me a thing or two about better channel-ing my abilities. We'll find out together.'

'Well, I'm sure it will all make sense,' he said. 'And if I can ever do anything to help or protect you, my love, here for us, or in the greater sense regarding your ultimate reunion and resumption, then I'll do whatever I can. And thank you for laying these items out for me. Even as I don't fully grasp all of the Athenaisms, I do appreciate them. Can I mix and match?'

'Whatever you like, my darling.'

'Okay, I'll have at it. I'll change after a shower.'

'The one here has nice massage jets on the wall. You'll figure it out, and take your time. I will go do likewise. I don't think I have time for a relaxing soak, but I can sprinkle some rose essence around the shower. Someone I know is on a mad rose kick!' She kissed him lightly on the cheek and then turned to go. 'Come in when you're ready, baby. I'll be waiting.'

'Oh!' he said, recalling her for a moment. 'Should I say my evening prayers here and now? Or in a few minutes?'

'You can do either or both, Josh. You will find that we will pray together extensively tonight. But you are most welcome to make your own orison aforehand.' She then walked down the hall. Josh, as it turned out, prayed both in his ordinary manner and then, later, with her in a completely different fashion. After his first, short, private supplication, he chose his nightwear and did his best to successfully operate the shower jets.

Feeling rather tired, yet also refreshed, Josh exited the guest room and made his way down the hall. He was wearing the new pajama bottoms along with his old Red Sox long-sleeved t-shirt. It all felt very comfortable together, and due to the washing in whatever secret solution she used, it possessed a smell that suggested pure nosegay bliss. He also, out of a bit of caution, wore a pair of loose athletic socks. *'Maybe our feet shouldn't touch?'* he thought as he approached her door. And inside her room, which was now lit only by a little reading lamp on one of the bed stands, he found her, looking as impressive as ever, even as she wore only what appeared to be silk pajamas.

'Socks?' she asked, looking at his feet. 'I do hear they keep the feet warmer in winter.'

'I didn't know, so, yeah,' he said bashfully.

'As you like, with or without them,' she said. 'But come here for one last touch and kiss before bed.' It was a soft, short hug with a sweet peck on the lips. Then she bid him to get under the covers on the far side from the lamp. As he climbed in and started to pull up the covers, she said, 'Do you normally sleep on your back?'

'Yes, I do,' he answered, adding, 'These are really nice sheets. Flannel?'

'Yes, dear. I just replaced them in advance of the cold weather. Warm and comfy under a wool blanket and a down comforter. Please make yourself reposeful and relaxed. Lie still and I'll tell you what we're going to do—two things.'

He found it easy to make himself comfortable in that bed, though he felt an uncertainty about what came next, and a silent thrill at being again so close to her. She leaned over on her side, and said, 'Just one more!' as she kissed his lips. Then she turned off the light. They were snug under the covers, which were up to their necks, and they were perhaps only a foot apart. He could smell her, the usual magnificent scent mingled with a hint of rose petals. He could feel her every movement rippling through the mattress. And he could feel warmth from her close body. Then she took his hand in hers beneath the top sheet, and the touch was magical. 'This is the only way we're touching in the dark, sweet Josh. And we don't have to, I just thought it would be nice. And it is. We are going to fall into a deep slumber together. And while we sleep, I will fully enter your thoughts. It won't be a dream, but a real and genuine conversation, one that won't even require language. We will talk, think, feel, see, research, read, and even pray together as one. You'll see shortly. And, baby, none of this will scare you, trust me. And, again, I love you.

'It will start in your toes, a relaxation that will creep up all the way to your hair even, and you will fall into the deepest, most healing sleep you've ever known. Flow under as you're pulled. And then, when you're there, I will be with you. Are you ready?'

Already feeling the tranquility overtaking his body and a placid aura building in his mind, he answered, 'Yes. And it feels so good. I love you, Athena. And a blessed good night.'

'Good night, my love,' she said, the last words he heard consciously that evening. In his first dream, which was not a dream but a waking thought experienced while asleep, he considered that the last word to his ear had been *love*. Now, the first he heard in this new unexplainable reality was the same. '*Love. I love you with all my heart and being, Josh. I. Love. You.*' She was speaking to him, in his thoughts, but also like she was face to face with him. He felt like he was standing. And floating. And flying. And completely at peace.

'*Hello, again, Athena. I love you too. I ache for you, and only you can complete me. And, um, welcome to my head?*'

They spoke in this manner for many hours, though the volume of information they processed and emotions they expressed and experienced, if conveyed conventionally, would have taken weeks or months. In several ways, they reintroduced themselves to each other, which had the hard effect of making their growing bond many times stronger than it had been. They discussed their hopes, dreams, aspirations, struggles, triumphs, and more. Athena finally felt like she had put Josh at ease concerning her background and the higher side of her tandem nature. And most important of all, they explored in great detail the questions of permissions Josh had raised. About an hour before dawn, with a course plotted, their parlay slowed, and, soon after, Athena said another kind goodbye and released Josh from her linkage. For a short while they slept, side by side, though in complete innocence, with blissful, cordial smiles on their faces.

Josh awoke to a tickling feeling on his face. Opening his eyes, he saw her, just like the previous Sunday morning, leaning over him from the bedside with her hair brushing against his features. 'Good morning, my love,' she said. 'How do you feel?'

Initially, he couldn't answer beyond a smile and a few sighs. Awakening a little more, he said, 'In my head, there is a feeling like everything has been cleaned by free-flowing, cool, fresh water; it's like I've lived another lifetime in order to gain great wisdom. And I have an image of you, your charms, and your being, etched in my mind. And, this is crazy good, my body feels like it's been completely disassembled and put back together again, overhauled. I feel like a kid! Good morning, Athena!'

'Those feelings will last quite a while,' she said. 'You did gain much mentally last night. And your body has indeed been refreshed. Also, a few things, four of them: First, whenever you need to or want to, you can now establish contact with me. At any time and in any place. I hope the needs are few and far between, but that the wants are many, frequent, and glad! I can also come to you, respectfully, of course.

'Second, I've already contacted Father Josias, who says he will happily meet with us after services today. The third thing is a little embarrassing, and I put all the blame on you! You see, I woke up bright and early, about half an hour ago. I looked at you sleeping, and you were so cute and cuddly looking that I broke the rule of contact for just a few minutes by slipping my arm beneath your head and wrapping around you. I was contented beyond description and you kind of purred like an overgrown kitten. Then, feeling a little guilty, I withdrew, kissed your nose, and ran away!'

'Bad girl!' he said merrily. 'But as I am so cute, I suppose you must be forgiven.'

'I'm still blaming cute little you,' she said. 'Also, the fourth thing: our coffee is ready and I will have breakfast started when you join me downstairs.' With that, she kissed his nose again, sighed, and left him, calling over her shoulder, 'Your fault! Irresistible!'

Nine

Josh's Prayer

The main bulk of the early snows had abated, though a few lingering flakes still fell intermittently. The air bordered on being cold by New England standards, and the sky was blustery and overcast. They walked together from the sanctuary of Saint Athanasius towards the fellowship hall. Father Josias spoke to them briefly in passing, saying that he would find them soon and that he wanted to talk. Walking on, Josh said to Athena, 'I sent a text to Father Griswald at my parish, both to let him know I was here and to apprise him of a few things.'

'Good. I think Father J has also spoken with him. After this meeting, and after this afternoon, we should probably pay him a full visit,' she said.

'A very good idea,' he concurred.

After they ate lunch, Father Josias appeared again and spoke to them: 'Father Andreas has agreed to cover for me here and as needed for a few hours. If you're both ready, I'd like to have you into my office for a chat. I think we have a miracle to work together!'

Seated in the man's pleasant little office, enjoying cups of rich coffee, he offered an opening prayer. Then out of several deferences, the floor was given to Athena. She spoke to them both, though initially primarily to the priest: 'Thank you so much, my sweet friend and confidant, for joining us in this process. As I

115

told you, Josh, here, now *knows*.' Josh nodded affirmatively. She continued, 'And we have in a relatively short amount of time, moved mountains in deciding what we want, if it may be so ordained. I will let Josh speak now, for this concerns him greatly and a mantle of responsibility is upon him. But first, I declare that I love him as I have never loved anyone on earth before.'

'Praise be to God!' said the excited priest. 'Josh?'

'Thank you, Father,' Josh said. 'Thank you, Athena, my love. And thanks and praise be to God for both of you and all of this! I would like to first say, Father, that I am completely, even hopelessly in love with Athena. To be completely honest, I loved her from the very first moment we met. In fact, I sensed her and started to love her before I ever laid eyes on her. In, yes, a short amount of time, that love grew immensely. And after our very deep talks yesterday, it has become overwhelming. I don't just love her, I must love her. If that makes sense. Or not. And as such, I want to marry her. I want her to be my wife, companion, lover, and the mother of my children. We discussed that blessed issue last night, and it led to our wondering if such a union is possible and permissible. I think part of the answer is wrapped up in seeking permission, via prayer, from God the Father, who made both of us and who is, literally in this sense, her father who I would have to ask anyway.'

'Athena,' Father Josias said. 'You said that you have already made your plea, and you told me you received what you took for a positive response. You said it was a two-fold answer. Is that correct?' Athena nodded and then recounted her experiences resulting in and from her prayers concerning Josh. The priest took great interest in what she said and nodded along in amazement as she spoke. He then turned back to Josh. 'What, now, do you think is the right way to approach this? For you, Josh?'

Josh answered, 'I think we three may agree this proposal may be without precedent. The best analogy I can think of would be the mention in *Genesis* Six of the Sons of God and the beautiful daughters of men.'

'The sons of men are beautiful too, one in particular,' Athena added. The priest smiled. Josh did too, started to blush, but still continued: 'And in *Matthew*, chapter Twenty-two, along with passages from *Mark*, Lord Jesus spoke to His disciples about love, marriage, the power of God, and Life beyond resurrection. He said that the angels of God remain unmarried. In Heaven. I do not know the strength of this analysis, but Athena is not, at present, in Heaven. By her own actions, and by a proportional response, she is here on earth with us, destined to live for a time as we do.

'I cannot begin to address certain matters. She told me that, as we might say, one of her first comforts was finding the Church during the first century. Or, rather, that it found her as it made its way around the eastern Mediterranean. As she suffered by our sides, so our great chance and hope in Christ became hers. And regarding she and I, especially she, she walks among men, endures with us, and has in many, maybe most regards, assumed a mortal way of life. With, of course, certain allowances and abilities. As she is allowed, doomed, or committed to such a temporary life, for so long as it lasts, it would seem to me that she is not immune from the lures of love. Nor that she should be barred from making a full sacramental commitment in love under the auspices of the Church. Even so far as marriage and child-rearing. I was awed by her revelation concerning, well, female matters. If it were not meant to be so, then why would she be given to preparations she never knew or needed before?

'In the end, as I cannot find any direct references, and I do not look to find that which may have never existed until now, I must simply ask and trust in the reply. So, with her help, I have decided to put this great question before the Lord, as I have ever trusted Him with all major matters in my life. I mean to make my prayer this afternoon or this evening.'

'Josh,' Father Josias said, 'I don't think anyone could have said that better. I have prayed mightily on these issues. And perhaps the answer Athena received to her pleas stands as our guide. What she has experienced is most certainly a miracle. So I now say it is up to you, young man. Ask, as they say, and thou shalt receive. Something. I feel that if this is right and permissible, then a sign or signs will come forth and that they will be unmistakable. Godspeed, Josh.'

'And Father,' Josh said again, 'and Athena, my love, if this works out as I hope it will, then I really do mean to marry my earth angel here.' He turned a kind but heated smile on her that could have melted lead. 'So, upon the answer, God willing and in His good time, I'd like to propose to her. I suppose that will mean rings and so forth—things I've no experience with. Yikes!'

They all laughed, though Athena said, soothingly, 'Josh, our ring of love is all I need. You don't have to—'

'Yes, I do,' he said. 'It may not be much, but I will have something for your hand when I ask for it.'

'Give him that, Athena,' Father said.

'Gladly,' she said. 'And as for not much, nothing could be greater than anything from you. And, my, aren't we moving this along?!'

'Someone recently told me time is really irrelevant,' Josh said with a wink.

'Hallelujah!' Father cried out. 'If, then, and I am in! This being a special case, even among special cases, I think we can, if the two of you decide, we can accelerate the ordinary process of formation. Still, even in an abbreviated form and with two extraordinary fiancés, I would like to conduct a pre-marriage course with both of you in advance of your wedding. Some semblance of the usual protocols, as or where they're applicable. We'll sort all of that out and I trust whatever we do will work. One of my growing joys and hopes is that your potential union may serve as a grand example for others to follow.

'In addition to serving, perhaps, as a vehicle for Athena's redemption, and maybe some related or expanded joinder of general salvation, I hope the example for other men and women is, at the least, one of the proper meeting of the spiritual and the physical, the real and true meaning of love. How wonderful would it be if your union forges at once the small church of the home while also rekindling the nearly lost, nearly impossible by modern standards, hierarchical family as was known for an age before the onset of false Enlightenment values. And maybe just for the two of you, though hopefully as a beacon for others, that your blessings together bring to life that ultimate reason for being happy as a man or a woman, to live with respect for one's righteous conscience. Some analysts and philosophers, seeking to reach beyond simplistic binaries, speak and write of the necessity of finding a real reason to be happy, not just artificially being so as is the late Western way. And what better reason could there be than to enjoy a deep unified new life together?! My two beloved friends, I could not be happier for you.'

'Thank you, Father,' Josh and Athena said together.

'And thank you,' he said. 'And I love the two of you more than I can say!' He did, however, say a parting prayer of thanks, and in due time, they left him and the parish.

Back in Athena's living room, they watched the wind and the sky out the window for a moment. Billowing gray clouds, threatening to almost turn black, sailed low across the dark horizon with some speed. It definitely felt like a winter day, just as the weatherman had promised, and due to the atmospheric conditions, the late afternoon almost had the look and feel of midnight. Suggestion was made of a dinner and perhaps with a bottle of wine beforehand. Small talk and small affections stirred haltingly. Suddenly, Josh turned to her and said, 'I have to do it. I have to ask Him now.'

'Would you like to be alone, Josh?'

'No. Please stay with me. I have to do this for us, and I need your presence, if I may have it.'

'Of course, my love. I'll just remain still and silent. I cannot read, hear, or see private prayers. So I'll just be here for you.'

'Can you hear them spoken aloud?' he asked.

'Yes,' she said. 'If that helps. But it is all up to you and what makes you most comfortable.'

'Then I will speak it out,' he said. 'I'd like to do so right now.'

'Okay. I'm here for you.'

Josh turned from the window and walked across the carpet until he was near the couch, more or less in the center of the room. He slowly knelt, bowed his head, and was quiet for a moment. She knelt as well, facing him at a distance of perhaps a foot or two. She folded her hands and watched him. Upon crossing himself, he began, 'Almighty God, my Father, my Lord God Jesus, my God the Holy Spirit, I am your least worthy subject and concern. It's just me, the same as I've always been. And as usual, I'm not sure what to say, what to ask for, or how. Please grant me the words and abilities I need at this moment. I know You know my mind and heart, but I would like to say all of this openly. This is my most important plea and request ever, and it is for something I do not deserve.

'My Lord, I am small, weak, and lonely. I am ever so grateful for everything You have bestowed in my life, including my life itself. I was lonely, physically and romantically lonely, though I never knew exactly what I missed. And now, I do. Again, and again, and again, thank You for sending Your daughter, Your angel, Athena, into my life. I love her. I am in love with her.' His voice became very soft, and he began to weep a little. She sat still and watched him. He continued: 'More than I deserved, You have provided in all things. I don't know who my parents are, nor what kind of people they are, or were. But You empowered them to give life to me, even if they wouldn't be present in that life. In place of an ordinary family, You sent powerful and kind friends who have ever helped me on my journeys. They have all led me here to this moment.

'And now, perhaps selfishly—and, if so, I repent—I desire a wife. A companion, a helper, a lover, and a partner in salvation. I love Athena, and I want to marry her. And I know she is, as a woman, and as a higher, better being, so far above and beyond me. I am not worthy of her affection, trust, or love. But if it is given, then I will dedicate my life to earning it and fulfilling all the cares and responsibilities as best I can. And, again, I'm just Joshua. I don't even really know what is involved in what I seek, but I vow to do whatever it takes, laying down my life if necessary, to try to do the right things for her, for You, and for me. There are two things, conjoined, that I must ask for.

'She has spoken to me about her earliest past. Lord, this is all plainly beyond my capabilities, but I have tried so hard to understand. I don't think that is really possible, but I have tried. And in trying, I am moved to sympathy. She repents, I see it and feel it, even without her telling me or my full understanding of it. I have no business in such high affairs, any of them. But some would call it fate, I call it Your Grace; You have brought us together. Thank You again, and please hear my humble questions and requests. I want to be her husband, but I am unsure if that is allowable. I believe her when she says You answered her prayers. And I don't assume or demand anything on my own behalf. This is only my calling out. If, as we have together imagined, she is, for whatever time, to be like a mortal woman, then I would ask that she be mine. And that I may be hers. That we may, with Your blessings, build a family with children, true love, and true obedience. With whatever that entails.

'I also imagine, again, a thing far beyond me, that this may be one small step in restoring her grace and position. I know, or I feel, that it is a great part in, or of restoring and furthering me. I ask that we be allowed to undertake the processes together. Saint Paul said that we mortals will judge the angels. It occurs to me that this could be my part in judging Athena in some way. I do not know of what I speak, precisely or even messily. But if it is to be, then I beg for Your permission to help her, or to judge her, or just to be there in any time of need she has. Without any knowledge or claim, I merely ask, Oh God.

'And as for the asking, if all these high matters be granted in a gift for which I can never fully comprehend or repay, then I must approach You not only as our Lord, Creator, and Ultimate Father, but also as I would the father of any woman. I do so love Your precious daughter, Athena, and I ask, I beg for Your blessing of our union. If that union may exist.

'I was Yours first, and I will be so forever. I will always abide by Your decisions and rules, even when I do not understand and when I falter through my own faults and shortcomings, ever seeking that mercy that I do not remotely qualify for. Please, God, help me.

Help me understand this. And if it is right, please allow me this unearned honor. As always, may Your Will be done in all things. Please, please, and thank You, God. In the name of the Father, and of the Son, and of the Holy Spirit. Amen.'

He crossed himself and opened his wet eyes just a little, but he remained bent down. Very slowly, she inched towards him on her knees. Completely at a loss for words, she simply reached out and touched his shoulders. With new tears flowing, he looked pitifully into her eyes, which were unusually dimmed at the moment. And they too were beginning to cry. Still, without speech, they embraced and held each other alone in the middle of the floor. Some time passed. They were now waiting for a hope beyond hope. 'I tried—' he started to say, failing.

'Josh—' she said, the word dying as it was born.

They came closer and rested their heads together. They both began to lower their wet eyelids. And just before they did completely close them, each caught a glimmer of light in the eyes of the other. And they opened their eyes again, fully, as the light continued to grow. And still, it grew. Still touching, they turned their heads to the window. Looks of sheer amazement burned across two faces streaked with tears. And they beheld it all as it inexplicably unfolded: outside, the dark black clouds rolled aside, opening a hole or channel in the early evening sky. And through the opening, there came a powerful blasting beam of flaming sunlight brighter than the noontime on a tropical beach. Blindingly, the rays came down and forth, falling into the window of Athena's living room. And there, on the floor, the beam illuminated two bent beings, making their small huddled mass shine like a vision of Heaven as painted by some great master of the Renaissance, man's best imagining of the Divine. And then, they knew!

As their tears evaporated, their faces glowed anew, and their eyes rekindled with fierce love, the light dimmed but did not disappear. Both lovers were now loudly babbling incoherent songs of joy. They stood and Josh took her in his arms. He raised her up and spun her around as they laughed and laughed. There was a crash as something on the coffee table was impacted by her flying feet. And still, they carried on. As the light outside dimmed further and the clouds began to mend themselves, the couple took to the couch, hugging and whispering sweet words to each other. They almost didn't hear her phone ringing. And she took the call at the last second possible.

'I take it Josh asked?!' Father Josias practically yelled breathlessly.

'He did!' she yelled back. 'Did you see the blinding sun?!'

'No,' he said. 'It is and it has been very dark here. But I take it you've seen a great sign. I heard mine. I've been sitting here in the study for some time reading. There is no one about to make a sound, not even the cat. And suddenly, from behind me, a strong, clear male voice of authority spoke two words to me. It said, *Bless them*. And so I will!'

They both spoke and prayed with the priest before hanging up. Athena sat on the couch, laughing and crying. Josh was crying as he ran around the room in wild, silly circles. Then he stopped and again fell to his knees. 'Thank you, God!' he cried out. 'Thank you, and I will do whatever I must to keep Your trust. But, God, this is still poor, silly, little Josh. Can You please also help me with the rings, and the timing, and all the things I have no ideas about? All of it really. Mercy, love, and thank You, Lord! Amen.'

He did have many things to do. As did she. And the following week was very busy and eventful, to say the least.

Ten

A Week of Thanksgiving

Sunday night, after a luxurious dinner and a bottle of the finest non-Rose wine on the couch, Josh and Athena refrained from a second bundling, each instead sleeping alone though a short distance down the same hallway. For once, he was up before her on Monday morning, and he had coffee brewing when she poked her lovely head into the kitchen. Even when she came in, he was thinking, '*I gotta do this right! Help me!*'

'Coffee smells so good, baby,' she said as she approached.

He grabbed her in a hug. 'Not as good as you,' he said, nibbling on her ear.

'I missed you last night if you know what I mean,' she said.

'I sure do,' he said. 'But this is just the beginning! Can I help with breakfast? I know how to boil an egg AND make toast!'

'You can help, baby. I'll do the heavy lifting at my usual speed. I have to go in today, and tomorrow. Hopefully, I can be out a little early on Tuesday. Then, that night, or Wednesday, we can go get everything for the big dinner. Are you going to see Sister and the girls today?'

'Yes. I'm going to take them all out for lunch. And we can get everything squared away. I know they'll love the idea. And love you all the more for offering. You're kinda special like that.'

'Not as special as my Joshy,' she said, taking a sip while opening the fridge.

'And in the afternoon, I need to drop by my place and run a few errands. Do I need to grab anything while I'm out?'

'No, we're good. Just pick up what you need and, later in the week, we'll do a big shopping trip. And, baby, I know you love them, but no roses are needed this week. I didn't want to tell you, but you, uh, forgot yesterday anyway.'

'NO!' he said loudly but dejectedly. 'Well, we were a little busy yesterday. But can I do roses or a rose just once this week? Pretty please?'

'If it makes you happy, then it will thrill and delight me! Sure. Now, would you like a yummy waffle?'

'Do angels deserve roses?!'

One did, and he knew it. But after more than a few 'you don't have to's' he let the petal matter drop—for a few days.

Athena bubbled around the Gallery that Monday in such a state of ecstasy that everyone assumed something truly wonderful was afoot and they didn't pry as they had the previous week. Marge and Bridget thought about it, especially after the shop received a phone call that morning, but they contented themselves to wait and wonder. As giddy as she was, the curator busied herself, further updating the plans for the new year, and going over some mandatory reviews and assessments. Josh ran a few errands and made a few calls, one of special importance. Around noon, he was driving the orphanage's van to town and a lunch for five followed by ice cream. The non-angelic women of his life, all still nearly angelic in his eyes, were very happy about the suggested Thanksgiving Day plans. Those arrangements were mostly firmed up, with the idea of everyone spending the night left open for a decision in the near future.

When he arrived home, to Athena's home, that is, though it had begun to feel like his too, she had a surprise waiting for him. 'Thanks. But do I really need these? Yet?' he asked as he looked at the gate RF badge, garage opener (for book access??), and the door key she'd just given him.

'Yes, of course, you do,' she said. 'We'll be in and out this week, and then, there's our beyond together.'

'I love this! But at the same time, I don't want us to feel like we're, what do they call it? Playing married? Before we are.'

'I know. And we're not. We'll not consummate this relationship until we are married. And, by the way, not one second later than necessary,' she said with a wink. 'But for this week, you are a glorified guest. You can return to your place until we're all set, but I'd like you to feel more at home and have access here when you need it until then. And, Josh, when the grand day arrives, you're moving in here, right?'

'You mean you don't want to share a tiny efficiency?'

'Any house with you in it would be a home. But ... no. We'll start here, and after we fill it up with kids, we'll move out to a farmhouse in the country or something!'

'Perfect!' he exclaimed. 'Farmer Josh can grow roses in the greenhouse!' She wrinkled her nose, and he added, 'And I like the idea of filling the place up with kids!'

'That we will, the good Lord willing. But now, how about filling up on lamb chops?!'

That night went spectacularly well, as did Tuesday. Athena was in until four, but she got a lot accomplished. There was only one hiccup when Sam reported a blocked drain in the basement, which he said required her attention. She didn't see why when she arrived, but she humored his explanations, his ideas, and several of his stories that she thought might have been contrived on the fly, almost as a way to buy time. She didn't know it, but his plan worked. Around the same time she was looking at a pool of water, Josh, feeling like a spy, snuck into the Gallery and headed to the gift shop. Marge and Bridget were waiting. It pained him to be so close and not see Athena, but after a laugh and a hug with the two ladies, he quickly departed. Back from the basement, Athena found the pair smirking about something, a joke she assumed, thinking no more of it.

Wednesday, as the weather again took a very wintery turn, with plummeting temperatures and more snow flurries, Josh and Athena were frantically busy preparing for the big party. They had gone ahead and deemed the dinner a party as a party felt more official. And fun. After a few runs for various inedible wares and whatnots, they journeyed to New Hampshire and a small farm that sold, during the season, smoked hams and freshly procured and prepared turkeys. The plan was to ice the meats in a cooler and hit Butcher Lads on the way home. As Josh was closing the rear door, his phone rang. It was a semi-serious conversation that would impact their doings, and it lasted for a few minutes. At intervals, he consulted with Athena, 'Is this okay?' She readily agreed to his requests, as she thought she knew what was going on. When he hung up and they were driving, he filled her in: 'Yeah, so Sister has a brother who lives alone down on the Cape. I met him once, a very nice fellow. But he's become ill, very ill, it seems, and there's no one else.'

'I hope the poor dear is okay,' she said.

'Me too. But as we arranged it, she'll go see him as soon as we pick up the girls tomorrow. And as it will help, all three of them have agreed to stay with us tomorrow night, and maybe Friday night too if needed. And they're really looking forward to it all.'

'Me too!' she said, coming more alive than even her perky ordinary. 'A house full of sweet girls! And a Joshy. And we'll do everything. Friday, maybe we can go to the city in the daytime for some extra fun. No Black Friday shopping—unless that's what they want—but we can look and play and have a wonderful time with the babies!'

'That's it!' he said, evidently extra excited about something. 'That's perfect! I mean, of course, we'll have a blast. And do you think they'd like ice skating? Maybe at the Frog Pond? Would you like it?'

'That does sound perfect! Little girls either love skating, or they learn to love it. And I love this idea, Josh!' They talked and schemed all the way to the market and even as they walked the aisles and sampled custom coffees at the kiosk. In fact, they talked of little else even as they bustled around the house that evening. That night, Athena dreamed of happy girls skating and laughing. Josh dreamed something similar, but his vision also included a rose, and something else.

On Thursday morning, after checking the bird and ham confined in the oven, they drove over to the home. There, while Josh fastened two booster seats in the GLS, Athena and Michelle consulted with Francisco. 'Call me on my cell if you need anything. I have here brother's number at home and his neighbor's number too. I will miss all the fun and good company, but I really need to do this,' the nun said.

'We'll miss you,' Athena said. 'And I hope he's okay. I'll say a prayer. And we'll save you a nice plate with everything.

After loading the girls' bags and with a goodbye hug to Francisco, they made their way back home. 'You have the nicest car, Miss Athena,' Isabella said as they walked up the steps Josh had deslushed only an hour earlier.

'And the nicest house,' Michelle said. 'Thank you so much for having us over like this!'

'Thank you!' little Kara said sweetly while hugging Athena's legs.

'I should be thanking you, and sweet Joshy, for all this wonderment,' she said in return. 'In fact, thank you, ladies! And Josh. This has already been my best Thanksgiving ever.'

Inside, Athena assumed the role of their master chef, with Michelle as her understudy and assistant. The more they talked and interacted, the more the pair bonded. Josh and the little girls were given various assignments, which they were proud to attempt—even if the completion may have been lacking here or there. Outside, a real snow shower began to fall faster, deeper, and heavier. Athena went to the living room and found Josh preloading the fireplace for later. She then spent a while longer with Michelle, girl-talking and cooking with abandon. About an hour later, they were a little surprised by the surrounding quiet and decided to look in on the trio. And they were not to be found in the house. Eventually, Michelle heard voices outside when she passed by the front door. She and Athena poked their heads out and heard the voices clearly. Following them, they found Josh, Isabella, and Kara hard at work in the small yard on the side of the townhome.

'Whaddya think?!' Josh said from inside a construction project that was beginning to look like a snow fort.

'And how about them?' Isabella said, pointing to three snowmen nearby. 'They need noses, and sticks, and hats, and all.'

'And how about my angel?' Kara asked as she flapped her arms and legs in the snow.

Michelle didn't answer, instead diving down and making her own angel. 'I love it all!' Athena said as she clapped her hands.

'One can never have enough angels,' Josh said as he walked up and put his wet, slushy arm around her. She kissed him, before dropping and producing a white copy of herself.

Athena, Josh, and Michelle took turns checking on the kitchen while they all played in their little winter wonderland. Around five, Athena suggested they go in, tidy up, and prepare for supper. As it turned out, they'd all worked up healthy appetites during their play. And so it was that around six, Josh and Athena sat down at the large, formal table for their first holiday meal together. And it very much looked and felt like a loving family scene, perhaps as painted by Rockwell. Josh led them in a special blessing, during which he had to stifle tears. And then they ate, and talked, and ate, and laughed, and ate until they were as content as could be.

When the women moved to the kitchen once again to prepare desserts, Josh lit his fire and tended it until it crackled merrily. He was admiring it when someone tapped his shoulder. 'A special adult drink for my most favorite special adult,' Athena said as she handed him a glass of champagne. She sat down next to him in the glow of the flames and they raised a toast to life well lived. 'Josh, this is the best day ever,' she said. 'These three and I can't stop having fun. And I feel we owe it all to you, sweetest man.'

'None of you owe me,' he said, rubbing her back. 'I'm the lucky one. I finally know what I've missed in life. And I love every bit of it.'

'Just the beginning, baby,' she said as she stood up and started walking back to help the girls. Josh smiled as he watched her. Her touch, her voice, her scent, her sway, and this whole scene were beyond his wildest dreams.

Soon he was rejoined by all the women and various dessert items, and they all ate and drank and laughed and basked in the warmth from the hearth until relatively late. Eventually, Athena stood and asked for their collective attention. 'Mr. Josh shall repose on the couch here for the night. Josh, there's a half bath and you can shower up in my bedroom in the morning. And girls, if you'll accompany me, I'll show you to your rooms. But don't plan on settling in just yet. We may still have a few fun games to play.'

The girls were most excited by the prospects, and quickly followed her away. Josh took the time to relax and reflect. He kept hearing giggles and feet upstairs, which made him smile. He poked the fire and thought about bedding down. Or, in his case, settling down on the couch. He was pleasantly surprised when that same someone tapped him again and handed him a beer, one of his favorites. 'Old Fezzi for young Joshy,' she said. Then she gave him a deep, long, mouthwatering kiss, winked, and returned to the little sorority party upstairs. Finally alone, and buzzing from that last kiss and the drinks, he decided to turn in for the night.

He lay still for a while thinking about sleep. The constant giggles, sometimes rising hysterically, made him chuckle. But they also made dozing off a chore. Around midnight, or so he sensed, he thought his time had come. The voices up the stairs were still and the only sound he could hear was the occasional crackle from the embers. He'd not long said his prayers, and closed his eyes, and he was just about to nod off when he felt something or someone or some *ones* grabbing his arms!

He opened his eyes to see Athena and Michelle holding his hands down, with the little girls standing by with some makeup and other torture implements. 'This game is called Get Joshy!' Isabella said as she approached sweetly but menacingly with a tube of lipstick. All four ladies burst out laughing and Josh managed to get out a, 'GAH!!!'

Get Joshy turned into a little series of running, jumping, and belly-laughing games that had him up off the sofa. The silly five-some frolicked until they were utterly exhausted. And at last, with a kiss from Athena, hugs from the girls, and a promise he'd be truly left in peace, they all departed for dreamland. On her way up, his beautiful girlfriend, the new light of his life, paused and whispered to him, 'Best holiday ever.' And so it was.

Eleven

Roses on Ice

All of them slept exceedingly well, a testament to tryptophan, hard play, joy, and more. Josh and Athena were up first and delighted in a little adult time with coffee in the kitchen, even introducing a little Irish cream to mark the occasion. They were seated at the table, sipping and cooing together, when Michelle walked in. She made straight for them and, dropping down between them, took them both in a hug. 'Thank you,' she said as she suddenly bordered on tears. 'You're the sweetest, kindest people. For me and those two baby dolls. Joshy, Athena, I really love you.' She hugged them harder, an affection they gladly returned.

'*A daughter?*' Josh thought as he hugged her and kissed her hair. '*Daughters?*' He liked the thought.

'*A daughter?*' Athena thought as she hugged her and kissed her hair. '*Daughters?*' She liked the thought. And as she guided the child towards the coffee pot and the juicer, she winked at Josh. He returned it with a wonderful smile.

The three of them talked for a while and then Michelle went to wake Isabella and Kara. Soon they all five sat down for breakfast. The girls stuffed themselves silly with pancakes soaked in butter and dusted with confectioner's sugar. Josh and Athena, working together to better their fasting habits, yet wanting enough energy for the day, ate reduced portions. And while the women made ready for their day trip, Josh ventured out to check the weather

133

and defrost the GLS. Soon they were on I-93, heading south. Josh tuned the radio to WODS and the never-ending Christmas tune cavalcade. They caught the DJ in between songs:

That was Sleeper Agent with their pop version of "Winter Wonderland." Next, we've got Darlene Love, "Alone on Christmas", and, soon, the first daily playing of "Dominick the Donkey." But first, this!

After navigating into the city and its notorious traffic, a process that Josh found remarkably light and easy for Black Friday, they parked at a centrally-located deck between the Commons and Faneuil Hall, though closer to the Commons, with the idea of looping around the area, nosing, perhaps shopping, and more likely than not, dining (Friday-friendly, for the adults), finally ending their tour at the skating rink at the Frog Pond. They had a delightful day, many hours of it. The girls did very little in the way of shopping, which Josh had originally feared they might. Thus, he didn't have to carry much in the way of baggage, though he did have to carry Issy and Kara at intervals when they grew a little weary. In the mid-afternoon, with a daytime high just above freezing and with mostly clear skies, they at last arrived at the ovalesque skating rink.

'Do you girls know how to skate?' Josh asked the young trio while they paused at the Pavilion. Three heads shook negatively.

'I've never been,' Michelle said.

'Nope,' said Isabella.

'Is it hard?' Kara asked.

'It can be a little tricky,' Athena said. 'But once you get the hang of it, it's a lot of fun. Josh and I will help you get started. I'm not sure about him, but I'm a pretty good skater.'

'She's pretty good at everything,' he said with a smirk.

For a little while, the adults assisted the girls, tutoring them in the ways of balance, steering, stopping, and all. Michelle took to it like a frog in a pond. And it happened that the rink had little animal figures mounted on flat ski runners that made perfect training and assist devices for the small girls. None of the ladies noticed Josh sometimes checking his watch or sending a quick text now and then. When the girls took a break, with Josh standing by at the tables in front of the Pavilion, it so happened that a lull on the ice emerged. With the rink mostly empty, Athena decided to go out solo to test or exhibit her skill. For a few minutes she sailed around effortlessly and placidly, but her momentum and performance built as she circled. Soon onlookers wondered if a professional ballet skater or Olympic competitor was on the ice, so graceful and impressive were her movements.

'That's what we want to be like when we grow up, girls,' Michelle said as they excitedly watched her perform with abandon, as she even dared a few flying leaps and turns. All around, everyone watched, most of them with growing awe. Some clapped and cheered. But then, a new performer challenged her show. Michelle saw him from the corner of her eye as he worked himself up at the end of the rink. With a bound of great energy, Josh launched away, running on the foretips of his skates. He immediately shifted into a series of powerful thrusts and caught Athena mid-rink. As she floated along, still most impressively, he showed off moves of his own, his being far less artful than hers, but still commanding of attention. He deftly slid this way and that, keeping pace with her. In fact, he began to circle her, in close, even turning and skating backward as he passed. He then engaged her in a not-quite-taunting conversation.

'What's this?! Maybe you have a rival? Well, we can't always be the best at everything, now can we?'

'That's really good, Josh. I didn't know.'

He held up four fingers, wiggling them, as he looped her again. 'Four. Four years a starter on the intramural hockey team in college! And I found out I was an as-good if not better skater than a player. So how's this?' He had become downright cocky, smirking mercilessly as he talked.

'Wonderful,' she said with a little smirk of her own. 'Well, come on. Let's see what you can do!'

'Just wait,' he said. He motioned for her to slow down, and they came to a stop at one end of the rink. Then he circled her again and said, 'Just wait right here. Don't move your pretty little feet an inch. I'm going to show you my very best move!'

'I can't—' she started to say.

But he was already off. He went behind her and then traveled back down the entire length of the rink, building speed as he went. When he turned, hard, leaning down and bracing with his hand on the ice, he flew towards her like a thunderbolt on blades. And at the right moment, he dropped to his knees with the skates tucked behind him. And he coasted, kneeling, until he was right in front of her. He'd impressed himself with how well he timed it, coming to rest only a foot or so from her legs. They looked at each other for a good minute, her standing, him kneeling. The entire crowd looked on in near-total silence. She was about to say something when he beat her to it. As he reached into his coat pocket, he said, 'Athena.' He produced a little box, flipped it open, and presented it to her. The cockiness was replaced by a gentle, hopeful look. 'Will you marry me?'

A complete hush fell on the pond, collective anticipation at its height. Then she dropped down with him, took the box in her trembling hands, and screamed, 'YEEESSSS!!!' He took out the ring, made of the finest nickel bordered with gold and topped by a small diamond, and slipped it on her waiting finger. Through tears of joy, she said, 'Oh, Josh! YES! I love you! I love you! I LOVE you!' With that, she wrapped her arms around him and took him in their most passionate kiss yet, one that seriously threatened to melt the ice beneath them. All around, voices shouted out with good cheer. They remained still in place, talking, weeping, and kissing. Directly, Michelle led the girls to them, sans the training critters, and they all shared an excited hug. As a few more skaters took to the now quiet rink, several of them passed by with congratulatory well wishes. As a group, they rose and made their way slowly back towards the Pavilion.

Josh said to Michelle, 'Hey, if you could, please hold on to the girls for a few minutes. I'm hoping, with this music from wherever the little Misses might like to dance! Then after a bit, please, bring them back out to us.' The children toddled over to the wall and eventually took seats so they could watch. Neither newly-betrothed had ever danced on ice, so, after a few tentative attempts to do, well, something, they simply settled for holding close and slowly spinning as they glided aimlessly along.

'It's beautiful, and I absolutely love it, Josh! Where'd you find it?'

'You don't recognize it?! It seems Doris Harper makes a very limited line of engagement and wedding rings. I hear they're popular coast to coast and even in Europe.'

'The shop!' she said. 'Wait. Did this have anything to do with Mr. Sam's mysterious water emergency the other day?'

'I dunno,' he mumbled with a look of faux guilt on his face. She reached up and stroked her ringed hand down his cheek.

'That makes it doubly special,' she said.

'I, uh, I could only afford this one,' he said. 'But in a week or two, I'll have enough for the other two, yours and mine. Or on Monday, I could dip into my retirement or see HR for a little loan. I want the best for my girl, my angel. If you want, you can pick out different designs, or when I have the money, we can replace—'

'Never!' she said emphatically. 'This is my ring, and I only want those that match it. Because it came from you it's worth more to me than all the gold and gems in the whole world. And don't you dare take out any loan; take your time, my love, and don't put yourself out.'

'I'd put myself anywhere for you,' he said. 'But, okay. Now that the secret is out, I'll consult with you at the shop for the others. Soon, too! And with you in on the scheme, I won't have to have Sam set those newspapers on fire next time.'

'You silly!' she said, playfully slapping his shoulder.

They held, kissed, cuddled, and swayed, eventually making their way back to the center of the rink in front of the girls.

Michelle, Isabella, and Kara joined them again, and they held a small private dance party. Josh cavorted with the little girls and spun them around, and Michelle talked and cherished incessantly with Athena about the ring and the event. Finally, Athena asked if the young ladies were ready for a change of scenery or something to eat and drink. All present, except Josh, readily agreed they were, and the girls began to pull him back towards the lockers. But the show wasn't quite over yet. When they were a few feet from the opening in the sidewall, Josh stalled and held Athena back. 'And ... now!' he suddenly yelled, making a cueing motion with his hand. And abruptly, a street performer, a man (or woman) dressed in an oversized rose flower costume made of colorful foam, moonwalked onto the rink's surface wearing ice shoes. The rose bore a small boombox that was playing "Angel" by Aerosmith. The booming, sliding figure came right up to them and did a little dance. The girls squealed and clapped. And when the big rose finished its rendition, it handed Athena a single real red rose. She took it, and yelled, 'JOSHY!' before kissing him again.

Back in the GLS, they prepared to leave the city, all of them deciding they wanted to go home to eat, play, and loaf about. After merging back onto the freeway, heading north, Josh looked over his shoulder, and asked the girls, 'Radio anyone?' When they agreed, he tuned right back in to WODS. Two DJs were explaining something to the audience:

> *Now, some say it isn't a Christmas song. And they might be technically correct. However, we have decreed—*
>
> *We have DECREED! Or at least you did, Bert.*
>
> *Hahaha. Yes, I did, Clyde. You know, their next few best-known songs were Christmas ditties, so that helps, right? This one might as well be Christmassy. Or whatever. We're just gonna play it! Folks, it's the Penguins, "Earth Angel..."*

Josh and Athena made eyes at each other and grinned. As the doo-wop Christmas carol stand-in commenced, her hand slowly connected with his on the center console. That soft thrill, which he never, even to his dying day, got tired of, made his hand jump an inch, bumping the electronic tap shifter, causing the machine to drop a gear. As the drivetrain lugged down, the RPMs jumped in sync with Josh's heart. 'Paddle,' she quickly said, temporarily releasing his hand. With a flick, he corrected and drove on. Their hands met again and didn't part—one taken phone call aside— until they pulled up to her townhouse. The call was from Sister Francisco, who informed them her brother was improving, though she also asked them to watch the girls for one more night if it wasn't any trouble. After hanging up the call, Josh looked in the mirror at his sweet, bubbly "trouble", and decided he couldn't be any happier.

Back home, because Athena made a really mean stack of pancakes, they had a second breakfast for supper. 'We're doing okay with the meats,' Josh privately, encouragingly noted to a smiling, approving Athena. Later, after they checked the remains of their snowmen and fort, Josh built another splendid fire. The night was more subdued, and no one even attempted to attack him with makeup. But they didn't leave him alone. While Athena and Michelle talked, like sisters, or, rather, more like a mother and daughter, Issy came over to Josh on the couch. She held her hands out and he scooped her up. They had nuzzled for a moment when they were joined by Kara. It wasn't clear who played the role of the teddy bear, but they were all happy. Eventually, the girls declared they were sleepy and excused themselves upstairs to prepare for bed. Michelle and Athena had been watching the girls with Josh, smiling and sighing about the spectacle. Michelle then looked at Athena, almost sadly, and said, 'Since it, you know, it happened, I haven't been comfortable with, well, men.'

'Those weren't men, my dear,' Athena said kindly.

'No, but it confirmed some experiences I'd already had.' She stifled a tear. 'I've just never been comfortable with, well, whatever they are. But Josh is different. He's a real man, isn't he?'

'I don't think they come more real.'

'I do like him, and I wish I could— Would it be okay if I went over and—'

'Baby! Look at him. He'd love to. Just go over there.'

Michelle walked over and sat next to Josh. He smiled at her and she leaned over. 'Joshy, Josh, Mr. Williams. I've never been— I mean— Would you please—'

'Come here,' he said kindly, offering his arms. She cuddled into his hug and stayed there with her eyes closed. He rested his head on hers, the way a big brother would to his little sister. Or, more likely, a father would to his daughter.

'Thank you, for being so nice to me. And to Issy and Kara,' she said, still holding on tight. 'I knew you two would get married. You're the best people I've ever known. And like I said, I really love you.'

Athena joined them and enveloped both in an over-hug, 'We love you too, precious child,' she said before kissing the back of the girl's head. They all three held together until Michelle broke out in laughter.

'So this is what a family feels like!' she said most jovially. 'Even if this is as close as I ever get, it makes me so warm and glad.' They talked with her for a while, assuring her of her great worth, and promising they'd always be around for her. Later, Athena walked her upstairs, talked with her a little more, and tucked her, Issy, and Kara snugly into their beds.

When she came down again, she found Josh with a fresh bottle of champagne. 'Another special drink for a most special day? This is, I suppose, another allowance for us,' he offered. She accepted a glass and he held her on the couch. They talked in whispers until well after midnight. Then they thought together without words. 'This was the most wonderful day in a great series of wonderful days,' she said aloud at last. 'Thank God Almighty for sending us to each other. I love you so, so much, Josh.'

'I love you too,' he said, rubbing his nose against hers. 'And, as if it wasn't special enough, along come those three.' He looked into her eyes a while before asking, 'You know, are you thinking about anything?'

'I'm thinking about it!' she said.

Later, after she went up, they continued to think about it, him on the sofa, and her in her bed. They prayed about it. They even dreamed about it. Of course, their dreams naturally turned to each other and their unbelievable new happiness and life together. Both were smiling when they woke up.

Around noon on Saturday, they drove the girls back to a waiting Francisco, complete with several plates of leftover turkey, trimmings, and pancakes. After saying bittersweet goodbyes, they went home and talked again until midnight. Sunday after church and lunch, they had their first marriage meeting with an over-the-moon Father Josias. And when Josh arrived back at his little apartment, while he felt at home, he really didn't. Something, or someone, or some ones, was missing. But he gave thanks to the Lord for it, for the joy, longing, trepidation, and all. Just as he was closing his eyes, she said to him from a distance, *'I love you. Goodnight, sweet Josh.'* He replied, just as he nodded off, *'Goodnight, sweet wife-to-be, my Athena. I love you.'*

Twelve

Hallelujah, Hallelujah!

Back in the department on Monday morning, Josh sat down in Professor Johnson's corner office for a debriefing of sorts. 'You wanted to see me, sir? And I wanted to ask how your holiday went.'

'It went far better than an old man deserves,' Johnson said. 'Kids, grandkids, and so forth. But enough about me; I'm the curious one. There are a couple of things I want to thank you for and ask you about. First, and this involves several things in one, how did your new love with Miss Athena develop?! I've heard the most amazing things.'

'Since I saw you last, I've had the best week and a half in my life! You and I talked about moving along, and about taking the timing as it comes. Well, we've taken it all at the speed of light. And that speed feels appropriate like it's the only kind we're allowed. Friday afternoon, I proposed to her down at the Commons. And she said yes! We've already started our marriage classes, and we'd like to keep the speed up and have our ceremony as soon as possible, maybe even before the year is over!'

'Have mercy, son! That's fantastic!' the older man said. 'With anyone else, or in any other scenario this insane world might present, I might have reservations. The adages about taking it slow and careful and whatever. Not here, with you though! Best news I've received in years, boy. Tell me a little more.'

'So, we took the three little girls from the home down to Boston for a day's outing. We finished with ice skating on the Frog Pond. She's an outstanding skater, but, you know, I can hold my own in that area. And we had a little competition on the rink, and I ended by sliding up to her on my knees. I popped out a special little ring and gave it to her. Then we had a little party. The ring is doubly important to us, maybe especially to me. I met her when I was shopping for Isabella. Athena helped me pick out a necklace with a locket. And the shop, or the jewelry maker, rather, has a wedding and engagement line. So I snuck in and got an engagement ring. Very unique, if not as posh as some. It took all my cash and I had to dip into my savings a little. In a week or so, or when I get the money, I'm going to get the two wedding rings.'

'How much,' Johnson asked, 'do those rings cost? Not that it's my business, I'm just interested and all. Like a father to a son.'

'Thanks,' Josh said. 'The two I looked at, well, she's going to give me her input, but I think the right pair will come in, regardless, at around two thousand dollars. That's what I paid for my car! But with her, for her, it'll be worth it.'

'That it will, young man. But, two grand, huh? What a very odd coincidence!'

'How's that coincidental, sir?'

Johnson took out his checkbook and started writing. As he did, he said, 'Very odd, but that's exactly what I owe you. So gimme a second, and I'll have the money for you.' He kept scribbling, adding, 'And this check's good. No bouncing about it ... I think.' He stopped inking, grinned, and handed Josh a check.

Josh looked at it timorously, and said, 'No, I can't take this. What on earth have I done for you?'

'What have you done?! Well, there was the matter of the two classes. A part of your duties, maybe. But there's also all the independent work you've done for me. I owe you, and I'd been meaning to catch up. And we need to talk about that as you'll soon be a husband and then a father.'

'Independent work?'

'Yes.' Johnson then pulled up some emails on his computer and motioned for Josh to look at them. 'See these?' he asked. 'You've been researching and editing for my latest textbook, and some outside things, and I've been reporting on you. These are to my publisher, a larger house that handles far more than academic books. See? I said *Josh did it, this was Josh, we should thank Josh*, and so forth. I've been giving you credit. You deserved it, of course, and I've got them curious as to who you are. But I now think my doing so was also predestined for other reasons. They have a slew of other kinds of jobs like this, and I think they're looking for a remote editor or two. All things you'd be an ideal fit for. You can keep working, of course, and do these on the side. Or they might want you full-time one day. Either way, this will be a nice new source of additional income, and it will expand your already tremendous reputation. Later this week, when I have my usual call with them, I'm going to introduce you and get this rolling!'

Josh was overwhelmed for a minute. 'Thank you, sir! I had no idea.'

'The thanks is all for you, son. And now, I need to keep it coming.' He clicked on a web browser, and said, 'See, here. You already have an entry on this professor rating site. Josh Williams, Merrimack. All I see are five stars, smiley faces, and a few red peppers. The peppers are from the girls, and they're a good sign! And the comments I've read match those I've been getting privately for a week from the students. You did a heckuva job, above and beyond. I noticed it. And, Lord, so did the kids. They're wild about you.'

Josh blushed, as one might have expected. 'They're all really wonderful,' he said. 'Bright kids and each one has a heart of gold. I love them.'

'The feeling is mutual, son. They were impressed enough, but when they saw Miss Athena, they were blown away. As was I when Lisa and the gang reported on Athena's answer to my riddle. I didn't have any expectation that anyone would be able to understand it, let alone answer it. Judging by what I've been told—and I kick myself for not being there—she didn't just answer it, she redefined it. No need to tell me everything, but she is VERY special, isn't she?'

Josh nodded affirmatively. 'She certainly is, sir. I didn't even really understand what she said that night. Really not in all the languages she spoke. But the mystery fits with who she is. I can't really describe it, other than to say she's as smart as she is pretty. Maybe more, and then some. Waaay above me, and I'm so lucky to have found her. Like a unicorn or something.'

'I'd say something beyond a mythical creature,' Johnson added. 'And that leads me to the next item: the country club had a raffle, and I won four tickets to see and hear Handel's *Messiah*, this Saturday evening, down at the Beantown Symphony. Laura and I had been thinking about who to invite for a double date. Now it's clear, and I've already got her in agreement. We want to meet your fiancé, and this seems like the perfect venue. Check and see if she, and you, are free. If so, then please accept. We can do the European thing and grab a late dinner when the show lets out. Somewhere nice like Top of the Hub! My treat all the way around. Do it for me?'

'That sounds fantastic! Thank you, and Laura, Misses Johnson. I'll call Athena in a second, and get right back with you. Pencil us in, in advance.'

The two talked for a little longer, and, in the afternoon, had lunch together after Josh deposited the check. His phone call with Athena went as expected, and so, their greater date for that week was set. They had minor dates every night of the week. Two of them stood out from the others. On Wednesday, once Johnson's check had cleared, Josh went to the Gallery, found Athena, and took her back into the gift shop where they'd met.

'This is going to be the most exciting sale in the history of this store!' Bridget said as she stood a few feet away from the couple at the back wall.

'What about these two?' Athena asked Josh.

'Those look perfect,' he said. 'I like the simple band design with that little stripe of gold running around the edge.'

'These are perfect,' she said. 'They certainly match their mate I'm already wearing. And they'd match just about anything. Including, that is, our love.' She stopped for a second, kissed his nose, watched him turn pink, and then said, 'Want to try them on now?'

'Sure,' he said. They slipped them on, with Athena maybe murmuring something under her breath, and they found that in addition to looking perfect, the rings happened to fit their fingers perfectly. Josh found that fact flabbergasting. 'This is just like with the engagement at the rink: my random size guess worked and fit like a glove. Like a measured ring, rather. What are the odds?'

'You just have a talent,' she said, winking at him, then raising her eyebrows. 'Now, can I help with these?'

'No,' he said. 'As it happens, I have some new side work I didn't even know about that pays very decently. I even had a little extra left over, which I've already spent on something else. Miss Bridget will show you what I got in advance when she rings up the rings!'

At the register, before Josh bought the rings, Bridget bent down and then handed Athena a dozen red roses. 'Someone sent these to you a little earlier, A. I can't remember who, but they look and smell great!'

'Yes, I too wonder about that,' Athena said while looking sideways at Josh. He was about to say something demure but silly, but she cut him off, preemptively, with another long, steamy kiss. That kiss, and a few others, still lingered on his lips, and in his mind, when they sat down for their minor date on Friday afternoon, another session with Father Josias.

'Really,' he told them towards the very end of their meeting, 'your speed in this Holy matter does not surprise me. And it would with nearly any other couple. But the Lord's time and timing are just that: His. I'd just like to mention a few things to close us out. And perhaps we've reached the end of mandatory utility. But let me say that I love and adore marriages. They are works of productive joy and beauty in their own way. They embody the kind of deep participation that is vitally necessary for fulfilling and understanding any sacramental activity, where faith meets eternity by the act of doing. And they stand, any real Christian marriages, in stark defiance of the world. And I mean the very fallen modern world, which, like so many societies of ages past, hates men and women, hates civilization, and hates God.

'Those are some reasons why today's people are taught to shun tradition and each other, the total atomization of mankind and, thereby, its possible death. The lies are many, such as that men and women are equal or essentially interchangeable. I need not blame any particular philosophy, as this idiotic worldview has sadly become the norm across much of the West. As I've said, may that your blessed union serve as a living example of renewed tradition, with two very different people, not at all alike nor replaceable, becoming something new and wonderful, a family. As the two of you know, men and women are markedly different. One to the other might, and probably should, be viewed as a great mystery. The sexes, both of them, should not ever compete with each other, a notion of ridiculous impossibility. A man should regard a woman, especially his woman, as an eternal being of extreme power and grace, and deserving of great respect and love. And vice versa, of course. Rather than distrust each other or otherwise be at odds, they should meld and compliment each other, with both growing far stronger for being so complimented, for producing, in essence, a new and hardier life. And both of them, together, are then in an ideal position to do and become those things, those purposes, for which our Lord intended men and women in the beginning.

'I know the two of you are with me, so, thank you for listening, my little choir. As I said, again, I hope your joining together in a new life will serve as an inspiration for others, both for all those unborn children in your future life and for any and all hopeful outside observers. You, both of you, dear children, are very unique, and this is a very different kind of marriage. Praise be to God, the Almighty, and the Mysterious. Then again, all of us are unique, and all marriages are special. Special blessings no men or women deserve, but with which we may all be blessed nonetheless by a God of infinite love, mercy, and kind, happy wisdom.'

They sat, holding hands, and smiling as they listened. Both nodded along in full agreement. And he then moved on to other related matters. 'Now, have you thought of any date or dates?'

'We have,' Josh said, looking back and forth between Athena and Father Josias. 'We'd like to do it sooner than later, and, as we both love the Season, and it is rapidly approaching, we thought a Christmas wedding would be nice, and appropriate.'

'By our calendar? Our Revised Julian, which, come to think of it, is the same, Christmas-wise, as the OCA's? And about, not on, of course,' he said to them. 'And, of course, with our ceremonies?'

'We've talked about this, Father,' Athena said. 'Both of us try to keep fully Orthodox, across the whole spectrum, and it's fun that way! Another thing we have in common is celebrating from the twenty-fifth through the seventh, two wonderful weeks of Christmas. So, Josh, would you like to go ahead with the Greek tradition?'

'And a partridge in a pear tree! Yes, I would,' he said. 'Honestly, I'm ready right now. But,' he laughed, 'we have protocols and invitations and so forth. I love the December Nativity. And, yes, I'd like the Greek services. Since we can't do it on Christmas, could we have the day after?'

Father laughed. 'Absolutely. Dutiful, loving surrender, I love it! And if it serves the heart in matters of expediency, so much the better. This is going to put the two of you, and me, under the gun, as they say, regarding planning and such, but, very well. I'll prepare for a ceremony on December twenty-sixth. To think, Josh, that I met you just after preaching about Crowns of Glory! Amazing and wonderful is life. Ah!'

'Thank you and bless you, Father,' Josh said sweetly.

'We love you,' Athena added.

'I will,' Father said, 'consult with Josh's parish, with Father Griswald, and prepare all internal matters accordingly. And speaking of formality, I sense the two of you share in my, ahem, great respect for the laws of our benevolent and benign Commonwealth. I hear they have regulations too. If you'll play their games, and get me the necessary—I hate this word—licenses, I'll happily do my part in that regard too. Rendering unto Caesar and so forth.'

At that point, Athena smiled and surprised the men. She reached into her folder and produced a few forms. 'I took the liberty,' she said, 'with the application nonsense, and with man's sad stand-in for lawful authority. Done, as they say. And the dates can be altered by true power as needed. And, no, I never mind overriding any such system that so deserves correction!'

'Boston gets as Boston deserves,' Father said with a chuckle as he looked at the documents. Not long afterward, they dined with him and his family, later taking their reluctant leave in order to prepare for a more divine and appropriate interaction with Boston.

The next afternoon, Athena stood in her guest bedroom. She was neatly smoothing Josh's only suit, a humble gray number from JCPenney when he came out of the bathroom. 'How do you like it, love?' she asked as he stood there admiring his new attire in a standing mirror by the door.

'It's perfect!' he said a little proudly, and at the same time, shyly. 'I've never had a tuxedo before. I don't know who Tom Ford is, but I like his work. But you shouldn't have.'

'I should have, and I did,' she corrected. 'And you look amazing in it! So handsome! It complements your classic features and your loveable … loveableness! And it matches my dress too.'

It did, in fact, as Athena wore a long, full black party dress, anchored by tasteful mid-heel shoes, and topped by a velvety black shawl. Her hair was up, in a grand display of feminine elegance, and the few pieces of unobtrusive jewelry she wore, including her new ring, served only to accentuate her poise and presence. 'You really look amazing,' he said, walking over to her and taking her hand. He kissed it, and then said, 'Maybe I can wear this tux for our wedding! It fits, feels like a second skin even. So soft and comfortable. I'd have never guessed formalwear was like that.'

'It feels that way when done correctly,' she said, picking up her purse. 'And I suppose the correct time has come to drive over?'

'Right,' he said. 'And thank you, again. For this, the night, and everything. I love you.'

'I love you, my sweet Joshy.'

Soon they were driving back down 93 in Athena's GLS with the Johnsons. Josh was at the wheel, a position he'd come to enjoy, with Hale seated next to him. Vivaldi's *Winter Violin Concerto*, as perhaps performed by Karolina Podorska, played very low on the stereo, soon ending and giving way to a Russian Christmas orchestral concert. The ladies sat behind their men, chatting away. Laura Johnson, a year or two younger than her husband, looked like and was dressed like a slightly older Athena, and not at all like a vision of Mrs. S. Claus. 'It's marvelous, my dear!' she said as she made over Athena's ring. 'Very impressive, and very unique. Much like the young fella who gave it to you!' Hale punched Josh's arm up front.

'He really is,' Athena said. 'Even if he forgot our customary roses tonight.'

'Uh, oh!' Hale said.

Josh only smiled and slipped the man a sly wink.

'And, Joshua!' Laura said, almost commandingly. 'You have outdone any expectations with this exquisite woman! She's a legitimate, a very real godd— She's a real angel!'

'She really is,' Josh said, winking back to Athena in the rearview mirror.

Their talk meandered along, merrily, until they arrived at the symphony hall. Inside, the show was everything they'd hoped for and more. Athena surprised Josh yet again by starting to sing along with the oratorio, in a whisper that was, while plainly audible, plainly natural sounding and demanding of joyous accompaniment. Soon all four of them were softly singing along, soon being joined by a decent number of patrons surrounding them.

King of kings,

For ever and ever, hallelujah, hallelujah!

And Lord of lords,

For ever and ever, hallelujah, hallelujah!

King of kings!

For ever and ever, hallelujah, hallelujah!

When the concert ended, more than a few of their fellow audience members paid her, and them, compliments for such a stirring and alluring chance to add to the general musical glory. In the lobby, the foursome posed for a few pictures, and Josh and Athena were singled out for special treatment by several different higher society outlets. 'With this, our kids will ace their finals without even trying! Wait'll they find these pictures!' Hale said to Josh as he engaged the boy in a walking hug near the doors.

About half an hour later, on the top floor of the Prudential Tower, the two men glanced out the corner windows at the city lights and the dreamy-looking Charles River below. They then turned back, pushed in the ladies they'd just helped seat a moment earlier, and sat down themselves. They'd just ordered hors d'oeuvres when Hale raised his champagne glass for a toast. 'My good ladies and very gentle man, I offer you, and I, this moment to reflect upon—'

He was cut short, and their attentions were diverted (along with those of all the customers around them), when up to the table marched a man dressed like Paul Revere, flanked by two Minutemen. 'Hear ye! Hear ye!' Revere announced. 'One if by land, and two if by sea. Roses for the ladies, who are so very pretty!' With that, and with a bow the Minutemen presented Laura and Athena with boutiques of two dozen red roses each.

As the Revolutionaries marched away, the women fawned over their flowers, Hale chuckled wide-eyed, and several other tables applauded, Josh smugly asked, 'Who forgot what, now?'

'Joshy!' both girls exclaimed.

'It was Professor Johnson's idea, part of it,' Josh said with another wink.

'Yes, yes, of course,' Hale said. In a moment, after the delight and surprise subsided, he continued his toast, 'Well, then. As I said, I offer us all the merriest sentiments on this merriest of nights. Now we have had delectations of sight, sound, and smell. To us!' They happily clinked glasses, with a rousing, 'To us!'

The dinner unfolded splendidly. Hale fussed over Josh's work and ability, along with complimenting Athena's unusual philological talents, even suggesting that one book Josh might want to edit should be a treatise on *Beowulf* as perhaps to be written by his future wife. Josh was rather enthusiastic about the idea, though Athena downplayed both a book and her little recitation. Additionally, much and great talk was made about a coming wedding. 'Would you really?' Josh asked.

'Certainly, son,' Hale answered. 'I keep calling you *son*, and I think the title fits well enough. I'd be honored to stand in as your father, or as your best man. The Greeks may call it the man's sponsor. Whatever the title, I'd be honored. Just an idea.'

'How about both roles?! By any title,' Josh said excitedly. He hadn't previously thought about the matter, and now this offer had great appeal.

'Just let me know, boy.'

'I will, sir. But I'd also ask if it's no trouble if Mrs. Johnson could stand in with you.'

'Certainly, Josh! I, we, would love to. Now, Athena?' Laura said. 'Have you picked a maid of honor or anyone to give your sweetness away to this little rogue?'

'I've mentioned something about it to Milley and Sam from the Gallery,' she answered. 'They're the older married couple who serve as our house wonder workers. They've both become like parents to me in many ways. And good friends. Family, by some description, rather than mere co-workers. And for a maid, what we call my *Koumbara*, I was thinking about Margarette. She's known Joshy almost as long as I have, and she thinks the world of him.'

'Darling,' Laura said. 'Most people do! And in whatever capacity, Hale and I will do whatever we can to help kickstart your eternal union. All others will help you too. As you two exude love, so you are greatly loved.' Her comments left all heads nodding in agreement. And Josh's blushing a little.

Later they removed to the little dancefloor by the bar for a few embracing, whispering twirls and circles. Athena found herself working up her low verbal intimations, drifting closer and closer to Josh's face and lips. After her fifth 'thank you' for the roses of the day, she leaned in and kissed him with such abandon it nearly knocked him off his feet. Hale and Laura, dancing nearby, noticed, and gave a few hoots, before enacting their own amorous shenanigans. As Athena kissed him and kissed him, and squeezed him tight, she couldn't help but feel the now-expected racing of his heart. Something, perhaps in the way he reacted, as more of a sub-reaction below his obvious desire for being kissed by her, caused her to focus on the patterns of his heart rate, patterns that she sensed were erratic. When she withdrew, and saw his look, both excited and mildly concerned, she placed her calming hand on his chest. With that, he smiled, pecked her cute nose, and they finished their imitation waltz. The rest of the outing passed like a pleasant summer breeze.

After dropping the Johnsons off at their home, with several hugs, kisses, and merry words, the couple returned to Athena's townhouse. 'Come on in, silly!' she said on the doorstep. 'I insist. In fact, I insist on you staying the night. Without bundling, and in the comforts of the guest room, but here the same. It's too late, and, besides, we need to coo and cuddle more, and have a nightcap.' He was in no position to resist, and so they made their way inside.

'More champagne,' she said, entering the living room from the kitchen.

'Thank you, most beautiful bride-to-be!'

'Thank you, beloved Joshy,' she said. But then, she put the bottle and glasses down and beckoned him to stand in front of her. She placed one hand on his chest, over his heart, and the other on his back, as if scanning or feeling for something. 'Baby,' she said softly, 'I've noticed something a few times. Not to pry, but this has become my business. When you get overly excited, or nervous, your dear little heart races. As to be expected, and it is so charming. But I must ask, and don't feel shy or concerned, have you ever been diagnosed with valve arrhythmia or what's called tachycardia?'

'Is that when my heart skips or flutters when I'm excited?' he asked. 'And beats irregularly and very fast?'

'Yes, baby.'

'Well, yes. I've always known about it. When I was at Dartmouth, I had a physical for hockey. They mentioned it, but I didn't think it was a big deal. Didn't stop me from playing. Later, I looked into the Army and they did a physical. They flagged it, and it prevented me from going forward. Their doctor said it probably wasn't life-threatening, but they, you know... I hear it can be corrected with a little balloon or something. I haven't looked into that, but, yes, I'm aware of it.'

'Does it hurt? Or cause you alarm?'

'Sometimes it scares me a little. And I'm a little afraid of doctors too, so there's that.'

'Would you like me to fix it, baby?' she asked kindly.

'Could you?!'

'Of course. The balloon, or possibly a current treatment, is designed, in this case, for your darling heart, to gently assist your cute little ventricle or mitral valve.' She looked at his chest closely for a moment. 'Mitral. It doesn't close all the way sometimes. Thus, the funny flow and rhythm. As it kind of sags open a little, it presses on a tiny little nerve. And that speeds up the beats. It's a simple fix, and I could do it right now.'

'Will it hurt?'

'No, not the way I'll do it.'

'Well, I trust you. And I love you. Okay, then, uh, Doctor Athena.'

'Good, baby. Now, I could just do it like that,' she said as she snapped her fingers for effect, 'but I'd like to do it softly inside, as much for me as for you. It won't hurt, but it might look a little weird to your eyes. Maybe look up, or close them?'

'Okay,' he said, as he did both. 'I'm ready.'

He, of course, didn't see what she did, but he felt it. A pleasant pressure built in his chest, and suddenly, he could feel every bit of his heart: the beats, flow, nerves, impulses, and all. He didn't know what she experienced, as she lovingly held his beating heart in her hands for only a second. First, she rubbed her thumb over the valve and nerve endings, healing them. Then she just held his heart and felt it working away. '*His life, his heart, his warm, gentle inner being,*' she thought in amazement as she cradled his most vital organ. Then she took her hands back, smiled, and said, 'All done! How do we feel?'

Josh felt and thought for a moment. 'I feel great! That was incredible.' He tried to work himself up a few times to check, but the issue appeared to have completely and permanently resolved itself under her kind, expert care. 'You're simply amazing, Athena. Thank you. You literally fixed my heart!'

'I owed you, love, as you've already healed mine!' She then kissed him with great force, providing a real heart check in more ways than one.

They settled in, enjoying their drinks and company on the couch. They talked about rectified hearts, music, friends, their evening adventures, their pending wedding, true love, and more. It all ended with a nuzzling embrace that sent their souls soaring together into high clouds of free fantasy. Before either became too sleepy, they jointly agreed it was time for bed. That night, she merely walked with him upstairs and escorted him to his room. She waited until he changed into his night clothes, and then lovingly tucked him into bed. She sat on the edge for a second, stroking his hair and kissing him.

'Josh, soon, very soon, we'll enter into a bedroom the way real lovers do. Can you believe it? Or wait for it?'

'I believe it with all my heart, Athena. And I'd say, I can't wait, but I can and will wait. Just a short while more to savor what is to come. I long for your touch, and to touch you, my love. Selfishly, I admit, I want your embraces and deepest affections.'

'And I, yours, sweet baby. And, yes, soon. Soon we will have each other, with all the fulfilling excitement two hearts can bear. But for now, I shall repose and simply dream of what is, and of what shall soon be. As always, if you need me, just call. Or think. And I love you with all my soul and being, gentle hero.'

'I love you, Athena, true angel of whose grace I will forever strive to deserve, keep, and cherish. Goodnight.'

'Goodnight, baby.' She kissed his lips briefly, softly, but persuasively, and then left him to his prayers and dreams. In her bed, her prayers flowed tearfully, full of thanksgiving for forgiveness and for a gift, neither of which she felt entitled to. Then, each under their own covers, deep pleasant sleep took them into its most caring protection and nourishment. And as they drifted under, they both thought one final word for such a wonderful night: Hallelujah!

Thirteen

Two Out of Three Ain't Bad

Good news, or as good a word of news about a certain subject that might have been expected, reached Josh one afternoon as he was leaving work. Over dinner at his place, again honoring the frozen aisle at Market Basket, he opened up their main discussion with his new tidbit and something related that now weighed a little heavier on his mind, and especially, on his heart. 'So, Sister Francisco called me this afternoon, and she was very excited about something!' he said.

'Do tell,' she said as she sipped her wine.

'Well, whoever makes the big decisions about group homes, and money, and the lives of poor children, all of that, they have granted a short extension for our home! It's probably not going to be that long, but it will get the gang through Christmas and into next year. My hope, which is hers, is that a miracle or two, or three, will let the girls find real families before the time to shuffle the deck comes.'

'That's wonderful,' Athena said. 'Did she say if she knew of any prospects for any of them?'

'Not so outright. But I know her, and I think she may have heard something. Whatever it is, I just pray it's not another fake runaround and heartbreak for anyone.' He sounded sincere but a little sad. She knew that, having lived through the system, he knew what he was talking about. They ate, drank, and thought in silence for a few minutes, when he said, 'That leads me to something else I wanted to discuss and get your opinion on. Something maybe just a little important.'

'Yes!' was all she said.

'Thanks. It's been on my mind for a little while, and sometimes I get choked up if I dwell on it for too long. There's—'

'I said, yes, silly!' she said. 'I mean we should discuss it obviously, but if you want my opinion first off, then I'm all in. I think it's a beautiful idea!'

'Do you know what I mean?'

'I do if our thoughts have been similar,' she said. 'Let me go first, if I may.'

'Ladies first, of course. The floor, or the table, is yours, beautiful.'

'We all but came out and admitted it to Father the other day, didn't we?' she asked. Josh nodded along, and she continued, 'You've been thinking it, and so have I. We've both seen them, all of them, and we love them. So if you're about to propose we, as soon as we're legally ready and all, adopt those three sweethearts, then, YES, I agree. Josh, when we spend time with them, it already feels like they're ours. And we're theirs. Let's do it!' She was smiling while a few tears brewed around the edges of her eyes.

'That's it! Do you really want to? I know I do! I want to have as many children of our own as the Lord allows, but, you're correct, they already feel like daughters,' he said. He was getting downright excited and a few tears rolled down his happy face. 'And, Athena, I'm curious about something. With Michelle, on the day she told you about the bad stuff in her past ... did you call down our Mother Mary for her?'

'Not exactly,' she answered. 'I cannot summon anyone, or I can't any more than you or anyone else. But I did pray for her intercession with Michelle. For her peace and protection. I trust she heard me, though I can't say whether she showed up then and there.'

'She did,' he said flatly. 'I saw her, or a glimmer of her radiance. You'd soon after asked me if I'd ever seen a sign from God. I wasn't thinking right, but I think that certainly counted for one! Glory.'

'Glory, indeed,' she said thoughtfully.

'But back on the proper aspects of what we're talking about,' he said, 'we need to discuss how to do it, of course. And then, there's the matter of whether we're able to. Money, and space, and all. I guess that's what we need to talk about.'

'Yes, it is extremely important. But first things first. As for space, we have enough room at my place, rather, at our place. And, if or when a few more additions start coming, we can always find a larger home. Maybe somewhere out in the country like we've mentioned or mused about. And as for money, do not worry about that.'

'I'm not worried,' he said. 'I just want to be ready to provide the right way. I'm going to start picking up some outside projects early next year, and I may have a lead on a side job doing some book editing for a publisher. That won't be bad money. And someday, out in the country, I wouldn't mind trying my hand at farming. Or something more hands-on in addition to the other stuff, most of which I can do remotely from anywhere. I just want to take care of my family.'

'And you will, don't worry,' she said kindly but affirmatively. 'That's never been a concern in my mind. And you will contribute in all the right ways, and it will work perfectly. But in general, as for us, I really meant don't worry about money. I'm not wealthy, but the very long years have led to a little accumulation. It's far more than I need, ever, a little trust fund if you like, that I set up a long time ago. Most of it goes, as it should, to charities. I admit that my current trappings are a reflection of the life, station, and society I've worked myself into this time, but I can always do with less so that others have more.

'Also, and I wish more people understood this, money should never be a bar to life and, especially, family and children. Like time, money is really irrelevant. Today, in places like this, it's a false or nonexistent commodity anyway. There will never be enough, but there's always enough. With a little kind effort from a mother and father, our Father makes certain of that! And all the other things, well, we'll just do them! How's that, baby?'

'Wow,' he said. 'Have I told you that I love you lately? Because I love you. Head over heels. Well, how about we dedicate a little more time to planning this out tonight?' They did, spending a few hours discussing logistics, timing, and how and when to broach the subject to their potential daughters.

As she was leaving for the night, she said, at the door, 'All good! You make the call, and then let's take off an hour or so early Friday afternoon and pay them a visit!'

'A perfect plan, my angel,' he said. With a kiss, a hug, another kiss, and a wink, they cemented that plan and parted for the evening.

On Friday afternoon, after driving down the cold but well-plowed streets, they arrived at the home. An extra car or two awaited them in the little parking lot. Walking inside, they were immediately greeted by Kara, who was bouncing around, obviously happy about something but, at the same time, seemingly a little nervous. 'Have you met them yet?' she asked Josh.

'Why, no,' he said. 'Who are we talking about?'

Just then, Sister Francisco appeared and took Josh by the arm. She looked at his face, then glanced at Athena, and suddenly guessed why they were there. She didn't know how their plans would be impacted by what she was about to say, but she told Josh anyway, 'Josh, my baby, there are a few people here that I'd like to introduce you to.' She then led them, following Kara, into the sitting room. There, a man, a woman, and two older children waited. 'Josh, this is Todd and Sarah Smith, and their children, from South Carolina. Mr. Smith is Kara's father's brother, and he and his family are taking her home. They're adopting her as their own. Isn't that wonderful? Mr. and Mrs. Smith, this is Josh and his fiancé, Athena. Josh was a resident here, and now the dear is little Isabella's big brother.'

Josh's face fell a little, which was painfully obvious to Athena, and probably only a little less so to Francisco. But he perked up, or tried to act perked up, and greeted the family. He spoke highly of Kara and she gushed about him. After a short while, he sat down and talked in earnest with them. Francisco joined them. Athena took a seat near the hall. And so she was in an ideal place to intercept a rather upset Issy when she came huffing down the hall. She spoke to her kindly, but after a few minutes, the little girl ran off to her room. Athena thought about the situation and decided to merely stand by for Josh. After some time more, the Smiths collected Kara and her things and removed them to their cars. When the sun was starting to dip low on the western horizon, they left. Josh, Athena, and Francisco stood silently in the hall.

'I'm going out to see Michelle!' Issy cried out, evidently in a fit, as she marched to the front door. She exited and turned to the right, stalking along, still in a huff.

'She's making for the grove in the back,' Josh said to Francisco from experience. 'That's probably where Michelle is. May we go out and talk to them?'

'Of course,' the nun said. 'They both love and respect you both greatly.'

'Sister,' Athena said, 'why don't you come with us? This may concern you too.'

The three walked around the house and, just as Josh had predicted, they found the girls in the yard. Michelle was sitting with her back propped against a tree with her feet squished into the accumulated snow. Her head was down on her knees and she was obviously crying. Issy now sat beside her, looking down, and was fighting back tears of her own. The women stood near but Josh simply plopped down on his knees in the snow right in front of the girls. 'Tough day?' he asked.

Isabella spoke first, with a little irritation, 'She was like my sister. Now she's gone! You saw them all. You talked to them.'

'I did,' he said. 'But I also know that while you're upset, you, like I, are also happy for Kara. That's her real blood family, so that's important. I know it's hard to think of being here without her, but she's going to be fine and so are both of you.'

'How?' the little girl asked through tears. 'I am happy for her. She's lucky. But where do I go? We don't have much longer here and I'm scared about going from one place to another and never really having a real home. No one wanted me last time.'

Michelle spoke up, quietly and sorrowfully, 'And nobody wants an older girl. A wicked teen girl. Especially with all the cruel rumors. Only creeps will take me now. To touch and hurt me. I wish— I wish I was dead.'

'NO!' Athena cried out. 'Never wish for that, baby. I know you're venting, but you are far too precious for those words. And we have something to ask and offer you. Hey, Josh, why don't you tell them how you and I feel about everything and what we're thinking.'

Josh was starting to tear up, but he forced control over his emotions, for the most part, and addressed the girls, 'You are two of the dearest people in my life. And I know, I really know what you're going through. Remember me? I did the bouncing all over creation only to never have anyone or anything for eighteen years. I know it hurts. But I'm proof that even if things don't work out, they still do. Trust me. And I know the three of you had become inseparable. Until you were separated. I know because I've been there with you, laughing and playing and loving. Athena and I had the privilege of acting as temporary guardians, maybe even parents for you. And we loved every second of it. So much so, that we'd come here today to offer the three of you our home. When we're married, in just a short time, we had wanted to adopt all three of you little sweethearts as our daughters. But now one of you is gone. To a good home, no doubt, but away nonetheless. And that hurts.'

The girls had become very quiet, though they were crying less. Josh was looking pityingly but sincerely at them. He went silent and Athena spoke up, even as she kneeled down next to Michelle. 'What Josh is trying to say,' she said sweetly, 'is that, if you agree, only if you want, and when it works out, then the two of you can be stuck with us as a consolation prize.'

After a few seconds, Michelle looked up at them, and said, 'Do you mean?'

'Yes,' Athena said.

'Do you really mean it?!' Isabella asked in excited disbelief.

'Yes,' Josh said.

Michelle continued, saying, 'You'd have us?! You want us? You'll adopt us and we'll be a family?!'

'Only if that's what the two of you want,' Josh said, very, very kindly and from the depths of his heart.

'I could have Joshy as a daddy?' Isabella asked as she started to stand up.

'We'd be your daughters?!' Michelle said, rising up from the tree. She looked at Issy and they both started nodding, then grinning, then laughing. 'Of course, that's what we want! We want to live with you guys and love you.'

'Then, love us—' Josh began to say. He was cut short when the girls launched into his arms, knocking him over on his back. They kicked their legs, latched onto him like two vice grips, and chattered away excitedly. Athena and Francisco laughed and cried at the same time as they watched the tackle unfold.

'Joshy, you're the best big brother ever,' Issy said. 'And you'll be the best daddy too. Daddy Joshy!'

'I love both of you so much! You are the best people I've ever met. I so want you,' Michelle said.

'Happy day! And hallelujah!' Sister Francisco cried out, clutching her Rosary beads. 'This is the greatest! Absolutely the greatest!'

'Look at us!' Athena said loudly and joyously as she added to the pile on top of Josh. 'Insta family!'

'God—' Josh said, muffled, 'I landed on a root...'

Back inside, Francisco wasted no time in assembling some paperwork, while Athena, aided by the girls, gingerly tended to a swelling bruise on Josh's back. 'This will take some time, a little while, at least,' the nun said. 'But we have time. You'll need to get married. And then jump through some hoops. But we have time and feet to jump with. Girls, I'll make a call or two, and a demand or three, and make sure you're settled here until it's time to make this dream family a reality.'

They all then pitched in and made a fine Friday-friendly dinner for five. After laughs, hugs, long chats, and more hugs, Josh and Athena finally left. While driving her home, he said to her, 'That went well, didn't it?'

'Yes,' she said. 'I'm as upset as you and they are about Kara. But all things serve the will of God. I'm glad you took all the contact information. Maybe, hopefully, all three of them, and the rest of us, can keep in touch and become like an extended family.'

'I hope so too,' he said. 'Now I suppose we can start on all of this paperwork. Probably going to need an attorney for that. Well, not until after the wedding and when I'm properly moved in. That should give us a little while to, you know, just have you and I for a bit.'

'I like the sound of that, as much as I love the idea of the adoption,' she said, winking at him and squeezing his arm. 'And an attorney, yes. I think I know one, associated with the Gallery fund that can help. I'll make a call. But leave the details and so forth to me.'

'It can be a difficult, sometimes lengthy process,' he noted.

'The time will give us time,' she said. 'And leave the difficulty to me. The more they complicate a bureaucracy, the easier it is for me to, well, work it.'

'The Lord works in mysterious ways, my angel, Athena.'

'He does,' she agreed with another wink. 'Also, with our newly-wed times, we've yet to talk about a honeymoon. Any ideas?'

'You're the great traveler,' he said. 'The furthest away I've been was up to the middle of nowhere in Maine last year, and, in college, down to New York City for a conference at Columbia. My idea is to trust in your better judgement.'

'Not a bad choice,' she said. 'I haven't been everywhere, but I've been further than most. I've even been to some places none of you have visited yet.'

'That sounds exotic. But I don't even have a passport.'

'I'd say you don't need one, and you won't, traveling with me, but we'll take care of it. Do you have a little more time to talk this evening about all the new, exciting developments?'

'All weekend, in fact,' he said. 'And as we did so well with our posting commitments lately, might another little indulgence be okay?'

'Like what?' she asked.

'Reach behind your seat for the little paper bag.'

She did, finding a bottle of rose Zinfandel with a little handwritten note attached to it:

My love,

More roses, of the drinkable kind. Just because! Well, that and I hope our visit goes very well! To celebrate.

I love you,

Josh

'Roses!' she laughed out. 'And the visit went better than could have been expected!' She then looked out through the windshield as fresh snow began to fall. Back at her townhome, they nestled together in front of the fireplace. In half an hour, Josh had it roaring, and so they sat, sipping, and enjoyed the warmth. They talked, as usual, until rather late. Then, as had become a habit, they shared a deep hug that threatened to sweep them both away. Then she began to kiss him, a kiss that threatened to sweep them further along, right up against their mutual boundaries. But that threat they broke away from, each tenderly turning down the passion at just the right, and last, moment. The wine finished, the fire still crackling away, he held her again in pure bliss. Their minds connected. '*We've covered a lot, baby,*' she said. '*Want to delve deeper into a few things. Maybe with added relaxation?*'

'*Another bundling?*' he asked, hoping that was what she meant.

'*Yes, my love,*' she said. '*We can plot and plan, and you can ask me some of those questions you have. Want to go up and get ready?*'

'No,' he said, openly. 'We can get ready. But then I'd like to come back down.' She gave him a curious look and he continued, 'We can do it anywhere, right?'

'We can. Why?'

'Then how about we build a little snuggly pallet bed right here and, as they say or sing, dream by the fire?'

'Okay!' she said. 'Quick showers, and then while you puff up the fire, I'll make a warm, soft bed here.'

'Deal!'

And just as before, with the addition of the hearth, they held hands, connected, and co-directed a dreamy talk that lasted until nearly dawn. When the first light of Saturday fell through the window it landed on them. Though they still held hands beneath the covers, she had begun to half turn over. Her other hand rested on their clasp, and their smiling faces were turned towards each other. In the night, they had somehow moved a little closer together, and now, their sweet, curled lips almost touched. Now and again, one of them would sigh contentedly. Their smiles would last until they awoke. But that would wait until midmorning, as they now simply slumbered happily without conscious thoughts, simply enjoying daylight dreams of love.

They spoke that afternoon about something, serious but also trivial, or so it had felt the night before, that they had agreed to get to later. When later came, she jumped ahead of him and asked, 'So, Joshy, whatcha want for Christmas?!'

'I want a wife!' he said somewhat jubilantly if smugly. 'I gotz mah eyes on this one chick. Think she's the one. She's sooo hot!' For his answer, he got a kiss.

'Weird,' she said. 'If anyone asked me, then I'd say I wanted a husband. There's this really, really cute, sweet boy I've been thinking of, and he'd be just perfect!' For that, she got a kiss. And they laughed at their cleverness. In the end, they indeed decided that they would simply give themselves to each other, gifts delayed one day after Western Christmas. And instead of any other presents for each other, they would lavish their material attention on Isabella, Michelle, and their close friends.

The next few weeks flew by. Josh and Athena continued their unusual courtship, with each call, date, and tryst feeling like a joyous meeting for the very first time. Josh, especially, was astounded to realize, even many, many years later, that he never once found the love of his life faded, mundane, or in any way ordinary. But in those weeks, he and his soon-to-be bride felt the rush of a hectic frenzy of what might have otherwise been monotonous activities. They laid fast but efficient plans. The church was readied for their betrothal and crowning. Invitations were hastily written and delivered. Friends, old and new, were consulted and, in some cases, requisitioned. Josh endured the fascinating, but frightening experience of wedding dress shopping and fitting, and he found there was one garment she wanted crafted and sized the old-fashioned way. She had tried to talk him into foregoing his new tuxedo in favor of his old budget suit, treads she insisted were dearer as they represented him as he had first found her. He almost conceded, but in the end, he argued the tux represented a newness in his life and hers, and that it thereby symbolized their new, growing chapter together. And he reasoned to her satisfaction that it just fit better. Many things were found, or rediscovered, and some things were altered by circumstance. One such change involved Josh's determination to join her church, a decision made upon a lunch consultation with Fathers Josias and Griswald. The two men, long and fast friends, helped convince Josh, who otherwise might have been prone to a reluctant overanalysis, that the adjustment was more than natural given its sequence and seeming predestination. And so the days passed until Christmas dawned, cold and white. At a certain time, the lovers kissed and began their ritualistic seclusion.

Crown Them

The early morning of the twenty-sixth found Josh awake and sitting alone, somewhat nervously, with a cup of coffee. He had tried to sleep the night before, finding only fleeting moderate success. In lieu of a bachelor party, a tradition he'd always assumed jaded at best, he'd stayed in the previous evening. His building anticipation he'd quelled, as was his way, by staying busy with a few little projects, checking, re-checking, and, then, checking again his clothes, his hair, and the short, stubbly beard she had convinced him to adore as much as she did. And as always, he turned his contemplations inwards with thought and outwards with prayer. With a glance at the clock, he decided the time was right for a final invocation before the greatest event of his young life. Kneeling down on the floor, he began to pray:

'Heavenly Father, dear Lord God, it's me, just little Josh, again. As You know well and far better than I, I have not changed. So my words, as usual, will probably fail me. Please forgive me for that and for all my many other failings. I remain most unworthy of what You are about to grant me from the infinite bounty of Your love.

'But I thank and praise You for that great gift, for a woman beyond my comprehension. Thank You, forever, for the happiness she has brought into my life, and for what lies ahead for both of us. Your will and Spirit have moved the two of us to this momentous event, the happiest in my life. And I looked up several things and found a new word, or a word I hadn't considered before: *theo-anthropos*, the very nature of Your Church, at once empowered with Your divine grace, and with our, or, in this case, my lowly and deeply flawed mortal ways. Please forgive this comparison if it doesn't make any sense, God, but in this new word, I think I've caught the barest look at my relationship with Athena. And maybe it all flows both ways and melds together, her greater carriage and my, well, Joshness.

'I know my pitiful sinful ways, my errors and falterings. And I know what she has told me of hers, or as she has tried to describe them to me in words I can understand. I, of course, was not there on that terrible day, and if I had been, I'm probably too stupid to have understood what happened. All I really know or sense is the great betrayal that must have wounded You the same way my original parents did in Eden. The serpent is the only true constant if I'm not mistaken. And as we were driven out, though still blessed with forgiveness and renewed hope we did not and do not deserve, so I think or feel went the suspension of Athena and the others of her faltered order. And these are matters I simply do not grasp in their entirety, or even in any measurable part. Still, if I am allowed, I beg and pray that, in Your good time and graces, that she and they be atoned and readmitted into Heaven and their place by Your side.

'If Saint Paul's words mean something, directly, for me right now, then might I help judge Athena? If her time on earth was a trial, may I assist with her sentencing and disposition? Her return to Your glory? I don't even know what I'm asking, Father. But I will do anything You require if it helps her. Even if that means losing her as my earthly companion. Even if that means my taking on her burdens. Please have mercy on her and on me. In whatever capacity, please help us each to help the other so that we may prove as worthy as possible in fulfilling Your grand ideals of marriage and family, and Your far grander designs for existence, renewal, and true Holy Life.

'With all things, at Your mercy, and by Your will, alone, I thank You for my role in them. In the name of the Father, and of the Son, and of the Holy Spirit. Amen.'

With those words, he crossed himself upon sitting back up on his knees. During his prayer, as rarely but sometimes did happen, he had sunk and bowed his head all the way to the floor, so great was the weight of his plea and concentration. In that moment, he reflected, and not for the first time, that one of the great many things he loved about his Muslim friends, those he knew and those he'd read about, was their *Sujūd*, their dedication in prayer and prostrating themselves upon the ground before God. '*That is,*' he thought, '*our proper low place in this hierarchy and for making these addresses. Salam.*' Then he rose and prepared in earnest for the coming day of sacrament. And he'd not been ready long, standing and looking at his reflection in a window pane, when a knock came at his door. Opening it, he found Hale Johnson waiting. 'Ready, son?' his mentor and great friend asked.

'As ready as I'll ever be.'

Laura had elected to go in advance to assist Athena, so the men drove to the church alone. The invitation list had been on the short side, consisting mostly of their work and church friends, honored guests from the group home, and a few of Josh's college chums and teammates. So when they pulled up, Josh was most surprised to find the grounds, parking lot, and surrounding sidewalks overflowing with a great host of people, most of them younger to look at. Noticing Josh's expression, Johnson began to laugh. It all made sense when they got out of the car. The instant Josh was spotted by the multitude, a shout went up in his honor. It appeared that many, if not most, of the students from Johnson's class had decided to crash the wedding. Many of them had brought significant others, some had brought friends, and some had even brought their parents and family members.

Given the excitement and the number of extra bodies, it took a few minutes longer than expected for the two to enter the building through a side door. When the time soon came, it was rather crowded inside though there was just enough room to keep everyone from the chill outside. Josh had, of course, no such problem with coolness, at once feeling a fire sweep through him when he first saw her in her wedding dress. It was simple, without any extravagant designs or embroideries, and it was long and flowing, with a short, clean train. But it was the upper region that stood out in his mind for an instant. *'I've never seen so much of her skin!'* he thought, before saying a quick and self-chastising prayer of penance. *'Still not quite yet, Josh,'* he thought after. Technically, however, he was correct; the dress, while still moderately conservative and very tasteful, did reveal the skin of her upper chest, back, shoulders, and, of course, her arms. Her long wedding veil made of a thin mesh did obscure some of her features. But he had, in fact, never seen so much of her smooth, toned skin. Or, if he dared admit it, ever seen such beautiful skin anywhere. And just when his mind was tempted to race, there at the finish line, with a soft, single-note chuckle some might have mistaken for a cough, he corrected and steadied himself.

Around the exact same time, Athena was taken and again smitten by the sight of him, as he stood there proudly but calmly with his cute, short beard and the tuxedo she'd bought for him. His face, those same features she'd instantly fallen in love with, were what arrested her attention. In a rare happenstance, her heart skipped a beat as she thought, *'He's about to be mine!'* Her quick, standing prayer was one of pure joy and thanksgiving. And it was reflected in the angelic smile on her face, which could not have been mistaken for anything else.

Both of them took a moment to look around at the gathering. She did not know any of the students, but automatically understood who they were. Those young people certainly knew who she was, though none of them imagined she would look so impossibly beautiful and subtly commanding in person. 'Brah...' was all the one young man could say before he had to brace himself for fear of fainting. The young women alternated their looks between indulging in a fascination with Athena and their immense fondness for Josh. Their expansive, dueling view of the couple was shared, if concentrated a bit more, by Isabella and Michelle, who were front and center with the bride and groom. Sister Francisco stood by, smiling, weeping, and praying happily. Margarette, Milley, Sam, Lisa, Allison, and the rest were nearby, all enraptured in glee. The church overflowed with tears, smiles, and joyous anticipation.

The betrothal and crowning services were conducted by Father Josias, assisted by the stalwart Fathers Andreas and Griswald. Josias commenced the first service with a doxology. The petitions and prayers were offered, two rings of finest nickel were exchanged thrice, and then, the final and longest prayer was made. At the end of it, the words stirred something deep in the hearts of Josh and his loving bride: 'Lord, may Your angel go before them in all the days of their united life, for You are He that blesses and sanctifies all things.'

'Please, God, Father,' Josh quickly prayed. 'One to guide and protect, please. But she too is Your angel, Yours and, now, ours. Amen. And thank you! Amen.'

When the crowning ceremony began, Josh's mind stuck for a second on the recited one hundred, twenty-seventh Psalm: 'Blessed are all they that fear the Lord; that walk in His ways ... Thy wife as a fruitful vine, on the sides of thy house.'

'My rose vine,' he thought, 'each rose, a wonderful child!'

Petitioned and named as servants of God, at last, their hands were joined. And with that connection, both of them felt a warm thrill and a calm, but also, an electricity! 'Oh, Lord our God, crown them with glory and honor,' Father Josias said. And, upon a triple reciprocation, the Stefana came to rest atop their giddy heads. Those crowns were of a custom design. They were most simple, though they were also pleasing to look at: each was a halo formed from several braided cords of a fine white textile, interwoven, and each was gently embellished by a row of small white roses. (And, yes, the roses had been Josh's primary idea and suggestion.)

The Scriptures were read and the Lord's Prayer was offered. Josh and Athena drank from the Common Cup, and then, processed with their lit candles. They were exhorted, with a few, most heartfelt words of kindness, wisdom, and joy by Father Josias, pertinent words for the miracle and blessing of matrimony in general, and for the specific happiness and fruitfulness of the bride and groom. At last, the crowns were removed and Josh pulled Athena's veil back behind her head. She held in one hand a boutique of pink roses, the stems bound together with a white cloth. Her other hand was on his arm. And that hand slowly rode around to his shoulder and back as he leaned in, reached around her with both his hands, and took her in the first embrace of their married lives. Eventually, one of his hands rose to hold and caress her head as their first kiss of marriage played out. For a long time. A very long time. The 'oohs' and 'ahs' of the party rose and fell and then were replaced by soft laughter as the embrace lasted and lasted. As the moment, that, for others, drifted perilously close to embarrassment, continued without abatement, at least two of the three priests loudly coughed into their hands. Then, opening their eyes, seeing one another as if for the very first time, the couple finally broke their kiss. As their voices fought off laughter, ultimately failing in that endeavor, they did manage a joint message to each other: 'I love you!' Oddly, at that second in time and of speech, they only heard those three plain, caring words, while all others present heard a constant roar of congratulatory cheer. And so, two such different, yet similar, and altogether wonderful children of God were wed.

Outside the church doors, on their way to the fellowship hall, amidst a hail of welcomes and praise, Josh swept her off her feet. He carried her into the hall, there lightly setting her down before kissing her again. Kissing her, again, for a very long time. In the interests of decorum, without words, they decided to postpone their affections until a short while later. And then, for a time, they mixed and mingled among the happy crowd.

It was a simple reception, though it remained etched in their minds, along with those of all attendees, forever due to its lighthearted but sincere tone and ambiance. Their kiss might have become a bit of a legend, factoring into future wedding preparations at the church (*'And then, you kiss her. And maybe not exactly like THE kiss, if you'll remember...'*) Their plans had not envisioned such a large impromptu gathering, and so they might have otherwise been short here and there with refreshments. Yet, just as in the earlier-read Gospel according to Saint John, there was enough, and with some to spare. They had, it seemed, kept their good wine just until it was needed. The available floor space, however, was slightly incommodious, with a portion of the party forced to spill over, beyond the doors and into the yard. Yet despite the cold air and snow on the ground, no one appeared to mind.

At one point, Issy found Josh and ordered him to lift her up into his arms. He did so happily, and she said, 'Joshy! This is the most amazing day! All because of you and her, and for all of us. When I first met you, you quickly became like a real big brother to me. Now with what you've both promised Michelle and I and with your marriage, you're about to become like my real big daddy! Can I start calling you that, Daddy Joshy?!'

'Babydoll,' he said after he kissed her, 'you can call me anything. Absolutely anything. But I would be most honored to be your real big daddy. And can I call you my baby girl, my sweet little daughter?!'

'Daddy Joshy,' she said, hugging his neck, 'I want to be your baby daughter!'

'Then, soon, it will be done and so,' he said. 'How's that? And as it turns out, we already have very good pictures in your locket!'

'Yes, but we need to modify it so we have one of you, me, Athena—mommy, and Michelle.'

'We can do that!'

'I love you, Joshy!'

'I love you too, Issy. And if it's okay, I plan to still call you Issy from time to time.' They then winked at each other, with a few Eskimo and butterfly kisses thrown in for good measure.

Nearby, Michelle approached Athena with a big, long hug. 'You are so beautiful!' the girl said.

'Thank you, baby,' Athena said back. 'And look at you! You were always so beautiful, though now, it's like a whole new vision of loveliness!'

'Happy day, and congratulations!' Michelle said. 'I'm so happy we were able to be here with you.'

'We wouldn't have had it any other way, darling.'

'Now that you're married,' Michelle said close to Athena's face, 'I really hope that Issy and I can become your real daughters. I really, really hope so. I love you so much!'

'That too,' Athena said, taking her in a closer, tighter embrace, 'we'd also have no other way!'

'I know the two of you need a little time for, um, things,' Michelle said, 'but will it be soon?'

'Darling, I think it takes a little time, but it's time we have without sorrow or worry. Soon!'

'And are you, you know, looking forward to the, um, things??' the girl asked her gleefully, in an almost silly way.

'More than I can say!'

'You're the perfect couple. Can I have something like this one day?'

'Michelle,' Athena said, squeezing her near daughter, 'something exactly like this will come to you one day. I and Josh will move mountains to see to it.' They then, in a silly, almost secretive fashion, discussed a few secret, silly girly girl items. Athena took a short break to toss away her roses, which were caught by Bridget.

Amid all of the excitement, Athena noticed Sister Francisco motioning to her, or, more exactly, calling her over towards a corner with a hooking finger. The happy bride approached and Francisco produced a little gift bag from behind her back. 'Again, my lovely angel, I couldn't be any happier for you and my sweet Joshua. And, my goodness, you are the picture of beauty!' the nun said.

'Thank you, Sister!' Athena replied.

'Well, speaking of pictures, I have another little gift for you,' Francisco said. 'It's not much, but it will, I think, greatly interest you. I saw you looking at our resident portraits at the home the other day and maybe you were looking for someone in particular. If so, then you wouldn't have seen him in the hall or the living room with the others. A few years ago, I moved these into my room to hang by my family. They're all of them my favorites, but he might have been the favorite of the favs. I made copies and doubled framed them the way I keep the originals. Eighteen and three.' She pulled a picture frame from the bag and handed it to Athena, who studied it intensely.

Two photos were arranged side by side, though the one on the right was set higher than the one on the left. That picture on the left was of a young man wearing a cap and gown. He was holding a diploma in his hands and smiling broadly and happily. He looked an awful lot like someone who'd only recently ventured into a certain gift shop one evening. The photo on the right was of a small boy with semi-messy brown hair. He was wearing a rugby shirt, which might have been a size or two too large for him, and he was holding a toy car in both hands. He was looking up at the camera with the sweetest open-mouthed smile Athena had ever seen. His adorable brown eyes stared straight out of the picture at her. As she looked at him she began to laugh and weep at the same time. She held the pictures to her side and hugged Francisco mightily.

'I was looking that day,' she said into the woman's ear. 'He's always been the same perfect sweetheart, hasn't he?'

'I got him when he was a baby,' the nun said, returning Athena's hug and tears. 'He ain't never changed. And he never will. Except that now, with you, he's happier and sweeter than ever.'

'Thank you, Sister,' Athena said. 'And thank you again! Your fav of favs just became my favorite gift and possession. I love it. And him. And you!' It was a few minutes before either of the ladies could rejoin the party, so great was their enthusiasm for Josh of all ages.

Towards the end of the festivities, a few short speeches were given, sweet but solemn, most notably by Father Josias and Margarette for Athena, and Sister Francisco and Professor Johnson for Josh. A wedding cake was presented, and the couple took their places to cut it. Upon the traditional smushing of the first pieces into each other's faces, the vaunted interest of decorum took a serious hit. At first, laughing, they picked up napkins, intending to clean each other. Then together, wholly unplanned, they tossed the cloths aside and began to lick the icing off. Much like their kissing, this tidying process also might have made it into premarital planning sessions; it was in-depth and thorough and the sight of it led to more laughs, 'ahs,' and coughs. At last, someone, perhaps Sam, shouted, 'Get a room!'

They took that spectacle, and their building desires as their cue to make ready to leave. Still, it took a while before they were finally free and making their way out to the waiting GLS that was now clad with the usual markings and streamers of marriage. As a hundred voices wished them all the best in life and love, Josh neatly assisted her into her seat and then took his place behind the wheel. After driving out of the lot, passing more and more waving, shouting, hooting well-wishers, he asked her, 'So, did you get anything to eat?'

'No,' she said as she leaned over and wrapped her arms around his upper right arm, 'all I had was some cake icing. Not very filling, but, my Lord, it was yummy. Well, that and the, uh, *cake* underneath it!'

'Hey! That was my experience. The icing was so-so itself, but I tell ya, I could eat that entire, uh, *cake!*' he said slyly.

'The whole sweet, delicious, sexy thing!' she rejoined seductively.

'But, serious for a second, did you eat anything?'

'Nothing all day.'

'Me neither. Wanna stop somewhere?!'

'I want to go home, to OUR home. There, now having my cake, I want to eat him too! But while we're on the way, yeah, wanna grab drive-thru?'

'Perfect!'

The window crew at the burger joint were a little surprised, and a little elated when the fully-dressed bride and groom drove up for cheeseburgers and fries. The couple's honeymoon plans, hastily yet generously contrived, were not set to commence for a few days. They had planned to use that short time to get to know each other better in certain areas where they were still strangers. And so, with two bags of the finest fast food in hand, they drove back to her former townhouse, which was now their home. As she clutched those bags, he carried her laughing across the threshold.

'Should we change first?' she asked.

'I'm hungry now. Your, er, cake needs a little energy. No. I propose that, upon donning bibs or something for garment safety, we dine just as we're dressed.'

'I happen to know where some bibs are!' she said, even then marching off to find them. And they ate at the kitchen table that was now theirs, and not her's alone. They ended up feeding each other the last few fries in their bags, and at the same time, they both exclaimed, 'Stuffed!'

'Tummy rubs?' she asked.

'Right after we change,' he said, loosening his collar. 'And we should set out some champagne too.'

They set out a bottle and two glasses before engaging in a little race to see who could change clothes first. Even as he carefully hung up his tux, he thought he'd set a fairly decent pace. But when he bounded down the stairs, wearing soft older shorts and a t-shirt, he found her already on the couch opening the bottle. She was dressed to match him, and now he saw more of that enchanting skin: her shorts were very short, as was her top. Still, after he joined her, nestling right up to and around her, feeling her warmth and their now-burning desires, they still did the proper thing and raised a toast.

'To the most wonderful man I've ever met,' she said. 'Josh, I will love you forever.'

'And to my Athena, my wife, who I will cherish forever,' he said back. 'I love you, baby!'

'To us!' they both said before hooking their arms and sipping together.

'Tummy rubs!' she sang, as she pushed her hand under his shirt and began stroking his skin in a circular motion. He reciprocated her actions. Their tummy rubs quickly led to general caressing, far deeper and more passionate than anything they'd dared before, and more involved and satisfying than anything either of them had ever known. That passion was accompanied by a kiss that shamed all their previous attempts. Their play lasted for hours without count. Finally, panting in the fires of mutual desire, they looked out the window, only then noticing that deep night had fallen. And they, instantly and without words or thoughts, determined it was time to consummate their love, to engage in their final deep exploration together. Accordingly, arm in arm, and smile by smile, they made their way towards their marital bed.

Fifteen

True Affections

At last, they stood looking at each other, again as if for the very first time, in their bedroom. The little reading lamp on the nightstand provided the only light, warm and, suddenly, suggestive and seductive. The soft covers and sheets, already turned down, added more suggestions. 'Hi, there,' she said playfully.

'Hello!' he said with bashful excitement.

'Do you want to hug and kiss some more?' she asked.

'Yes, but maybe, you know, maybe it's finally time to, uh, undress?' The sweet puppy, in fact, had some wolf in him.

'I think it is time,' she said, as her fingers found the bottom of her top and began to inch it upwards.

He audibly gasped in genuine excitement, with one of his hands stealthily approaching the waistband of his shorts. Then with a quick expression of greater purpose, he stopped and extended his hands to her. 'Wait!' he said. She paused, letting her shirt fall back into place, and looked at him. He continued, 'First, we have to pray in thanksgiving for each other.'

'Yes, we do, baby!'

So together, facing each other, they knelt in the circle of light from the little lamp. They crossed themselves and then placed their hands on each other's shoulders. And he began, saying, 'Heavenly

Father, Creator of all life, and of man and woman, and Designer of their interwoven fates, we thank You for all Your blessings. In particular, we give our humble gratitude for Your supreme generosity, unearned by us, in the gift of having each other as husband and wife. We are doubly grateful for the knowledge of each other we are about to gain and enjoy, given by You, and for Your grander purposes. As we experience deep physical love, we ask that You guide, bless, and secure all things in Your infinite grace and that our love satisfy all of Your intended purposes for a man, a woman, a marriage, and, as You will and intend, a family. And, personally, I thank and praise You for allowing me to wait and find someone as utterly special as Athena, a being of whose touch and affection I am simply unworthy. My God, may I please her and earn her love to the best of my abilities.' He paused before concluding, sensing she might want to add something. And she did.

'God Almighty, my Father, who I failed so pitifully in the beginning, please hear and love me. I ask that You guide and bless the union between Josh and me so that it may flourish in accordance with Your plans and by Your will. It is I who am most unworthy, both of Your forgiveness and mercy, and for Your acceptance of my pleas, but also of the love of this man, Your dear, gentle, and manly creation, Josh. I pray that I might satisfy him, for his own sake, for Your honor, and in continuing atonement for my mistakes. Please let our example echo those highest tenants of the relationship between God the Son, of whom I am unworthy, and His blessed Church. May that I please and serve my husband so that he may better please and serve You, O Lord. Guide us in all things, Father.'

Dispensing with habit, his eyes were open, locked onto her moving lips, and full of sweet tears. When she finished speaking, he said, 'In the name of the Father, and of the Son, and of the Holy Spirit.'

And together, they said, 'Amen.' She then wiped his tears away and hugged him. As they rose, they crossed themselves, and then, standing, hugged again. And began to kiss.

After a breathless minute, he said to her, 'I hope that was right. I hope we are both worthy or may become so. And I do love you, my blessed wife.'

She said, 'I hope so too, darling husband. And I also love you, completely and fully. Now, may I demonstrate my full affection?'

He just nodded, as if he was rapidly falling into a trance. With a finger, she instructed him to stand still. She then carefully and gently removed his clothing, and then removed hers. She stepped back two paces, and they again looked at each other. It occurred to her that she had never fully seen a man, not dreaming one might offer as much as Josh did, and she quickly thought, *'Thank you, Lord! And I'll take him.'* She then openly said, 'Wow! Just wow!'

'I know what you mean,' he said, as he stared at her very appreciatively. He knew in his heart that he was looking at the most wonderful design of all Creation. Yet suddenly, he did feel worthy of her. 'You know,' he said again, 'I had thought that when the great and terrible wait was over, and this moment finally came, that I would be my ordinary self, that I would feel bashful, and perhaps even ashamed, standing disrobed before your gaze and your complete perfection.'

He paused and she asked through a warm smile of desire, 'So, do you, baby?'

'Not at all!' he said, moving slowly towards her. 'Instead, I'm excited!'

'I know,' she said with a laugh, smoldering with yearning. 'I can plainly see that! Now, come here!'

This time, when they embraced they each and together felt something previously unknown and unimaginable: the thrill of pure unfettered passion born of Heavenly acquiescence. And that passion now drove their thoughts and actions in a way giddy and free from inhibition. The little lamp was forgotten and stayed lit. In fact, everything not related to their immediate being and activity was forgotten. And as they climbed into their bed, she lifted up her head and told him, 'Josh, I promised you that I'd never hurt you, and I won't. But, well, you're about to get a real workout, baby.'

But they were both ready, and their exercises commenced in full, proceeding with wild abandon deep into the night and, further, until not long before dawn.

At some point, before the sun rose, he woke up just enough to appreciate his blessings and fortune. They were under the covers, with their heads resting on the same pillow. Or at least, his head was on it. Hers was warmly, heavily resting on his shoulder and chest, as she cuddled into him. Under soft sheets of flannel, he could feel their bodies entwined together as one. And he felt, again and again, that crushing tidal wave of current surging up his spine and reaching out to every single inch of him. He could feel it running through her too. He even imagined he could feel it coursing back and forth between them. Physically, it was the most amazing thing he had ever experienced. But there were other sensations too. He could feel both of their heartbeats, and he swore their hearts were beating in time together. There was the intense warmth of the moment, and he realized and enjoyed the degree to which so much of it poured forth from her. It was something beyond pleasant, beyond intoxicating even. And it was all maddeningly heightened by the sound of her softly breathing. She also purred a little now and again as she nuzzled against him in her slumber. And her smell overwhelmed him, a scent so rich and deep he could also taste it. He was just licking a bit of drool when she stirred slightly. She stretched a little, tucked right back into him, and whispered into his skin.

'This is how we're going to sleep, Joshy. Every night, forever. Warm, naked, and wrapped into something beyond the reaches of the world. I am now one with you, and, in our private, most intimate couplings, I must continue to be one with you. Like this. There is no other answer, so just say *yes*,' she said, her eyes still closed.

'Yes,' he said without hesitation. 'I've been lying here in bliss thinking the same thing. And more. How are you on this, at this, uh, whatever time it is?'

'I exploded into little gooey pieces,' she said dreamily. 'No apologies, and you'll have to put them back together.'

'Sorry, no can do,' he said with a sigh. 'I'm in pieces myself, and I might not have the energy otherwise.'

'We're doomed...' she slurred as she rubbed her lips on him.

A short silence followed, with each of them starting to softly caress the other's body wherever their hands fell. Suddenly, he surprised her, and himself, when he exclaimed, 'Gooey! You're a genius, Athena!'

'What? What's so intelligent about being turned into love putty?' she asked, now nibbling somewhat determinately on his chest.

He stopped her by lifting up her head. They looked each other deep in the eye, and he said, 'Gooey is the answer to what I was wondering.'

'Have you gone mad?'

'Well, yes, madly, helplessly mad, my sweet-smelling wife.' He started to rub her head and told her with his thoughts, '*So you always smell good, so good. Too good. And I've been trying to put my nose on it. There's your shampoo, obviously.*' He paused, leaned over, and smelled her hair. Then, as he moved his head down her body, he openly said, 'Roses and other sweet flowers and such. And it's a similar note with your perfume, all dainty and girly.' She giggled a little, and, upon hearing her, he lightly tickled her ribs.

'Stop!' she said. 'No, really, DON'T stop.'

He didn't, though he continued to move down until his head was right next to the spot where her ribcage rolled smoothly and invitingly over and down to her stomach. He knew it must be the perfect place, and he lowered his nose and began deeply inhaling over her skin. The actions caused her giggles to burst into hard laughter. Still, with one hand lightly tracing her side in an attempt to keep the tickles going, he ardently continued to smell her. He let his nose ride along as he made his way back up the center of her chest, up her neck, and over her chin. He then started to kiss her pretty laughing mouth, though he managed to keep his eyes open and focused on hers. Finally, he said, 'At the base, under it all, I've finally figured out your smell, yours, and yours alone!'

'Well,' she said as she stretched mightily, yawning a bit, 'what is it, silly?'

'You, Athena, bearer of the sweetest, richest scent known to man, smell like warm, fresh cookie dough. Or possibly, ooey, gooey, soft, warm, sweet partially-baked cookies. Full of sugar!'

She stared at him for a moment with a wonderful smile of amazement on her face. 'Sugar and spice and all things nice. That was the sweetest thing, ever, Joshy.'

'You're the sweetest thing ever,' he said. 'Deliciousness in woman's form.'

'You're making me hungry, baby,' she thrummed as she moved in to embrace him.

Just before she pulled him fully back under the covers, he asked, 'What are you hungry for?'

'Fresh baked Joshy!' she said even as she pulled the covers over their heads.

At an unknown time during the great festivities, the poor little lamp took a tumble off the nightstand. Its cord pulled free from the wall socket, it lay quiet and dark on the carpet. But at an early hour, the first rays of sunlight had begun to relieve it of its illuminating duties. Josh sat on the edge of the bed and stretched in those rays. Behind him, he felt her hand find and stroke his back. She murmured or purred something indecipherable.

'That was incredible. And intense,' he said.

'Oh, Josh—' she moaned as she grabbed and pulled him backward.

A bit later, the full light of morning fell into the room as they both finally set their feet on the floor. He met her after circling the bed, and they hugged again. Fearful of being drawn back in, just at that moment, they reluctantly broke the embrace and quickly dressed. Down in the kitchen a few minutes later, he made coffee while she obtained the ingredients for her patented pancakes. He handed her a mug and they drank the first happiness of the day together. Then he watched her mix the batter. While her back was to him, he crept up behind her. Leaning against her, he slid his hands along the smooth skin of her lower abdomen, pausing, and then gently patting it with both hands. 'I wonder...' he said.

'One never knows,' she said, reading his fuller thoughts while greatly enjoying his touch.

They dined on a felicitous breakfast. As they munched and sipped, they chatted about their evening, more, less, all about all things, and about nothing at all. They came close together and fed each other the last few bites of their fluffy, sugary stacks. Rubbing and kissing, she said, 'Let's pretend we're in need and indulge in tummy rubs, eh? Tummy rubs in bed!'

As the mid-afternoon sun drifted lazily along, and, of its movements, they did not reckon or care, she lay there cradling his head on her soft shoulder. He purred, or spluttered, so it at first sounded, as she gently rubbed her nose across his closed eyelid. She became aware of the fact that, in her arms, he was softly singing something about, '...*my heart pierced by flaming sword, my heart pierced by flaming sword...*'

'What's that? Part of a song, my love?' she asked him, though still schnozily addressing his dear eye.

'Oh,' he whispered. 'Lying here, being pampered, I was thinking that you, my angel, are a wonder worker. For all you've done for me and given me. Those words were some of the chorus or whatever they call it, the refrain? Anyway, they're from a neat little jazzy folksy song called "Wonder Worker." Because you're my wonder worker and all, setting my heart on fire. And you fixed it, in more ways than one, with or without a blade.'

'Lovely!' she said, still concentrating on his eye. 'I've never heard of it.'

'It's by a wonderful woman from Lebanon, Sima Itayim,' he told her. 'It's, of course, not made specifically for us, but it could have been. It fits.' He then sang for her as much as he could remember. She continued to hold him as she listened. When he stopped and grew still, she began to kiss his eye and his nose.

'I could get used to this,' he said.

'Me too.'

'And just every once in a while, can we switch it up and do this?' he asked.

'Do what, baby?'

'I love holding you in our permanent, committed sleeping embrace, our oneness of onenesses. But just every so often, would you, Athena, hold me?' He snuggled deeper into her softness and warmth with a pacified sigh.

There was something so fond and emotional in his request that she started to cry a little. Holding him much tighter, she said, 'Yes, baby, of course. I love comforting you. Doing so gives me something I never knew I wanted, but that I now couldn't imagine living without. Back and forth we shall go, dearest man. When we make love, we will always complete it like this, one of us deep in the other's arms. Now, shhh, let me hold you. Let me be with you. Be yours as you are mine.'

From where he cuddled in quiet ecstasy, he could not object, which, of course, he didn't want to. And in this back and forth, up and down, soft and firm manner, they continued to gain knowledge of each other along with abundant satisfaction. They found that it worked so well and that they enjoyed it so much that neither left the house for a few days. And when they did leave it, arm in arm, they carried suitcases with them.

Sixteen

Corinthian Bridges

A s they walked towards the terminal at Logan International, still arm and arm, and in a state of sheer bliss, Josh suddenly panicked. 'I don't have a passport!' he told her, a look of shame and terror in his eyes, the concurrent tone echoing in his voice.

'Sure you do, baby! Here it is,' she said as she handed him the document, previously concealed in her purse. 'I told you not to worry about anything.'

He took it and glanced at it in captivation. 'Well, you do have your ways.' His fear gave way to a chuckling calm that quickly returned to bliss. He had never been inside an airport and found the experience interesting though slightly nerve-racking, even as their processing was sped along and smoothed by Athena's unusual methods. A few hours later, they canoodled in a private first-class mini cabin on a Swiss Air flight bound for Zurich. Josh had never been on an airplane either and found it all exciting if mildly tedious. But he was very impressed with the front-end luxury inside the Airbus A330. Looking out the window, and back towards an engine as it began to spool up, he asked her, 'These things are safe, right?'

'Airlines would go out of business if their flights weren't safe, baby. Safer than driving, on average. This one is perfectly safe, one hundred percent, of course,' she said sweetly while stroking his arm.

He sat back and said, 'This is all so much. Thank you for handling everything, my love. I'm about to become a world traveler. With the best guide possible.'

'You, and you must accept this fact, you deserve this little treat, baby. I want you to enjoy it, just as much as I'm going to relish enjoying it with you,' she said from the little bench seat adjacent to his main chair.

Technically, they had two such little cabins, side by side, but separated by a little wall, a boon for ordinary privacy, though a hindrance for those wishing to intimately connect. No one, however, appeared to care, or even notice, that Athena remained with Josh in his little pod the entire time. After the rush of takeoff, some pampering from the crew, and a bite to eat, she suggested he recline his, or their seat into a bed. Theirs was a night departure, due in Switzerland mid-morning, local time. As she closed the little sliding door, severing them from the rest of the passengers, she said, 'You'll want to be rested when we arrive. So why don't we cuddle up, hold hands, sleep, and talk?!' He liked that idea immensely, and soon, high over the North Atlantic, they were off on a different kind of utterly private journey.

'*Hi there, angel! Welcome back,*' he said to her inside his thoughts.

'*Hello, sweet baby,*' she whispered to his buzzing brain. '*I'm glad to be here again. Now, before we go over all that we're going to see and do—and I have some special side trips planned as surprises—please ask me anything you like that we haven't covered before. Or haven't covered enough.*'

Their hands tightened and released in little rolling waves of silent affection as, within their minds, passion and intellectualization raged. '*Well, okay,*' he thought, somewhat shyly. '*Tell me, in this state, can we, uh, you know???*'

'*Yes,*' she said. '*But it's probably not the best idea. I can keep us still and well concealed, as we are. But if I lose my concentration, well, then we might make a scene. Let's just converse and cavort, and save the infatuated fervor for later.*'

'Gotcha! So, anyway, I have a few things, and I'm not sure about the order. Where to start?'

'Start anywhere, love,' she said.

'Well, you mentioned, a while back, that you thought your original mistake ran along the lines of those made by my original parents. But you said it was also different. If I can ever help you move on, and back up, what, exactly, did you mean by it all?' he asked.

'That's both easy and difficult to explain,' she said. 'Adam and Eve used their free will not, I think, out of an overt desire to do evil, but, rather, from a misunderstanding of what obedience meant to them and God. In a way, they disregarded His commands out of a sense of trusting that perhaps He would be forgiving. He was and is, of course, but not in the way they expected. And again, due to that most dangerous concept of unfettered freedom of thought, they probably also expected, or perhaps half-expected to be able to impose their wills against or even over His.

'Their punishment was quite similar to mine, to ours, our little group, in many ways. They had been warned they would die if they disobeyed, and their bodies did die eventually. Their souls live on, like yours and mine. But they lived physically with pain and suffering and consequences previously impossible for them to witness or understand. All because of that first lie. And the enemy always lies, even when he tells the truth. In that first case, by gaining the ability to understand, they did in a sense become like gods, or, rather, like we higher original spirits. The lie was that they did not and could not gain the capacity to understand or use that new, expanded ability. By gaining, they thereby lost; the disastrous power of corruption comes not from total erasure or destruction, but from the maddening or clouding of the right and the proper. Inversion is worse than annihilation. The devil's worst trick is offering people what they think they want.

'And a similar lie kicked off our troubles Above. And we, to our discredit, some of us, did have both the means to identify problems and the skills to avoid or defeat them. Those who fell, both under his influence, and completely from Grace, disregarded all caution and love out of greed and pride. Their dark story is more familiar than mine, even to you who lack any first-hand knowledge of what happened. You know or sense because, in addition to the cautions of the Bible and the teachings of the Church, you are semi-doomed to a similar if potentially less eternal turmoil and temptation, and, sadly, mortal life is perpetually afflicted by the threat and hatred of the fallen. Very, very sad.

'We, who were reluctant, much like Adam and Eve, were innocent of the fallens' will to dominate and corrupt, to rebel. We, rather, partly trusted that, well, things would work out a certain way, even without entitling or safeguarding action from us. Laziness, or sloth, played a role in our errors. The Regulars, on the other hand, immediately both realized what evil was emerging in our midst and also instantly sought to quell it. They were completely faithful, the polar opposite of lucifer's intention. We, alas, were too complacent, too slow to act. Some say doing nothing is the worst course of action. Aside from doing rank evil just for the sake of doing evil, they may have a point. By the time we decided to join the battle, it was already over. The day was saved and with no thanks to us. Accordingly, we earned our fates and sentences. My existence since, while walking with and trying to help you, has consisted of trying to understand my failure and rectify it in God's eyes.

'That, I think, truly, is like, if not entirely like the plight of Mankind: mostly gentle souls, prone to great error, who still strive for the perfection of forgiveness. In that way, I feel bound to you, to your race, as much as I now feel bound to and one with, you, dearest Josh, gentlest of souls. Also, on a very personal note, please pardon this side notion: you have questioned why I chose you. Self-deprecating as ever, you over-complimented me, while stating a general truth about female hypergamy: no, women, mortal women, don't tend to date downwards, as they say. If I must be compared, then I am of a similar nature. My problem in that regard is that, in almost all ways, I have no choice. If you know what I mean, and I know you do. In beauty, strength, intelligence, longevity, and almost all areas, I have no equal or any close associates. But with you, and with piety and constant *humble deference and penance, I at last met my equal. THAT! That as much as your cuteness and kindness, earned you my heart. When I first sensed your approach, I let my usual guard down, thus allowing you a mere hint of the real Athena. And I'm glad I did and that things have proceeded as they have. I love you all the more, even as our mutual consideration makes me digress at times...*

'In my mind, after thousands of years of internal contemplation, my way out is almost, if not exactly like yours. In Angelic terms, I made myself into a Gentile. Ergo, my salvation, even as assisted by you, my love, comes from the supreme gift of Jesus Christ, the Lord God, True Light From True Light, of Whom I was aware when I first awoke, but of Whom I did not understand until around two-thousand years ago. You've asked me how I came into the Church; and, while I witnessed its rise from as close as I felt comfortable, and while I sensed it was coming, it found me. I'll show you where I made my conversion, in Corinth, Josh. In so many ways, it was like a preview of returning Home. Every Mass is too, in fact, as is my interaction with you.'

'You're amazing, is all I can say,' he said. 'I can barely understand what you say, but I do understand it. Or, rather, I trust it. That's really the only way, isn't it?'

'For you, yes. And for me,' she mused. 'Even for higher orders of beings and souls, logic, while very important, only goes so far. I, even in my original state, could not fathom the inner thoughts of the Father. Nor, sweet boy, can you. So we resort to the apophatic. We trust the mysteries and delight in their fulfillment. But, of course, as we discussed with Father Josias, trust is fulfilled, it is completed by participation. The larger Church among our fellows, and the smaller church of our home, is our chance for active involvement with God.'

'Do all angels do that?' he asked like a child.

'Yes, all but the fallens,' she said. 'They arrogantly assume too much, a faith in themselves absent real dialectic interpretation. They have blinded and deluded themselves as much as damned themselves.'

'*Can you see and communicate with your kind? With those who were slow, and with the Regulars, as you call them? I'm just curious,*' he said, still like a little boy in awe and under learning's spell of excitement.

'*My sad kind, yes; we can see and interact, though we generally do not,*' she said. '*We have many unspoken rules governing our probation. We failed together, yet due to our individual mistakes and misgivings. So perhaps it is better if we proceed in our recompense alone. The Regulars are a more regulated matter. I can see them and understand their ways—on earth, that is; I suppose they could, of their own accord, initiate contact with me and, thus, coax or allow my participation. That is something I have contemplated but have not experienced. Heaven, beyond remembrance and prayer, is closed to me. But I suppose those who were faithful have little need for any input from me. So I merely watch, witness, and sense them. I try to learn what I can from their better examples.*'

'*This kind of goes to the old worn-out atheist question or the forgivable lament of the downtrodden,*' he said, a child reflecting deeper. '*Why don't you, or the Regulars intervene more to stop bad things from happening here? I know firsthand that you can influence or even control minor things like car heaters, passports, and, well, me. And I know that the Regulars, or so I read in the Bible, are capable of tremendous ability—when ordered by God. But, really, what about stopping wars and plagues and great suffering?*'

'*The fraught peril of free will still must be respected because it was and is a gift from God, even if a dangerous gift,*' she said, somewhat sadly. '*Now, bad things can be any kind of things that people don't like or that cause simple harm. A tree limb falling on your head is bad, but it is not caused by evil malice. Sometimes, gravity is just gravity. Little things like that, I can, and sometimes do, avert or fix. You know, like speeding trucks on icy streets, or overworked nerves caused by slouching heart valves? Remedies like that still must have some greater purpose, whether of convenience for a task, love, or learning. It is much* more difficult to stem the negative effects of mass events like diseases and hurricanes. Too many variables. And physical phenomena, we must remember, are still part of God's plan whether we understand it or not. And it's far, far more difficult to fix evil. I, we, and especially He, Above, try very hard to do what we can do, without overriding human thought, intuition, and even ambition, so as to instruct against wicked deeds before they happen. Or, afterward, as a basis for voluntary rejection, repentance, and amelioration.

'I've watched all of your wars, and I have detested every single one of them without exception. But to stop them would be to exert a level of control impermissible because it would compromise some of the fundamental aspects of humanity. It is, in too many ways, what lucifer does. A terrible quandary. And I do not know, exactly, but I trust, so much stronger a trust as to surpass mere knowing, that for every heartache I feel about violence, suffering, and sin, God is infinitely more aggrieved by the betrayals and abject casting aside of His designs.'

'I feel small and guilty,' he said.

'In a way, you are,' she said. 'We all are.'

'What is your true form? Are you taller, grander, with wings, or—' He hesitated, then asked, 'Am I like a small bug to you? And your beauty? What do you really look like? And if I may ask, what is your real, original name?'

'So many questions, my love!' she laughed. 'But I know all of them are born out of innocence. No, you are certainly not like a bug to me. And you know that I even revere the smallest and least creatures, anyway, all of them created and empowered beings of great worth. But you and all Men are much dearer, you being the dearest of them all to me. We are not equal or alike, but for that, I love you all the more. Size-wise, I might be a little larger. Our physicality is different, being both of matter and energy, and in no way bound by the confines of either. It would be virtually impossible to explain. Instead, trust that one day, you will see, understand, and even join! My looks are a dimmed reflection of the soul I was. The Regulars, as you read about in the Bible, for instance, assume a muted form when appearing to mankind. A middle state, if you will. My form you see is muted again, and I usually try to mute that appearance even further. When you first saw me, you must have caught the barest glimpse of something closer to the middle state. All of us are, in ways, in all ways, formed in His Image. I chose this female body and appearance based on who I had been. And I modified it slightly to honor two women of renown, Mother Eve and Mother Mary.'

'Did you meet them?'

'No, but I saw them and appreciated them, Mary in particular. I never tried to approach certain figures out of both respect and a little shame.'

'Could you show me, sometime, what you really look like, Athena? Your beauty, as-is, is impossible, but part of me yearns for more, for the full truth.'

'No,' she said flatly. 'Not even in this dream state. First, I was stripped of my highest form when I came here among you. And even if I could still recall it, I perceive that you could not withstand it. That it would blind you or that you would simply be unable to see what was revealed. Worse, I fear it could destroy you, my baby. And I could not ever risk that. You again remember from the Scriptures that the Regulars usually approach mortals in one of two ways: they either appear with words of comfort, assuring they mean no harm, or else; they appear in middle-state glory, as a warning. Think about the different revelations to the poor shepherds and to Balaam. Even the half-state can be overpowering. Also, I do have another name, an eternal name. But as with my appearance, you could not hear or understand the language. Again, just trust and wait. All in His good time, my love. And, by the way, you, sweet Joshua, also have a hidden identity, one I deeply desire to witness!'

'You make the most compelling cases,' he said, mentally falling deeper into her. 'Oh! And, speaking of witnessing ... can anyone, like the crew, see what we're doing now?'

She laughed and hugged his little soul closer, saying, '*We are, in a critical thinking manner, veiled to prying eyes. But, yes, one or two may see something. A kind young woman just passed by on her way to the galley. She looked over the divider and saw us, and she thought our cuddling and hand-holding were sweet. Which it is! But none shall think anything inofficious or untoward about us.*'

'*Oh, back to your name, again, your earth name, Athena,*' he said after a moment. '*I understand why you don't like association with a name or a being from ancient mythology. I get that. My question is, as such, why'd you keep her name?*'

'*I like it,*' she said somewhat wryly though innocently and honestly. '*On my own, early on, I'd never really given much thought to a human name. Before my Grecian mistake, I had interacted with people before. And at times some of them would address me by one name or another, frequently as a kind of nickname or a case of mistaken identity. But no one had ever given me a specific, formal name. So when they finally did, even after the way it happened, I just decided to take it. Oh! A funny side note: I think I had said something in an understated attempt to defuse my error, and someone misheard me. Or else they just conjured up the title based on a series of conversational mishearings. Or something like that. More mysterious than funny maybe. Regardless, I thought it was a pretty name. Don't you agree?*'

'*I had always found it striking as a name, regal even,*' he said. '*But now I think it's the most beautiful name in the world. It matches the owner.*' His response met with her approval and she mentally squeezed him tight for it. The squeeze led to a nuzzle that led to a pause in their discussion. He thought for some time in her embrace, before venturing most cautiously, '*So, something scary. You can see your kind, my kind, and the Regulars. Can you see or feel the others? Them. Are, as we suppose, demons and evil spirits real and sometimes visible?*'

'*All too real, and ever on the prowl for the corruption, consumption, and death of souls, Josh, yes,*' she said, a bit sternly. '*Evidence of their misdeeds is so abundant that even your atheists oftentimes admit to the presence of darkness beyond conscious description. Again, I am not a warrior, and I cannot engage or have not engaged them as a Power or a Champion does. And I do not interact with them. But I feel their nearness or their curses at times. They hate my being and, while not fleeing, soon depart from me. Our hatred is mutual, and I just as soon have them leave. One day, forever.'*

'You, child, should fear what they represent, even as you should never fear the illusions of their power or their pitiful innate emptiness. Your faith and piety or honesty are excellent bulwarks against the enemy, though, as someone nominally incorruptible, you are considered a great prize if any daring opportunity might ever present itself. Do not let it! Christ is your best protection. And mine. Faith in Him alone defeats them in their attempts. Do not ever forget that, lest, on one miserable day, you receive a visitor for which you are unprepared. Speak His name boldly but sincerely and also humbly, and they will flee from you. You may also ever seek my assistance, though I pray the need never arises. In summation, while honest caution is warranted in all things, fear is unnatural to you—except fear of losing your soul. Trust and faith, my love. Let us speak of more pleasant things!'

Together, they spoke of more kind and well-lit subjects, including their plans for the coming weeks, and for those times beyond, until the announcement was made that the final descent had begun into Zurich. There, they caught a connecting flight to Athens. On that plane, they were both pleased with less luxurious seats as it afforded them the honor of sitting side by side and hand in hand, watching out the window, and chatting gaily, as they prepared to see Athena's ancient eponymous stomping grounds. On their way, Josh was astounded, as usual, and he reckoned he could have no better tour guide. She knew the names and histories of every mountain, town, river, and feature they flew over. If he'd asked, he assumed she could have named each tree or bird, and probably have conversed with them. Better yet, she allowed him to see with her eyes as she pointed down and described. And in that manner, he saw even when clouds were in the way. His mind was giddy and his heart glad when they arrived. But he also felt a rather pent-up desire to again express his affections for her.

'This is all expensive, isn't it?' he asked her when they were checking into their wonderful, older, private hotel near the base of the Acropolis. He was trying to add it up, and it felt like they'd spent as much that day as he made in a year.

'My treat, all of it, baby,' she said. 'I owe you everything, and, as I said, let's pretend money is no object.'

'I just don't want us, or want you going through everything.'

'My money is your money, and there's plenty,' she reassured him. 'Or, if you like, we can pretend someone can completely take control of things like, oh, I don't know, SWIFT and Fedwire with a flick of her thoughts.' She smiled so convincingly that he let his concerns fade away.

In the room, a spacious suite and well-appointed, as they unpacked, she asked him, 'What do you want to do first?' Her question was met by his amassed desires to which she ardently acceded and enjoyed. A few hours later, as the sun sank lower, she said, 'Sight-seeing tomorrow, then! But now, how about dinner?'

Their hotel featured a lovely rooftop restaurant with abundant outdoor patio seating. They welcomed the warm Mediterranean-Myrtoan breeze that softly wafted by and around them, fluttering the flowers and trees so as to bring forth a sweet mixed aroma. While looking out at the growing lights in the central city and, higher up, on the Acropolis, they dined on local lobster with linguine and black truffles. At her suggestion, they sipped a choice white wine from Santorini. While they sipped, held hands, and looked out at the scenery, he said to her, 'This city is named after you, you know.'

'It was named after a myth,' she said. 'One that would have been better if it had never been concocted. But, yes, I am tied to this city. Tomorrow, I look forward to connecting you with it. As much as I've looked forward to connecting with you here over our wine!' Together, they enjoyed the bottle and their company. Later, at his suggestion, they enjoyed a bottle of Cristal Rose on the balcony of their room. After that, they did what newlyweds are known to do. They did so until very late.

The next day, Josh awoke to the feeling that he was floating in the bed, moored only by her embrace. When she looked into his surprised eyes, he said, 'What's happened?! I almost feel paralyzed, though in the most pleasant way imaginable. Everything feels so loose and relaxed. I've never had a morning like this. What gives?!'

'Oh,' she said sweetly as she caressed his head, 'last night, while you looked so sweet as always, I thought you might have felt weary from our travels. So I spent half the night giving you a nice, deep massage. I hope that was okay.'

'Okay?! Lord, we need to travel more often,' he said in relaxed excitement. They then rejoined their prior activities from the time just before he'd fallen asleep for the night. After a leisurely breakfast, which was delayed just a tad by their fond canoodling, they approached the famed Acropolis. In the museum, Josh turned to a statue of a goddess adjusting her shoe, and said, 'It kind of looks like you, but kind of not.'

'It most certainly is not,' she said.

'By the looks, a little maybe,' he added sweetly. 'Maybe not as pretty though.'

'A similar image was on Tiberius's accursed coin held by the Pharisees too,' she said, not quite in a sad scoff. 'Insult to injury.' But as with all his sweet ways, she found it easy to forgive him, and she indulged his remarks and his fascinated viewing of the many items and venues. Additionally, she was able to add insights about the various monuments and sites that literally no one else alive knew. High up on the outcrop, they toured just about everything. He noticed that she turned her back on the Temple of Athena, though she otherwise remained most jovial during their visit.

He helped her mood return to its jubilant natural state by hugging her and whispering as he kissed her ear, 'A mistake maybe, true. But it was the residents so long ago who went crazy with it. In their madness, they did name the city after you. Or you as they wildly imagined. A grand mistake, but right now, I'm having trouble blaming them. You're driving me mad with love!' More of his kisses, hugs, and silly, innocent laughter convinced her to dispense with some of her ancient reservations. She allowed him to lead them about in a state of wonderment, wandering here and there without much care or prescription. Later they toured narrow streets looking and poking into small shops. In one, Josh was delighted to find a set of small, delicate rose earrings. 'Look at these!' he said happily. 'I'm buying them for you. And that will take care of the roses today, and perhaps on any future days when I forget!'

'Let me see the mechanisms,' she said. 'Oh, Joshy, I'm sorry. These are standard piercings, and I only wear clip-ons.'

'Really? I never noticed,' he said. She unhooked the small pearl she was wearing on one ear and he saw plainly there was no hole in her pretty lobe. 'I get it,' he said. 'You don't want to tarnish perfection or dishonor it.'

'No,' she said, adding with a faux stern face, 'I love earrings as much as the next girl, and I would wear the standards, but no needle can pierce my skin.'

'So much awe and mystery around here,' he said with a laugh. 'Can I still buy them for you? Maybe with my tools, I can convert them to clips!'

'With that, I would love them even more, Joshy. I accept!'

They spent a few days, sometimes taking extended excursions, seeing all of the usual sights and scenes, historical and modern. For New Year's Eve, they watched fireworks over the Acropolis from the hotel rooftop, complete with excellent champagne, a wonderful slow dance, and an extraordinary kiss. They had already done and seen much, but she evidently had one special place to show him and a very unique story to tell. But first, on the afternoon of a special New Year's Day, as they gave thought to another lovely dinner, she asked him about something else very special, another detour, though one of a slightly different variety and destination. 'Josh, would you like to take a few quick side trips? Maybe way outside? My way of traveling? I have at least two places I'd like to show you, and it won't take long at all. Then we can eat. These are very, very special places. You will be the first man to ever see them.'

'Wow, sure,' he said excitedly. 'Anywhere with you. And I'd be honored to be the first. But how and all?'

'Well,' she said, 'you'll just hold my hand and we'll go. They, honestly, might be a little scary at first. But do you trust me?'

'Implicitly,' he said.

'Ready, right now?'

'Sure, baby!'

'Okay. Hold my hand—and it won't hurt if you let go. And for a surprise, please close your eyes, and it's off to our first destination!'

He took her hand, smiled, closed his eyes, and felt a slight buzz. Then she said, 'Open them!'

He did but nothing changed that he could see. In fact, it was even darker, completely black, and he could see nothing at all. He had the feeling that something strong and cold was touching him everywhere, but also that the touch didn't affect him in any way. But the only other things he could sense was her hand in his and that it vaguely felt like his shoes rested in sand or dirt. 'Where are we? And what's this?' he asked.

'Welcome to the bottom of the Mariana Trench!' she said. 'Here, let me provide a little light.' With that, Josh could suddenly see around them. They were on the ocean floor and bits of dust or debris flowed by slowly and silently in a mild current. Ahead of them, something was bubbling from the sand. 'Like it?' she asked.

'U-u-uh—' he stammered.

'During the Great Flood, I made my way down here after checking in on Noah and company. Water begot water and so forth.'

'Shouldn't I be crushed right about now?' he asked with a little concern.

'Ordinarily, yes, you'd be dead. But not with me here. Now, if you'll look over there, I do think we've got a little venting going on!'

He tried to humor her, but he honestly didn't share her thrill in that cold, dark place. She soon sensed as much and kindly suggested a new venue. 'This one's out of this world, baby. Ready?'

'Yes,' he answered.

'Close your sweet eyes.'

When she told him to open them again he did. And then, he felt absolutely nothing, aside from an idea that he should be cold, though he was not. But he could see, if he didn't know what he was looking at. It appeared they were suspended in a void with stars all around them, even under them, and all very far away. And before them, he saw what appeared to be a large milky ball of white dust.

'Okaaaay—' he said to her. 'What is that thing?'

'That's the Oort Cloud, sweetie! That's our entire Solar System!'

'And where are we to so observe it?!'

'We're quite a few billion kilometers into deep space, baby. I first came out here an age ago, relatively new into my exile so I could get a feel for things. Do you like it?'

'Uh, maybe a little better than the sea. But shouldn't I have frozen or exploded?'

'Yes, probably choked and frozen, but not now,' she said kindly. 'I just wanted to show you a few things.'

'Wait. Just how far away have you been before?'

'Just a system or two over. Not that it matters, but I've also been inside the Sun and a few other stars. Just to check. It's all really the same outside of the Earth's narrow confines. And that leads me to something: temptation and its futility. Look around us. God made all of this. Do you remember how satan allegedly tempted Jesus with control of Creation?'

'Yes, on earth, in the world.'

'He, of course, couldn't really be tempted by what was already His. But the devil has stupid ideas and lame tricks. All that is around us, the entire vastness of Creation, is His work. And it all serves a purpose. But all that really concerns you and me and all mankind is right back there in that cloud. Look with my eyes now!'

She pointed and he looked. And he could plainly see, even at that extreme distance, the planet Earth as it made its jolly way around the Sun. 'It does look like a blue marble,' he said.

'And that blue marble is unique in all the universe,' she said. 'Of all the matter in this expanse, only there, back home, will one find sentience, soul, and true life. All for us. Why be tempted with anything else, when we've been granted the most amazing gift in all reality?'

The gravity of her comment made sense to him, even in the near-total absence of regular gravity. But again, he didn't really feel at ease way out beyond. 'I understand, and I appreciate this, but I'm not a spaceman, Athena. I didn't even like the *Star Forces* movie or whatever it was called. It's beautiful and humbling, but—'

'Time to go?'

'Yes.'

And just like that, they were back in the suite. 'A little too out there?' she asked.

'Yes, but I'm glad for the experience. And glad to be back. I do love this wild ride I've signed up for. And that last part about satisfaction makes great sense. I'm happy with what we have here. On Earth and above water.'

She laughed and hugged him. 'Tomorrow, I want to show you and tell you something special for me regarding my reformation as a soul. It all happened not far away and it's better than anything in outer space. Now, how about a bite to eat and then some terrestrial fun?! A nice celebration to ring in the New Year.'

'Lead on, lovely guide!'

They ate and then played, and then wrapped into their standard nightly marital embrace. In the morning, she had plans for them, plans originally forged in ancient times by a troupe of traveling preachers and miracle workers. In the night, as he cuddled her, she mentally reviewed each and every aspect of those first special meetings some two millennia earlier.

'Peter,' Athena said, with perhaps distant fondness. 'Saint Peter the Apostle of Christ stood on this very spot.' She had rented a car, and herself drove the two of them the short distance along the coast to Corinth late that morning. Now they stood several blocks from a church in a place that didn't exactly look like it had ever hosted any Disciples. But he believed her when she said it had, and he listened as she told him more: 'I hope you're having a fantastic trip, my love, and you deserve it. But for me, this little reveal was a strong motivation for coming here with you. I wanted to show you. So much, nearly all, of what I knew long ago has vanished with time. But my memory of this place, and of a meeting, lives on until this moment. And I am so glad to be able to share it with you, the dearest man I have ever met.'

'I'm having the time of my life, beautiful!' he said, giving her a hug. 'I would have agreed to go anywhere with you—and we've already been to some outlandish places! But I want to know more as I can see this is very, very special to you. Tell me.'

She turned away to face the area in front of them, though she happily allowed him, and encouraged him, to keep his arm wrapped around her from behind. She placed her left hand on his as it rested on her upper chest and squeezed his fingers with hers. Her other hand pointed around as she spoke. 'In *First Corinthians*, Saint Paul spoke to the earliest Christians here. Matters with which you are familiar by reading the Missive. But Saint Peter came here as well, as is not so well recorded, an issue of relative speculation. Here, very briefly, and he did not know who or what I was, I met the man upon whom the Church was founded. It was a high honor in its own right, but the experience provided me with something beyond price.

'And in the First Letter to these good if reluctant people, Paul mentions carrying a woman—a woman, or a sister. Some say it was a wife, perhaps even Peter's. I will not say as much to that end. Instead, I will only tell you the way those words, woman and sister, and, especially, *woman*, affected me. Carrying a woman! Before the terms were recorded, during that time, and afterward, general talk to the same effect permeated conversations all across Greece. And beyond. The chattering lips, of course, didn't dwell on the fact of the woman, but that is what I heard, and it convinced me. I knew of the Lord's mighty gift and presence. And a few times, I dared to go near enough to come close enough to sense if not witness some of the scenes and matters noted in the *Gospels* and *Acts*. But even then, I did not know exactly how, or if, the Word impacted me.

'I correctly thought of myself as an angel, someone better suited to messaging or guarding. But I had diminished my abilities as you know. I was no longer chosen as were the Regulars. So, in a way, and again, I had made myself a Gentile among my kind. When I first heard rumors of His preaching in Palestine, and then later, heard that the message and miracle was to be shared beyond the Hebrews, I drew a comparison between my plight and those of the people here and elsewhere. I began to wonder if Christ's sacrifice and offer of new life were not meant for me as well. So, having lingered around Greece for so long, I ventured here, to this spot, so many years ago. On my way, as if to motivate me, came the rumored mention of the carried woman. I heard Peter say something almost identical when he and I arrived. And in my heart, I realized that any Power that could, in any capacity, carry a human woman, Hebrew or Gentile, towards salvation, might also carry my self-tortured earth-bound image of a woman.

'That is what led me to the Church, Josh. They, or It, as it happened, did come to me, by way of location and proximity. But I was drawn in because I already expected and hoped for something. And I found it. Here. Christ's Bride, the Christian Church, provided me with a home and a glimpse of the to-be restored Heaven, a glimpse of what I'd lost and wished with all my heart to regain. And if it were remade, better than before, then, hoping the same thing for myself, I desired it all the more so. I received my Baptism just over there, beyond that hill,' she gestured towards it, 'where that warehouse now stands, in a little creek long dried up. The sacrament and the mystery. Many, nearly all, of these kinds of mysteries, for me and all of us, run in ribbons. They rise and fall, ebb and flow, but they remain connected as they stretch out over time and space like bridges.

'There is also the matter, a concern you have previously invoked, and one recorded in the sixth chapter of *First Corinthians* of a certain judgement. Paul asked, *Know you not that we shall judge angels? How much more the things of this world?* That deeply touched me, being, then and now, a subject of judgement both angelic and of the world. I do not know, but I trust: I hope and believe that all these matters, concerning my eternal fate, are woven together in a ribbon that leads like a bridge, someday, to Paradise. Now you know, sweet Josh. Maybe we're overcoming the past, and bridging to the future, and it's like this trip is connecting my past, and my restart, with the present and beyond, with you. And regardless of my hopes in, prayers for, and faith about the future, I praise God that you are part of my part in it!'

He held her hand lightly but firmly and walked around so he could face her. Leaning in and kissing her several times, he said, 'I've been praying in my own faltering little words for the same, Athena. And as for having you, I too praise God. And I couldn't be happier. I also hope against all that our actions together somehow foster your redemption and return. And,' he added with a little laugh, 'if I get to directly participate in your case, then I think I'll have to vote to acquit! You're a giant part of my personal miracle, thank you, very much and forever; and, I hope I can play a part in yours. And I'm pleased to have learned where and how it started. In our case, woman means wife, and I ask that you let me carry you. Now and for all our life together. Carrying with, for, and out of pure love. Let's pass over our bridge together!' He finished and, not waiting for any reply, hugged her tightly and kissed her with a strength worthy of eternal recordation.

Later that afternoon, as they walked back through the hotel lobby, she asked him, 'So, what's this surprise for tonight?'

'Well, I was feeling a little like it was a corny thing, really. But when you mentioned bridges connecting here and there and then and now, it made me feel better about the choice,' he said as they entered an elevator. She looked at him expectantly and he went on,

'The other day, I passed by the concierge desk and saw a little sign. I asked about some tickets, and they arranged them and a limo ride over to the venue, which I think you'll like. I found it a little odd but rather fitting that it's an American band, but, baby, we're going to a concert!'

'Really? Who is it?' she asked as they started walking down their hall.

'You'll see inside. They were supposed to leave the tickets and something else while we were out.'

And inside the suite, on the table near the door, they found what Josh had expected. Room service had left a dozen roses in a nice vase for Athena. And propped against it was an envelope. She opened it, read over the tickets, and said, 'I'm all in! This sounds fun, though I've never heard of them. How'd you know about this Dandy and the Bass Slayers?'

'I'm really not that familiar,' he admitted. 'But I've heard of them—kind of a Southern rock-country-jazz-opera band without a real description. Pretty popular, I guess, and this is their first time playing in Greece. Hopefully, it will be fun. I know the dinner beforehand will be, along with the wine and relaxation afterward!'

'Well,' she said. 'Let's go find out!'

After eating, they stepped into a limousine and were driven a short distance to the ancient Odeon of Herodes Atticus where the concert was held, midway up the hill, and ironically, under the temple Athena disliked. During the show, she was pleased her back was again turned to the structure. However, both of them, despite not knowing any of the songs played—and Josh thanked God all the lyrics were in English, even if accented with a deep Southern twang—had a marvelous time. The Bass Slayers, true to their patented ways, soon had the whole arena up and dancing, mostly in popular, freestyle form. But Josh and Athena found a special time to hold and sway together slowly, and they found added meaning in the evening, when the band played a classic off of their older album, *One Ton Dually*. Lead singer Andy "Dandy" Fitzdale spoke to the audience at the end of a break, 'How y'all likin' our lil' show?! Eh? Good, good. We're so happy to be here in Greece for the first time. And we were reminded that one of our songs has something to do with some words said not too far away from this very spot. We took our inspiration from *First Corinthians* when we wrote the last song from *One Ton*. Well, like all our stuff, we took inspiration and ran Southern country wild with it. Hope y'all enjoy it; folks, here's "Carrying a Woman."' Athena and Josh took the song as an apropos happy sign about things. And they also thought it was a pretty good ballad in its own right.

Back in the room, she asked him, 'Wine or champagne on the porch?'

'That would be nice,' he said. 'But just maybe I have a better idea. You decide.' She, in fact, thought highly of his idea and accepted it. It meant sacrificing some of her roses, but she enjoyed watching him tear their petals off, gathering them in a bowl. Those petals were strewn about the oversized bathtub where they held and bathed each other while enjoying the last bottle of the night.

The next morning, they bid a fond farewell to Athens, a city neither of them would ever visit again, and headed back towards New England. Once home, and not at all tired, they attended services at her, or now, their church, along with those at Josh's old OCA home. They spent the last full day of their honeymoon and Josh's Merrimack Christmas break moving his things from his apartment and into the townhouse they now shared which now began to truly feel like a home. One aspect of family life still remained outstanding, though they had excellent plans for capturing that missing piece. Or, in their case, pieces.

Seventeen

Fruit Begins To Grow

They both returned to work, each spending an hour or two on the first day back gushing about their trip and their new life together. In the evenings that week, Josh sorted many of his belongings, temporarily stored in the garage where Athena had moved out a number of book boxes. Most of his modest furniture wasn't worth hanging on to, though she requested he keep the couch where they'd enjoyed each other's company on a few occasions. All of his clothes and other personal items fit right in as if they'd always belonged next to hers. Their new and blissful married life continued to unfurl, grow, excite, and enlighten. And towards the end of January, they prepared for another important meeting.

One afternoon, upon leaving their respective jobs a little early, they sat down in the office of Steven Dandelion, attorney-at-law. He came highly recommended by the lawyer who handled many of the endowment fund affairs for the Anderson Gallery and was a widely respected family law expert, well-known across New England. Whereas in most law offices, family law really meant divorces and other unpleasant matters, in his it only stood for adoptions and for strengthening or creating families. He liked to make that distinction and happily did so as soon as he met them. They were joined by Sister Francisco in Dandelion's office. And when the kind man learned they were present and waiting in his reception room, he invited Michelle and Isabella to join the party of which they were the primary subjects.

'No case, in any area of law,' he said, 'is more important than an adoption. And only a capital criminal case is as important.' Depending on how one looked at jurisprudence, he had a point. 'And I am delighted to make all of your acquaintances, early in this process, sure to be a happy one, and I'm pleased to see we have already started on our tedious paperwork. And I get to meet the two children! How are you, today, young ladies?' He and the girls chatted for a few minutes, with a little input here and there, from the adults. While they talked, Josh looked thoughtfully at Athena.

'*Here we go!*' he said mentally.

'*Yes, I'm so excited,*' she replied, the rest of the room oblivious to their discussion. '*I took the liberty of, well, fast-tracking just about everything. I'll just produce it all as needed or when he requests.*'

'*Athena, I had that idea again today, the thing or things I mentioned a week or so back,*' he said. '*As they're very real girls, and we're going to be a real family, might we want to let the process work, more or less, along its ordinary course? I have all of the things I was told to obtain: work records, background check, and so forth. Wanna give it a try?*'

'*You make an excellent argument as always, darling,*' she said. '*Yes, let's try it, as far as it goes. I will have to fudge a few tests, if the DNA or blood thing is required, because, you know. And I always manipulate my database information as I don't really, truly exist in their world. Or, you know, I don't fit in like anyone else, that is.*'

'*Fair enough,*' he said. '*But with the home study, and letting the department do its work, the Indian registry, the timing of the process, and all that, how about we just see? I figure that if there's a snag or slow down somewhere, then you can, uh, bump it along.*'

'*Deal!*' she said, giving him a mental kiss. The kiss broke their respective concentrations and, at the same moment, they both laughed and sighed a little, the spectacle of which caught the attention of the others. 'We're very excited,' Athena explained with another more open laugh.

They were then brought back, fully, into the meeting. They signed off on a number of documents and listened to Dandelion's instructions. Several petitions would be filed and there was an apparent order as to how they would progress. Guardianship, and a slow-walking transfer from the Catholic home, would come first, he explained to them. Then, after the girls were comfortably living in the couple's care, the regular adoption process would proceed. 'Based on what I see here, and what I've learned about the two of you, Josh and Athena, I have no doubts that this one will go smoothly. I don't foresee any parties contesting anything or any other roadblocks. But I will say that I never make ultimate predictions or guarantees, and I caution against trusting any attorney or other professional who does. My job is to keep things moving, keep you apprised, and to answer any questions you come up with.

'I'll get all of this filed, and then we'll get rolling. The department will, at some point, meet with you and perform a little home inspection. Just be honest with them, and nice to them. They get a lot of flack, much of it deserved ['*Like with that social worker!*' Josh mentally noted to Athena.], so when people are friendly and helpful, it makes their work a little easier and it makes them easier to work with. Once you are established as temporary guardians, the girls can move in with you. How's that sound, gang?!' All nodded in happy agreement and Michelle and Isabella loudly cheered the idea. 'And once you're living together, it can take six months to a year before we get a final hearing and we all become a full, permanent family. I see Miss Michelle here is a little shy of fourteen. That's the age where the process can be sped up by operation of law. Of course, this being a double, we'd have to wait on little Miss Isabella anyway.' He gave her a squint, and she made a funny face back at him.

'Outside the operation of law, in the realm of facts on the ground, if we can paint a picture of a smooth and happy family life, and no other issues arise, then the courts do sometimes speed things up on a case-by-case basis. This is not a prediction, but let's cross our fingers, say a prayer, and count on getting the wonderful final decrees by this fall. How's that?' They all eagerly agreed and hoped he was right. 'And, one more thing,' he said. 'I see that the girls both want to change their last names to Williams during the adoption, is that right, ladies?'

'Yes!' Michelle said quickly. 'I do.'

'Me too,' said Isabella. 'I want to be Issy, Isabella Daddy Joshy!'

'Well, when you put it like that...' Dandelion said with a laugh.

And so, they were off on the beginnings of making theirs a true family with children. Afterwards, Josh and Athena took Francisco and the girls out for dinner and they further discussed the exciting future. After seeing the three back into the little orphanage, Josh and his bride went home, where they kept talking about the adoption and a life with children, a discussion followed by several rounds of another kind of potential child creation. The weeks seemed to fly by at that point. Two representatives from the State, two who had worked very satisfactorily with Sister Francisco a number of times before, paid them a pleasant visit. Soon rumor, bordering on an offer, reached them that the girls could probably move in just after Saint Valentine's Day. If that pleased Athena and Josh, then it utterly elated Michelle and Isabella. Then, a day or two later, other good news, stemming originally from a rather bad incident, came to their attention.

Far away...

Two grungy men sat in the shadows of a dingy room at a drug motel in Fabens, Texas, not far from Interstate Ten. As he looked at his cards, one of them spoke to his companion who'd just finished off another can of cheap beer. Exhaling his cigarette smoke, the man said, 'Never thought I'd be sneaking into Mexico. Where is this dude anyway?'

'Carlos,' the other man said as his eyes alternated between his cards and a fifth can of beer. 'Dude is Carlos the coyote. Mexico may not be far enough away, but it's a start. May be a good start for us. Those stupid little girls won't remember much about me, and with your changed appearance, nobody'll make you after a while. We're headed towards freedom, man.'

'How much does Carlos the coyote charge? For a reverse trip?'

'Not that much. He's dropping off some migrants at the moment, and he's gonna slip back in with two more going south. Us! I gave him a couple hondos and the promise of some girl fun when we get rolling again. He's gonna be here soon.'

'Sounds okay, but I don't know, brother. I got a bad feeling about something. That old gut instinct is warning me.'

There came a series of light knocks on the door, a pattern that sounded very much like a signal. 'And that's our *hombre el liberte* now!' the one man, the one without the gut issues, said as he got up. The other man drew on his cigarette and felt something sour in his esophagus. He watched as his friend approached the door, started to look through the peephole, and said, 'Carlos?'

It happened too fast for the smoking pedophile to make sense of it. He watched as his partner was knocked back and then crushed beneath the falling door that was smashed into the room, hinges, lock, frame, and all. A large gray blur swept into the berth. In an instant, it had a death grip on his throat and the lowlife was horrified to see a golden Cross embossed on a vambrace just above the armored glove that silenced his breath and speech. 'You should've trusted your gut,' a deep, menacing voice growled. Then the criminal was lifted up, rammed into the wall, and slammed into the ceiling, before being pulverized through the table and into the floor. Everything went dark, a fitting irony for such a low and dastardly set of miscreants.

Back in their happy home...

Athena walked in whistling, or, he couldn't exactly tell, she could have been singing about something. 'I have the best news!' she exclaimed.

'What is it? What has you singing happy?' Josh asked her.

'You know what?' she said. 'I'm going to let you tell me!'

He gave her a puzzled look, but then his eyes returned to the online news story he'd just found. It was on an aggregation site he rarely if ever consulted. For some reason, something had told him to browse the page that day. So he quickly read the short crime news story. 'Hey! Wow! They caught those two worthless jerks who molested Michelle! Is this what you were talking about?'

'How'd they catch them?'

'Well, it says they turned themselves in. To the police, but to a hospital first. It seems they were dropped off at a Texas ER comatose and in critical condition. Says they should recover physically. Well, mostly. But when they came to, they immediately identified themselves and demanded the doctors call the police. Confessed on the spot in their traction beds. No one can make sense of it, but evidently, someone put the fear of God in them.'

'Someone did, indeed,' she said with a smile of deepest satisfaction.

'Someone named Christian?'

'Maybe...'

'Is he like you?' Josh asked sincerely.

'No,' she said. 'He's one of yours, only stronger, faster, and with a few more resources. Really, he's just a big, walking, talking millstone. If you know what I mean.'

'I certainly do now,' he said with a laugh. 'And justice is served. Sing on, my beloved!' In fact, they were so happy that they ended up singing about it together.

They decided to keep that knowledge between them and from Michelle, at least until she was older, or unless she asked, or it became widely-known information. And they saw her and Isabella more and more each week, making a point to spend as much time as possible with the two sweet sisters-to-be (and Francisco). On Saturday, they had the girls over and talked about rooms and related moving-in matters. The townhouse had, in addition to the master and guest rooms, two additional bedrooms on the third floor, each with a bathroom, one connected to the other via a common shower and tub area. The girls loved the tentative plans they drew up. Later that evening, after the little ladies departed, Athena led Josh in a related discussion in the guest room, 'He, or she, will, of course, start out with us. But the guest room here will make a fine nursery. When the time comes!'

'I can't wait for that time to arrive!' he said. 'Wanna go prod it along a little?' And prod they did, pretty much for the rest of the weekend. The next week was full of ordinary work and preparations for the pending expansion of their family. One night, a little after they both arrived home and began exploring dinner possibilities, he announced to her, 'Hey! I have something exciting to run by you! Two things really.'

'Great, baby!' she said. 'And I have something to tell you too. Or to run by you.'

'Okay,' he said. 'Ladies first.'

'No, Josh. You mentioned it first. I defer to my husband.'

'Well, since you put it that way,' he said, kissing her nose. 'The big thing, or the minor thing, depending on how you look at it, is that I've been hired part-time as a junior editor for that publisher! I can do it all remotely, it fits with my college work, and there's all kinds of room for growth. Seems I made an impression on them when we talked. And whatever Dr. Johnson's been telling them hasn't hurt. And for us, it'll mean a decent boost financially! Not to worry about money, but if or when you ever decide to, you know, take time off, it'll really help.

"The second thing, that feels kind of big at the moment, is about Valentine's Day. Since we can't decide on Meadowbanks again, or anywhere else, and you mentioned a romantic dinner here, well, I owe you for all the home cooking. So I checked out a cookbook at the school library, and, baby, how about I cook you a special dinner?!'

'Josh! That first part is wonderful, and it goes right to what I wanted to discuss with you.' She took him in her arms as she excitedly responded. 'And the dinner sounds so incredible. I'll take it. Anything from my man, even another round of frozen pot pies!'

'Real food, this time, my dear, real, real food.'

'Very well, I accept. And go, you! Now, here's what I've been thinking about—and talking to the board about at work. In a short time, we're gonna have two girls here who have never had a mother around. And they might really want to homeschool like you and I've mentioned before. And sooner or later, they're going to start getting little siblings. So—'

'Do it!' he said, increasing the pressure of his hug around her waist. 'I'm for whatever you're about to say.'

'Thank you, baby. And for now, I'm just planning some scenarios. But I really would like the experience and the chance for service as a stay-at-home mom.'

'The most important job ever created,' he added, beginning to sniff her hair, steadily making his way towards her sensitive ear.

She giggled, and said, 'Stop. No! Don't stop, keep going. But I do have some options. One would be to ease out. Another would be to— BABY! That's driving me crazy! T-to become a consultant. I could go part— This is, oh, my! Keep going, baby! I just want to make our babies as comfortable as possible. Should we go up—'

Josh's sniffing had become a nibbling that threatened to escalate into more, very soon. 'Work out whatever you need to, Athena. I love the idea, any part of it. In fact, let's go discuss it more and in greater detail. Especially the part about all those little siblings!' They did discuss the matter, with a special concentration on having more children. And eventually, they got around to dinner. Or, rather, they got up for a midnight snack.

As the days moved forward, they ramped up their work plans, his to increase his load, and hers essentially becoming an easing out process. At the end of each day, they shared their milestones with each other. And they also looked forward to their coming special date at home. Saint Valentine's Day came on a Thursday that year, and the day before he'd told her to take her time leaving work, or to find a way to kill an hour or so to allow him to get home first and get things baking. It was all to be another of his trademarked grand surprises. And all that day, she anxiously waited and looked forward to enjoying whatever he was up to. She loitered around the Gallery for as long as she felt she could, and then she tried to drive back home as slowly as possible. But she was humming with excitement, a permanent smile etched on her gorgeous face, as she pulled into the driveway.

Her smile fell a little when she walked in and was immediately greeted by the smell of smoke. It got stronger as she approached the kitchen, though she kept her hopes up. Those were encouraged when she passed by the dining room and saw the table nicely set for a dinner party of two, complete with better China, some candles, and roses on her place setting. On the kitchen table, she saw many more roses, a nice box of chocolates, and a red card waiting for her. But she also saw Josh sitting there, a beer in his washcloth-wrapped hand, with his head down. Glancing past him for a moment, she saw that a small calamity had unfolded earlier.

'I blew it,' he said with a cracking sound in his voice. He looked up at her sadly. She walked around and took stock of the situation. On the stove, in a pan, were the rather awful-looking remains of what had probably been intended to be mashed potatoes. He evidently had—and she guessed by sight—sliced up one or more uncooked tubers, diced them, and attempted to smash them (possibly with a hammer). Some sauce of milk, butter, or water had been added, and the concoction was left to cook. For too long. Way too long. On the floor, she saw proof that something had fallen and splattered. That something, a jumble of unidentifiable meat and some charred vegetables, lay within and without a glass pan in the sink. The oven door was cracked ajar and the hood fan was running. Peeking inside the open door, she saw what looked like a cake overflowing from a heart-shaped baking dish, but blackened and ruined into something resembling burned wood. A trail of thin smoke still wafted away from its surface.

After assessing the damage, she turned back to Josh, finding his eyes pleading with her. But her shock was giving way to a burning desire, tinged with the almost unbecoming urge to start making jokes. His next words put that little notion to rest. 'While I was burning everything else, I burned my hand.' He held up the cloth-covered paw as evidence. 'That's why I dropped the roast. Not that it was worth salvaging by that point. I'm sorry, darling. I wanted to give you something, and instead—'

'You gave me something greater!' she said, as she rushed to hold, hug, and kiss him mercilessly. Then she said, 'Let me see that sweet hand. We need to treat it. And then you and I will just go grab something. Anything from anywhere, as long as we're together.' He smiled at her better suggestion, and deeply appreciated the kisses and kid gloves treatment of his injury. About an hour later, having stopped at the first place that didn't look overly crowded, they sat at the bar of the local 99 enjoying cheap wine, hot wings, and stuffed potato skins. After running her hands through his hair for the fourth time, she took out her card and opened it. 'I wanna see what my sweet man was thinking!' It read:

> *Dearest Athena,*
>
> *Like the vaunted Saint, driving deviant serpents from Ireland, you have driven away all my loneliness, doubt, and pain. This little meal, and these gifts, are only a token of what I owe you. Cupid came calling in my life as if with a vengeance. And now, my heart burns with a great fire for you. Happy Saint Valentine's Day, my beautiful angel of a wife!*
>
> *Loving you more and more every second, I remain, forever, yours,*
>
> *Josh(y)*

He had even drawn a flaming heart below his script. She held the card to her breast and started crying. Then, carefully setting it on the bar, she seized his head in her hands and planted a long, wet kiss on him, into him, and through him with a fervor that finally made the bartender and other patrons blush. Upon releasing him, still holding his breathless body, she placed her forehead on his and said, teasingly, 'That was so sweet, baby! Even if you, uh, might have been talking about Saint Patrick there.'

'Oh, no,' he said with a little embarrassment. 'I was thinking about two things, trying to decide, and ended up writing both of them. Or, well, the wrong things. I messed up again.' He looked sad again for a second.

She laughed, kissed his forehead, and said, 'Well, you certainly got the burning fire part right!' She then proceeded to tickle him, a tickling that turned into a playful love fest that finally had them threatened with banishment from the pub. Taking the hint, they left for home. For some time, they enjoyed more wine on the couch, feeding each other chocolates before turning consumption of the little candies into a kind of game that would have made Ol' Cupid proud. At two in the morning, they took a laughing break and cleaned up the kitchen. The scrubbing was followed by a joint bath in the big tub, followed by more games that might have made even Cupid ruddle. Friday, they were both moving a little slowly, but they wrote it off to the happy trials of burning desire.

The following Friday hosted an event of a different character, different but very, very important. Isabella and Michelle both attended the local Catholic day school. Instead of walking back to the home, holding hands, skipping, and chatting, as they usually did, that afternoon, promptly at three-thirty, they were picked up by their new guardians. Josh and Athena had taken the day off and visited with Francisco, and they had gathered the girls' belongings as pre-packed into boxes. Those boxes, partly emptied, now awaited the girls in their new rooms on the third floor. The foursome stopped by the home, both to see Franciso again and to make sure nothing had been left behind. Around five, they walked into the townhouse that was truly becoming a loving family home.

Standing at the door of Issy's bedroom, watching the womenfolk pass around clothing, a giant bear, other stuffed animals, and toys, Josh said, 'If you girls want to keep going, please do. You can take a break in an hour or so; I'll have something nice and hot ready! I have a little cookbook from—'

'I'll get dinner!' Athena suddenly volunteered, a pronouncement that at once made Josh happy and a little embarrassed.

'Okay, then,' Josh said. 'I'm the loadmaster tonight.' The girls giggled.

'What would you sweeties like,' she asked them. 'Anything.'

'Pancakes!' Michelle said instantly.

'You're pancakes are so dreamy!' Isabella said.

'Come down and help me when or if you like. And take it easy on poor Joshy.' Athena then turned and went to start another breakfast supper.

'How can we decorate our rooms?' Issy asked Josh.

'Anyway you like!' he said. For close to an hour, he did as he was told, helping Michelle help Issy arrange things to her liking. Around six-thirty, a sweet smell filled the house, rising right up to their noses, and it drew them downstairs. Michelle quickly and smoothly shifted gears, from moving into waitressing, and started helping Athena prepare the kitchen table and their food. They all sat down together, and Josh said, 'Let us pray in thanks for our never-ending blessings!'

But Michelle jumped in with an offer to that end. 'May I say it, please?' she asked.

'Well, certainly, young lady,' Josh said. Athena and Isabella smiled approvingly at the idea.

'Thank you,' Michelle said as they all linked hands around the table. Then she prayed, 'Dear God, thank You for these pancakes, the very best in the whole world. And thank You very much for leading Isabella and me here to live with Josh and Athena, who I want so dearly to call Mom and Dad. They really are the best, kindest people I've ever met, and little Issy and I are so lucky to have them. And to have them want us. It seemed like forever that no one wanted us or would treat us right. But You have fixed that, God. I pray that we can always act as the best daughters for them. We love them. So please bless this food, Josh, Athena, Issy, and me. And thank You. Amen.'

'Amen!' they all said a little louder than normal. And they squeezed hands together a little harder and longer than they otherwise might. Then fighting back a few tears, Josh got up. He walked right around to Michelle and beckoned her to stand as well. When she did, he reached down and lifted her up in a huge, full-body hug that made her laugh and cry. He said nothing, but he kissed her head. Upon setting her down, he did the same thing with Issy, and then, with Athena, completely lifting her off the floor as well. A group hug was shared, still just with contact and without words. At last, as they stood around smiling at each other, Athena said, 'Now, please, let's eat before the cakes get cold!' It turned out they were just in time, with the temperature and taste being perfect, a description that also matched their long talk, many smiles, and the happy mood that settled over the kitchen.

Later that evening, and for the rest of the weekend, they turned their collective attention to the girls' rooms and their new roles of being the best daughters anyone could imagine. And on Sunday night as they were preparing for bed, Isabella made a somewhat prophetic statement: 'Poor Daddy Joshy is outnumbered by girls around here! What we need now is a little boy.'

Eighteen

More Flowers Bloom

As the days and weeks passed, the young family, each member, came to question how they had ever lived apart before, so natural was their association. Various things, of course, required a little adjusting. Josh became more involved in his new role as an editor, though the occupation meshed very well with his existing work, his personality and interests, and his new family obligations. Athena, still the director and curator of the Anderson Gallery, was slowly preparing to transition into being a full-time house mother and wife. That process, met only with professional encouragement, went just as well as Josh's. Every single day brought the budding parents closer into the lives of the girls, and vice versa, and the girls felt more and more like sisters than they ever had before. They all still saw Sister Francisco on a frequent basis, a tradition that continued for the rest of the nun's long and happy life in retirement. And, just as Athena had hoped, Kara and her family down in Dixie began to keep regular contact—a trend that lasted for a lifetime, in the future bringing many visits up and down the East Coast. The somewhat probationary guardianship rolled smoothly into the process of regular adoption, as overseen very well by Dandelion. Two other areas of great importance involved Michelle and Isabella's places in church and school.

Thanks to the Herculean efforts of Sister Francisco, and in spite of the ways of the world and their particular fates, both girls had been raised, like Josh before them, in a mostly Roman Catholic fashion. Both had been Baptized and were somewhat regular attendees at Sunday services. However, now living with Josh and Athena and feeling both a connection and a powerful lure, they quickly became interested in Orthodoxy, as represented by the Greek church led by Father Josias they now began attending. Josias instantly fell in love with both of them, a feeling they reciprocated. So without prompting and of their own curious accord, the sisters soon catechised into Saint Athanasius.

Education was another supremely important issue. The girls had off and on, as dictated by their foster trials, attended the local Catholic day system. Josh and Athena, by their own research and with Josh's previous experiences, and in consultation with the principal, felt the curriculum and the environment were good enough, or, at least, decent enough for the remainder of the school year. As genuinely loving parents, their true problem was that good or decent enough in the case of their daughters didn't feel sufficient. 'How would you girls like to learn here in our home?' Athena asked them one day.

Both were more than open to the possibility as both also felt their schooling was acceptable though not something they would really miss or regret losing. 'We'd love to stay here,' Michelle answered. 'You're both so smart, and you have all these books everywhere. And you know all the answers to our questions and then some. Would you be our teacher?'

'Yes!' Athena said, very excited at the job prospect.

Dandelion added his own decent if cautious advice regarding the homeschooling plan, which he endorsed and, in fact, practiced at his own house. 'It's really the only way to go,' he said. 'But let's time it out right. If there was trouble, I'd say yank them yesterday. As-is, as long as they're happy, maybe let them ride out the end of this year. One fewer change might actually be better for them, for you, and it probably wouldn't hurt our case progress. Nice and smooth and so forth. When the fall rolls around, then it'll be time! Homeschool away. Doing it all that way might even help push us to an early decree.' Trusting his expertise, which turned out to be right, they all agreed. However, Josh and Athena did a comprehensive audit of what the girls had learned and were being taught, ultimately finding none of it overly objectionable. For the rest of the school year, they kept a close eye on everything. Josh made semi-regular visits on various school days, something few if any other parents did, and he and Athena attended all special events and meetings. Additionally, while sometimes she was seen, other times not, Athena began making daily inspections—being ever generally pleased with what she found, but as any mother should be, also remaining ever on guard.

As winter progressed towards spring, virtually everything in their lives was working well and producing great happiness. Still, life must slope downwards sometimes, just as it goes up. They caught a small, sad reminder of that fact one snowy weekend in March. Even early, it was shaping up to be a lazy Saturday. Athena had gone downstairs to make coffee and investigate breakfast, leaving Josh to slowly make his way from the bedroom at his leisure. By the running of smaller feet and the happy chattering of little female voices, he knew the girls were up. He decided it was the right morning to try out the new bathrobe Athena had given him, so he put it on over his pajama bottoms and t-shirt. He'd just slipped on some comfy lay-about bedroom shoes, when he heard a set of little feet pounding back up the stairs, coming up rather quickly. He was almost to the hall when he met an alarmed-looking Isabella. 'Josh! Daddy! Athena— Mommy's upset about something in the kitchen! I've never seen her crying!' the poor girl said, almost out of breath. They quickly hurried down and into the kitchen.

Michelle was standing by Athena at the sink. Athena was looking at the window sill and crying, not quite uncontrollably, but still hard enough to stir concern in the teenager—and in Josh.

'Baby!' he said as he rushed to her, going around to the side opposite Michelle. 'What's wrong?!' Then, looking at where she was staring, he saw the matter. Down on the sill, between the lower edge of the window and the vase they used for flowers, lay a tiny motionless figure. Proud, noble, and independent Charlotte was frozen with her eight little legs curled up almost into a tiny ball. 'No. Baby, I'm so sorry,' he said as he hugged her, immediately being joined by the girls.

After comforting Athena and giving her some coffee, Josh, assisted by the girls, made ready. He removed the two remaining matches from a little box and then very gingerly lifted and placed Charlotte into it. Unlike so many, too many people, especially men, he'd never been afraid of spiders nor hated them, instead admiring the little jobs they did so well. But even just six months earlier, he would have hardly batted an eye at the sight of a deceased one. Now his eyes were a little moist and his throat was dry. He closed the matchbox and sought a little relief for his voice from a mug of coffee. Then dressed just as they were, heedless of the cold and fallen snow, they all made their way into the little backyard. Isabella swept the ice and snow from a patch in a flower bed near the garden wall, and Michelle dug a small hole with a flower spade. Then Josh gently lowered the little casket into the fresh grave. None of them noticed, but up on a few icey branches, a Blue Jay and a Black-capped Chickadee, ordinarily dread adversaries of arachnids, stopped, bowed their heads, and paid their respects.

'Let us pray and show final honors to our departed friend,' Josh said, breaking their collective silence. They all crossed themselves, and he began, 'Lord, into Your all-knowing and all-caring love and keeping, we commend the spirit and body of our good friend, Charlotte. She lived a grand life, and evidently, a long one, filled with good deeds to earn her keep here in our fallen vision of Eden. Man, woman, and child have never known so good a little being, one ever dedicated to all the purposes You in Your wisdom intended for her. And she brightened our days. Please welcome her so that she may continue to brighten Yours. And as we remember her always, we hope to be comforted in our loss of her. We humbly ask this of Your infinite wisdom and mercy, O Lord. In the name of the Father, and of the Son, and of the Holy Spirit. Amen.'

They crossed themselves again. Then Josh and the girls replaced the dirt and mulch atop the little tomb, finally covering it all with snow again. Athena then stooped and placed a dried rose on the memorial. 'She did live a good life, and she was a very dear girl,' she said as a tear rolled down her lovely face. Life did go on for the family, even that day returning to a normal kind of happy existence. But as they made their way back inside, and for much of their breakfast, they were mostly silent. In the inevitable yet tragic circumstances, they all learned or were reminded that even the smallest life, dearly lived and given, has the ability to touch others with a magnitude most unexpected. Not long after the sad event, however, the loss of one small life was corrected by the addition of another, and one, no disrespect to spiders, of almost incomparably greater magnitude.

One fine morning during coffee time before breakfast, Josh was sitting on the couch, flanked by Athena on his right and Michelle on his left. Isabella, destined to forever be a daddy's girl, sat on his lap facing him. All three ladies, in some form or fashion, were affectionately petting or adoring the man of the house. Their happy conversation went nowhere and everywhere, generally eased whichever way by smatterings of laughter. Breakfast was slowly becoming the topic of the time, with the girls giving hints about what they wanted. 'And I want that many pancakes,' Isabella said, holding apart her hands for effect.

Athena, who'd been smiling an awful lot that morning (and for a few days before), knew the time was right. She rubbed Isabella's back and said, 'Pancakes it is! And very soon, baby girl. But first, would you mind switching places with me? I have something, a bit of show and tell, for you girls and Daddy Joshy.' The little one happily switched places, a change conditioned on a hug from Athena first, and Athena took a family-friendly but still rather romantic seat on Josh's lap. She was sort of sitting up on her knees, her upper body erect, and she leaned in a little towards Josh's face. 'I want pancakes too. This many,' she said, holding up her hands as an illustrative example. 'But, Joshy, you know, for wives and mommies, pancakes can be a little like, well, buns.' She then used one hand to lower her waistband just a little while her other raised her shirt until it was up to the bottom of her ribs. They all looked at her lower tummy, Josh with keen affection and interest as he always admired her soft, smooth skin and all of the delightful curves of her figure. But then he and the girls noticed that Athena's ordinarily flat stomach, while still toned and lovely, had a slight but observable bulge just below her cute navel. She looked deep into Josh's eyes, even as they were tilted downwards, and he caught her look from the upper edge of his vision, which was still primarily locked onto her stomach. Then she gave the area a little pat and rub for emphasis. His hands immediately joined hers as a look of unconquerable joy leaped to his face. The girls then began smiling with their mouths open.

'ARE WE?!' he yelled out, a bit too loudly for them but still to their liking. 'Are you?'

'Yes, and YES!' she said back, also in a somewhat louder than necessary voice. She was smiling and sighing happily, an expressed feeling that grew warmer when she felt the girls' hands joining Josh's on her skin. 'We're having a baby!'

'Is it going to be another sister? Or the little brother I mentioned?!' Isabella asked excitedly.

'We'll have to wait and see,' Michelle said. 'Whichever, he or she is going to be so cute and cuddly. I can't wait!'

'Well, Daddy is both cute and cuddly,' Josh said as he pulled Athena closer and nuzzled his face against her belly and the little bun inside. As he caught more hints of the warm, fresh cookie dough smell he'd become crazy over, he decided to second Issy's questions. 'I'll happily take a boy or a girl. But like lil' sis here, I'm a little curious.'

Athena, smiling and adoring their adoration, thought for a moment. She caressed the girls' heads and then ran her fingers through Josh's hair, down his temples, and across his beard. Then she lifted his chin a little so his eyes were peeking up at her over her rolled shirt. 'I think I know,' she said with a grin.

'How?' Michelle asked.

'Which?' Issy asked.

'I half expected you to know or guess,' Josh said. 'We'll all trust you. Wanna share?' The girls immediately echoed his request.

'Well,' Athena said, relishing her thoughts. 'Since poor Joshy is so outnumbered here, I'm thinking he's going to be joined before long by a little baby boy!'

'Woo!' Josh said happily. 'I need reinforcement.'

'What will we name him?' Michelle asked.

Josh and Athena had already talked about that eventuality a few times before. So they were elated when Isabella just happened to throw out the very name they had fallen in love with. The little girl giggled and said, 'He'll be baby Joshy, Junior. Named after his daddy, of course.'

'Little Joshua, Junior. I love it. Love him!' Michelle said.

'So I think it's unanimous, then,' Josh said. 'Any objections to a mini-me?' There were no objections, although, after a minute, Michelle did a little strategic assessment.

'What if he turns out to be a she? What would her name be?' she asked.

Athena was about to drop the female contingency name she and Josh had arrived at when Issy beat her right to it: 'Eve!' the baby girl said. 'Just like in the Bible.'

'Lemme make notes for later,' Josh said, pretending to write on Michelle's head. 'Biblical names. Eve, Adam, Peter, Mary, et cetera.'

'How many will we have?' Issy asked.

'As many as the Lord gives,' Athena said.

'Praying He is generous, I'd like to be on the cover of National Geographic one of these days. Maybe we'll have to move into a shoe or something,' Josh said.

'Or a farmhouse in the country,' Athena added.

'With a big farm kitchen?' Michelle asked. 'Where they cook pancakes all the time?'

'Is that a hint?' Josh and Athena asked together.

It was, in fact, a syrupy, sugary, battered suggestion, and they soon settled at the kitchen table for breakfast. Josh, half-joking with Issy and half unknowingly serious, babbled a little about ice cream and pickles. Michelle took an even deeper interest in assisting her guardian-mother. 'When or if you ever need to rest, then I can take over breakfast and stuff!' she sweetly volunteered. 'And right now, I want to learn more of your secrets.'

'Very well, sweetheart, I'll be happy to start sharing a few now,' Athena said. She also quickly pondered if or when the time would come to reveal another of her secrets, but at the moment, she left that for some future divulgence and simply started discussing ingredients and cooking times. She also added, with a wink and a chuckle, 'And I'd love to have help in the future. Joshy is so thoughtful, but when it comes to domestic timing and logistics, he needs a little help. Especially with cooking.' They laughed about the Valentine's meltdown, which Athena had evidently already shared with the girl.

Michelle said something, and Athena added, looking at Josh, 'But his cakes are … hunks of burning love! Get it?!' Their laughter grew louder.

Josh looked over, perplexed, and said, 'I can get ice cream later!'

'Don't burn it,' Michelle said, feeling a little flushed even as she did.

'No,' Athena countered. 'It was funny, but the poor dear meant so well. He was even willing to endure pain to make us happy. And it was so cute. Well, it was funny!' Silly girl talk, punctuated with serious remarks about loving husbands and the importance of allowing the batter to rise properly, flowed until a fluffy, delicious breakfast was on the table. And their merriment flowed for the rest of the day.

That night as they lay in bed, and she lay in his arms, Josh said to her, 'Three! Soon, we're gonna have three children. Can you believe it?'

'Like a dream, baby, but yes,' she said. 'The first three of as many as we can get.'

'Maybe we can, when space dictates, move out somewhere. I'd love to try my hand at gentleman's farming one day. And I know just the first crop I'd plant. And when the time comes, I think we'll be ready, financially and so forth. I know you say to not worry about money, and I don't, but I think we should try to do this, well, as on our own as we can. Know what I mean?' He was happy, earnest, and very optimistic-sounding.

'I do,' she said. 'My life, here, has gone in cycles. I've been a hermit, an interloper, an observer, and, at times like the past few decades, a kind of participant. And the roles I play rather dictate how my life moves along, materially and socially. Here and now, with the Gallery and coming out of Paris, that's meant higher society, this home, the Mercedes, and the like. The station was easy for me to fall into, with my talents, both earthly-natural and extraordinary. But this is a totally and radically different change for me, and I love it. I'll do whatever it takes to transition into it properly.'

'You're making outstanding progress, beautiful,' he said, kissing her cheek. 'Who knows? Maybe this phase is what's needed for, you know, the real mission. Of getting back in and up. And regardless, we can do this! If I edit and write and maybe teach, along with growing my super-special crop, we'll be fine. Especially if you want to start that translation business on the side one day. High demand for the woman who can outrun a computer, without errors, in any language! We'll figure it out as it comes to us, baby. We could trade our coats for swords, or just sell it all and follow along. And I'm so happy it comes along and is to be followed with me being here with you! I love you, more today than yesterday, and I'd have thought that impossible yesterday. PS: and if we ever need to, you can just manipulate the commercial banks or something.' They had a good but tender laugh about it all.

'You are the best, Josh. Thank you for everything. Life is going to work! I think it was just meant to be so. Now, what's that first crop you're thinking about?'

'Not going to read my mind?'

'Not tonight. Not with this, baby.'

'Well then, you, the little ladies, and baby Joshy here will just have to wait and see. I might give you a preview sooner than expected though. But for now, if you'll excuse me, I'd like to talk to our little bun for a minute or three. Luckily for you, that comes with a tummy rub. Well, kinda lucky for me too!' He then rubbed, whispered, nuzzled, and generally loved his wife and unborn baby boy into a deep, dreamy sleep. And one day a few months later, he found the chance for that little preview.

It was leaning towards the middle of June, and the last week of Spring. The girls had not long before finished their institutional school careers—forever. The adoption was hitting on all cylinders and they were told to expect an official court blessing sometime in the fall. Athena had gone part-time and was preparing to start consulting, again, part-time, from home as summer worked its way forward. Josh was busier than a bee, but one day he found an opportunity to explore something new. Once he got a message that the delivery had just been made, he rushed home as fast as he could. Athena, slowly swelling and flourishing with glowing maternal beauty, and the girls were still inside so far as he could tell when he sped up. None of them had disturbed the boxes sitting on the driveway even if they had seen them. He later learned that while they had been aware of the truck, they attested they had not gone out for an inspection, a matter they felt better suited for a boy's work. He believed them and was glad the matter was still a secret. And for that time he kept it that way, lugging the boxes into a corner in the garage and covering them with other boxes, bits and things, and an old beach towel. Now all he needed was the right distraction, an opening of several hours he reckoned, and he could get to work with this latest surprise, one he hoped would have a lasting impact and constant productive giving presence.

The opportunity presented itself a few days later on a Saturday when the girls begged and demanded Athena to let them join her in shopping for new baby clothes. Josh, of course, was invited and half-expected. However, ever since he'd learned of their plans, he'd alternately insisted he was coming down with a cold or that he had a mountain of paperwork to climb. Still, he'd been overly anxious for them to get off, and kind of ushered them along, telling them to take as long as they needed or wanted, and maybe even a little longer than that. All three women found his behavior a little suspicious, but they knew him, and they imagined that when they returned, his odd ways would manifest into something wonderful. And so, without him, they drove off.

Josh immediately ran to the backyard with a rake and moved aside the mulch and straw he'd used to conceal the construction site he'd previously broken in clandestine fashion. Next, he fetched the new boxes to the site. Then he brought out his tools, a six-pack of some lighter summer ale (because why not?), and got to work. And the project took every bit of time he was allowed. He was dirty, tired, sweaty, and out of beer by the time he slipped the pieces of paper into their places, little picture representations of what was to come. And he had not a minute to spare.

Knowing and loving her husband as she did, Athena knew to take as long as possible and give him all the time he needed ... for whatever. When they walked back into the house, they found him, very sweaty and dirty, as he'd just come into the kitchen in search of water (or a seventh beer). 'Hello, mystery man,' she said. 'You're gonna love what we bought! Care to give us a hand? If your hands aren't too dirty, that is.'

'Baby, in just a bit, I'll give you two,' he said, holding up his hands. 'But first, grab the girls and all of you come see it!' He made them close their eyes, and he helped each of them out the back door, across the patio, and into the yard. 'Open them!' he said triumphantly.

There in the yard, between two small trees not far from the back of the house and the patio, and just beside where Charlotte physically reposed for eternity, Josh had planted a row of a few rose bushes. A few small flowers and buds were already visible on two of them. Next to the last one in the little row sat the cutest little greenhouse made of painted aluminum strips and plexiglass.

'Joshy!' Athena said, wanting to hug him but fearing contact with the grime of labor.

'What's that cute little house?' Isabella asked.

'That's the cutest little greenhouse I've ever seen,' Michelle said. 'It's for growing plants when it gets cold, Issy.'

'May we look inside?' Athena asked the beaming general contractor.

'Absolutely!' he said. 'That's where the hint of what it's for is.'

He led them inside the little door, and the four of them occupied almost all of the available floor space. At the back was a little heater of some kind, not yet plugged in or made ready. Along the sidewalls were a double set of shelves, one shelf set back above the other like stair steps. And on the side nearest the house, on the bottom shelf, Josh had arranged a few pots. And inside each pot, propped up and standing proudly for all to see, he had set a series of printed pictures of roses. 'Welcome to Old MacJoshy's Rose Farm,' he said. In response, after a few 'oos,' 'ahs,' and 'oh, sweetnesses,' he was veritably mauled with hugs and kisses in spite of his grungy bedraggled appearance.

His roses, in the garden and in the cold frame, were a hit. It took him a while, but he showed great natural talent and a truly green thumb. And he delighted in always being able to deliver the freshest roses to his angel. In fact, he soon had so many and it seemed like such a natural idea, that his daughters—and they had firmly established themselves as *his* daughters—received similar gifts on a most regular basis. All throughout that marvelous summer and into the fall, their lives continued to sprout like a well-tended garden. And as with a hothouse, the growth didn't abate when the cooler weather returned.

Nineteen

Even Fuller Circle

November rolled in much the same as it had the year before, with an early harbinger of a white, snowy winter to come behind it. As a side project, Josh had taken to restoring his little Civic. The kindly mechanic was surprised to learn the radiator and heater core had lasted an entire year. But he was ever so glad to assist Josh in replacing them nearly twelve months after their last conversation about the work. Josh thought the car might make a good starter vehicle for Michelle. Or Issy. Or maybe just a continuing starter for him. In addition to engine tinkering, rose pottering, and fathering, he'd been busier than ever, both at Merrimack, where he'd been semi-promoted to an irregular lecturer in addition to his usual tasks, and as an in-demand editor. Athena made an excellent wife, mother, and teacher, though she still consulted with the Gallery as needed. She even crafted or rewrote a few covert translations here and there, usually for longer academic works, though she felt open to trying anything. Little Josh was due towards the middle of the month, which gave them all something to be extra excited about, a dream and a reward about to come true.

Timing was everything that fall and just ten days before their baby boy's due date, the good courts of the Commonwealth gave them another sweet dream in the form of two official daughters. At their first and final court hearing, the judge, after orally reviewing

239

their file and making general pleasantries about adoption, said to the couple, 'This is the best part of being a judge. It really is. I see crimes and disputes and horrible travesties of anti-family law, but today, I have the privilege of helping build and better a family and precious lives. Tell me, before we attest this matter into reality, why do you, Mr. and Mrs. Williams, want to adopt these girls, Michelle and Isabella?'

After looking and nodding at each other, Josh, appearing fatherly in his JC Penney suit and brown beard, went first: 'Your honor, these two angels mean the world to me. I know much of what their lives have been like because that was the life I led, the life of an orphan. Now having lived with them for this year, I finally understand what a family is supposed to be. They've given me and my wife as much or even more than we've given them. A real family where all members love, protect, and grow with each other.'

Athena, looking the part of the perfect pregnant lady and mother, went next: 'Judge, thank you. I can only add to what my Josh said that I too am an orphan. Or I was. Within the past year, I've gained him, the girls, and, soon, a baby boy. Believe it or not, I met him because of Isabella and Michelle. In a way, we've all adopted each other in the most amazing, almost inexplicable love story. And for as to why we really want to adopt these sweet babies, well,'

'We love them!' she said, being joined instantaneously and word for word by Josh. And in that moment, they had joined hands.

'And we love them!' Isabella and Michelle blasted out from just behind, neither being able to contain their joy in the instant.

'That is what I wanted to hear,' the judge said, smiling and sniffling a little. 'This is my honor, and I thank the four or, well, the five of you! Let me just sign right here, and ... I pronounce you the Williams family!' A little ceremony commenced in the courtroom, with the new family being photographed together as such for the first, official time. The judge was happily roped into another picture. As was Sister Francisco, Father Josias, Attorney Dandelion, Dr. and Mrs. Johnson, Milley, and more. The last photo even included the bailiff and the court reporter. And just a week and a half later, the joy continued to grow.

Joshua Williams, Jr. was born at home on his parents' bed. He was delivered, naturally, by his mother, with the careful assistance of Doctor Daddy and two big sister nurses. After the umbilical cord was cut, no needless vaccines or foolish pin-pricks were administered, and mother and son were made comfortable, Big Josh climbed into bed with them to snuggle. After looking at Little Josh's nearly bald head for a second, studying it carefully, Isabella remarked, 'You know, we really do look like a family.'

'We are a family, silly,' Michelle said.

'Yes, and you can see it,' Issy said. 'Look at baby brother's cute thin hair. It's a perfect mix of black and brown. Yours is raven black just like mommy's. And mine is the curly version of Daddy Joshy's brown hair. I'm not sure enough about all of our eyes, mom's in particular, but we really all do look alike. But special in our own ways. And nobody's more special than that little critter!' She happily pointed to Josh, Jr. as he lay cuddling between their parents. He (and they) were soon joined by the little nurses, but first, the girls held a short side conference, with Michelle at one point running off to grab a calendar. Upon her return and a little more consultation with her sister, she said, 'You want to tell them, Issy?'

Isabella, nearly nine, turned towards the bed, and said, 'Yes, thank you, dear sister, and co-nurse. Mom and Dad, do you know what day this is? In addition to baby bunny's birthday, of course, and that just makes it sweeter!' Being met with two blank faces, both of them a little tired-looking, she continued, 'Look at my locket for a reminder. One year ago, today, a sweet, cute, young man walked into a gift shop looking for something. He found it, but he also met the sweetest, cutest, young woman ever! And the rest, as they say, is history!'

'Happy first anniversary,' Josh and Athena said softly to each other as they cradled their little miracle. The girls then presented them both with roses previously concealed. Then they climbed into the bed, where the five of them remained, snug and warm, for the rest of the day and through the night.

Little Josh was a big celebrity in certain ways: he could always bring them all together, frequently, in those early days, on his parents' bed. One such occasion came on (Western or Greek) Christmas Eve. Big Josh, Joshy, Sr., was lying in the middle of the bed. His arms were stretched out. On his left, Michelle rested her head on his shoulder, with Issy nestled between them. Athena occupied the other shoulder. They were all of them looking at the little man sleeping on Josh's chest and stomach. Little Josh, on his tummy with his legs tucked up beneath him, was the picture of sweet happiness. And in his green onesie, he put on a most convincing imitation of a cute tree frog. His father was busy stroking the hair on his mother's and oldest sister's heads. And his mother was busy rubbing his little back. His eldest sister was rubbing his little, sparsely-haired head, and, without knowing it, he was holding his youngest older sister's pinky in one of his little closed hands. All at once, the dearness of the moment became too much, and he started receiving kisses from all three women in his life. Still, he slept on. He was small, but his ways and habits were powerful. When they finally got enough kisses in, the women noticed that Big Josh had also fallen asleep. Three winks were given, and then, Michelle lightly turned and quieted the little reading lamp. She and her mother then pulled up the comforter over all their bodies. They were all asleep with the boys in an instant, a slumber to last them until Christmas dawned. Or, rather, it lasted maybe twenty minutes, before the little frog announced his diaper needed changing.

But the dawn came, bringing Christmas joy and wonder. As a bundled family, they made their way to church. Afterward, foregoing the fellowship brunch, they returned home to lounge, munch, baby-dote, and to exchange presents. It was their first Christmas as a full family and they made the most of forging the beginnings of as many household traditions as they could. Few if any other families had a Christmas tree with so many roses added to the usual decorations. And no other tree was topped by a semi-preserved, star-shaped pancake. Like most families, however, there was a good assortment of presents under the curious fir. Athena and Josh gave modestly to each other, choosing instead to lavish (in a still modest way) their babies. Even at the tender ages of nine and fourteen, young ladies can still amaze when it comes to donatives. When they counted, Little Josh had received the most gifts, though in exchange he'd given the best present of all to them—himself. Of course, little Joshy could still sometimes make a little mischief, though usually of the sweetest kind.

One evening, Josh had heard his son fussing from the nursery just down the hall. There might have been a younger female voice that way too. Athena had quickly gone to check on the situation and Josh had half drifted back to sleep. But after his wife didn't return, he decided to investigate. He walked into the baby's room and noticed the crib rail-gate was down. A closer look revealed the occupant was missing. Still a little foggy, Josh glanced around, immediately noticing a picnic-like gathering on the floor. In his haze, he considered that the girls had intercepted their brother first, addressing his needs while also making a mattress of blankets and towels on the carpet. There, they enveloped their sleeping baby sibling, all of them dreaming away. Athena, coming along a little later, had simply joined them. Curling right up behind her, Josh coalesced with the rest. Little moments like that kept the family in mirth, sleepy or otherwise.

And so the days and months marched blissfully forward. It is possible for a love at first sight to grow, and to grow daily, almost hourly, as Josh and Athena's marriage testified. And few things can polish the diamonds of two already seemingly perfect daughters, a snuggly baby brother being one of them. Or two of them, as just a little over a year after little Josh was born, the family welcomed their second boy, Adam. The brothers shared the room formerly reserved for guests until a year or so later when they moved upstairs to Isabella's old room when she decided she wanted to be her sister's roommate. The moves were prompted by the arrival of a new sister, little Eve.

With the townhouse beginning to fill up and their hearts and spirits overflowing to match it, on a summer day, the family decided to investigate a new home, one further off the beaten path. After plotting it all out, and with a certain nod from fate, they loaded up the GLS, which they completely filled to capacity, and drove north on a little vacation and house-hunting trip. Josh safely navigated them out of the bustle of the Greater Boston area. Then out on the open highway after a stop for late breakfast or brunch by the sea, and after they crossed into Maine, Michelle took the wheel as part of her continuing driver's education in advance of obtaining a full license, a process she had delayed a little longer than was the norm in those times, feeling it was important but that it could wait. Josh sat up front next to her, giving advice, ever without admonishment. The babies reclined snugly in their little seats within the seats of the second row. Isabella and Athena sat in the back row, chatting and sometimes poking around the seats to attend to Josh, Jr., Adam, and Eve. Athena also maintained unusually close attention to the road and their driver, though she quashed any notion of acting as the ultimate backseat driver, instead simply trusting Michelle's growth, Josh's instructional ability, and Lord Jesus. She made mention of her latter trust to Isabella, and Issy quickly said a short prayer about the drive: '...and keep all, uh, seven(!) of us safe. Amen.'

Athena added quietly and only to Issy, 'Well, it may be the eight of us...' She was patting her tummy and grinning.

Josh intended to begin piloting again after another rest and a late lunch around Bangor, but Athena had a new idea, or one she'd held private until then. 'Allow me to drive a little, baby!' she said happily and with a hint of a deeper purpose.

'Absolutely,' Josh said. 'It's your car, after all. Did you research us a little place to spend the night?'

'I did, and something else,' she said. She then switched places with Michelle, complimenting the young woman's driving as they jostled over and past a baby's car seat. 'You'll see,' she told Josh. 'And maybe you'll remember! Maybe it's the place.'

On that picture-perfect afternoon, she drove them on to the east, into an area just past Bar Harbor, maybe halfway between there and New Brunswick, and perhaps halfway between the coast and the low, rolling, tree-covered hills there Downeast. Some distance off of the main highway, as they drifted from one little forest to another, passing quaint farms, hills, and little streams, she brought up something from Josh's not-so-distant bachelor past. 'When you bought the Civic and made your getaway here to the north, do you remember when you started having problems and had to turn around?'

'Oh, yes,' he said. 'It was so thrilling, and not scary, but I didn't really want to be stranded.' He laughed about it.

'So you stopped and tinkered by the roadside, then turned back?' she asked as she started to slow down considerably.

'Yep. I stopped in the grass out in front of a little farm. It was my tinkering and, more importantly, my prayers that saved me and the car. A farmer passed and waved, but thankfully no one had to give me a tow. Or a laugh.'

'Would you recognize that little farm if you saw it again?' she asked, coming to a stop in the grass just off the road.

'Maybe.'

'Is that it, right there?' she asked with a smile as she pointed towards his window. 'The little farm with the for sale sign out front?'

Josh now looked with great interest, as did Michelle and Isabella, who had both found themselves drawn into the little story. Adam and Eve continued to doze. Little Josh was looking out the window too, though it was a mystery whether he understood what he was looking at or what it meant. Big Josh, however, did know. 'That's it!' he said, turning back to Athena. 'And it's for sale? How on earth did you know about it?!'

'Woman's intuition,' she said smugly. 'Right girls?' The older girls concurred. 'And would anyone like to look at it? Maybe as a new home or anything?'

'Wow!' Josh said. 'Yes! We'll need to call the real estate broker, I suppose. Maybe something to do first thing tomorrow.'

'Or we could do it right now,' she said as she leaned back and gestured towards the car that had just pulled up behind them. 'That should be Mr. MacVay, the broker listed on the sign!'

Thad MacVay met with them and then followed them down the drive to a parking area that linked together the farmhouse, a barn, and a separate garage. As the owners were present and had something in progress in the house that afternoon, they would have to come back. But they could do that the very next morning, and they were free to look around the outside at the moment. They did so, making a cursory inspection of the expansive grounds, before heading off to a little motel in the nearby town. The next day, they returned and spent most of the daylight hours touring around the property, asking questions, making calculations, and dreaming about the future. On the third day, they tooled around town and the area, getting a feel for the lay of the land. On the fourth day, MacVay graciously allowed them to reinspect the property for a few more hours. At the end of their latest, and last visit, substantive family talk about the matter continued, with all of them sitting and standing around the patio behind the large farmhouse full of many bedrooms, nooks, and features. Josh continued summing up their prospects: 'Well, right now, we're cramped for space, and the cramping will continue, I think, to get worse as our family gets better. And bigger. Here, we'd have twenty fine acres, maybe more, with fields, woods, a creek and a pond, and all kinds of room for children of all ages to run around.

'Mom and I will have all kinds of opportunities here, the same and better than we have now, to continue providing for all of us, those here and those to join us eventually. I think we're all falling for the area, I know I am. It'll be a bit of a departure from the city, but I think we're all ready for that now. There's a little church between here and our motel. Before we pull the trigger—and, here, the boys and I, maybe you ladies, could start hunting in addition to fishing! Before we decide, do you have anything to add, Athena? Girls?'

'We love it!' Isabella said, not waiting.

'When could we move in?' Michella asked excitedly.

'Athena?' Josh asked with a laugh.

Athena smiled, beautifully and sincerely as always, and said, 'I agree with the girls and you, Josh. This chance appears to have been put here for us for a reason. Everything you've said, and everything we've talked about is not only true, but it's that kind of happy truth people should be on watch for. We can swing the price, and then when we sell the townhouse, we'll be paying ourselves back with some left for renovations and so forth. I say we should do it!'

'Okay,' Josh said. 'Show of hands?' Four hands immediately shot into the air. Then, assisted by Michelle and Issy, Josh, Jr., Adam, and Eve raised theirs too.

'See,' Michelle said. 'The babies are all for it!'

'It's unanimous, then,' Josh said. They all cheered.

They called MacVay over and made an offer on the spot. Just a few hours later, he met them at a restaurant with some papers; their offer was accepted. A few weeks later, the farm was theirs. For the remainder of the summer, they listed the townhouse, which sold quickly, Josh made arrangements with his jobs, and they packed up and moved to the Pine Tree State. There, many more chapters in their beautiful family saga would unfold for decades and decades.

Michelle, Isabella, Little Joshua, Adam, and Eve were eventually joined by, in this order: Noah, Mary, Peter, Abigail, Paul, Ruth, and Michael. As Issy had observed earlier, they all had hair to match their parents, each according to his or her sex. And their eyes ranged from Josh-brown to some combination that hinted at Athena's ever-shifting kaleidoscope. 'Cheaper by the dozen!' and 'All we need is twelve,' became Josh's hallmark sayings, soon adopted at times by Athena and the children. The babies were all born at home in the welcoming company of their family, each being gifted with natural immunity, and, because theirs was a Christian home governed by loving parents, none of them, especially not the boys, were physically mutilated. Those children, all of them, grew up in an idyllic environment, full of discipline (for which rarely was more than a word required), the fascination of learning, the frivolity and character-building that comes naturally from a life led nearer to nature, and, most importantly, held fast by great love. They, each and every one of them, knew without any shadow of doubt their mother and father loved them as much as each parent loved the other, and even more so; and, the children, returning the affections of their elders, also gleefully but jealously cared for each other. As an added bonus, mystery, and delight of timing, the maturation and births of Ruth and Michael coincided with Michelle's first two pregnancies and the coming of Josh and Athena's first grandchildren—with many, many more to follow. And it so happened that just a street or two away from the little church Josh had noticed during their first foray, Doris Harper lived and worked in her home factory cottage. Thus it became a tradition that, while the boys welcomed other kinds of gifts, all of the Williams women received at one point or another in their lives, a locket, a bracelet, or a ring made of the finest nickel.

Josh became a (mostly) full-time senior editor, ever sought after and compensated accordingly. He taught editing and research methodologies on occasion at the local community college. He also became locally famous for his astounding rose business, which he supplemented with additional flowers, Christmas trees, and a few edible crops. In time, the old reliable GLS, with its capable all-wheel drive, became Josh's farm truck. He was sometimes the talk of the town over it, a semi-eccentric mixture of rugged hauling power and a hint of faded luxury. The Civic, rebuilt several times, was passed around as a starter vehicle. Given the size of the family, their mainstay transportation became a small bus, a used model purchased from an airport auction and overhauled by Josh. All of his laborious endeavors, mechanical and agrarian, were assisted greatly by his children. Athena busied herself as a mother and wife, a homeschool teacher, and, when she had the time and felt like it, the best translator of any text in any language anywhere in the world. But unlike her revelation to Josh, she kept her inner nature and eternal secret between her and her husband and away from their children. That is until one day when her singularity and Josh's farm work collided with each other.

When Ruth and Michael were still but a wee toddler and an infant, respectively, one fall afternoon, Josh took the older children into the woods to fell a few older, dying, and nuisance trees for the next year's firewood and to tidy the forest. So it happened that due to a slip of attention, Josh, Jr., then a strong and ordinarily wary young man, accidentally but severely injured himself with a chainsaw. Upon hearing his cries, his siblings quickly gathered around him. His father came running through the trees from a short distance. But his mother arrived first. Athena's instantaneous appearance among her children was enough to awe them, but her healing touch upon their brother's leg was too much of a miracle to ignore. She held her firstborn and said, 'Only a small cut, healed, and you're fine, my baby!'

Just as the questions began to echo through the stands, Josh arrived and quieted them. 'Praise the Lord! And I do suppose the time has come, eh? Gather all of your siblings together; call the older girls back home; and, we have something to share with you about your mother,' he said. When they were all twelve informed, they took the news gladly though as a matter of deep mystery. Beyond acknowledging the miraculous fact itself, there was little Athena or Josh could do to further explain exactly how it affected the family. They did the best they could, even as they had always done with themselves. In the end, all of the children agreed that as astounding as it sounded, having an angel for a mother didn't really impact them any more than the general excellence of love she and Josh had always showered them with.

'I've always known,' Isabella said. 'Or I suspected. There was just always something about mommy, something, well, angelic.' Michelle said something similar, as did all of the older children. And together, one aiding the other in the building of it, the two eldest girls voiced a question that neither Josh nor Athena had ever thought of before. Isabella asked it directly for the sisterly duo, 'Mommy, are you daddy's guardian angel?'

Josh nodded along; he'd never really considered the matter, though he now assumed quite obviously that the answer was 'Yes.' So he was surprised when Athena quickly said, 'No.' She further explained, 'I lost the potential for such a privileged and responsible office early on. It may be that my love for your father, my helping him, in some ways counts as something similar. But, no. He has, like all of you, one or more angels that assist him. I can sense them at times, though I could not say who they are or, really, how they work. I'm just happy to do my part anyway I can.'

Many deep and long conversations about these matters, most similar to those shared between Josh and Athena, took place for years and years to come. More than once, from more than one mouth, questions were asked about whether the children would "be more like" their mother or their father. At the time, there was no indication of supernatural ability or predisposition among any of them and, in fact, Josh, Jr.'s injury, along with countless minor ailments and sprains, indicated the ten naturally-born offspring favored their father—a point which made Athena the gladdest of them all. And indeed, as the future bore out, the Lord's limit of one hundred twenty years upon all children of men held true. None of the unusual family heritage was fretted over, but the secret went no further, within the family than the twelve children. There was no written rule, but that was the way it turned out. And without the family, Athena's revelation was only ever shared with one more person.

Now partly thanks to that one man, all twelve children and their parents basked in the love and worship found at their new church, the Russian Orthodox Mission Church of Saints Boris and Gleb. There, from the first day they arrived as a family of seven-plus, and for many years thereafter, they were led by the kindly and capable Father Alexander. And he ended up playing, like Josias before him, a substantial role in fostering the family and its extra precocious wife and mother.

Twenty

Signa Et Orationes

Not long after the woodland accident and Athena's revelation to their children, the couple decided it would be a good idea to include their spiritual father and earthly advisor in the knowledge of her and their secret. One afternoon, they joined him alone in his office. After a short prayer and a little pleasant chit-chat, they had intended to get down to business. What Father Alexander said to them first, however, left them momentarily speechless. 'So, Athena,' he said, 'you're an angel. A real angel of the Lord.'

When they recovered enough to reply, she asked, 'How did you know that?'

'Yes, exactly how? That's what we came to reveal to you!' Josh said.

'All praise and glory! Hallelujah!' Father said. 'How? It came to me in a dream just the other night! I was in between two dreams, an intermission break from the ordinary, when suddenly I saw you both together, just as you are sitting here now in my office. And a voice said very matter-of-factly, *She's an angel*. That's how I knew. And now, as by your reaction, I take it the voice, probably THE or A Voice, was correct, I have questions about it all. So please do proceed, my friends!'

There was something in the way he'd said his words that made Josh and Athena laugh out with gladness. He followed them, and their further explanation was delayed for half a minute. Then she told him an abbreviated version of what her husband had heard some years before, punctuated at intervals by input from Josh. He then caught Alexander up to date on what they had been thinking, and hoping, lately, and a key reason for them coming in for their meeting, 'We've had and we continue to have the most amazing and blessed union, Father. In two different ways, she and I were orphans and people seemingly destined to be alone. Neither of us had ever experienced real romance either. So coming together, meeting, and joining as we did, has provided us with everything we ever imagined we were missing. And it turns out, we didn't even know or suspect the half of it, so much have we joyously discovered and gained in our marriage. Those three primary reasons behind matrimony that we heard explained so well in our first Mass together keep coming to mind. We have a most, well, healthy physical relationship. That and the Lord's unending gifts have afforded us our large family we love more than we can say. Or that I can. I'd almost say we love the children more than we do each other, but that isn't exactly right. For me, and I suspect for her, as I was God's first, so I am Athena's second, and my sons' and daughters' third. But it's not mathematical. Each one of our babies does more than complete us, and there is no palpable order to it. How can I put this? Rather than coming last in a hierarchy, they, all of them, all of us, really, just add ... more. So much more than I'd ever suspected possible, and now, it's a great addition I really couldn't live without. Do I have that right, baby?'

'Yes, and then some,' she said as she squeezed his hand and rubbed his arm lovingly. 'Each child, a product of sanctioned intercourse, flows from our oneness and expands our concept of being. I know you, Father, with seven yourself, understand us here.' The man nodded with a smile. She continued, 'So that brings us to our somewhat unique version of marital joint salvation. May I go on, Josh?'

'Please,' he said sweetly and appreciatively.

'Backing up for a second, as to our salvation and to our first meeting,' she said as she remembered that icy evening; 'This goes beyond the contrasting and complementary aspects of true femininity and masculinity, those physical and emotional components we enjoy: here I mean of the spiritual nature of our existences. In Josh, I finally found something I'd never seen or felt before and that I had essentially written off as impossible. As for a companion, a lover, a soulmate, or even just an extraordinary friend, I had all but given up. Then I sensed him before I saw him. With his humble piety and constant penance, I had at last found an equal. A genuine soulmate. A one love forever. So sensing it, I dropped that guard of visual perception I wear nearly perpetually, and for an instant, he saw me as I am, in my real higher middle state of being. And just then, I saw him for what he really was. Forgive me a moment, Father.' She then turned and kissed Josh intensely. 'I love you, forever, baby!

'Now, as for salvation!' she continued. 'Our paths are interwoven like those of any good man and woman. But we also have the added aspect, as we perceive it, of what to do about me in my well-earned predicament. We see the two elements as being linked, in and around our earthly relationship, and with the divine and the eternal, all with fostering via the love of Christ and His Church. Miracle compounding miracle! He Above leads us all, or, here, we both, and we follow. Josh leads our family and I follow. Josh carries me, as his woman, as a woman, and as a different womanly being in need of everlasting forgiveness. He, more perhaps than I, hopes and deeply prays that his efforts and love with and for me may play some role—a role neither of us pretend to understand—in the judging of one specific angel as Saint Paul put it two millennia ago. Am I leaving anything out, Josh?'

'No, and yes,' he said. 'Even without a full comprehension of what we're talking about, if we tried to explain it all, we'd be here for another twenty centuries. But as always, you've made a concise and moving summary, my love. And thank you for the kiss too! Is it now, do you suppose, time to conduct the check?'

'I think so,' she said, then saying to Father Alexander, 'I am greatly heartened by the Words spoken to you in advance of our company. They give me comfort that our test of sorts is right and will work. Given what you know of us, what we've just told you, and given what you surmise, might you be open to telling us a summary of your thoughts? If as we pray, they match ours, then perhaps our journey is, indeed, fruitful by all accounts.'

Father Alexander sighed contentedly and smiled, then said, 'Yes, I would love to add my own words and notions to yours. I think I know what result you're hoping for, a true concurrence, and it is also now my own hope! So, if you will, I would simply like to make a few remarks about how I see you both, and then we can conclude and go forth, hopefully into further productive bliss. Shall I now?!' They both eagerly agreed and he continued, 'So Josh and Athena, in you and in your relationship, I see great examples, love, and mystery. I also note the many metaphors, which in your case, might point towards absolute truth.

'You certainly capture the first and second elements of a Christian marriage, as you have described them, and the third. Both of the first two are self-proving and you provide much proof in addition. Also, the birth and growth of children testifies to the benefits of carnal relations, a self-fulfilling and harmonious cycle. In those two areas alone, I think you serve as a sterling example of Christian love. That could be a sign of resolving your unique situation. But back to your very different, yet similar backgrounds, I should say that across the vastness of our planet, all its real estate, and across the long ages of time, you were destined to meet and love. God ordained it. As such, and supported by the symbolism you've witnessed and your initial miracles when you asked for permission to embark on this novel quest, it all further explains His Will through you and His plans for you. Might I add that, just as you've lived the Christian benchmarks of piety, chastity, and humility, you, of course, sought permission. Glory and Praise! Answered prayers! Answered because they both served Him and were not selfishly offered.

'Athena, your analogy to becoming an angelic Gentile is priceless, as was your solution to join Christ's Church. Only do we, all of us, come to the Father but through the Son. I suppose it applies to those who once knew and saw God. Perfectly fitting and beautiful.

And yes, woman, you are being carried, in multiple ways, those of your own and those held in common with all females. And we carry each other, man and woman, in so many ways as well. Josh, I cannot ultimately say that I know you are helping judge Athena for her worth, her omissions, and more. In fact, I cannot even say conclusively that I really understand Paul's general concept. But if you are in any way correct, as I hope you are, then, well, you're doing a fine job! Is this the concurrence of thought you envisioned?'

'Yes,' Athena said.

'It's perfect, if not verbatim,' Josh said. 'Please go on if you'd like to expound further.' Father did, and the three of them spoke for another hour or so about the family, their commitments and responsibilities, and more.

As Alexander wrapped up his remarks, he said, 'From what you've said and seen, I think you are getting little signs along the way that you're on the right path. Will there be greater or more pronounced signs? I do not know. I was touched that Josh has twice now said he offered both to pick up Athena's cross, so to speak and to selflessly endure her burden. Perhaps he already has in many regards. And you also said, good man, that you would also endure the pain of losing Athena if you are preemptively successful and she might be called Home earlier than expected or before you fully lived out your joint life. Man has no greater love than to lay down his life; it may also be said he has a great near-peer love if he is willing to sacrifice the happiness of his life for the gain of another. Blessed joy!

'So we will continue to look for greater markings, while also observing those of more ordinary or mundane character. We shall see what we see. It is very important, in this as with all things, that the two of you continue to ever communicate with each other. Always know I am here to help if or when possible. And most importantly, always continue to pray and to defer your wills, thoughts, judgements, and desires to the infinitely more knowing and honest Will of God. Ever only seek that It shall be done; by doing so, you will both help yourselves helping each other and will also make it easier for God's Will and His Holy Spirit to do

Their work and to thrive as intended. We are in the world but not of it. Ultimately, aside from obedient worship, whereby we find ourselves and our true happiness where we might not otherwise think to look, we must put ourselves aside and fully submit. These things you obviously know. And I relish in being a witness to their fulfillment through you.'

'Thank you, Father, and this was precisely what we hoped to accomplish here today,' Josh said. 'We can't even see the track before us, but via meetings like this, small miracles, we certainly feel that it is the right one!'

Alexander led them in a short parting prayer and then they all stood and the couple prepared to leave. 'Thank you and bless you, Father,' Athena said. 'All things in our Lord's time and by His graces. And you are a magnificent example of His grace in action!'

'Let me say this in closing and before we part,' Father said as they moved towards the door. 'I hope and pray there will be signs to guide you and to indicate that a reprieve is coming or at hand. As always, praise be the Lord's. However, something else in all of these potentialities and possibilities has occurred to me; I don't like to think about it, but I have, and I will share it with you. If as we suppose, divine signs, small or great, do start coming, then it can only mean, as best we the faithful can tell, that a door or a window may be opening under the weight of redemption. This is the barest speculation on my part, but we are admonished to keep hope, look for miracles and signs, and not to deride prophecies. For all those things, here, perhaps especially, signs we might observe, will show that Athena is regaining favor, with or without her own efforts and thanksgiving, those of our good Joshua and your wonderful family, but supremely with the Grace of God.

'Here and now, a warning of a different kind of sign of which to be watchful and guarded against. If such comes to pass, then in its own inverse way it will be a good and true thing. But also a dangerous thing, for the sign itself must be read without heed or reverence to its earthly author. For if penance and atonement are true, and a return to that glorious station and Place begins, just as we may notice what is happening, then so too might, and very likely could, someone else. Growth of love, obedience, and all things sacred, all the things we must strive for, are anathema to someone else. And this process, if or when it happens, will make him extremely angry. Perhaps it would be unwise and utterly futile for him to direct his anger at a re-emerging angel of the Lord, just as it would be plainly stupid, as we say, for him to direct that anger and malice at God Himself. Yet, of course, we know he does and has done even that for all ages. And I, of course, do not know precisely and I cannot even guess accurately. But he might have other, more accessible targets upon whom to vent his hatreds: a helpful and loving family, for instance. Or in the case of our speculative joint salvation analogies and examples: a husband. In that warning, I still pray I am wrong entirely. Still, a caution...'

Even as he said it without precision, and without him naming the party of negative signage examples, they knew what and who he was warning against. They merely nodded along as he spoke, appreciating every word. Then, saying merrier parting words and well wishes of their own to him, they bid Alexander a good evening and drove back home.

It had not been long since Father Alexander reluctantly alluded to some vague, terrible possibility. Father Josias had warned them years before, as had other assorted good, Godly men and women. It was a caution they had both come to know and understand, if by nothing more than merely observing the fallen world around them. Athena had alluded to it, years earlier, as they had crossed the ocean. She knew it for all ages, better than any of them, and Josh had understood for most of his time spent living in that era; they knew the dark truth: the enemy hated. A deep and abiding hatred had the dark prince for the Glory of God, for His Creation, and for His Children. He hated the young. He hated the mothers who bore the young. He hated the women who married to become mothers. And he hated the men who became husbands and fathers. Atavistically, he hated the sons of Adam and the servants of Christ. A lesson never to be forgotten, with or without any direct confrontation.

Athena had gathered the children into the bus that day, and they had made a small pilgrimage to town, the farmer's market, and other pleasant places. Alone in his own pleasant spot later on one particular afternoon, Josh, then nearly fifty years old, sat at the dining room table in an empty house. Before him lay two different sets of work. On his left side, he saw some papers and a manuscript in need of review. On his right, he beheld several small trays of rose seedlings, the products of his own imaginative breeding endeavors. He was taking a short break, an emptied coffee mug testifying to that fact. And he, right then, was deciding which project deserved his immediate attention. Owing to great interest in both, he was a bit torn, though he felt himself leaning towards the cute, tiny plants. Behind him, through a window pane crossed with thin slats of wood, a breeze blew down from lofty gray clouds of some magnitude. And to that window pane, there came a tapping.

Knowing what the sound was, though not what caused it, he started to lean his head around for a closer listening. But the tapping moved. To the next window, it went: *tap, tap, tap*. Just as he thought to cock his ears that way, it moved again to a window in the kitchen. *Tap, tap, tap*. Then it moved on to the next. From window to window, the tapping sound circled the house. It passed him in his room again and returned to the kitchen. It stopped at the glass in the back door leading out to the patio, his greenhouses, and the field yard beyond. On that pane, the tapping became incessant, louder, and even violent. *TAP, TAP, TAP, TAP, TAP!!!!!!* Under the reverberating pressure, as if a strong finger probed dynamically, the glass rippled and the door shook in its frame.

Josh was sitting upright, attentively listening in that direction, a look of concerned annoyance on his face, when the noise ended. He narrowed his eyes, still glancing that way, when a dreadful voice spoke from beyond the door in a low, dark hiss: *'I win...'*

Without seeing, Josh knew where the voice came from, and upon uttering the steeling name, 'Jesus,' while rising in mild wrath, he moved steadily in that direction. Through the kitchen he walked, through the shaken door, out over the patio, and past the greenhouses. Stepping into the lusher grass behind their farm-house, he walked on, determined to answer the hiss. A face ever soft and kind had hardened without sign of flinching. Brown eyes accustomed to gentle peering now burned hot and did not blink. Hands calloused by hard work, that had never before been raised in anger or tumult, now clenched into fists. Stalking along, like a soldier at the head of a great column of warriors, he marched into the backyard. And he beheld his adversary, more or less where he'd expected to find it.

Down the long, faintly sloping yard, right in front of the stand of small trees beside and afore the impounded fishing pond, stood a vision of evil risen from the depths of hell. It took the form of a tall cloud of smoke, utterly black, blacker than midnight, and vaguely in human shape. Within the cloud lurked an even blacker shape, the vibrating image of a hideous man. Both the man shape and the encompassing cloud hosted burning eyes and a jagged mouth, both features blacker than impossibility. The eyes raged at him in hatred. And the mouth released a torrent of low but discernible curses and wicked laughter.

Undeterred, in fact, emboldened, Josh marched forward, increasing his pace. 'NO!' he thundered at the fiend. 'You lose! And you will leave my family alone!'

The obscene creature took a step forward, its laughter and fury deepening, with its clawed hands outstretched. It uttered a contin-uous hiss both freezing cold and scalding hot.

On walked Josh. And he then said, 'In the name of Jesus Christ, the Risen Lord God! Leave now!' He intended to say more, but those words had been enough. They, and what appeared to the wraith, though Josh did not see it behind him, proved far too mighty. But the monster suddenly went silent, retreated two steps, and began to vacillate with fear. What the beast observed up the slope, beyond marching Josh, above the house, and towering over a billowing gray cloud was a scene of glory, power, and, to its darkness, an answering menace. Two impossibly tall figures of white stood there, each glowing and glowering down at the thing, each with a sword in hand. And between them, far loftier and grander, stood the form of a Great Shepard holding up His hand.

Josh did not see his Allies, but he did witness Their onslaught. From above and behind him, there rolled and blasted an intense light that covered everything. The light's awful illuminating power should have blinded him. In fact, it should have incinerated him. But it did not. Instead, he saw it as it gathered, racing towards the shadow, focusing down to a sharp, hard point. And like a bat striking a baseball, it hit the foul spirit with a crack of finality. Just like that, the shadow sailed like a line drive straight over the horizon and out of sight, taking with it any lingering threat and malice. Peace immediately returned to the field. Josh stopped, blinked, and released his hands. Then he dropped to his knees and converted his exorcising incantation into a micro prayer of gratitude, 'Lord God, Lord Jesus, Lord the Holy Spirit, thank you! And well done! Amen.' He smiled broadly.

He had not called to her in any way, but suddenly Athena appeared in a flash, kneeling at his side with her arms around him. Concerned, she asked, 'Josh! What happened?' Even then, she sensed, and sprung to her feet, taking a fighting stance. With a scowl, her eyes burning with that white fire, she looked to where the demon had stood. Then, her face shifting to awe, she looked back up towards the clouds behind them. She looked back down at him and asked, 'You had a visitor, didn't you?'

'Yes,' he said, more put out sounding than alarmed, 'a most unwanted solicitor. But gone, now, with no worries or harm.'

'I felt it, she said quietly. 'Though, gratefully, I also felt Them.'

She reached down her hand to help him stand and he took it. As he rose, still grimly smiling, he hoped that she didn't hear the slight sandy rolling and grinding sound that came from his knees. Once on his feet, he looked at her somewhat skeptically, and said, 'You know, I don't think that guy is ever going to learn!' She took his arm and they walked back towards the house. As they went, he shook his head a little, rolled his eyes, and muttered, 'Stupid devil.'

The incident with ol' scratch or one of his minions did upon a little more reflection, bother them, though not as much as either would have previously thought, particularly Josh. Both came to see it as the kind of double-edged sign that Father Alexander had mentioned, approval of their course by forces both dark and Light. And there was no doubt that the Light had intervened on Josh's (and the family's) behalf, a fact that emphatically affirmed divine love and protection and which also contributed to their lack of extreme concern—theirs was a feeling of security and serenity rather than apprehension or anxiety. He made mention of that distinction in his first prayer after the incident. Before joining Athena in bed, he bowed down in his private vespers: 'Lord God, it's only me again, Josh. If I felt unworthy of all You've bestowed upon me before, I now doubly feel inferior. Thank You, and thank You again, for Your protection today. For me, and especially for my family. I meant it when I said *well done*. For as I called, and only called out, the only power or ability given me in such circumstances, You delivered. Literally.

'God, thank You for all of our blessings, each and every one of them. Those and our late conversations lead me back again to my central topic and request of the past quarter century: Athena. All these years and prayers, I have tried to put my feelings and thoughts into words both to honor and beg You. I am thankful that You, the Author of all knowledge, speculation, and hope, know best. Once again, here I am out of my reckoning when it comes to her. So I will just plainly ask You to save her, God, save her as You promise to save all of us who believe. Please welcome her back one day. I know nothing of the great and final eschaton or whether it figures into Your plans of redemption for my wife, Your daughter. I will, as ever, do anything You ask to further this process along, so long as my doing so honors Your Will in these matters.

'And for my part, and I'm beginning to see this not completely as the selfish part, which it still is, in some ways—for my part, I thank You for the unimaginable and nearly unbelievable gift of her in my life. I know or trust without knowing that our meeting and our lives together are a part of Your plan. Thank You for including me in it, and allowing me to experience it with her. And for the family, the children You've blessed us with, thank You again and again. I love my babies as I love my wife as I love You. Thank You for blessing us all, and please grant us Your mercy.

'In the name of the Father, You, my God, and of the Son no man deserves, and of the Holy Spirit, Giver of life. Amen.'

He then joined her under the covers, finding her saying a short prayer, the first of several she'd make that night. They expressed their usual gentle affections, and talked for some time about life, love, demon-besting, rose farming, and more, before snuggling together into their perpetual embrace of unison. And sometime in the night, after checking and holding him, and after resuming and pausing her prayers and powerful inner thoughts, she added a kind of postscript to her Father.

'Almighty, eternal, and merciful, God, my Father and Creator,' she said. 'I wish to complete my last thought upon deeper reflection. Once more, I thank You for protecting this home, our family, and my beloved Joshua, the man, the only man, You have given me, a gift I could have never earned and may never pay for properly. In that kind man, I continue to learn things of a kind I have never understood before. The praise is Yours, but his small actions on this earth testify to Your power, truth, and love. Whereas I, once confronted by a similar attack, quailed and dallied, Your more worthy son and servant did not. He instinctively turned to Your Thrice Holy Being, calling upon Your Son, my Lord Jesus. Faith, not blind, nor calculated, but utterly and blissfully trusting.

'And he is ever thankful for every facet of his life. Following him, loving him, helping him, instructing him, and lovingly learning from him is also a series of gifts from You that I most certainly could not merit by my own worth or effort alone. So as I ever apologize for my inexcusable actions and failures, ever seeking to atone, I am also grateful for this life. It is, I now realize, not a final sentence, but a reprieve of a different character, an enhanced opportunity to grow. To fully understand the impact of sin and evil by witnessing it as a woman. I hope and pray that all my previous explorations, understandings, and actions have pleased You. But in my union with sweet Josh, by fully embracing all that a human woman can feel and be, I find myself totally complete on Your good earth. Thank You for the amalgam of factors that have led me here and which I pray will one day lead me home to Heaven and the Glory of Your Presence.

'To those ends, I continue to learn and grow as a wife and mother, and as Your child. I love You more dearly than ever, a love I intend to see expand forever. Thank You for this wonderful, unlooked-for, and undeserved opportunity. Thank You for my Josh and our babies and all the blessings of life. Please continue to bless, protect, and rescue all of us. All in Your time, and all only ever serving Your interests and Will.'

'I pray to You, God the Father, God the Son Jesus, and God the Holy Spirit. Amen.'

When she opened her teary eyes for a moment, she immediately noticed him lying there, still holding her close, and looking at her. 'It's four-sixteen in the morning,' he said. 'And I get to tell you my favorite words again on this new and glorious day. I love you, Athena. I love you almost as much as our Father does. Almost as much as He loves us both.'

Unlike true love and good families, material things do wear out from time to time. Theirs was a nice little garden tractor, but it was older, already well-used when Josh bought it a few years earlier. Having grown his mechanical skills alongside his family and the farm, having traveled far from his radiator flake days, he diagnosed the new inconvenience and set a fix-it plan in motion. On a morning, he was in the back of the supply store in Bangor, in the corner at the far end of the last row. In retrospect, it was about the last place he'd have ever expected such an encounter to occur. And yet, it did. He'd just stood up and was looking at the replacement PTO over-clutch, trying to read the fine print on its labeling, when from the corner of his eye, he saw the man coming down that last aisle adjacent to the shop's outside wall.

The man was tall and very well-dressed. He was walking briskly, and Josh sensed as much as saw a faint glow about him. His face, which many would have described as handsome, if perhaps rugged, really then and there lacked a genuine description. Nor could the man's age be guessed beyond a vague notion of representing the younger middle years. But Josh plainly saw he was smiling. Coming to a stop at the end of the aisle where it merged into Josh's corner, he suddenly bowed and then said, 'Hail, Joshua, strong in Faith! The Lord our Father is pleased with thee.' He then bowed again before extending his hand.

Josh took it, suddenly feeling an electric yet calming sensation, somewhat like one he realized he had already become acquainted with but of a stronger, more piercing nature. 'Thank you, sir,' he said. 'Well met and thank you. Do we know each other?'

'I certainly know you, young man,' the visitor said. 'And I know you have heard of me, though we have never met. My name is Gabriel, and I have been sent to bring you good tidings. That one in your hands has the proper facings, but do not forget the housing gasket!'

Josh looked back at the clutch, only then remembering that he did need a gasket or, better yet, several of them just in case and for future repairs.

'In the bin next to the cardboard box, on the third shelf, an arm's length to your right,' Gabriel helpfully noted.

Josh glanced over and saw the parts. Turning back, he said, 'Thank you again, uh, Mr. Gabriel. How did you know?'

'I noticed it, the whole failed assembly, right off, as soon as We arrived at your house that day,' Gabriel said with a smile.

'At my house?' Josh said haltingly. He was only slightly confused, though the perplexity, like all parts of this sudden meeting, began to fill him with great joy.

'Yes, and that is why I was dispatched to give you this message,' Gabriel said. 'In all these important matters, you are a rare find, sadly all too rare, a firm but gentle mixture of conviction and caution. Let your heart be at ease, Joshua. As for the late unpleasantness, your boldness along with your humble deference to the Triune, was rewarded as it was and is appreciated and loved. As for your far-reaching quest, know as you trust, that humble and honest prayers are answered. They are answered in the manner that you so meekly suggest at every call. Praise be to Our Father! And, to that noble end, towards salvation joint and intertwined, I was instructed to return a quote of your words back to you: *Well done!* Blessed are you and yours and all those who follow the path of righteousness. God bless you, Joshua. And He dearly loves you.' With that, Gabriel bowed again and turned to leave.

'Amen,' Josh said very happily, 'and God bless you, Gabriel!'

Now nearly halfway back down the aisle, Gabriel stopped for a moment, He tilted his head to his right though he did not fully look back. '*And on a personal note, Josh, thank you eternally for your kind and courageous treatment of and your love for my sister,*' he said mentally.

'*I do love her, and it's my honor,*' Josh silently replied. Then he openly exclaimed, 'I love her! And you. And the Great God Who created and blessed us all.' He wiped his eyes and then looked up again, but Gabriel was nowhere to be seen.

Late that afternoon, Athena walked down the path from the back of the house towards the barn and Josh's shop. Halfway along, she met their good, kindly, and utterly Christian next-door neighbors, an older couple though forever young at heart, Bobby and Gloria. 'Your boy is in a great mood for a man working on a machine,' Bobby said with a smile as the three briefly greeted each other.

'He's always in a good mood,' Gloria added.

'He always is,' Athena said with a sweet grin. 'It might have something to do with the good company we keep around these parts.'

'Maybe,' Bobby said, not quite rolling his eyes. 'But I think he had some divine intervention fixing that old clunker.'

'He always has that too,' Gloria said. 'Might go with his mood, all of it well deserved. Now, supper, Bobby?'

Athena gave them a parting hug and walked on, finding Josh sitting in the tractor's seat with his hand on the key. He saw her when she walked in. 'Did anyone ever tell you you're beautiful?!' he asked.

'There's this one guy,' she said. 'A sweet little rose farmer. I think he has a crush on me.'

'He just might!' Josh said. 'He also might have, with a little miracle, fixed this thing. Let's see!' With that, he turned the key, revved the little engine, and engaged the PTO. They both watched, her from the door and him over his shoulder from the seat, as the shaft link spun hecticly but happily around. With a satisfied smile, he shut it back down and turned off the engine.

As silence returned to the barn, Athena smiled and broke the still air when she clapped. 'Well done!' she said.

Josh hopped off and ran to hug her. Face to face, between sweet little nibbling kisses, he said, 'That's what he said They said I said!' Whatever lay behind his little riddle, he appeared pleased by it.

'Do tell,' she said, rubbing her hands up and down his back and across his shoulders.

'Well, in the big city today at the store,' he said, 'I had another visitor. A little family reunion of sorts. Your side.' He then deeply kissed her and held her tight in a squeezing hug. Later, after dinner, the family prayers, and after seeing the children in their rooms with several kisses, they spoke more about the meeting. They spoke about it, openly face to face, and sleepily mind to mind, and of little else until deep into the night, even unto the early hours near dawn.

Twenty-One

Judgement: The Way Home

Almost every single day they had together was new and glorious, and they never tired of reaffirming their love for one another. Concerning the eyes and thoughts of those around them, even after long years passed them all by, no one ever once mentioned any perceived difference between their ages. It could have been her continued graceful alteration, a veil to comfort and ease, though of it they never spoke. To his eyes, and in unveiled reality, she did not age. He did, however, and one evening, ever thinking of others, he made his thoughts and concerns known to her while they slept. *'Athena,'* he thought.

'Yes, my baby?' she said.

'I've again had a worry about or for you,' he said. *'One I may have never mentioned before as it all makes me sad.'*

'What is it, Josh?'

'I don't want you to be alone and hurt,' he said. *'What happens when I get old? Really old, or, older? And I become weak or sick? What will you do when I die and leave you?'* Though the words were in his mind, the tears fell on his sleeping face.

She said in response, *'I have thought of these questions too, sad though they be, sweet husband. Let me tell you my answers, wherein I meet sadness with resolve. First, at any age, I love you. Completely. When you are old and weak, I will care for you.*

And when you die, I shall mourn for you and look forward to the Resurrection and Final Judgement. Do not trouble yourself with these notions again. I now have all the children and their children. And do not fret over them or my potential loss at their passing. For I also have the Lord, the God of eternity. We both do, and He is enough. Be comforted in my love, Josh. Joshy.' And even in sleep, even after all those years, she again had a miraculous effect on him. His tears turned into a slumbering smile of ease.

The thought of death, his death, which had never really troubled him of his own accord, never again was a specter in his mind. But he did age, growing through his midlife and beyond. Her childbearing had ended one day, much as it had come to her, at about the same time and of the usual age that an ordinary woman would encounter menopause. They took that mystery in stride, giving thanks, as ever, in all things.

The vine of life and love did grow and it bore great fruit: the long years saw children, grandchildren, and great-grandchildren come, play, grow, and thrive. Josh's rose gardens performed much the same, and he tended them daily, even as he settled pleasantly and gracefully into old age. Again, no one ever noticed or, at least, mentioned any perceived age difference between him and his bride, though, to outside eyes, she remained forever youthful and radiant. But in virtually every second of every day, in each year that passed, he ever remained in her thoughts and cares, and she remained cheerfully, adamantly dedicated, caring, and mindful of him. Deep into his later years, three things happened that deeply affected both of them. There was a final adoption, an illness, and a death.

Not for the first time, a dog, some mixture of Shepard and Retriever, had come calling around the rose beds. Josh, ever a softy, and Athena, ever in love with life, happily made the dog, an older girl that they ever-so-creatively named Rosebud on the spot, a member of their family. Like Josh, she was up in her years, and the two elderly friends enjoyed each other's company. Athena also loved Rosebud dearly and frequently conversed with her in her own raspy language. So when she died, only a year or so after joining them, they were hard hit. But nothing could have prepared them for what came next. It happened two months after Rosebud's departure. The next event shook them horribly and likely contributed to the acceleration of Josh's easing process.

He sobbed uncontrollably on her shoulder late one night. 'She was only a child yesterday,' he cried. 'The sweet girl in my old room. Then she was ours. All ours and an anchor of our family. How can we lose her? We can't. Never. How would we ever endure this?' They ultimately found answers, only through accepting the possibility of loss and trusting as always in God's plan, but that night there had been no real rejoinder to his pitiful questions. Michelle had lived to the respectable age of eighty-five, she had lived a remarkable life, a gift to her parents, siblings, husband, many children, and grandchildren. But even as Josh lived on, seemingly untouched by any major ailment, and as ever did Athena, their eldest child did not. Her illness came like a storm of rapid onset and steep decline. For her part, she accepted the doctors' assessment that she only had, at best, a few months to live. She certainly accepted the news better than her parents, her father especially. But then, nearing the end of a hard, dark journey, she miraculously recovered her full health; and, it was not a miracle directed by her wonder worker mother. Great praise and thanks were given, and things moved forward. But things also began to change. As might be expected of a woman her age, Michelle began to earnestly slow down. She took to spending most of her time living with one of her daughters and her visits to Josh and Athena were substantially reduced to the point they often missed her presence.

On a Thursday afternoon, a little late though in a time still graced with sunlight, Athena suddenly missed Michelle again as she frequently did. She was standing in their kitchen when the thoughts took her, recalling the closest shave with the kind of mortality no parent ever wishes to understand, and she quietly wept. Then something, some kindness tinged with sorrow, presented her with an image of old Rosebud, whom she also missed. That mental image was of the dear old dog alongside Josh, both of them slowly trodding through a field. And at that hour in time, she missed him and immediately desired to see and hold him. Suspecting where she might find him again, she sought out his usual hobby and pre-cinct. Out back, she saw the greenhouse door was open. It was his first, original hotbed, the one he'd smuggled in and assembled in secret over seven decades earlier. Despite the regular additions of newer, nicer, and larger conservatories, it continued to serve as his favorite. Walking to the open door, she once again found him inside, a freshly cut red rose grasped in one hand.

She shrieked and cried out, 'Josh! No,' upon seeing him as he lay on the pea gravel floor, the rose tightly in one hand, the other hand clutching his chest and with a look of angst and fading light on his face and in his eyes. Those sunken but partially alert eyes connected with hers and he opened his mouth, repeatedly, gasping like a fish out of water, though he emitted no sounds. In a flash, she held him on their bed.

'Stay still, baby. I can do this,' she said reassuringly, her voice once more calm and soothing. She placed her hands over his chest, closed her eyes, and prepared to mend his dying heart. But to her surprise, and it was the surprise of a long-considered understand-ing or agreement in place of shock, she felt him weakly take hold of her wrists, then push her hands back and away. She opened her eyes and saw his glinting back at her—soft, pleading, but contented and resolved. His mouth, the same sweet mouth she'd loved, lis-tened to, and kissed for an age, opened slightly and his lips curled upwards into a fragile though sincere smile.

'Not this time, my love,' he said very softly, almost in a hoarse whisper. 'I think at last all my debts are paid, my work is finished, and I have picked my last rose.'

She held his hands tenderly and bent over him, her hair cascading over his head until their noses nearly touched. 'Is it really time?' she asked quietly and sadly.

'Someone once told me that time is irrelevant,' he whispered with a smile. 'But, yes, I'm being called away at last, my sweetest, dearest wife.'

'Still,' she said as tears rolled down her cheeks, a few beginning to drip upon his face below, 'I don't want to lose you, baby. You first came to me for a gift, but you ended up giving me one. One precious beyond words.'

'You can't lose me, angel,' he said. 'You are my great gift. You fixed my heart once, and then, it became yours. As did I. I'm part of you as you are part of me. One. So we may never really part. I simply must go forward a step before you, advancing over the bridge a bit. I'll be waiting, come the Resurrection.' As he spoke, he, and she, felt his mortal life's energy draining away. A deep and lasting calm took him, and he passed some of its kind touch to her.

'Then wait for me, as I will await you. With, in, and for our Lord God.' She kissed his lips, feeling his last few soft breaths ease out. 'And, Josh, my husband, friend, and saving judge—forever, I will love you. I love you, Josh.'

With his last breath on earth, he told her, 'I love you, Athena.'

And with a smile still on his sweet face, now looking younger than she'd seen it in years, he left her.

She held him and cried for hours. Composing herself as best she could, she uttered an open prayer for the peace and love of his soul. 'Almighty God my Father, You have defeated Hell and given all life, destroying death forever. Please, my Lord, grant rest and salvation to my dearest Josh, my husband, and true love, Your good, worthy, and humble servant. Pardon him of all his transgressions, God, and restore him to glory in Your Holy sight. Please receive him and heal him. As You deliver all Mankind, bask him in the light of Thy truth and righteousness forever. And please allow me to one day see his beautiful face and feel his gentle being in the presence of your Holy life-giving embraces. Forever and ever, I pray, unto the ages of ages, my Lord God, the Father, the Son, the Holy Spirit. Forever and ever. Amen.'

Josh was buried following a funeral that, like their wedding, was overrun with loving friends and admirers. The priest recalled the nature of that special speculative theology concerning the Resurrection and eternal life in the Glory of the Almighty, a new Heaven for souls reborn and remade. 'May that Joshua, our friend, wait and rise anew one day,' he said. 'Followed in Thine good time,

O Lord, by all of us unworthy sinners.' There was no doubt among those gathered that Josh had defeated, was defeating, or would defeat his last enemy, as Saint Paul so termed death, that Josh's victory was assured by the might and love of Christ. None of them knew for certain where Josh's soul reposed, now separated from his body, nor when he would reunite and enter into Paradise. But all of them trusted that his middle state, like theirs, was ordained and would proceed by God's plan until the Final Judgment and the commencement of the life ever-lasting and free from all agony, feeling instead of pain, blissfully and perpetually renewed in Glory. None knew it better, or rather, faithfully trusted in it more than Athena, who then, and for all ages, would unconditionally love the man she had helped save, the man who had helped save her.

Many, many years in the future, no one else was around, and so no one saw what happened. Had there been eyes to see, then most might have found it a curious sight in the dwindling dusk of that rather cold and inclement mid-November day. In an open field, stamped here and there with trees, in the remains of an old cemetery in what was once called New England, a young woman, beautiful beyond description, stood looking at the weathered tombstone of a man who had lived and died several centuries earlier. It was a double marker, and his side read, in barely legible characters:

Joshua O. Williams

AD 2000 ~ 2099

Husband, Father, Unworthy Servant of God

The other side of the stone was similar, though it bore no dates, merely reading, as a companion ledger:

Athena N. Williams

~

Wife, Mother, Recalcitrant Daughter

She'd come to the double grave, regularly, for years, oftentimes singing "Summer Rain" by Belinda Carlisle, along with a variety of other mournful love songs. That day, without song, the woman was more interested in the name and being of Joshua, and she stood silently before his side for a long time. No one saw her tears or heard her soft words. She knelt and placed a single red rose at the base of Josh's monument. Next, she leaned over to the woman's side of the marker and etched dates into the stone with her finely manicured fingernail harder than steel. Turning back to her husband's side, she quietly said, 'Just a moment, and I'll be there. How you helped me, sir.' Then, crying, she spread herself out on the tall grass that covered his grave, completely flattening down so as to be as close as possible to the man long departed. She remained there, motionless, for a very long time. As her tears ceased, she whispered into the ground, 'I love you, Joshy.' Then her sorrowful face became glad, and she at last smiled. And then, most unusually, her form and essence, her body, her clothing, and all, appeared to melt, fade, and, finally, vanish altogether. Seeing that would have been enough to convince any, again, absent onlooker of the power of possibility. But what soon followed would have left no doubt whatsoever as to the potential and legitimacy of miracles.

At the end of Josh's plot, opposite his name, dates, and vocations, she once again stood. But she did not stand as she had before, nor like at any time during the living memory of all Mankind. She was taller now, her beauty had become exceeding, blinding, nearly imperceptible and indescribable, and utterly white were her face, her features, her flowing robes, the wing-like appendages upon her back, and the light that fell from, into, and all around her. She raised both her arms and her face upwards to the sky, as she uttered, 'Glory to God the Most High. Holy!' At that instant, a beam of pure white energy and light fell from the heavens. It pierced the damp gloom and illuminated the field like a dazzling fire, and she ascended into it, rising to her Home of Homes.

Her penance was made and accepted, she was restored. Athena was judged worthy.

To his mind and eyes, it was not exactly how Athena had suggested it might look. In her defense, she had only seen, long before, the initial version, which this new and eternal edition outshone ten million times over. But as she had accurately noted about all such concepts of Elysian Sion and related paradisiacal matters, he instantly knew that no artistic estimation, no matter how well inspired, came close to capturing the encompassing grandeur, beauty, truth, and glory. Josh was moving, with utter happiness, amidst a throng of righteous souls, into his new and genuine Home. They had all lately returned to a place they'd always longed for though one they had never seen before, the fulfillment of *hiraeth*.

He saw that they, all of them, looked perfect—exactly, utterly perfect. His own body, what he could see of it, and he wasn't paying much attention to himself apart from his joy, looked like he remembered it from his youth, perhaps his early twenties, though it had been reformed in impeccability. Everyone else presented the same way. And he found that he knew all of them, really knew them, all like close friends or family members. Some of them he remembered from before. Others, he had heard of, seen remotely, or had read about. And yet others, he just knew without the benefit of having met them in any particular way. At that moment, right before him, chatting happily, went Isabella and Michelle, flawless young women and sisters forever. Their other siblings walked with them. Everyone he'd ever known was also there, and he could see them clearly, whether they were near to him or far. And as he proceeded, he held hands with two comely adults, a man and a woman, who he had never seen before with his knowing eyes; and they had not seen him since he was merely a baby boy born into their destitute and downtrodden household. Not that any of the previous circumstances mattered at all; for there, none of them knew sorrow or pain.

At once, they all began to sing out in praise and joy. The song remade reality again and again, each time better than before. And they all, as they sang, beheld the Holiest of Presences, seated high upon His White Throne. The glow of His Face and Being melted and forged all things together, all of them rededicated to perpetual bliss and true purpose. Yet and still, they each retained a new and surpassing characteristic of their own, which all flowed together, one individual after another, nation beside nation, rank upon rank, joy through great joy. At once it all appeared as One, yet, upon closer inspection, the One yielded into the many.

Around the Throne, Josh observed the high chorus, the leaders of the unending song. Those faces, while he understood them, were new to him. The newness felt natural, beyond natural, and brought him further happiness, the novel discovery of a child. But at last, in the center of one row, he found a face he did recall, though, like all those around him, its beauty would have been incomprehensible in any previous age. He at once saw the perfect truth in the words, perfect as always, of Lord Jesus: in Heaven, the angels did not marry. There was simply no need, as this relationship was far better. And she saw him, revealed as he really was, better than at their first meeting when he had, even as he then appeared, stolen her heart. Athena smiled. And, wrinkling her nose, she blew him a kiss. Everything within and everything without made pure sense, and forever and ever, they sang. They were all judged worthy.

The End

Afterword

by the Author

The preceding is what I fancifully refer to—and let's not dwell on exact genre classifications, my friends—as a Christian fantasy romance novel. It certainly is a love story, one I sincerely hope the reader deeply enjoys. It does involve various elements which, at first glance, may appear fantastical. To that end, one should remember that our natural world is graced with the supernatural. And it is a Christian tale, an exposition or apology of several combined Biblical themes, dramatized, of course, and to some extent, possibly to a great extent, dramatized fantastically via highly or even novel theological speculation. Athena's nature, or a question as to the same, came to me as a series of evolving ideas, as did how she and Josh handle their unusual circumstances. In the end, this fantasy element is a central plot vehicle—I am not suggesting anyone wait around in order to marry an earth-bound angel any more than one should look for and try to live in a magical medieval kingdom ruled by a talking lion. Rather, by weaving things together as I have, I hope this story showcases the importance, beauty, and righteous feasibility of true love, marriage, family and child creation, and joint or family salvation through Christ. My hope is that the book in all ways serves, showcases, and promotes the good, the true, and the beautiful. Early on, in the pre-review process, I received encouragement that I was on the right track. Dr. Clyde Wilson, only part of the way through the manuscript, emailed me that I had crafted "...a beautiful portrayal of the relation of man and woman at the highest level." A bit like Josh, I do infrequently blush.

Athena came along at precisely the right time for me, a welcome reprieve from the geopolitical madness of our times, which had, by the fall of 2024, begun to take a toll on me. Remarkably, this book kind of wrote itself with, of course, generous help from me. I was walking about the neighborhood one evening, when the idea popped into my head. As I stumbled around, limping pitifully, I ran a few scenarios through my head. Once safely back in my cave, I cranked up the magic word machine, intending to see how much of the idea I could translate into text. My plan was to just type and see where it went. The process did not at all follow my long standing practice of mulling thoughts, tinkering, scatter-shooting bits and pieces, and generally procrastinating. In a hair over three weeks, I had written a first draft of the full book, essentially going straight from page one to the end. The clean-up procedures took a while longer, but I was most impressed with how fast and easily it all came together. I strongly suspect there was a tad of Divine inspiration and assistance. (Thank You!) I think of all the longer or major works I have written, published or otherwise, *Athena* is my favorite even as it is completely outside my ordinary fare. I genuinely like this story and I hope my gentle readers do too!

Speaking of gratitude, I want to thank all those in my life, and others I have read about, who gave me various ideas here and there, who helped, directly or indirectly, to make this tome a reality. I owe a special debt of gratitude to those who humored me along as this project came together—Annie, Lynne, Walt, Dr. Clyde Wilson, and the rest. Of course, none of this would have been possible without the expert professionalism of Paul Graham (and Suzette and Boo!) of Green Altar Books. Many, many thanks, my friends. Now among many other ordinary or common items, like car brands and commercial locations, several songs are mentioned throughout the text, by title, artist, or both. However, as noted way back in the copyright language, some of the lyrics from "Wonder Worker" by Palestinian-Lebanese-Cypriotic artist Sima Itayim are included as spoken words, part of the lovey-dovey dialogue during the honeymoon phase towards the middle of the book in chapter fifteen. The version of the song Josh remembers and sings may be found here: https://www.youtube.com/watch?v=haRJNXQBH9U. While writing and imagining what a young husband might sing to his bride, I recalled the song and knew I had to include it in the manner I chose. Your author greatly thanks Sima Itayim, a tremendous grace and talent within her, both for creating such beautiful, soulful music and for her permission to use a few of her words in this story. As one Youtube commenter said about another of Itayim's songs, "Dressing Up For Nobody": "The best Singer in this world by far. 100% original." I do wonder, however, if we shall ever read such high praise for Dandy & The Bass Slayers, Lincolnton's hometown heroes, who I suppose need no introduction.

Despite the inclusion of the Bass Slayers (and one other element most might not catch) in this work, I have decided that this book is NOT set in the Ironsides "universe." Call it noncanonical inclusion if one likes. Or not, just so long as one enjoys it all.

A note about words: No, unless it is the first word in a sentence, I do not capitalize any variant of our eternal enemy's name. I italicize Biblical books like any others. "Theoanthropos" is, in fact, a word, and the right one as mentioned by Josh, despite the existence of a similar and perhaps more widely recognized term. The first "o" makes all the difference.

Also, if only for one novel, I was ever so happy to revive the WODS Christmas songs of old and to restore Top of the Hub. You're welcome, *Bah-stin.*

God bless, cheers, and *Deo vindice,*

Perrin Lovett, Winter 2025

About The Author

Perrin **Lovett**, is a Christian traditionalist author from the South. His books include *The Happy Little Cigar Book* (2015), *Get Out!* (2020), *The Substitute* (Green Altar, 2023), and *Judging Athena* (Green Altar, 2025). His columns, essays, and short stories have appeared at *Reckonin'*, *Geopolitika*, *Katehon*, *Pravda English*, *The Fourth Political Theory*, *Nova Resistência*, the *Postil Magazine*, *Idee e Azione*, and various other thoughtful outlets, being translated in roughly a dozen languages, a few of which he is moderately fluent in. He holds some of those degreed credentials people like. Kindly follow him at www.perrinlovett.com and www.perrinlovettbooks.com.

Deo vindice!

Available From Green Altar Books

If you enjoyed this book, perhaps some of our other titles will pique your interest. The following titles are now available for your reading pleasure… Enjoy!

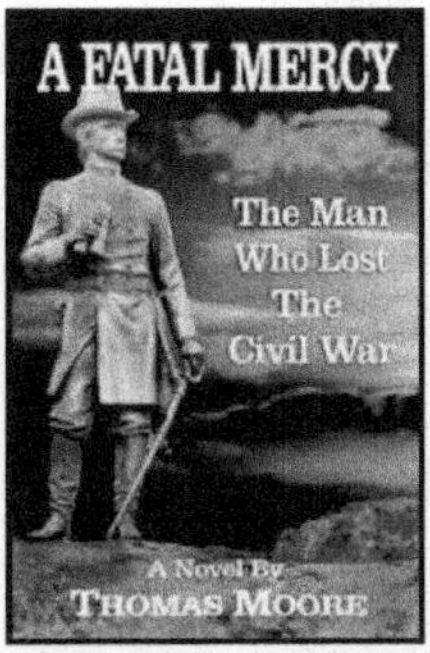

GA
GREEN ALTAR BOOKS
SHOTWELL PUBLISHING

Green Altar (Literary Imprint)

CATHARINE SAVAGE BROSMAN
*An Aesthetic Education
and Other Stories (2nd Ed)*

Chained Tree, Chained Owls: Poems

Aerosols and Other Poems

Partial Memoirs

RANDALL IVEY
*A New England Romance:
And Other Southern Stories*

The Gift of Gab

SUZANNE JOHNSON
Maxcy Gregg's Sporting Journals 1842-1858

JAMES E. KIBLER, JR.
Tiller : Claybank County Series, Vol. 4

The Gentler Gamester

*Beyond The Stone: Poems of Tribute
& Remembrance*

THOMAS MOORE
*A Fatal Mercy:
The Man Who Lost The Civil War*

PERRIN LOVETT
The Substitute, Tom Ironsides 1

KAREN STOKES
Belles

Carolina Twilight

Honor in the Dust

The Immortals

The Soldier's Ghost: A Tale of Charleston

WILLIAM THOMAS
*Runaway Haley:
An Imagined Family Saga*

*The Field of Justice: Moonshine
and Murder in North Georgia*

CLYDE N. WILSON
*Southern Poets and Poems, 1606 -1860:
The Land They Loved, Volume 1*

*Confederate Poets and Poems, Vol 1
The Land They Loved, Volume II*

Gold-Bug
(Mystery & Suspense Imprint)

BRANDI PERRY
Splintered: A New Orleans Tale

MARTIN WILSON
To Jekyll and Hide